The Sean O'Rourke Series

Book 4

O'Rourke's Law Or No Law At All

by

Michael E. Cook

TELEMACHUS PRESS

Cover art and design by Telemachus Press, LLC with assistance from Beatrice Gallaugher

Published by Telemachus Press, LLC
http://www.telemachuspress.com

Contact the author at cookorourkeseries@gmail.com

ISBN: 978-1-945330-00-1 (eBook)
ISBN: 978-1-945330-01-8 (Paperback)

Version 2016.06.06

Table of Contents

The Sean O'Rourke Series

Book 4

O'Rourke's Law Or No Law At All

CHAPTER ONE

Another month and a half rolled by and according to Doc Rawlins, Maggie was as good as new. Maggie and Sean were spending a lot of their time together. Everyone expected her to announce sometime soon that she was with child. Jesse had healed well. He and Dawn were on their way down to "The Nations" to visit her father and uncle. Jesse assured Sean that he would always be there for him if the need arose. Jon was still staying with Martha but nothing was ever mentioned about the two of them doing anything permanent. Cookie and Barbara still acted like they were newlyweds, and Michael and Betty were not seen from time to time. Construction continued for new businesses and the railroad got closer.

It was now the summer of 1866 and the warmer weather seemed to slow everyone down some. That is everyone except some of the Southern Cheyenne. Several raids had occured in western Kansas and several people had been killed. Black Kettle did not want to fight with anyone, but he could not control the "Dog Soldiers." Every treaty that the Cheyenne had signed up to this point had been broken, and some of his young men were tired of it. More and more white settlers were screaming for protection by the Army. Two colored cavalry regiments, the 9th and 10th, were formed. Many white folks did not believe the colored troops could handle the job. Those white folks were proved wrong many times over the years.

George Custer was offered the rank of full Colonel if he would take command of one of the newly formed colored cavalry regiments, but he did not want to command colored troops. Instead, he went to the newly formed 7th Cavalry at Ft. Riley Kansas as a Lt. Colonel. Sean was never in the Army of the Potomac, but he had heard of Custer's reputation. Custer was not afraid to lead his men in a charge, and although his units always had high casualty rates, Sean knew that Custer's recklessness helped end the war. Sean also knew that the tactics of a regular army would not work against the Cheyenne or any tribe for that matter. The people of Abilene were not worried about the Cheyenne raids yet because they were happening over to the west for now.

Another month rolled by and it was still quiet in Abilene. Sean and Maggie were having breakfast one morning at their regular table when a telegram came for Sean. The operator came running into the saloon all excited and yelling for Sean. "Marshal, Marshal, this here's an important telegram," he cried. "You'll be surprised when you see who it's from."

"All right, calm down there fella," said Sean. "Don't be callin' me Marshal anymore. Name's Sean. Now gimme that telegram." The operator stood there waiting for Sean's reaction. The telegram went as follows:

Sean O'Rourke
Abilene Kansas

O'Rourke<<stop>>with seventh cavalry Fort Riley Kansas<<stop>>understand you lived with Cheyenne several years<<stop>>would like to employ you as Chief Scout for campaigns against Cheyenne, Arapaho, and Sioux

George A. Custer
Fort Riley Kansas

"Well what do you think a that darlin'?" Sean asked Maggie. "The boy General wants me to scout for'm against my old friends."

"What do you mean boy General?" asked Maggie. "I heard he was just a Lt. Colonel."

"He is a Lt. Colonel now, but they called him the boy General during the war," answered Sean. "He was the youngest Brevet General during the war. I heard he was only 22 or 23 at the time. He made Brevet Major General near the end of the war."

"What is a Brevet General?" asked Maggie.

"Well during the war, some men get temporarily promoted to higher ranks," said Sean. "They're needed durin' the war, but when it's over, the army downsizes and all them Generals aren't needed. They made Custer go back ta bein' a Captain when the war was over. I think he was a Captain when they made him a Brevet General. I'd say it really hurt his pride. I heard he's a real ambitious man. I even heard that he wants ta be President of these United States someday. Couldn't give me that job."

"So what are you going to tell Mr. Custer?" asked Maggie. The operator was still there waiting for Sean's response.

"That's easy. Just send Custer a big "NO", said Sean.

"Are you sure this is what you want me to send?" asked the operator. "Custer's a famous man. He might not take kindly to you being that blunt."

"You let me worry about what Custer might think and send what I told you," said Sean. The operator mumbled something to himself and left.

After a few minutes, Maggie could see that Sean was doing some thinking. "What is it darlin'?" asked Maggie. "You're not worried about Custer. You're worried about the Cheyenne aren't you?"

"Yes I am," answered Sean. "If I was Black Kettle, I'd probly fight and get all my people killed. There's too many white folks and more comin' west all the time. The Cheyenne and all the tribes are gonna end up gettin' brushed aside. Their way a life is gonna be over soon and nothin' I can do'll change that. The buffalo herds'll get wiped out, and farmers and cattle ranchers'll take the land. Sooner or later the tribes'r gonna end up on some reservation dependin' on hand outs from white folks who don't wanna give'em hand outs. You mark my word. One day they'll even take the reservations away from'em."

"There's an awful lot of buffalo out there," said Maggie. "Do you really think white folks can kill that many of them?"

"They'll kill'em for hides, and once they understand that the buffalo is the main food source for the plains tribes, they'll kill'em to help starve the tribes," said Sean. "This'll happen darlin'. Not right away, but we'll see it happen before we have any grandkids."

"So you're expecting some grandkids someday," said Maggie. "We can't have any grandkids without kids first so maybe we better go work on that."

"Sounds good Maggie," said Sean. "I'd rather be in the throws of passion with you than thinkin' about what I was thinkin'."

"Throws of passion," said Maggie. "I've never heard you say that before. It sounded good. Let's get to that throwing."

"I don't know about you but I think we did some pretty good throwin'," said Sean when they were finished. "I know it's early, but I feel like soakin' in that tub with you."

"Sounds good darlin'," said Maggie. "Let's go."

~~~~

After they had been soaking for a good while, Maggie could tell that Sean still had something important on his mind. "I can tell by just being here with you that you have something on your mind," said Maggie. "Tell me about it. Maybe I can help ease your mind if there's something that's troubling you."

"It's not really troubling me," responded Sean. "I just been thinkin'. It's been some time since Lucas got himself killed, and we haven't heard one thing about him gettin' replaced. When Lucas got the job real quick, we thought it was odd. Now it's been all this time, and that seems odd too."

"Well darlin', it could be that no one will take that job right now," said Maggie. "Two Federal Judges killed so close together like that. Maybe anybody they have in mind is going to investigate and try to find out what actually happened and why. We have no idea how many people knew that Lucas was a crook. Anyone who did know probably won't say anything because they might be incriminated too."

"You could be right darlin'. No one'll say anything," said Sean. "I would expect some sort of investigation if I was gonna take a job where two men ahead a me got themself killed. All this thinkin' is makin' me hungry. Let's get dressed and see what Cookie and Barbara got goin' today. Whatever it is, I know it'll be good."

Sean was right. The food was good. Cookie had made some venison cooked slow with onions and mashed potatoes with gravy and some greens. Barbara had added some spices and they gave it a little bit of a kick. There was even apple pie for dessert. Sean and Maggie ate their fill. It was Saturday and there was always a huge crowd on Saturday. The place would start filling up early afternoon and stay full till the wee hours of the morning. Cookie and Barbara always had everything ready and were ready for the crowd.

About two hours before dark, three men that Sean had never seen before came into the saloon. With all the new things going on in town, new faces didn't bother Sean, but there was something about these three. When they entered the saloon, they stood at the sign that said to give your weapons to the bartender. The three of them stood there talking among themselves until Michael approached them. "Do you men need any help reading the sign?" Michael asked them.

"We don't need no help," one of them said. "We just never been no place that made you give up yer guns."

"That goes for knives too," said Michael. "Now if you're comin' in, please take your hardware over to the bar. If not, please remove yourself from this establishment."

"Damn, he said please," the one who had spoken earlier said. "Since he said please, I reckon we'll give'em up. Let's take'em to the bar boys. I'm gettin' thirsty." The three of them took off their gun belts and handed them to Tom.

"You'll get these back whenever you're ready to leave," said Tom. "Now what'll you have? There's a table over there. Have a seat if you want and I'll bring it to you."

"Give us some rye whiskey and three glasses. Name's Carl," the man said. "We'll be over at that table."

"Comin ' right up," said Tom. Carl paid for the bottle. The three men sat there quietly and sipped their whiskey. Michael went over to Sean.

"Let's keep an eye on those three," said Sean to Michael. "I just got me a feelin' about them. They're not slammin' down their whiskey so it looks ta me like they wanna stay sober for a spell."

"Well they turned in their weapons without too much fuss," said Michael. "I'll stay over by the piano and keep an eye on them. If I see Jon before you do, I'll tell him too."

"They did turn in their gun belts, but they could still have some weapons tucked away," said Sean. "We don't frisk anyone who comes in here. We rely on people's honesty. Trouble is, not everyone is honest." Maggie was still there with Sean. "Darlin', you make sure Jeb doesn't leave your side and make sure you're armed," said Sean.

"I'm always armed," said Maggie. "The only time I don't have a pistol on me is when you and I are making love or in the tub. Then there is always a pistol close by. You know I keep a pistol right beside my side of the bed."

"I know that," said Sean. "Sorry I seem edgy. I just got me a feelin' about them three fellas. Hope it's nothin'."

"Me too darlin'," said Maggie. "Sure would hate to have any trouble in here tonight with this big crowd."

~~~~

A couple of hours rolled by, and the three men were still drinking from the same bottle. A very well dressed middle aged man sporting a fancy cane now entered the saloon. Sean could tell that the three men's eyes never left that man. The man walked up to the bar where Tom was waiting. "I do not carry any weapons," said the man. "My name is Robert Sharpton. Could I get a glass of some Irish Whiskey?"

"You surely can Mr. Sharpton," answered Tom. "We always try to keep some Irish Whiskey on hand. Our owners fancy it."

"And who might the owners be?" asked Robert.

"Well you see that big Irishman over at the piano and that red headed beauty with that handsome dark haired man at that table over there?" said Tom as he pointed towards Sean's table. "Well this place belongs to the three of them."

"Is that painting on that wall over there the same woman at that table?" asked Robert.

"Yes it is," answered Tom. "That's Maggie and the place is named after her."

"She's uncommonly beautiful," said Robert. "I'll make it a point to meet her while I'm in here this evening."

"That won't be a problem," said Tom. "Maggie always goes around and mingles with the customers. Excuse me Robert. Got another customer."

When Tom went to wait on the other customer, Carl left his table and came up behind Robert. Robert could feel that something sharp and pointed was against his back. "You and me are gonna turn around and walk outta this place like everything is all right," Carl whispered to Robert.

Sean could see that Carl had come up behind Robert, but he couldn't tell exactly what was happening. The other two men that were with Carl were up now and heading for the door but they still kept their eyes on Carl and Robert. Michael and Sean saw the two men moving. Michael was closer so he went to the door to stop the two men.

Robert had no intention of going with Carl. He moved a little away from him, turned, and without saying a word, he cracked Carl on the head with his cane. Carl went down and when he did, a knife fell from his hand. When the other two men saw Carl go down, they both pulled small pistols that they had hidden in their boots and pointed them at Robert. Before they could get their hammers cocked, they were both falling backwards with holes in their chests. Sean stood there with the smoking pistol in his hand. Carl was up now and was reaching for something that was stuffed in his pants. Michael saw him reaching for something and didn't hesitate. His bullet passed through Carl's chest and struck next to the mirror behind the bar. Carl hit the floor dead. Sean checked to make sure the three men were dead.

"Are you all right mister?" Sean asked Robert. "Seems those three wanted to do you harm."

"I'd say you were right," said Robert. "I have no idea who those men were and why they would want to harm me. My name is Robert Sharpton and you must be Sean O'Rourke. I have heard about you and your reputation. I see what I have heard is true. I thank you for saving my life."

"Glad to be of service," said Sean. "We don't like it when bad things happen in our place. So you say you have no idea who those men were and why they would want to harm you."

"That's mostly true," said Robert. "I'd like to have some words with you when you have the time, but first I'd like to meet that wife of yours. She is uncommonly beautiful."

"Maggie, this gentleman would like to meet you," Sean said as he waved for Maggie to join them. "Maggie this is Robert Sharpton. Robert, this is Maggie." Robert took Maggie's hand and kissed it.

"I am so pleased to finally meet you," said Robert. "I have heard about you for a long time, and what they say about you is not quite true. You are more beautiful than I have heard."

"Thank you for your kindness," said Maggie. "I am glad that you are not hurt."

"That big Irishman over there that shot this one fella is Michael O'Connor," said Sean. Michael walked over to Robert and extended his hand. They shook.

"I'll get some help and we'll get these bodies out of here," said Michael. Jon walked in and walked over to Sean to see what had happened.

"I just took Dog out to do his necessaries, and I come back in and there's three dead men in here," said Jon. "What did I miss?"

"Jon, this well dressed fella is Robert Sharpton and Robert, this is Jon O'Brien," said Sean. Jon and Robert shook hands. "These three were tryin' to do harm to Robert here. They're dead and he's not."

"Well all right," said Jon. "I'll help get these bodies outta here. Don't shoot anyone else while I'm gone."

Jon and Michael drug the bodies outside. Then they had some more men help take the bodies over to the undertaker. The undertaker apparently was asleep in the back of his shop so they just laid the bodies on his back porch. They went through the dead men's pockets and found nothing that would identify them. They did have $500 between all three of them. "That's a good bit a money ta be carryin' around," said Michael. "I reckon sooner or later we'll find out what they were up to."

"Maybe they was hired ta kill that Robert fella," said Jon. "Maybe he's somebody important or rich or somethin' and someone wanted'm dead."

"Well let's tell young Sean about the money and such," said Michael. "The buryin' fund's gonna make some more money looks like. These three probly had horses too."

When Jon and Michael got back to the saloon, Robert and Sean were sitting at Sean's regular table enjoying some Irish Whiskey. Michael and Jon went over and joined them. "Those three had $500 on them all told, and there was nothin' that would identify them," Michael said. "We'll find out tomorrow if they had horses or not."

"What will you do with that money?" asked Robert.

"It'll go into the bank with the buryin' fund." said Sean.

"What's the buryin' fund?" asked Robert.

"Well sometime back I started it," Sean began. "Whenever we kill an outlaw, we take whatever money was on'm, sell his horse and guns, get'm buried, and then put what's left in the buryin' fund. If the next outlaw killed don't have any money or anything, we use the fund ta get'm buried."

"That sounds reasonable," said Robert. "Most folks would keep all that money."

"I don't need it," said Sean. "What with this place and reward money and money made from a cattle drive, I would probly never hafta work another day in my life if I didn't wanna. Last reward money we got, I give to Jesse Strong. He's not here now. He was a deputy for a short while. Just a short while back he took his wife down to "The Nations" ta visit her relatives. Jesse is a colored man, and his wife is Osage."

"I don't care what color a man is," said Robert. "If he worked for you, he must be a good man."

"He sure as hell is," said Sean. "And he is about the strongest man I ever did see. He took a bowie knife and rammed it into the top of a man's skull, and the tip was stickin' out below the man's chin."

"Damn, I just bet that he was a blacksmith too," said Robert.

"Yep, he was," said Sean. "He worked on a big horse farm in Kentucky before the war. He was in the 54th durin' the war too. Ended up in the cavalry, and he can shoot too. He killed two men in a gunfight not long ago. Anyway, let's get this place livened up some. Michael, how bout playin' somethin' fast on your piano. Maybe someone'll get up and dance."

"I'll see if I can get anyone movin'," said Michael. Michael went back to his piano and started playing. Jon grabbed Martha and started dancing. Then a few other men grabbed some girls and joined in.

"Now Robert, you said somethin' earlier about it being mostly true that you had no idea why them three fellas would want to harm you," said Sean. "Now just what did you mean by mostly true?"

"Mr. O'Rourke, you and I need to have a very private conversation," began Robert. "What say we meet here for breakfast. It is just too crowded in here now, and our conversation must be private."

"That's fine by me," said Sean. "Now I'm concerned for your safety tonight. Do you have a hotel room?"

"No I do not," said Robert. "I got into town late and I wanted to come right here first."

"Well I have a room for you out back," said Sean. "I'll have Jon's dog stay with you. That's Dog over there watching Jon dance. I can assure you that with Dog in your room, no one will get in there and live to tell about."

"So that dog is named Dog," said Robert. "What's the name of the other dog that goes everywhere Maggie goes?"

"That's Jeb," said Sean. "He's me and Maggie's dog. We got him and Dog from the Hawks. They was usin'em as cow dogs. The Hawks won't need'em anymore. Ole Jeb and Dog have both ripped out some men's throats. Jeb here bit a man's hand clean off. You won't hafta worry bout Dog. I'll get you two introduced. Be nice ta Dog and he'll be nice ta you."

When the song was finished Jon and Dog came back over to the table. "Jon, I'd like ta borrow Dog here ta spend the night with Robert," said Sean. "He'll be stayin' in your old room out back."

"In that case I better introduce Dog to Robert," said Jon. "Dog, this here is Robert. You'll be in his room tonight. Don't let nobody else in there unless you know'em."

"Did Dog understand what you just said to him?" asked Robert.

"Yes he did," said Jon. "Won't nobody get in your room that you don't want in there." Robert reached over and petted Dog. They made friends right off. "Dog just did his necessaries so he'll be good for the whole night," said Jon. "Whenever yer ready ta turn in, just tell'em to c'mon and he'll go with you."

~~~~

Robert finished his drink and told Sean that he would see him for breakfast. Dog went with him and slept at the foot of the bed. Nothing happened during the night. Robert woke up right after daylight and Dog was standing beside the bed staring at him. "I suppose you need to go out for a minute," said Robert. "All right, you go on out and I'll be out in a minute." When Robert came out the door to go to the saloon, Dog was there waiting for him. He and Dog went to the saloon together. Sean, Jon, and Michael were at their table drinking coffee.

"I guess you had a good sleep," said Sean. "Dog looks like he had one too. Have some coffee. Breakfast'll be ready shortly." Robert joined them at the table and Michael got Robert some coffee.

"I did sleep good last night," said Robert. "Haven't slept that good for a long time. Now I suppose you want to know why I need a private conversation with you."

"It's been on my mind some," said Sean. "And if you haven't figured it out yet, these two men were my deputies so anything you say here will be considered private."

"I figured that these two were your deputies," said Robert. "I'll get right to the point. I am here of my own free will to investigate the killings of the two Federal Judges. Now before we go on, can we go ahead and eat breakfast? I haven't eaten since yesterday afternoon, and I'm famished. I didn't feel like eating last night with everything that had happened."

Cookie brought them all out some ham and eggs and fresh coffee. Not a word was spoken while they ate. Then Michael spoke.

"Why did you say that you were here of own free will?" asked Michael.

"I have been selected as the new Federal Judge. No investigation has been ordered so I'm doing one myself," said Robert. "I have heard rumors about Lucas, and I would like to know if they are correct or not."

"Well I don't know what you've heard," said Sean. "Lucas was a thief and a murderer. He had Dave Simmons killed so he could be my boss. I have no idea how a man like that got to be a Judge in the first place."

"Well let's go back to Dave Simmons," said Robert. "When did you first meet him and how did you become his Marshal?"

"It was during the war," started Sean. "I had killed some deserters who had murdered a civilian family. They were raping a dead woman when I killed'em. I was takin' their bodies back to the Commanding General when I met Dave. He was a General's aide. He musta been impressed with what I'd done. He found out all about me. He said he was a Federal Judge and asked me to be a Marshal after the war."

"The way you were talking, it sounded to me like you knew that family who was killed," said Robert.

"I knew'em," said Sean. "I was raised in that part a Tennessee. That woman they raped was gonna be my wife after the war. We was childhood sweethearts and got back together when we was fightin' over that way."

"Sorry for your loss," said Robert. "Please continue."

"Well I took the Marshal's job," started Sean. "Spent a lotta time killin' the Hawks and the Anderson bunch. Found out that they worked together some. Ever once in a while, one a them outlaws would tell us that Anderson had a boss. There was several attempts on my life this whole time. Anderson had put $2000 on my head, and we heard that his boss put up another $2000. After we got Anderson killed, things slowed down some. Then we got sent to Kansas City. Every public official in that town was corrupt. We knew there was a bigger boss somewhere. One day we got a telegram from the Judge tellin' us that some border gang was causin' trouble over east and when we were on the trail, we found out that Dave had been killed. I figured it couldn't have been Dave who sent that telegram so we got back to town. Nothin' was goin' on. Then my friend Sam Draper got killed. Then we got a telegram from a Judge in Kansas City tellin' us that a Bo Billings was headed our way and there were three other men on the stage with him. Bo was wanted for murder in three states."

"So what happened next?" asked Robert.

"Well we found out them four was together and was part of a group of eleven killers who were comin' here ta kill all a us," said Sean. "We found out about the other ones and who their boss was, and we got'em killed. We also found out that Lucas was their boss."

"I'll not ask how you managed to find all this out," said Robert. "So do you have any idea who might have killed Lucas?"

"I'd say one a his own men did it," said Sean. "If he was a big a crook as they say, maybe one a his men decided he wanted a bigger share of the action. Maybe Lucas didn't wanna share anymore, and the man killed'em. I don't know. Just guessin'. We heard he was doin' a lotta black market stuff durin' the war. We heard he even had his own men killed. Maybe someone finally got even with'm."

"I have heard rumors about his war time experiences too," said Robert. "If any of it is true, then Lucas did have some friends in high places and probably still does. Maybe those three men who you killed yesterday work for such men."

"So you think it's possible that those three men were after you because you might know somethin' about Lucas, and who worked for him or who got him appointed?" asked Sean.

"It's possible," said Robert. "A man would have to know some powerful people to get himself appointed as a Federal Judge. Those powerful people would have the President's ear."

"So are you worried that if you take the job you'll get killed too?" asked Sean.

"No, I'm not worried about getting killed," said Robert. "I was in the war too. I commanded an infantry battalion most of the war. Got shot up a couple of times. My wife died right after the surrender so I'm not worried about making some woman a widow. All I really want to know is what I'm up against. I hate corruption, especially when the corruption is by men who were placed in positions of trust by their fellow citizens. I intend to make it my personal duty to clean up any corruption that I find."

"Good luck with that," said Sean. "I imagine that some places were just a terrible mess after the war. Some politicians want revenge for the war and others just want us all to be brothers again. I think we been lucky out here so far. Haven't even heard anyone around here call someone a carpetbagger."

"Let's move on to some other things," said Robert. "I know that Judge Simmons told you to hang George Anderson when you caught him, but did you hang any other men without being told?"

"Yes I did," answered Sean. "I hung some a the Hawks and that Sheriff in Kansas City. I also hung some a that bunch that was sent here ta kill us by Lucas."

"And you feel that you had the authority to hang them?" asked Robert.

"Weren't nobody else around to do it," said Sean. "They was all guilty a murder and it needed done. I did it. You got a problem with that?"

"I could be removed from the bench for what I'm going to say," said Robert. "If you will become my Marshal, I will want you to do just what you've been doing. One day we will have more law and more courts and such, but right now we don't. For the time being, we need a quick and firm hand. When I accept my appointment next week, will you be my Marshal?"

"I have thought about this for a good while," said Sean. "Maggie will go along with whatever I do. She knows that even if I weren't a lawman, there would always be trouble from an old enemy. Yes sir Robert, I'll be your Marshal," said Sean. "I can't speak for Michael and Jon though."

"I reckon we've been this far with you Sean darlin'," said Michael. "I reckon we'll go the rest of the way."

"I reckon we will," said Jon.

"I want to thank you men," said Robert. "After I'm sworn in I'll send a telegram. When you get that telegram, consider yourself sworn in again. Now let's have some Irish Whiskey and have a toast. I know it's early in the day yet, but a toast seems appropriate."

"Michael and me been doin' a special toast ever since the war," said Sean. "I think you'll like it." The glasses were filled and each man raised his glass. "Here's to not getting killed," toasted Sean.

"Here's to not getting killed," all of them repeated.

"That is a good toast," said Robert. "Now I'll be leaving on the next stage. I look forward to working with all of you. We'll have O'Rourke's law or no law at all."

CHAPTER TWO

Robert left on the next stage as planned. Sean let it be known that if anything bad happened to Robert while he was on the stage line, he would take it very personally and individuals would be held accountable. Shotgun riders were armed with shotguns, Winchesters, two pistols, and plenty of ammunition. The drivers were armed with Winchesters and pistols. Robert made it safely to Kansas City and then took the train to St. Louis.

~~~~

Four days after Robert Sharpton left town, two soldiers came into town. One was a Major and the other was a Captain. When they got off the stage, they went straight to Maggie's Place. It was mid morning, and there were only a few customers in the place finishing a late breakfast. Michael was setting at his piano practicing a new tune that he had written and Jon was at the regular table drinking coffee. Dog was with him. Tom was behind the bar and Cookie and Barbara were in the kitchen. Maggie and Sean were still upstairs in their room.

Michael was the first to see the soldiers. He eyed them for a moment and then yelled over to Jon. "What do you think there

Jon?" said Michael. "Should we make the boys in blue give up their side arms or not?"

"I'm not sure," answered Jon. "These fellas is officers. I bet they got some kinda regulation that says they can't surrender their side arms or somethin' like that. Is that so blue boys? You got some regulation says you can't give up your side arms to no one?"

"That is correct," answered the Major. "And I appreciate it if you didn't call us blue boys. We are officers in the United States Army. I am Major Dunlap, and this is Captain Pierce."

"Sounds like these fellas been educated," said Jon. "Too much proper speakin' makes my ears hurt. You talk to'em Michael. I bet they got nothin' ta say that I wanna hear anyway."

"You two'll hafta excuse my friend there," said Michael. "He was an officer in the war, but he didn't wear the blue. Now just what is it we can do for you this mornin'?"

"We are here to speak with Mr. O'Rourke," said the Major.

"And why would you be needin' to speak with our friend?" asked Michael.

"That would be between him and us," said the Major. "Would you please tell Mr. O'Rourke that we are here?"

"No I will not," answered Michael. "He will be here whenever he shows up. You two will hafta just wait. We have us a very good cook if you want somethin' ta eat and we have plenty to drink if you're drinkin' men."

"We are on duty and cannot drink, but since we must wait, we might as well have a meal," said the Major. "We'll have whatever the cook is making today."

"I'll have the cook get two meals ready," said Michael. Michael was looking at the Captain now. "Can't you speak?" Michael asked the Captain. "Hasn't been one word come outta your mouth yet."

"I just bet you were a Sergeant," said the Captain. "You act like a Sergeant. If you were a Sergeant, you would know that a superior officer should be doing the talking."

"Yes I was a Sergeant, but I always figured that when there's somethin' ta be said, it should be said no matter the person's rank," said Michael. "Rank doesn't always make a person smarter. So what unit do you two belong? You're not with the 7th Cavalry are you?"

"As a matter of fact we are," answered the Major.

"Well we already know why you're here and you've wasted a trip," said Michael. "Now you two enjoy your meal and think about what you'll tell your boss when you get back empty handed." Not another word was spoken. Cookie brought the food to the officers and got them some coffee. After they were finished eating, both of them agreed that they had eaten a very good meal. They were finishing their coffee when Maggie and Sean finally came downstairs. Jeb followed them. Sean spotted the boys in blue right away.

"You boys can go back and tell George Armstrong Custer that I will not scout for him or anyone else," said Sean as he came down the stairs. "I got nothin' against the Cheyenne, Arapaho, or Sioux and I'll not help anyone who wants to do them harm."

"The General will not take it kindly that you feel this way," said the Major. "He's used to getting his way."

"I couldn't care less about how Custer feels," said Sean. "And what's this General crap? He's a Lt. Colonel."

"We call him General out of respect for his former rank during the war," said the Major.

"Well I'm not in the army anymore, and I'll call Custer whatever I want," said Sean. "Now why don't you two save your breath and head on back to your boss?"

"Mr. O'Rourke, don't you know that the Cheyenne are raiding over west and killing innocent people? They must be stopped," said the Major.

"Why are those people innocent?" asked Sean. "They're over there takin' land that the Cheyenne believe has been theirs since the beginning of time. Wouldn't you fight for your land?"

"I wouldn't kill women and children," answered the Major.

"And just how many women and children did Chivington massacre at Sand Creek?" asked Sean.

"Chivington wasn't regular army," said the Major.

"He wore blue didn't he?" said Sean. "Do you reckon the Cheyenne know the difference between regulars and militia or whatever Chivington was. They see the blue."

"Those are Christian families being killed out there," said the Major. "Doesn't that mean anything to you?"

"How do you know what religion them folks are?" said Sean. "Just cause they're white, don't make'em Christians. I'l l bet anything you want that Chivington claims ta be a Christian. And who says so-called Christians is better than other folks?" Seems ta me a lotta Christians don't pay much attention to the New Testament."

"So you know about the New Testament do you?" asked the Captain.

"I was raised Catholic," said Sean. "I can quote from the Old or New Testament as well as any Bible thumper. I know what the Cheyenne believe too."

"So you know all these things, and you don't practice any certain religion?" asked the Captain.

"The only thing I practice is "right or wrong," said Sean.

"So you think you're always right?" asked the Major.

"No I do not," answered Sean. "Now we're about done here. You fellas should get yourself back to your boss before I lose my temper."

"I assume that this beautiful woman here is your wife," said the Major. "Why would a man have his wife in a place like this?"

"You just crossed the line mister," said Sean. He grabbed the Major by the front of his uniform at his chest and stood him up. Sean let go with a right to his body, and when he buckled over, Sean gave him a left uppercut and put him flat on his back. The Captain stood now.

"So you like to use your fists," said the Captain. "I boxed some in college. I think I'll give you some lessons." Before the Captain did anything, Sean shoved the table into the Captain and knocked him down. Before he could get back up, Sean was on him. A right to the jaw, then a left, and the Captain was knocked out. The Major was up now and was about to hit Sean with a chair. Jeb came over and let out a vicious growl. The Major put down the chair.

"Someone throw some water on the Captain here," said Sean. "I believe if he's gonna gimme some lessons, he needs ta be awake." Tom came from behind the bar and threw a bucket of water into the Captain's face. He came to wondering what had happened. "Thanks for the lessons Captain," said Sean. Now you two set down and have a drink. I think you need it."

"I believe you are right Mr. O'Rourke," said the Major. "Do you have any good bourbon?"

"Yes we do," answered Sean. "Me and the boys'll join you if you don't mind."

"We won't mind," said the Major. "We apologize for causing trouble in your establishment."

"Apology accepted," said Sean. "Now have you two seen the elephant?"

"We were both in the war," said the Major. "We saw plenty of death."

"Well I'm gonna tell you some things about Indians," said Sean. "They might help you sometime and they might not. Indians mainly just wanna be left alone ta live their lives like they have for years. You leave them alone, and they'll leave you alone. I can't speak for Comanche though. Indians don't fight like soldier boys. They won't line up and let you shoot at'em. They can put three arrows in you while you're reloadin' a carbine. They know their land and you don't. They know every water hole and stream and every rise and dip. There can be hundreds of'em watchin' you and you'll never know they're around. I reckon the army'll still be usin' Pawnee as scouts. We had some scrapes with the Pawnee when I was with the Cheyenne. Don't have no use for no Pawnee. Well I talked enough. You fellas remember some a what I said, and maybe you'll be alive in a few years. If I was you, I'd get myself in another unit before too long. I've heard all about Custer's luck. Some day it'll run out."

"Mr. O'Rourke, would you mind if I asked you some questions about how you came to be with the Cheyenne and how their way of life was?" asked the Major. "Most white folks know nothing about Indians. All anyone ever hears is bad things. I personally know nothing. I refuse to believe all the bad things I have heard. I refuse to believe that just because they are different and not Christians that they are inferior to the white race. I do not believe that colored folks are inferior to the whites. I saw colored troops in action during the war and they fought as well and as bravely as any white troops I saw. Maybe even better. They knew if they were captured they would be murdered. That would make me fight harder. So what do you say, Mr. O'Rourke, will you tell me about the Cheyenne?"

"First off, you can call me by my name," said Sean. "It's Sean. I will talk with you if you set here and sip some whiskey while we talk. Second, make sure you remember what I tell you. Them are some a my friends out there. Maybe one day, they'll be your friends too."

"I promise that we will not forget one word you tell us Sean," said the Major. "I'm ready to listen."

"All right, I'll start back in '54," Sean began. "I was raised in Tennessee not far from Chattanooga. There was my Pa, Ma, and me. We had a 300 acre farm and my Pa was a blacksmith and horse trainer. We never had no slaves. We had a colored family that worked and lived on our farm too. We had a big shoot out one time with some white trash. We killed eight men that night, but Jim got killed and little Jim was wounded. That was the colored man and his son. The woman had died earlier from pneumonia. My Ma and Pa decided we needed to go west before the war started. Everyone knew it was comin'. Our small wagon train was massacred by white outlaws. I was out huntin' at the time. I had my Sharps and a Colt Walker with me, and I killed some a the outlaws. Some Cheyenne happened by. They had one a the outlaws with'em. I had wounded him and he was tryin' ta get away when he run into them. I killed that man and told the Cheyenne they could have whatever they needed from the wagons except what was with my wagons. They took me in."

"So your folks were killed?" asked the Major.

"Yes they were," said Sean. "Them outlaws shot everyone several times. Don't know if it was ta make sure they was dead, or they did it for fun. Anyway, I lived with a Cheyenne woman and her mountain man husband. They had a daughter who later became my wife. The man, Braddock, taught me how ta track and hunt and everything I needed ta stay alive. The daughter, Katie, taught me their language and all about other tribes and such. We lived by following the game. You spend warm months gettin' ready for the cold just like white folks do. We had some scrapes with the Pawnee and the Comanche. You need to remember that some tribes hate other tribes just like some white folks hate other white folks. I always carried a Sharps rifle and a Colt Walker pistol. I was a very good shot. They started callin' me "the one who kills with the long gun and the big pistol." Anyway, the Cheyenne are good people. They are very polite and believe in good manners. They just wanna be left alone to live like they have for hundreds of years. They can be fierce fighters when they have to. They know about certain medicines and how to treat wounds so they won't get infected. I took a Comanche arrow in my side once, and I got healed up no problem." "So Cheyenne and Comanche don't get along?" asked the Major.

"No, the Comanche don't get along with no one except the Kiowa," said Sean. "And the Pawnee don't get along well with anyone. Them scoutin' for the army don't make the other tribes like'em any better either."

"So who do the Cheyenne get along with?" asked the Major.

"The Cheyenne, Arapaho, and the Sioux are good friends and allies," said Sean. "You may wanna make sure your boss knows that when he's out lookin' for glory. Could find hisself outnumbered sometime. Now back to my life with the Cheyenne. Katie and I were married when we turned fifteen. We had a daughter, and Katie was pregnant again when the cholera came. I lost them, and every lodge lost people. That was early '61. I left the Cheyenne then cause I didn't know what I wanted to do. That piano player there was a Sergeant and on patrol when I met'm. The war started, and I scouted for the army through Indian land when they was ordered back east. I joined the army on the way. I'm sure you know the rest."

"We heard that you were a sharpshooter and you only shot non-commissioned officers," said the Captain. "Is that true. Why did you do that?"

"Because Sergeants and Corporals are the ones who make sure things gets done," said Sean. "Sure some officer give the orders, but the men with the stripes make sure it gets carried out."

"That's true," said the Captain. "Most officers give the orders then get out of the way. Now Custer wasn't like that. His men loved him. He always led the charges."

"I heard he was like that," said Sean. "He was out for glory. He was probably sad when the war ended. Now he's out here lookin' for more glory killin' Indians. As I said earlier, his luck'll run out one a these days."

"So let's get back to the Cheyenne," said the Major. "You really did enjoy your life with them?"

"Yes I did," said Sean. "It was a good life. It was hard, but it was good. I loved it."

"So do you think Indians and white folks will ever get along?" asked the Major.

"We won't see it in our lifetime," said Sean. It'll be the same with colored folks. Just cause the war freed the slaves, don't mean attitudes'r gonna change. I just got no idea where all this stuff about inferior races comes from. It makes me sick thinkin' bout it. I heard your boss turned down being a full Colonel with the 9th or

10th. He musta figured there'd be no glory with colored troops. Why don't you ask'm about that next time you see'm?"

"I doubt we'll get the chance," said the Major. "After we give him the news about you, he'll probably call us incompetent and tell us to get out. He's used to getting his way. Now is that story we heard about when you first met General Sherman true? Were you really going to brain that Captain?"

"The story is true," said Sean. "I'm surprised so many people know about that."

"I think General Sherman tells it more than anyone," said the Major.

"I wonder what Sherman thinks about all this Indian stuff?" said Sean. "He's probly gotta be a politician now more than he is a General."

"I don't know what they have him doing now," said the Major. "We all know that Grant'll be the next President of the United States. I'd say his friends'll get good jobs when he is." Before the Major could get out another word, Jason came running into the saloon.

"Sean, better get over to the livery right now," Jason cried. "There's two men there and they're fixin' to lynch a colored man. Young Billy was there by himself. He tried to help that man, and one of'em clubbed him with an ax handle. When they saw me, they pointed a shotgun at me and told me to mind my own business."

"Excuse me Major," said Sean. "I best get over there before that fella gets lynched." Sean got up and ran to the livery. As he was running he checked his two pistols to make sure they were fully loaded. When he entered the livery, the first thing he saw was young Billy laying there unconscious. Then he saw two dirty rough looking men. Both of them had double barreled shotguns, and they were pointed at the colored man. The colored man was on a horse and a noose was around his neck. His hands were tied behind his back. One of the two men had the other end of the rope in his hand.

"Get outta here and mind yer own damn business," said the taller of the two. "We're gonna hang us a horse thief."

"You with the rope, drop it now," said Sean.

"Go ta hell," the one with the rope said. "We're hangin' this nigger, and there's nothin' you'r anybody else is gonna do bout it."

Sean could see that neither man had cocked the hammers on their shotgun. Young Billy was starting to come to. He was behind Sean. "Billy, soon as you can git up, you back on outta here," said Sean. "Gonna be some dead men in here in a little bit." Billy made his way out of there. When he cleared the door, Jason was there and picked him up and took him to the Doc's. The Major and the Captain were there and were trying to peek in and see what was happening.

"You boys don't know me, but the name's O'Rourke," Sean began. "I can kill you before you can get them hammers cocked. Now I'm gonna ask this fella you threwed up on this horse some questions. If I even think I see your thumbs movin', I'll kill you."

"I heard a you," the taller one said. "Go ahead and ask yer questions."

"So mister, these two fellas say yer a horse thief," said Sean. "Is that so?"

"No it's not so," he answered. "It's not stealin' when you take yer own horse back. Them two stole that horse from me bout two weeks ago. Look at that brand. It hasn't healed yet."

"So how am I s'posed ta know that it's yer horse?" asked Sean.

"I raised that horse from a colt," said the colored man. "There's a real small brand on the under side of his tail bout four inches from the tip. Move the hair around and you'll see it It's two letters, S and C. Stands for Sam Carver. That's my name." Sean checked the horse's tail.

"Looks like an S and a C," said Sean. "Looks like you boys'r the horse thieves, and I should be hangin' you. Now you know what really gets me ticked off besides horse thieves? It's people that beat kids. Now you two got two choices. You can keep holdin' them shotguns and I'll shoot you dead, or you can put them down and I'll beat the hell outta you. I might still kill you after I beat you. Don't know yet. What'll it be?"

"I think we'll take our chances with our fists," the taller one said. "I don't think you can take both of us. After we beat the hell outta you, we'll hang this nigger." The two men put down the shotguns and made a run at Sean. The taller one reached Sean first and made a dive to grab him. Sean simply sidestepped him and kicked him in the ribs as he flew past. The other man was close now and took a swing at Sean with his right hand. Sean blocked it with his left arm and then hit the man with a tremendous right to the jaw. The man flew backwards moaning. Before he hit the ground, Sean hit him with a left to the jaw and the man was unconscious. The other man was up now and grabbed Sean from behind. Sean stomped the man's right foot with his right foot and the man let go. Sean turned to face him and put a left hook into his mid section. When the man doubled over, Sean brought up his left knee and put it into the man's face. Blood went everywhere."

"You broke my nose you son of a bitch," the man said. The man reached into a pocket and pulled out a very big pocket knife. Sean figured the blade was at least six inches long.

"You shouldn't a pulled that knife," said Sean. "Now I might hafta kill you."

"You won't be doin' nothin' but bleedin' with yer guts hangin' out," said the man. Then he put the knife in his right hand and came after Sean. He held the knife above his head with the blade downward. He closed in on Sean and struck downward at him. Sean blocked the blow with both of his arms, and at the same time, he kicked the man square in his privates. The man let out a groan and fell to the ground. The knife was still in his right hand. Sean thought that he might stab himself as he was falling, but the knife stuck in the ground instead.

"I think you can git down off yer horse now Sam," said Sean. "Sorry this took so long." Sean took the knife from the other man and was cutting the ropes from Sam's hands. Sean still had his gun belt on. The two men had charged him before he could remove it. When the ropes were almost cut, Sean heard what he knew was a hammer being cocked. He turned and drew and fired twice. The man who had been knocked unconscious had come to and had crawled over to his shotgun. He had cocked one hammer and was cocking the other when Sean's bullet caught him in the forehead. The other man had reached his shotgun and was attempting to raise it when he too was struck in the forehead. Michael and Jon were at the livery now.

"So what did we miss this time?" asked Jon.

"We'll sit down and talk about all this over a drink," started Sean. "Are you a drinkin' man Sam?"

"I been known ta have a few at times," said Sam. "Now seems like a good time."

"Well let's all go back to the saloon and Sam can tell us all about himself and such," said Sean. "Michael, check their pockets and such. We'll sell their hardware and horses as always. Jon, let the undertaker know he's got some more business." Jason met them at the saloon.

"Doc says Billy'll be all right," said Jason. "Just got a bad bump. He's a brave little boy tryin' ta help that man."

"Yep, he is," said Sean. "I wonder where his dogs were. They wouldn't a let anything happen ta Billy if they was there."

"I asked him that myself," said Jason. "He said he left'em home cause he wasn't gonna be at the livery long."

"I bet at least one of'em'll go everywhere he goes from now on," said Sean. They got back to the saloon, and they all sat at Sean's table. Sean invited the soldiers to be with them too. "So will whiskey be all right with everyone, or would anyone like a beer too?" asked Sean. No one asked for a beer, so Tom brought over a couple of bottles and several glasses. Sean filled everyone's glass. "Now Sam, tell us all about yourself," said Sean. "I don't just mean about them horse thieves. Tell us everything about yourself."

"Well I was born a free man," Sam began. "My family lived in Cincinnati. My folks was servants for some rich white man. He had a big horse farm just outside a town. When I got bigger, I worked with the horses. Mr. Parsons, that was the man's name, well he liked me cause I was good with the horses. When I turned eighteen, he gimme that horse. The war was goin' on then too and the army wanted a lotta our horses. We convinced the army that Charlie, that's what I named him, had a terrible temper and couldn't be broken. We just used'em for breedin'. Ya see, that was somewhat true. I was the only one that Charlie would let ride'm. The army sent several men to try and ride Charlie, but he hurt'em bad. They give up. Them two that stole Charlie from me must notta tried ta ride'em, or they wouldn't a been able ta follow me."

"So how was things in Cincinnati?" asked Sean.

"Well my folks both died in early '63," said Sam. "Mr. Parsons' wife and his oldest son died then too from the coughin' sickness. Mr. Parsons said he was gonna sell out. I didn't wanna work for nobody else, so I went over and joined the 54th Massachusetts."

"I got two good friends who were in the 54th, Jim O'Rourke and Jesse Strong," said Sean. "Did you know'em?"

"Jim was my platoon Sergeant," said Sam. "Him and Jesse was best friends. I seen'em do some things durin' the war. I don't know how they didn't git killed."

"Well Jim's dead now," said Sean. "He came out here cause he heard they was gonna form a couple a colored cavalry regiments, and he was bein' my deputy while he was waitin'. He got killed by a bad outlaw. Jesse Strong was here for a while and now he's with his wife visitin' her kin down in "The Nations."

"It don't seem possible Jim could be dead," said Sam. "I seen him and Jesse fightin' off reb after reb when we was on that wall at Fort Wagner. Back then it didn't seem like he could be killed. I sure woulda liked ta seen Jim again. Mebbe one day I'll see Jesse again."

"He might come up this way again," said Sean. "So what'r you gonna do with yourself?"

"I came out here ta join the 10th," said Sam. "They're formin' up at Fort Leavonworth. There was three of us when we left Ohio, but the further west we got, the more them other two decided that they had enough a the army. They was both with the 54th too." Major Dunlap joined in the conversation.

"Sam Carver, my name is Major Dunlap and this is Captain Pierce," said the Major. "Would you mind if I asked you some questions about your army service?"

"No Major, I don't," said Sam. "You might not like what I say dependin' on what you ask."

"Don't worry. I will not be offended," said the Major. "Now I would like to know if you liked having all white officers."

"I never minded'em. A lot of'em sure minded us though," said Sam. "Some of'em treated us pretty bad. Our Colonel was a good man though. He was right there with us chargin' that fort when he got killed."

"So you say that most of the white officers treated you badly," said the Major.

"Yes they did," said Sam. "They treated us like we was too stupid ta tie our own shoes most a the time. They finally found out that our blood was red too."

"So do you think it'll be any different with the 10th?" asked the Major.

"I don't know, but I hope so," answered Sam. "Mebbe we'll get some white officers that know we're just as good or better fighters than white boys. Who knows, mebbe one day they'll be some colored officers."

"What rank were you when you mustered out?" asked the Captain.

"I was a Sergeant," answered Sam. "I had me a platoon and they was pretty good. I bet we coulda taken Richmond all by ourselves."

"It's good that you had that attitude," said Captain Pierce. "I hope you can keep that attitude where you're going. You'll be in the middle of nowhere. Most of your officers will not want to be there, and they'll take it out on you. Any white folks you see probably won't like you either."

"So things'll be the same as they already are, huh Captain?" said Sam.

"I guess so," said Captain Pierce. "Anyway, I wish you the best."

"Thank you Captain. Who knows, mebbe one day you'll end up bein' one a my officers," said Sam.

"At least I'll know that I have a good man in my unit," said the Captain. Then the Captain reached across the table and extended his hand to Sam. Sam stood, and they shook.

"So Sam, just how in the hell did come across them two horse thieves?" asked Sean.

"I got no idea," said Sam. "They musta seen me and Charlie somewhere and decided Charlie was worth stealin'. I was really surprised they took Charlie that night without me wakin' up. I musta been dead tired and like I said before, they must notta tried ta ride'em. I tracked'em on foot for two days. They went ta some little town and got drunk. I slipped in and took Charlie back. Got all the way here before they found me. I didn't have my pistol on me when they showed up, or I'd a killed'em. Would you have hung me if I'd a killed them two? I've heard that you don't mind hangin' folks."

"We've hung a few, but we knew for sure that them that was hanged needed it," said Sean. "We'd hear you out before any hangin' decision would be made."

"That's good ta know," said Sam. "Now can a man get somethin' ta eat in here. It's been a while since I et last."

"We'll get you somethin'," said Michael. "We got the best cooks in town right here."

"Well I have whatever they got goin' today," said Sam. It wasn't long and Cookie brought out a plate for Sam. Sam tore into it like he hadn't eaten for a year.

"No one's gonna steal your food," said Jon. "There's more if ya need it." Maggie walked over to the table now.

"Introduce me to your new friend darlin'," said Maggie.

"Well Maggie, this is Sam Carver, and Sam, this is my wife Maggie," said Sean. Sam stood and nodded his head.

"It's a pleasure ma'am," said Sam.

"I'm pleased to met you too Sam," said Maggie. "And you can call me Maggie. That's my name."

"Yes Maggie," said Sam.

"Maggie, Sam here was with the 54th too and knew Jim and Jesse both," said Sean. "He's joinin' up with the 10th."

"I wish you well," said Maggie. Maggie then excused herself, and she and Jeb headed out the door. "I'm going to the bank. Be back shortly." Sam took a look at Jeb and looked like he had swallowed a frog.

"What kinda dog is that?" asked Sam. "Scares me just ta look at'm."

"Don't know what kinda dog he is, but if I don't like someone or Maggie don't like someone, he don't like'em either," said Sean. "He's ripped out some throats, and he bit a man's hand clean off. We like you. You got nothin' ta worry bout. So when will you be headin' to Leavonworth?"

"I'll be leavin' first thing in the mornin'," said Sam. "I'll get me a good sleep and head out right after daylight."

"Well I got a room you can use for the night. It's right out back," said Sean. "Charlie'll be all right at the livery. I'll tell'em over there ta make sure nobody tries ta ride'm."

"This is mighty nice a you," said Sam. "You know I can't afford ta pay you."

"Did you hear anyone ask you for money?" asked Sean.

"No I didn't ," answered Sam.

"Well finish eatin', and I'll show you to your room," said Sean. Sam was impressed with the room and the bed.

"I'll repay you one day," said Sam.

"You can repay me by stayin' alive," said Sean.

"I'll do my best," said Sam.

The next morning Sam left for Fort Leavonworth, and Major Dunlap and Captain Pierce left for Fort Riley.

CHAPTER THREE

A few days later, the telegram came from Robert telling Sean that he had been sworn in as Federal Judge, and Sean was now a Federal Marshal again. It went as follows:

Sean O'Rourke
Abilene Kansas

O'Rourke<<stop>>have been sworn in as Federal Judge<<stop>>you are Federal Marshal again<<stop>> nothing pressing at this time<<stop>>expect letter from Susie at Palace<<stop>>trouble with new owner

Robert Sharpton
Federal Judge
St. Louis

"Well boys, we're lawmen again," said Sean. They had all been eating breakfast together when the telegram arrived. "I wonder how Robert got himself acquainted with Susie," said Sean. "I reckon she'll tell me when her letter gets here. I hope that new owner is not one a them fellas that was tied up with Lucas. If he is, I believe I'll go up there and straighten him out."

"You mean kill'm, don't you?" said Jon.

"If I hafta," said Sean. "If that fella or any a his boys'r mistreatin' them girls, his days as owner'r numbered."

"That'd look good to our new boss," said Michael. "We just get sworn back in, and we go kill some thugs right there is St. Louis. I wonder if that Marshal, Mike Kiley knows there's trouble."

"Hard ta say," said Sean. "Maybe the girls are afraid ta speak up to someone in town. Maybe they think he can't be trusted. Like I said, we'll find out more when Susie's letter gets here." Maggie had been in the back room and was coming over to the table. She had heard part of the conversation, but not all of it.

"What's this about Susie?" asked Maggie. "Is she in trouble?"

"Don't know much yet," said Sean. "We got that telegram from our new boss saying he was sworn in, and we were lawmen again. But he said to expect a letter from Susie. There's trouble with the new owner."

"Well Sean darlin', if that new owner is mistreating them girls in any way, I expect you to go up there and straighten things out," said Maggie. "Susie and those other girls are a nice lot. I won't stand for them being mistreated. Now just how do you think Robert came to know Susie?"

"I'm sure she'll tell us in her letter," said Sean. "How bout you and me goin' upstairs for a while? I'm gettin' worked up listening to you." Maggie grabbed Sean by the arm and they ran upstairs to their room. A good while later, they were still wrapped in each others arms, but were exhausted.

"I got me an idea darlin'," Sean said to Maggie as he looked into her eyes. "This all depends on what that letter from Susie says."

"Well fill me in," said Maggie.

"Well I would just bet that the new owner practically stole "The Palace" at that public auction," said Sean. "I bet him and his thugs had everyone else afraid ta bid. Sam's relatives didn't want the place and were glad ta git rid of it at any price. I figure they already made enough money off the place. Anyway, if Susie confirms what I already think, I'll go up there and convince that new owner ta sell ta me."

"You won't do anything illegal, will you darlin'?" asked Maggie.

"Heavens no, I'm an officer of the law," answered Sean. "Anything I do'll be legal, maybe."

"So how much are you willing to pay?" asked Maggie.

"Depends on what the new owner paid," answered Sean. "I'll pay him more than what he paid so he can make a profit. If he isn't agreeable, I'll convince him otherwise. He'll hafta agree ta leave town too."

"So I suppose him and his thugs, I'm assuming he'll have some thugs, will go right along with everything, and there won't be any trouble," said Maggie.

"We'll see," said Sean. "I suspect that they were tied in with Lucas. If they were, maybe we'll get lucky, and we'll find out who their boss is now."

"So we end up owning "The Palace," said Maggie. "Do we stay here or do we go there?"

"I'd rather stay here," answered Sean. "St. Louis is too big a town for me. We'll get someone reliable ta run the place for us. We'll visit on a regular basis."

"I don't want to live in St. Louis either," said Maggie. "We'll see what that letter says when it gets here. Who knows? Maybe we won't want to live here when the cattle drives start."

"Maybe we won't," said Sean. "It could get rowdy here when them Texas boys arrive."

"Let's go soak in the tub," said Maggie. "I think that would be nice right now."

"I'll go get some water heated up," said Sean.

~~~~

Two days later, the letter from Susie arrived. It went as follows:

Dear Sean,

I have no right to ask this of you, but I know that if you were here, things wouldn't be as they are. The new owner practically stole the place at the auction. Him and his thugs intimidated folks, and everyone else was afraid to bid. He got the place for $5000. You and I know it's worth ten times that. The first thing he did was fire all the bartenders and dealers and put his thugs in. He made us raise our rates and he takes a huge portion of it. We are forced to give him and his thugs free ones whenever they want. Some of the girls have been beaten. We are too afraid to leave. Mike Kiley retired as Marshal and the new Marshal is easily intimidated. When I heard about the new Judge, I went to him. He told me it was a local matter and he was a Federal Judge. I told him I was a friend of yours and he suggested I contact you. I told him I would. Can you help us?

Susie

Sean and Maggie were eating breakfast when the letter arrived. "Well darlin', I'll be goin' ta St. Louis," said Sean. "Sound like what I thought is true. Sounds ta me like the Judge doesn't care if I straighten things out either. I'll be sendin' him a telegram before we go."

"Who will you take with you this time?" asked Maggie. "I bet Michael would like to go. It seems like you always have him stay here when something's going on."

"I leave Michael here because he's a good man and can handle anything," said Sean. "I was thinkin' that I would take him and Jon both with me this time. Would you be all right with that?"

"We'll be all right here," said Maggie. "I can shoot. Betty can shoot. Tom'll be here. Cookie'll be here. And most of all, Jeb'll be here. Nothing will get past him."

"Well I'll talk to the boys and make sure they're all right with this," said Sean. "If they are, we'll be leavin' on the next stage." Sean found Michael and Jon and told them what he wanted to do. They were excited about going. After talking with them, Sean went to the telegraph office. He sent the following telegram to Judge Sharpton.

Federal Judge Sharpton
St. Louis

Will be coming to St. Louis<<stop>>received letter from Susie<<stop>>suspect that new owner had ties to Lucas<<stop>>will investigate

O'Rourke

The next morning, the three men and Dog left Abilene on the stage headed for Kansas City. Sean made sure the men had their repeating rifles, pistols, and plenty of ammunition. Sean also took his double barreled ten gauge. The stage ride was uneventful. They would spend the night in Kansas City and catch the train the next morning. When they got to the hotel, there was a new sign on it. It said Cutright's Hotel and Restaurant. Alex was at the desk when Sean and his men arrived. "I see your name on the sign," said Sean to Alex. "You musta figured out who ta buy this place from."

"It's good to see you again Sean and you can call me Mayor," said Alex. "You can call Roger Sheriff when you see him too. Still don't know who to buy this place from. If anybody in the future wants to know, I'll tell'em the previous owner give it to me."

"Sounds like you folks'r gettin' things sorted out," said Sean. "Did you get yourself a good Town Marshal?"

"Yes we did," answered Alex. "He was with you when we had that shoot out. His name is Jake Solomon. There hasn't been much for him to do since you took care of that bunch. I hope it stays that way. Lawrence Todd'll be wantin' to see you while you're here."

"I'll be wantin' ta see him too," said Sean. "He helped us out a while back, and I need ta thank'm."

"Well your rooms and drinks and meals are on the house Sean," said Alex. "If you want to go have a drink or a meal, I'll get your things up to your room."

"That'd be nice Alex," said Sean. "I believe me and the boys'll go get us a drink." Sean and the boys went to the restaurant, and Alex took their things to their rooms. They had just gotten a drink when Lawrence Todd showed up.

"What brings you back to our town?" asked Lawrence as he shook hands with Sean and then his men. "Nothing bad I hope."

"We'll find out how bad it is when we get ta St. Louis," said Sean. "Now before I forget, I wanna thank you for sendin' me that telegram bout Bo Billings."

"I read that he was dead," said Lawrence. "I thought I read that someone stuck a bowie knife in his head."

"They sure did," said Sean. "Jesse shoved that thing in the top a his head and it stuck out below his chin."

"Damn, that Jesse must have been a very strong man," said Lawrence.

"Yes he was," said Sean. "That Bo Billings was with ten other men who were sent ta kill me and my men. They're all dead and we're not."

"I just bet that Judge Lucas was their boss," said Lawrence. "He got that job kind of quick. Seemed suspicious to me."

"Yep, he was their boss," said Sean. "We're goin' ta St. Louis cause we think we got some folks who had ties ta Lucas."

"Well good luck to you," said Lawrence. "I have a feeling that Judge Lucas had a very big organization. Now if you'll excuse me, I have a small dispute to settle between a couple of our citizens. I always hate it when someone dies and there's no will. Take care of yourself."

~~~~

The boys had a good meal and a few drinks and Michael and Jon turned in early. Sean wanted to pay Sally a visit and see how her new place was doing. When Sean arrived at "Sally's Gentleman Club", the same dark haired beauty who was at the desk before, greeted him again. Sean didn't need to say anything and the dark haired woman went to the back room and came back with Sally. Sally ran to Sean and kissed him on the cheek. "It's always good to see you, Marshal," said Sally. "What brings you here?"

"I'm on my way to St. Louis and we're spendin' the night here," said Sean. "I just thought I'd check on you and make sure you're doing all right."

"Well we are doing very well," replied Sally. "My husband is always a perfect gentleman, and he makes sure my girls are treated like ladies. He took a job as loan officer at one of the banks. He's very good with numbers. We're hoping to expand here. Maybe we can have a restaurant and a hotel. We'll see. How's that wife of yours? I bet she misses you already."

"Well I miss her already," said Sean. "Hopefully we'll get things sorted out in St. Louis and I'll be home soon. Now I'll take my leave."

"Nonsense, you'll sit and have a drink with me," said Sally. "I couldn't give you a free one before so now I'll give you a free drink."

"All right Sally, I'll gladly drink with you," said Sean.

"I have a feeling that you are a bourbon man," said Sally. "And I bet you like Irish Whiskey too."

"I am a bourbon man and I do like Irish Whiskey," said Sean. "I'll take whatever you have."

"I have some of this brand new bourbon that I just received," said Sally. "I have not tried it yet. You'll be the first to try it." Sally made a motion to the dark haired beauty and she left and returned with a bottle and two glasses. Sally filled the glasses.

"Shall we have a toast?" asked Sean.

"Sure, let's drink to friendship," said Sally.

"To friendship," toasted Sean. As soon as the bourbon hit Sean tongue, he knew that this was the best bourbon he had ever tasted. "Sally, this is some very good stuff," said Sean. "Have you got somethin' ta write with and some paper.? I wanna write this down so I don't forget. Well be gettin' this stuff back home."

"Well I'm glad you like it," said Sally. "My husband picked it. There was a drummer here not long ago and he had all kinds of samples."

Sean finished his drink and gave Sally a kiss on the cheek. "I'll be leavin' now," said Sean. "If you ever need me for anything, don't hesitate to get ahold of me. If you can't get ahold a me in Abilene, Judge Sharpton in St. Louis will know my whereabouts. Just tell'm you're a friend a mine. He'll understand."

"Always a pleasure to see you Sean," said Sally. "Don't be a stranger."

Sean went back to his hotel and went straight to bed. It took him a while to get to sleep because he kept thinking about Maggie. The next morning after a good breakfast, Sean and the boys were on a train for St. Louis.

~~~~

When they got to St. Louis, they checked into the same hotel that Sean and Maggie had used on their honeymoon. Nothing was said about Dog. They took separate rooms. "You men get your gear to your rooms and we'll meet down here in the lobby in fifteen minutes," said Sean. "We'll be paying the Town Marshal a visit." They all went to their rooms and then met back down at the lobby. Sean had the ten gauge with him.

"Are we expecting trouble?" Michael asked.

"A ten gauge can make people listen," said Sean. "Hopefully it'll just be for show." The men and Dog exited the hotel and went straight to the Town Marshal's office. The Marshal was at his desk looking at some wanted posters and another man, probably a deputy, was behind him looking over his shoulder. He was wearing a tied down Colt. When they entered the office, the deputy placed his hand on the Colt. The Marshal stood now. He was also wearing a tied down Colt.

"Name's O'Rourke, Federal Marshal O'Rourke," said Sean. "Tell your man ta get his hand off that Colt and I mean right now."

"Better do as he says," said the Marshal. "I hear he could probably kill you with his pistol before you could get that thing outta the holster. And that ten gauge'll rip you ta pieces if he uses it." The deputy did as he was instructed, but Sean could tell that he was not too happy about it. "I'm Mark Turner and this is one a my deputies," said Mark. "Why are you Federal boys here?"

"I got a question for you, and I want a straight answer," said Sean. "And I'll tell you right now that I'm very good at spottin' a liar."

"Well I'm no liar, so ask away," said Mark.

"All right, here goes. Are you tied in with them fellas that own "The Palace" now?" asked Sean.

"Just why in the hell would I be tied in with them?" asked Mark.

"Just answer the question," said Sean.

"No I'm not," answered Mark. "I don't know them fellas. I never go there either. I'm not a drinkin' man. I got me a wife so I don't need them lady's neither."

"Well that fella damn near stole the place at the auction," started Sean. "He fired all the good help and put in his thugs. He beats and abuses his girls."

"Nobody has ever come ta me with a complaint," said Mark. "I seen some a the girls around town. None of 'em ever looked like they took a beatin' ta me."

"Well they must be afraid ta speak up," said Sean. "Now we know for a fact that they do abuse the girls and me and my men are gonna go straighten things out. You can help us or stay out of the way. We'd prefer that you stayed outta the way." When Sean said they'd prefer they stayed outta the way, the deputy put his hand back on his Colt. When he did, Dog got right in front of him and had his teeth bared with a good growl going.

"Better get that hand off that pistol," said Jon. "Dog here just loves rippin' out a man's throat. You'll be dead before you can get that thing pulled."

"Do as he says Bill," said Mark. "Just look at that dog. He'll kill ya sure." Reluctantly, Bill did as he was told. Dog quit his growl but stayed right in front of Bill.

"Don't look 'm in the eye," said Jon. "He don't like that." Bill kept looking into Dog's eyes. Dog started his growl again. Bill looked away, and Dog stopped the growl. The jail cells were about ten feet behind the Marshal's desk and were empty. Bill turned and ran to the nearest one and locked himself inside. "That damn dog can't get me now," said Bill.

"No he can't," said Mark. "I think mebbe you just better stay in there a while and cool off. Hand me your Colt. You won't need it in there."

"Why should I give you my Colt?" asked Bill.

"So you won't try somethin' stupid with it," said Mark. "Now hand it over or I'll fire your ass." Bill said a few cuss words to himself and then handed his Colt through the bars to the Marshal. "Now you fellas do whatever it is you gotta do," Mark said to

Sean. "If ya need help, I'm here. I heard a you and your deputies. I doubt you'll need my help."

"First thing we're gonna do is get somethin' ta eat," said Sean. "Then we'll visit an old friend a mine. After that, we'll get down ta business. So if there's gonna be any gun play, it should start in maybe an hour and a half'r so. Maybe we'll have some customers for your jail. Take care a that deputy. He's young. Mebbe he'll learn." Sean and the boys left and went to a small eatery and had a meal. Then they went to Susie's place.

Sean knocked on the door and waited. About a minute later, Susie came to the door. When she opened the door and saw that it was Sean, she grabbed him and gave him a huge hug. When Sean hugged her back, she let out a groan. "What is it Susie? Are you hurt?" asked Sean.

"You and your men step inside and I'll show you," said Susie. Susie was wearing only a long robe and when the men were inside and the door closed, she opened the robe and showed them. There were bruises on her chest. Both of her sides were covered with bruises and her back and backside was covered with welts. Susie saw the look of extreme anger go into Sean's eyes. Michael and Jon stood there with their fists clenched. "They never hit us in the face," said Susie.

"Which one of them did this to you?" asked Sean. "Which one?"

"It was the one they call Mountain," answered Susie. "He's one of the bouncers. They call him Mountain because he is huge. He's bigger than Michael."

"Don't matter how big he is," said Sean. "He'll never beat another woman after this day. Now are you up to tellin' us about this new owner and his men?"

"His name is Delbert Owens," started Susie. "He's a small man but his men do what he says. His two bartenders are Steve and Larry. They are scum. They beat the girls too. The two dealers are Dan and Ed. Dan is a good man and I think he is just here because he needed a job. He doesn't mess with any of the girls, and he's a straight dealer. Ed is crooked, and he is scum. The two bouncers are Mountain and Wilson. Both of them are scum."

"Well get yourself dressed and we'll go pay Delbert a visit," said Sean. "I reckon we'll figure out which one is Mountain. If this Dan is a good man like you say, we want to know which one he is so we don't mess with him. Will they all be there this time of day?"

"They'll all be there somewhere," said Susie. "All of them but Dan hang out there even when they're not working. I don't know where Dan goes when he's not working. Maybe he's got a wife somewhere. He's working right now. I almost forgot. I expect you know this, but these men are always armed, and there's two shotguns behind the bar."

"I would expect them to be armed, and I figured on the shotguns," replied Sean. "Thanks for telling me anyway. Now finish dressin', and we'll get over there."

~~~~

When they got to "The Palace", Susie went in first. Sean came in next followed by Michael and then Jon and Dog. There were about fifteen customers in the place. Susie pointed out each of the workers to Sean. Steve was at one end of the bar and Larry was at the other. Dan was dealing blackjack but Ed was nowhere to be seen. Mountain was setting just inside the door to the right and

Wilson was standing in the middle of the bar having a drink. Susie told Sean that Delbert was probably in his office.

"Susie, you go have a seat where Michael and Jon can keep an eye on you," said Sean. "I'll be havin' some words with Mr. Mountain. Michael, Jon, keep your eyes peeled. Anybody gets edgy and goes for a gun or wants to butt in, kill'em. Jon, have Dog stay with Susie." Dog went over by Susie and Sean walked over to where Mountain was sitting. "I reckon I know why they call you Mountain," said Sean. "You're a big fella but you're probly dumber than a pile a rocks."

Mountain was a big man. He was probably about six feet six and weighed well over 250 pounds. He was stocky, but not fat. "Go away little man," said Mountain. "I eat small men like you for breakfast."

"Do you eat your breakfast before or after you beat up some women?" asked Sean.

When the customers in the place saw that there was going to be a fight, they all got up and ran out the door. Some of them stayed outside and peaked in the windows and door.

"Suit yourself little man," said Mountain. "I'm gonna break your back. Take off that gun belt so you don't accidentally shoot me or yourself. I'll lay my pistol on the table here." Sean took off his gun belt and laid it on the closest table. Mountain laid his pistol on his table, stood up, and came right at Sean. Sean was ready for him and hit him with a right to the jaw and then a left. His punches had no affect on Mountain. Mountain came in close and Sean hit him in the gut with a right. Still his punch had no effect. Mountain was in Sean's face now. He took his huge arms and wrapped them around Sean at his waist. Sean's arms were also pinned by his grip. Mountain picked up Sean and was shaking him. "I'm gonna break your back now little man," said Mountain.

When Mountain picked up Sean, Sean's head was just above Mountain's head. Sean knew he had to do something quick or Mountain would break his back. He opened his mouth as wide as he could and bit down as hard as he could on the top of Mountain's head. Mountain had short hair so Sean's teeth went right to his scalp and hit bone. Sean could feel his teeth rake along Mountain's skull as he bit down. Then Sean yanked back with his head as hard as he could and ripped off a piece of Mountain's scalp. Mountain started screaming in pain and let go of Sean. Blood ran down Mountain's forehead and into his eyes. "You scalped me you son of a bitch," yelled Mountain. "You're a dead man now."

Sean spit the scalp out of his mouth and bent down a little. Mountain had so much blood in his eyes he couldn't see at all. Sean hit Mountain with a right uppercut in his privates. Mountain went down hard. Sean then kicked him in the ribs a few times . Mountain tried to sit up but Sean hit him with a tremendous right and Mountain went back down and didn't move. Sean felt a sharp pain in his hand when he hit Mountain's jaw but he didn't think anything of it.

"Anybody else wanna dance?" asked Sean as he wiped blood from his mouth. No one said a word. "Now Susie, point out the other fellas here that like to beat up women?" Susie pointed to Wilson, Steve, and Larry. Ed was still not to be seen. Delbert had still not come out of the back room. "You three are gonna take a beatin'," said Sean.

"Like hell we are," said Steve as he reached for a shotgun behind the bar. Larry went for one too. Michael and Jon already had their pistols out and were ready for them. Wilson was still standing at the bar and started reaching for his pistol. Sean grabbed one of his pistols from the table where he had laid his gun belt before the fight with Mountain. When he grabbed the pistol, he felt a severe pain in his right hand and dropped the pistol. He was able to grab his other pistol off the table with his left hand and put a bullet in Wilson's head before Wilson had his pistol up to fire. Steve and Larry had stopped to watch Sean and Wilson, but as Wilson was falling, they both brought up their shotguns to fire.

"Don't even think it," said Michael. Steve and Larry ignored Michael and tried to cock the hammers on their shotguns. Michael and Jon fired at the same time. Both Larry and Steve were struck in the forehead. The backs of their heads exploded and blood, bone, and brains went all over the mirror behind the bar. The mirror did not break. Then another shot was heard. Sean turned to look and saw that Dan had shot Mountain. Mountain apparently had come to and pulled a derringer from a pocket and was trying to shoot Sean in the back.

"I thank you," said Sean. "Susie told me you were probly not with this bunch." Then Sean went over to Dan and extended his hand. "I'm Sean O'Rourke," said Sean. They shook.

"Name's Dan, Dan Taylor and I don't go for no back shootin'," said Dan. "And Susie's right. I just work here. I took this job just ta get by and save a little money so me and the wife can get ta California. The wife's been real sick though, and the doctor here can't figure out what's wrong with her. He's been sending telegrams back east somewhere tellin' them her symptoms and seein' if they can help. We won't be goin' anywhere till she gets better."

"Well I'm glad you were here and I hope your wife gets better," said Sean. "Just what's in California for you?"

"I got an uncle who runs a nice saloon and gamblin' house," said Dan. "He asked me ta be his partner. Soon as I had enough money saved and the wife was better, we was goin'."

"Well I wish the best for you," said Sean. "Now if you'll excuse me, I'll be payin' a visit to your boss."

Sean put his pistol in his belt and headed to the office. Jon went with him. "I'd say somethin' got broke in that right hand a yours," said Jon. "That man's jaw was probly like granite."

"Yes it was," said Sean. "Good thing I can shoot both ways." Sean had Michael stay in the saloon to keep an eye on things. "Susie, you tell Michael if that Ed fella shows up," said Sean as he left to go to the office. The door to the office was closed. Sean opened the door and walked in. Delbert Owens was sitting at the desk and had a pistol pointed at Sean. "You must be Delbert Owens," said Sean. "I'm Federal Marshal O'Rourke. I got a question for you, and you better answer it."

"So you're that famous Marshal that everyone is so afraid of," said Delbert. "You just killed some of my men. I can shoot you right now and claim self defense."

"I can kill you before your thumb even gets close to the hammer on that pistol you're holdin'," said Sean. "Now answer this question. Was Lucas your boss?"

"Lucas, you mean that Judge that got killed," said Delbert. "Just why in the hell would he be my boss?"

"We're not gettin' off to a very good start," said Sean. "You and your thugs stole this place at the auction, and you fired all the good people. You made the girls raise their rates, and you take a bigger piece from them. You make the girls give your thugs free ones, and you let them beat on'em. This is the kind of stuff that Lucas's people would do. Now I'll ask you again. Was Lucas your boss?"

"I don't hafta answer any a your questions," said Delbert. "Now get outta my office."

"Well if you won't answer my question, then there's somethin' you're gonna do before you leave," said Sean.

"What is it you think I'm gonna do," said Delbert.

"You're gonna sell me this place," said Sean.

"Like hell I will," said Delbert.

"All right, I'm gonna stand right here in front a you. You better use that pistol or you better sign this place over ta me," said Sean. Delbert never said another word. Five minutes rolled by. Then ten minutes passed and then fifteen. Delbert was shaking now.

"What's your offer?" Delbert finally asked.

"You stole this place for $5000," said Sean. "I'll give you $6000 and you can keep whatever you got in that safe over there."

"What if I refuse?" asked Delbert.

"You won't," answered Sean. "A fella like you is afraid a dyin'. Now get out that deed and sign it over." Delbert dropped the pistol and went to the safe and pulled out the deed. Sean could see that there was a lot of money in the safe. Sean handed a bank draft to Delbert and Delbert signed the deed over to Sean.

"Can I have a day to get my things out of here?" asked Delbert.

"Sure," said Sean. "Of course you won't mind if Michael here hangs around with you." A shot rang out, and Delbert fell to the floor. Sean looked out the small window on the left side of the office and saw a man running away. "Michael, get Jon and see if you can find that fella," said Sean. "I didn't see much but he had on a gray hat and a dark blue jacket. Have Dog stay with Susie." Sean checked Delbert. He was dead.

~ ~ ~ ~

When the Town Marshal heard the first shot, he decided he better get over there and see what was happening. He let his deputy out of jail and gave him back his Colt. "We'll git over there and see what's goin' on," said Mark. "You go around back and I'll go in the front. Don't shoot nobody unless they're shootin' at you." They both took off at a run towards "The Palace."

When the deputy finally got around behind the saloon, he saw a man running away. The man was wearing a gray hat and a blue jacket and was carrying a pistol. "Stop or I'll shoot," yelled Bill as he raised his pistol. The man stopped. He turned to face Bill. They were about fifty yards apart. Bill was so glad that the man had stopped that he got a little careless and lowered his pistol. When he lowered his pistol, the man raised his pistol and fired. Bill was struck in his right leg and went down. The man turned and started running again. Bill rolled onto his belly and took careful aim and fired. The man was struck dead center in the back and went down. Just as the man was falling, Jon, Michael and Mark showed up.

"That was some shot," said Mark. "Musta been seventy five yards'r so. Now where you hit?"

"I got careless, and he got me in the leg," answered Bill. "I believe that fella is one a them dealers in the saloon. I think they call'm Ed."

"Well Ed just killed his boss," said Michael. "I bet he done that ta keep'm from talkin'."

"So you figure this whole bunch was mebbe tied in with Lucas?" asked Mark.

"I would say that they were," said Michael. "But with all of'em dead, we might not ever know."

"I believe I'll be talkin' ta your boss now," said Mark. "Not every day we have six men shot and killed in town. You stay right where you are Bill. I'll send the Doc to look at you. Might be best if you're not moved yet."

"That Doc'll need ta have a look at Sean's hand too," said Jon. "I think he broke some bones when he hit that Mountain fella last time."

Mark got the Doctor and took him to Bill and then went into the saloon to talk with Sean. Sean was sitting in the saloon having a drink when Mark came in. "I hear you got an unusual way a scalpin'," said Mark. "Most folks use a knife when they scalp someone."

"Couldn't git my hands on one," said Sean. "Now what can I do for you?"

"Well we got six dead men, and I'd kinda like ta know how it all happened," said Mark.

"Well we came in here ta give them boys that was beatin' on the girls a good beatin'," said Sean. "After I knocked out Mountain, them other fellas decided they wanted ta shoot it out. They're dead. That Ed fella wasn't here."

"I know," said Mark. "My deputy killed'm out back. I guess Ed was the one that killed Delbert."

"Well if Ed had on a gray hat and dark blue jacket then he was the one," said Sean. "By the way, I own this place now. Delbert sold it to me right before that Ed fella killed'm."

"Why would Delbert sell this place ta you?" asked Mark.

"I showed him the error a his ways, and he decided ta move on," said Sean. "He made a little profit too."

"Well whatever," said Mark. "I'll have the Doc look at your hand soon as he gets done with Bill. He got careless and took one in the leg."

"He's young. He'll learn," said Sean. Mark left, and Jon and Michael came in and sat down with Sean. About fifteen minutes later, an undertaker showed up with some men and took away the bodies. Susie was still inside, and she came over and joined them. She gave Sean a hug and then sat down.

"Susie, do you reckon that them fellas that used ta work here are still around town?" asked Sean.

"I think most of them are," answered Susie.

"Well I own this place now and you go find all of'em and tell'em they got their jobs back," said Sean. Tell the girls they'll have no one stealin' their money. And before I forget it, I don't want that mirror cleaned off yet. It might come in handy for somethin' I'm gonna do later." Susie seemed perplexed about the mirror, but she was overjoyed about getting the help back and gave Sean a kiss on the cheek and went out to find the former help. The Doctor was there after another fifteen minutes.

"I'm Doc Barnes," he said as he approached Sean. "They tell me you mighta broke some bones in your hand. Let's have a look." Sean handed him his right hand. "Yep, you sure did," Doc said. "The bones between the palm of your hand and the first joint are broke on your middle two fingers. Feels like clean breaks. I'll fix ya up with a splint. You'll be good as new in no time."

"How was that deputy?" asked Sean.

"Bullet went clean through," said Doc. "He'll be up and around in no time." Doc finished with the splint and gave Sean a few instructions. When he was done, he looked at Sean and said, "that'll be $2.00." Sean reached into his pocket and pulled out the money and paid him. Doc took the money, smiled and left.

~~~~

It wasn't two hours later, and Susie was back with the whole crew. Sean had them come to his table for a short talk. "I guess Susie here told you I was the new owner," said Sean. "Things'll be like they were when Sam was here. You all know what to do so go and do it. I'll be lookin' for someone ta run this place cause me and Maggie don't wanna live up here. Soon as I find someone, I'll be goin' back ta Abilene." Sean could tell that everyone was glad that Delbert and his thugs were gone. "I'll be goin' to the telegraph office so I can let Maggie know what's goin' on," said Sean. "Michael, you and Jon just stay here and enjoy your drinks."

Sean made his way to the telegraph office and sent the following telegram to Maggie.

Maggie O'Rourke
Abilene Kansas

Maggie<<stop>>we own Palace now<<stop>>Michael Jon all right<<stop>>I broke two bones in right hand when punched big man<<stop>>will be all right<<stop>>will find someone to run place and be back

Much love
Sean

Maggie had been on her way to the bank when the telegraph operator found her. After she read the telegram, she sent one back to Sean. It went as follows:

Marshal O'Rourke
St. Louis

Sean<<stop>>let Susie run the place<<stop>>she can handle it

Miss you
Maggie

CHAPTER FOUR

When Sean read the telegram from Maggie, it didn't take him long to make up his mind about who would run the saloon. Dan Taylor was going to California to be a partner in a saloon and gambling house. Sean figured he must know what he's doing if his uncle wanted him to be his partner. Maybe while he was in St. Louis waiting for his wife to get better, he could help Susie learn anything she didn't already know. Dan was still in the saloon, so Sean went over to him for a talk.

"So Dan Taylor, why would your uncle in California want you ta be his partner?" asked Sean. "Is it just because you're related, or does he think you know what you're doin'? Have you ever been in charge of a group of people?"

"First off, my uncle knows that I am very capable," said Dan. "Bein' related's got nothin' ta do with it. I had my own place back in New York before the war. We did a good business. I sold it when I left for the war so the wife would never hafta worry about money when I was gone or if anything happened ta me."

"That was a wise move," said Sean. "What did you do in the war?"

"I started out as a plain old foot soldier," started Dan. "After Gettysburg, they made me a Sergeant. At Spotsylvania, they made me a Lieutenant. I was a Major when the war ended. I was in the infantry the whole time. I got out soon as I could after the surrender."

"Sounds like you know how to get things done," said Sean. "What did you do from after the war till now?"

"I went back to New York and worked for the man that I had sold my place to," said Dan. "I was there till I heard from my uncle in California. The wife started getting sick as soon as our trip started. When we got here, we decided we better stay here till she got better."

"Well I got a proposition for you Dan," said Sean. "How'd you like to help Susie run this place while you're waiting for your wife to get better? You can teach her what she doesn't know already. What do you say?"

"Sounds good ta me if it's all right with Susie," said Dan.

~~~~

Susie was at another table talking with some of the other girls so Sean went to her table and asked her to join him and Dan. "Susie, I got a proposition for you," Sean started. "Would you come over to our table so me and Dan can go over it with you?"

"I'm not in any trouble am I?" asked Susie.

"No you're not," said Sean. "I'm sure you'll like what you hear." They went to Sean's table. Sean pulled out a chair for Susie and then they got started. "I'll get right to the point Susie," Sean began. "How would you like to run this place for me? Dan here had his own place back before the war, and he will be with you and help you learn the ropes. He'll be here till his wife gets better. Then he's going to California. What do you say?"

"I say I'll make you and Maggie proud of me," said Susie. "I know I can handle it and I'll do my best for you. Dan and I are already friends. We'll do good together."

"All right, sounds good," said Sean. "I'll need to go over the books and such and get you both a respectable salary. I'll visit the bank so they'll know the place has a new owner and different people will be doing the business at the bank. Now I wish Maggie was here. She takes care of all the bookwork back home."

"Don't worry Sean," said Dan. "I'll look at the books and help you figure things out."

"I don't know what kind of books Delbert kept," said Susie, "But I'd say that Sam kept very good books when he was here."

"I'm sure he did," said Sean. "Now I think I'll go to the office and see if I can find out which bank we do business with. Another thing, there's a safe in the office. Delbert opened it to get the deed, but then he closed it back up. I don't s'pose anyone here would know the combination."

"I'd say the ones who might have known it are all dead," said Dan. "There's a locksmith in town. He can get it open for us."

"Well you go get that fella," said Sean. "Might be some important stuff in there that I need ta know." Dan left to find the locksmith, and Sean went to the office. Susie went back to the other girls and gave them the news. Sean could hear the cries of joy from the other girls. Sean couldn't find anything about the bank where "The Palace" did business, so he figured there would be something in the safe.

Dan was back in a half hour with the locksmith. The safe was open in about fifteen minutes. Sean paid the locksmith, had him write down the combination, and sent him on his way. Sean and Dan just stood there and stared into the safe for a few minutes. "There must be twenty, thirty thousand in there," said Dan.

"I'd say so," said Sean. "Get it out and get it counted. I see a bank statement in there." Sean took the statement out of the safe and looked at it. "I guess we do business at the Bank of St. Louis," said Sean. "According to this, we have $155,000 in the bank. Dan, you get that money counted, and I'll go over to the bank."

~~~~

The bank was a couple of streets from the saloon. Sean went to a teller and asked to see the bank President. "Who may I say is asking to see him?" asked the teller.

"You tell'em that the new owner of "The Palace" wants to see him," said Sean. "The name's O'Rourke, Sean O'Rourke." The teller went to a back office and returned with the President. He was a small, slender, middle aged man.

"Mr. O'Rourke, I am Steven Atwell," he said as he extended his hand to Sean. They shook. "I understand that you are the new owner of "The Palace." Would you mind if I asked what happened to Mr. Owens?"

"No I wouldn't mind," said Sean. "Some fella named Ed shot him dead. He had just signed the deed over to me when Ed killed'em. Was you a friend a Delbert's?"

"No, he was just a customer," said Steven. "Now what can we do for you?"

"Well I have two people who will be running the place for me," said Sean. "Their names are Susie Carson and Dan Taylor. As of right now, they will be the only people who will be doing our banking business. That is 'ceptin' me."

"That's fine," said Steven. "I'll just need you to sign a form that states that those two will be doing your banking business." Steven got the form and Sean filled it out. "Now would you mind if I asked you a question?" said Steven.

"Go ahead," said Sean.

"I know that you are a lawman," started Steven. "Will you still be a lawman now that you own this very successful business?"

"That's a good question," said Sean. "I have enough money that I'd never hafta work another day a my life. But there's just too many people out there with no respect for any law or other people. Someone's gotta ride herd on'em. Might as well be me. Besides, I'm good at it."

"Well I wish you well on your endeavors," said Steven. "It's been a pleasure meeting you."

"Same here," said Sean. "Thanks for your kindness. If you ever need me, Judge Sharpton will know how ta find me." Sean shook Steven's hand again and left. "I reckon I better go see the Judge and let him know everything," Sean said to himself as he was leaving.

~~~~

Judge Sharpton was in his office when Sean arrived at the courthouse. Sean lightly knocked on the door and went in. "Good to see you Sean," said Robert. "Fill me in on what went on over there. I've heard a few rumors already. I see you have an injury."

"Well me and the boys talked with Susie," said Sean. "She had bruises all over her so me and the boys went over there to straighten'em out. I had a fight with this big bear of a man called Mountain. I finally got him knocked out. I broke some bones in my hand when I hit Mountain's jaw. The others decided to shoot it out. They're dead."

"So what happened to Delbert Owens?" asked Robert.

"Well I had just convinced him to sell me the place when one a his own men shot him dead," said Sean. "Then that fella that shot Owens shot a town deputy and that deputy killed'em. We weren't able ta find out if Owens was tied ta Lucas'r not. But I just bet he was. I mighta got somethin' outta him if that fella hadn't a shot'm."

"So now that you own that place are you still gonna be my Marshal?" asked Robert.

"I am," said Sean. "Now while I'm here, is there anything important I need ta be doin'?"

"No, it's been pretty quiet for a while," said Robert. "Earlier in the year there was a bank that got robbed here in Missouri. No one's for sure who is responsible. I have heard that it might be some men calling themselves the James-Younger gang, but it's not certain. The local law is taking care of things."

"Well I'll be gettin' back to the saloon and probly head back to Abilene in a day'r two," said Sean. "Me'n the boys'r ready whenever you need us."

~~~~

Sean went back to the saloon, got Susie, and they went to the office. Dan was sitting at the desk just staring at the huge pile of money. "Well how much is there?" Sean asked him.

"There's $38,450.00 in bills and $300.00 in coin," said Dan.

"Damn, that's a fair amount," said Sean. "And I told Owens he could have what was in the safe. No wonder he wasn't too upset. Anyway, he's dead. He won't need it. If he's got kin somewhere, they'll never find out from me about this. If any show up, they can have the $6000 I paid him for the place. Does that sound good to you two?" Both of them nodded yes. "Now I need to figure out a good salary for both of you. Dan, what was you gettin' paid as a dealer?"

"I got $100 a month," answered Dan.

"Well how does $300 a month to start sound?" asked Sean.

"That sounds great to me," said Dan.

"You'll earn every penny a that," said Sean. "You'll be takin' care a all the books. You'll be makin' sure everybody gets paid. You and Susie'll work together on everything. I'm sure it'll take a while ta figure out how much of everything you need. Just make sure your suppliers don't try ta talk you into stuff you don't need. Now I want to give everyone that came back a raise. Whatever they was makin', give'em another $20 a month. Does that sound all right with you two?" They both nodded yes.

"Now Susie, how does $350 a month for your salary sound ta you?" asked Sean.

"Sounds very good," said Susie. "I'll do my best for you."

"Now Dan, does it bother you that Susie will make more money than you?" asked Sean.

"No, it won't bother me," answered Dan. "Susie's been here a good while, and she'll be here after I leave. She deserves it."

"Good, now there's something that we're gonna start en-forcin'," said Sean. "Not that many people carry guns in St. Louis, but some do. I am not sure what the local laws are about that, but we are gonna have customers start checkin' any weapons they are carrying at the bar when they come in. This will include any knife with a blade longer than four inches. Does this sound all right with you two?"

"Sounds good to me," said Susie. "How about you Dan?"

"Sounds good to me too," answered Dan. "Like you said, not that many people here carry guns but some do. I don't think we'll have any trouble."

"Now if any lawmen or soldier boys come in, they can keep their weapons if they're officers. Officers are s'posed to carry sidearms," said Sean. "Susie, you get someone ta make us a sign and we'll get started on that tomorrow. Just have it say somethin' like, "All guns and knives with a blade longer than four inches will be checked at the bar upon entering this establishment. Failure to do so will cause permanent expulsion from this establishment or worse. Weapons will be returned when leaving. Then put "The Management" at the bottom. Anyway, do somethin' like that. This is why I don't want that mirror cleaned yet. When someone asks what all that blood and stuff is about, you tell'em that's what happened to the last two fellas who didn't wanna check their guns."

"That'll probably make someone think. I know it would make me think. I know someone who can make us a good sign," said Susie. "I'll get that started right now."

"I got one more thing ta go over before I leave," started Sean. "I know you two will do a good job. I'm trustin' you. There'll be a lotta money ta work with. After all expenses, wages, salaries, and whatever is paid, I want the rest put in the bank. You two are the only two who are permitted to do banking business. Keep maybe a few thousand in the safe for any unforeseen expenses, but the rest goes to the bank. Me and Maggie will be checkin' out the books every so often. Me'n the boy's'll be leavin' day after tomorrow. Right now I'm gonna get Jon and Michael and get somethin' ta eat. You two can get started doin' what needs done. I just thought of somethin' else. I want you to put up a sign out front that says "Under New Management." Then inside behind the bar, I want a sign that says "Susie Carson – Manager, Dan Taylor – Assistant Manager." Does that sound all right to you two?"

"Yes it does," answered Susie. "How bout you <u>Dan?</u>"

"Sounds good. We'll get those signs made. I'll leave $3000 in the safe and get the rest of that money over to the bank right now," said Dan. "I'll have the books ready for you to check out before you leave."

Sean left Susie and Dan to their work, and he, Michael, and Jon went for a meal. "Well boys, we'll be headin' back home day after tomorrow," said Sean as they were eating their meal. "You two can do whatever you want till then. The Judge said there wasn't anything goin' on right now that needed our attention. We would be leavin' tomorrow, but I wanna be here when we start havin' customers check their guns and knives. Probly won't be a problem here, but you never know."

"I think I'll go down to the river, cut myself a pole, and do a little fishin'," said Jon. "Haven't done any fishin' for years. Maybe I'll just fall asleep on the bank in the shade."

"That sounds relaxin'," said Michael. "Maybe I'll join you if you don't mind. We might take a bottle with us too."

"Well don't you two get drunk and fall in and drown," said Sean. "I think I'll go over to the docks and see if Horace's boat is in and visit with him for a while. See you two later."

Sean left for the docks and Jon and Michael took off to go fishing. When Sean got to the docks, Horace's boat was just pulling in. Horace was at the helm, but he saw Sean and waved for him to come aboard. Sean went up to the control room. "Hello my friend," said Horace as he extended his hand to Sean. "What brings you here this time?"

Sean shook his hand. "Well I'm the new owner of "The Palace," said Sean. "Just gettin' things straightened out then goin' back to Abilene."

"Just how in the hell did you become the new owner of that place?" asked Horace.

"Well when they sold the place at auction after Sam was killed, it was practically stolen by that Delbert Owens and his bunch," started Sean. "One a the girls wrote me and told me what was goin' on and that they were mistreatin' the girls. We also figured he had ties to that crooked Judge Lucas. Me and the boys came up here ta straighten them out. Susie, she was the girl who wrote me. We saw her first when we got here. She had been beaten pretty bad. We went there to give them fellas a beatin'. I broke my hand punchin' out that fella called Mountain. The others wanted ta shoot it out. They're dead. I convinced Owens he oughta sell ta me. Right after he signed over the deed, one a his own men killed'm. Susie and a fella named Dan Taylor is gonna run the place for me."

"So you would never hafta work ever again in your life if you didn't want to," said Horace. "But you will. You like bein' a lawman, and you're good at it. Let's go have a drink to celebrate your good fortune."

"Sounds good," said Sean. "Me'n Maggie'll be comin' ta St. Louis every so often ta check on the place and I'm sure we'll be seein' you from time to time."

"So how's business for you?" asked Sean.

"We're doing very well," answered Horace. "We'll refuel and resupply today. We'll be back out tomorrow. We've been full up almost every trip out."

"That's good," said Sean. "Did that fella that took a swim ever come back?"

"Actually he did," said Horace. "He had a very nice looking woman with him. I believe she was his wife. At least that's how they were registered."

"Well good for him," said Sean. "Now maybe he won't be lookin' for any workin' girls."

"So how's your new boss?" asked Horace. "Haven't heard much about him."

"He's a good man," answered Sean. "He hates corruption, and he wants me ta keep doin' what I been doin'. We'll make a good team. Horace, I hate ta cut this short, but I just thought a somethin'. I best get back to the saloon and talk with Susie while I got this on my mind."

"I bet I know what you're thinking," said Horace. "You're worried about Susie being the manager now and how her regular customers will handle it if she quits her previous duties."

"That's just what I'm thinkin'," said Sean. "Some fellas might not be too happy if she quits."

"Well I don't know Susie in the biblical sense, but I have been around her and talked to her on several occasions," said Horace. "I think Susie has a good head on her shoulders, and she will be fine whatever she does."

"You're probly right. I worry too much," said Sean. "Let's enjoy our drinks."

While Sean was visiting Horace, a telegram came for Doc Barnes. It was news about Dan Taylor's wife. Doc went straight to

"The Palace" to give Dan the news. Dan was in the office going over the books, and Susie took Doc to him. "Dan, Doc's here," said Susie. "I'll leave you two alone."

"What is it Doc?" asked Dan. "Did you find anything out about my wife?"

"Mr. Taylor, every once in a while I gotta tell people something I'd rather not tell them and they'd rather not hear," started Doc. "I have suspected this from her first visit to me. There's no good way to say this. Your wife has a cancer. It appears to be all through her. I do not know the name of it as I am not a specialist. Cancer is something that not a lot of people know anything about. We don't know what causes it or anything. All we know is that your wife is gonna die. No one can save her. That laudanum I have been giving her is the only thing I can do for her. She can take more of it when the pain increases."

Dan held back his tears as best he could. "So you're sure about this?" asked Dan. "Maybe whoever you sent those telegrams to could be wrong."

"They could be wrong, but I doubt it," said Doc. "The way your wife's pain has been increasing and the way it hurts her when I examine her tells me that she has something I've never seen before. I've seen a lot of different illnesses."

"Well how long does she have?" asked Dan.

"I don't really know," answered Doc. "She could die tomorrow or five months from now. One thing I do know. The longer she lives, the more pain she'll be in. The laudanum will not help when it gets that bad. Now I know you are a brave man. Are you brave enough to tell her or would you want me to do it?"

"I'll do it Doc," said Dan. "I'll tell her today when I go home from work. I thank you for your kindness." Dan extended his hand to Doc. They shook and then Doc left. When Doc left the office, Susie went back in.

"What'd Doc want?" asked Susie. "When he asked for you, he said it was very important."

"Well everybody's gonna know sooner or later so you'll be the first to know," started Dan. "My wife is gonna die. She has somethin' called cancer. Nobody knows much about cancer except that if you get it, your're gonna die. It'll be agonizing and painful."

"I'm so sorry Dan," said Susie. "I don't know what to say. If you need to be with her, I'll be all right here. Go, be with her now. She needs you."

Dan let out a few tears, and nodded his head to Susie and left to go home. They were renting a small cottage not far from downtown. When Dan opened the front door, his wife was laying on the sofa. Dan went over and looked down at her. Her eyes were open, and she had a smile on her face. Dan said a few words to her but she didn't answer. Dan then put his hand on her neck. There was no pulse. She was still very warm. Dan figured she must have died less than a half hour ago. He got down on his knees, put his head on her chest, and cried for a good ten minutes. There was a knock on the door. Dan went to see who it was. It was Doc Barnes. "I just happened to see you, and I was headed this way on another call, so I figured I'd stop to see if I could be of help," said Doc.

"She's dead Doc," Dan said. "She must have died not long ago. She's still very warm. I came home from work and found her there on the sofa. Why would she have that smile on her face?" asked Dan.

"Maybe she was thinking of you when the end came," answered Doc. "I really have no idea but if I was you, that's what I would like to think. Now nobody likes to hear this either, but would you want me to set things up with the undertaker? I'll go right past there on the way back to my office."

"That would be nice Doc," said Dan. "I guess I better decide what she would want to be buried in and get it ready. Doc left and Dan started going through his wife's clothes to pick out a nice dress. Most of her things were still packed in a trunk as they were expecting to be moving on soon. When Dan came across her wedding dress, he broke down and cried some more. He cried for a good fifteen minutes. Then he pulled out a blue dress that he knew his wife was fond of and put it on the arm of the sofa. He went into the kitchen, got a bottle of whiskey and a glass, and returned to the living room. He sat down in a chair next to the sofa and poured himself a drink. He raised his glass to his wife. He said no words and then took a drink. He didn't slam it down. He sipped it. He sat there for another fifteen minutes finishing his whiskey. He filled his glass again but did not drink it yet. He sat there looking at her and remembering their life together. An hour later, the undertaker came. Dan thought he was very nice and he gave him instructions on what he wanted for a funeral. He decided that there would be no viewing as they had no relatives there and he only knew people from the saloon. There would be no service either. Dan just wanted them to do their work and then bury her. He would be there and have his own personal service. The undertaker told Dan that everything could be ready by ten o'clock the next morning.

Dan decided that he wasn't going to sit around and cry anymore. He wiped the remaining tears from his eyes and went back to the saloon. When Susie saw him, she knew that something had happened. She went to him. "What is it Dan?" she asked. "Is everything all right?"

"My wife died. Brenda died," said Dan. "She must have died not long before I got home. She was on the sofa and she had a smile on her face."

"I'm so sorry," said Susie. "Is there anything I can do? You don't need to be here now. You can go take care of things or just be by yourself for some time if you want."

"I'm all right Susie," answered Dan. "Everything is already being looked after. Doc happened by and we already have everything planned with the undertaker. She'll be buried tomorrow morning. There'll be no viewing or service. I'll be doing my own personal service."

"I can be at the service if you want me," said Susie. "Sometimes it helps to have someone around at those times."

"Well the burial will be at ten o'clock and if you want to be there, I will not mind," said Dan. "Now don't think me an unloving man, but I'm gonna go take a look at the books right now. That should help keep me from crying." Dan spent the rest of the day going over the books. About midnight, he finally decided to go home. When he got home, he stood and stared at the sofa remembering Brenda laying there with the smile on her face. Then he got himself a glass of whiskey and layed on the bed. He propped himself up and took small sips from the glass. He and Brenda had never been apart for even one night after the war ended. How long would it take him to get over this empty feeling? It wasn't long till he fell asleep. Not long after daylight, he woke up. He was amazed that he had slept so well. He felt guilty because his wife had just died and he slept so well. Was there something wrong with him? Shouldn't he be going crazy about now? He sat on the edge of the bed for a short while and decided that he was all right. He got himself cleaned up, put on some fresh clothes, and went to an eatery for some breakfast. He sat there till about nine o'clock drinking coffee. Susie was walking by the eatery and noticed him sitting there and stopped in.

"Mind if I have some coffee with you?" Susie asked.

"No, please sit down and join me," said Dan. He got up and pulled out a chair for her. "I feel guilty. I slept very well last night. I didn't cry or anything. Shouldn't I be going crazy or something?"

"Not everyone acts the same when they lose a loved one," said Susie. "Don't try to punish yourself for this. You know she loved you and you loved her. You will always remember this. Life must go on." The waiter brought Susie some coffee. "I'll go with you to the burial, and if you need to be by yourself for a while afterwards, it will be all right."

"I'll be goin' to work," said Dan. "Work will help me. Besides, it'll be an interesting day. We'll find out how customers feel about checking their weapons. Now I have a question for you. If you don't want to answer, It's all right."

"Go ahead and ask," said Susie. "I believe I know what it will be because I have been thinking about it myself."

"All right, here goes. Since you are the manager now, do you intend to give up your other duties?" asked Dan.

"I have thought about this ever since Sean asked me to run the place," answered Susie. "I do intend to stop being a working girl. I do have a lot of regular customers who may not be too happy about this, but they'll have to get used to it. I'll be finding another girl to take my place. Maybe they'll like her more than they do me. Time will tell."

"Well we'll just have to make sure that no one gets nasty about this," said Dan. "If you even think that there will be trouble, just let out a yell and I'll be there."

"Thank you," said Susie. "I'll be carrying a derringer in a pocket too. Hopefully, it will never be needed."

They sat there and talked till almost ten o'clock. Talk was mostly about the saloon. Dan decided it was time to head to the undertaker's place, so he and Susie headed that way. Everything was ready. They followed the hearse to the graveyard. As they were walking the short walk to the graveyard, Susie took Dan by the arm. He looked over at her and smiled. As they placed the casket in the grave, Dan let out a few tears. "You were the love of my life," said Dan. "I will miss you forever." Dan gave a nod and the undertaker had his men start filling the grave. Dan went to the undertaker, shook his hand, and he and Susie went back to the saloon.

Sean's visit with Horace turned into a day long visit. Finally at about dark, Sean decided it was time to leave. He thanked Horace for the drinks and the meal and headed back to his hotel room. He decided he would not go to the saloon till late the next morning. Michael and Jon had a full day too. They went to a general store and bought some line and some hooks and then headed to the river bank. They cut some poles, dug a few worms, and tossed out their lines. They passed the bottle back and forth, told a few war stories, and then they both fell asleep in the shade. About dark they both woke up and decided to get something to eat. "We didn't catch supper," said Jon. "I really didn't want to clean fish anyway. I had me a good relaxin' sleep though. Dog had a good sleep too."

"I had one too," said Michael. "I was dreamin' about Betty. Yep, I had me a good dream. Let's just leave these poles and such here and go get somethin' to eat. Maybe some young fella'll come along and he can use these poles and such." They went to the small eatery close to their hotel and afterwards, they went to their hotel rooms.

~~~~

When Sean got to "The Palace" late morning, he saw that all the new signs were in place. Susie and Dan were sitting at a table talking. Everyone else was getting ready for the day's business. Sean went to Susie's table. "I have something I'd like to discuss with you Susie," said Sean.

"I bet I already know what it is," said Susie. "Dan and I have already talked about it. I will be quitting my duties as a working girl. I will be getting a new girl to take my place. Hopefully, there will not be any trouble from my regular customers."

"Sounds like you have everything under control," said Sean. "I reckon we'll see how things go as the day goes along."

"Susie, if you'd excuse us for a few minutes, I'd like to have some private words with Sean," said Dan.

"No, go ahead and talk," replied Susie. "I'll go out back and check supplies. Yell if you need me."

When Susie left, Dan began. "My wife died yesterday," Dan said. "We got her buried this morning. As of right now, I'm considering staying here in St. Louis and not going to California if you would want me to stay."

"I'm deeply sorry about your wife," said Sean. "I never knew she was that sick."

"We found out that she had something called cancer," said Dan. "They don't know much about it except that if you get it, you're gonna die. I'm glad that her suffering is over. Doc said that the longer it went on, the more pain she would be in. I really didn't want to go to California in the first place. My wife had read so much about San Francisco and other places and decided it would be a wonderful place to live. With good employment waiting on me, I went along with her wishes."

"Does Susie know all of this?" asked Sean.

"She knows my wife died and such," said Dan. "I have not told her that I might stay here."

"Well you go ahead and tell her," said Sean. "If she doesn't mind you being here, I won't either."

"I'll go tell her right now," said Dan as he got up and went to find Susie.

"We'll make a great team," said Susie when Dan told her his intentions. "I'm sure we will make Sean proud."

~~~~

Around noon, business started picking up. Everyone that came in stopped and read the sign about checking their weapons. Sean counted them as they arrived. The first twenty men were not armed. Of the next ten men, only one man was armed and he checked his pistol at the bar without grumbling. The next five men that came in were all armed. They read the sign and then went to a table. Dan saw them too and went straight to their table. "Gentlemen, you will check your weapons at the bar or you will not be welcome here," he said. "Now please do as I ask." Dan was right handed and had his Colt on his left hip for a cross draw.

"So what's gonna happen if we don't?" asked the biggest man in the group.

"You will be leaving on your own power or you might get carried out," said Dan. The big man went for his pistol but before he had it out of the holster, Dan's Colt was out and about two inches from the man's forehead. "Now you five will stand up and drop your gun belts," said Dan. "Any one a you makes a wrong move and your friend here will get the top of his head blown off."

"He won't shoot boys," the big man said. "Go ahead and take'm."

"I don't know Roy," one of the other men said. "I think he'd kill ya."

"Fine buncha boys I got workin' fer me," Roy said. "Hell, he won't shoot me. He's no gunman. I think I'll go ahead and shoot 'm myself."

"If you wanna die mister, you go ahead and pull that shooter," said Dan. "But I wanna tell you, I never, and I mean never, miss at this range." Roy started laughing and as he was laughing, he went for his pistol. Dan's Colt fired and Roy was thrown backwards. Blood and brain and bone went everywhere. Dan did not watch as Roy was falling. He cocked his Colt again and pointed it at the other men. "Now drop them gun belts boys and I mean right now," Dan said. They did as instructed. "Now git out of here," yelled Dan. "I'll give these back to you soon as you get out the door. Any one a you thinks he's gonna come back here and get even, better try it soon as you get your guns back cause if I see you later, I'll just start shootin' and claim self defense." The four men never said a word. When they got out the door, Dan gave them back their gun belts. They mumbled a few words to themselves, and then started walking away. Sean was by the door now so he could help Dan if necessary.

Michael and Jon had just left the hotel when they heard the shot. They were on the sidewalk almost to "The Palace" when they passed the four men who had been kicked out of the saloon. As they had passed them, Michael accidentally bumped against one of them. Michael immediately apologized to the man. "Please excuse me kind sir," said Michael.

"Watch where you're goin' you stupid mick," the man said. The man turned to face Michael as if he was going to draw on him. Michael stopped and stared at him. "What are you lookin' at you stupid mick?" the man asked.

"I'm lookin' at a man who's about to get a good thrashin'," said Michael.

"What a ya say boys. Do ya think we should give this dumb mick a good beatin?" the man said.

"I think we oughta whoop that breed friend a his too," another one of them said. "And then we'll shoot that ugly dog."

Jon looked down at Dog and told him to stay. Then Jon charged like a bull. He had his head down and rammed it into the man's gut. They both went down. Jon got on top of him and was beating him senseless. The man closest to Jon kicked Jon in the side and knocked him off his friend. The other two men thought they would get after Michael but when they closed in, Michael hit one with a tremendous right to the jaw, and then he gave the other one a left to the jaw. Both of them went down and didn't move. Sean and Dan stood there watching from the saloon door. "Should we go help them?" Dan asked Sean.

"No, they'll be just fine," said Sean. "They won't even get a good sweat goin'."

Sean was right. The two that Michael had hit were out cold and the first one that Jon had tangled with was out too. Jon had the one who had kicked him up against a wall and was beating him senseless. "That's enough now," Michael said to Jon. "He's out on his feet. You don't wanna be breakin' a hand hittin' a man who's already out."

~~~~

Marshal Turner had heard the shot too and was on his way to the saloon. When he got closer he saw the four men laying on the sidewalk and Michael and Jon beside them. "Just what the hell went on here?" asked the Marshal. "These four look pretty beat up."

"We were on our way to the saloon after we heard that shot when these fellas picked a fight with us," said Michael. "I want'em arrested for disturbin' the peace and assault on a Federal Officer."

"I'll throw'em in jail," said Mark. "But it looks ta me that they didn't get much assaultin' done. Now what was that shot?"

"We don't know Marshal," said Jon. "We didn't make it over there yet." Sean walked over to Mark.

"Come on inside Mark," said Sean. "Got a dead man in there." Mark went in and looked at the dead body.

"Well somebody tell me what happened," said Mark. "Did it have somethin' ta do with that new sign?"

"I'd say so Marshal," said Dan. "Name's Dan Taylor. We got a new policy here about weapons. Just started it. That dead fella and them four fellas outside didn't want to abide by our rules. That dead one over there tried to shoot me and I killed'em. I kicked them other four out."

"Is that right Sean? Is that what happened?" Mark asked Sean.

"Sure is," answered Sean. "Dan tried ta talk that fella inta givin' up his gun but that fella wouldn't have no part of it. He tried ta pull on Dan. He's dead and Dan's not."

"Well I'll git the undertaker over here," said Mark. "I don't s'pose anybody knows who this fella is."

"We never seen'm before," said Dan. "But I remember that he said that them other four worked for'm. You can most likely find out from them. That is if they're not wanted'r somethin'.""

Mark left and it wasn't five minutes later and someone from the undertaker was there for the body.

After the body was removed, Susie had some of the help clean things. "I hope we have no more of that," Susie said to Sean. "That can't be good for business."

"You never know," said Sean. "Sometimes a shootin'll make more people come. Curiosity I guess. We had some shootins' back in Abilene, and it never hurt our business one bit."

"That's because of that reputation of yours," said Susie. "I guess I remember when you saved Sam that night. Business really picked up after that. Well anyway, I hope we have no more shootings."

"Me too," said Dan as he approached Susie and Sean. "I didn't wanna shoot that man. I never figured I'd ever hafta kill another man once I got outta the war."

"Well sometimes it might just happen that if you don't kill someone, they might just kill you," said Sean. "Are you sure you never been a lawman? You handled yourself pretty darn good."

"I had a few scrapes back in New York when I had my own place," said Dan. "But there weren't any guns involved."

"Well me and the boys'll hang around today and help with anything if we're needed," said Sean. "We'll be leavin' for Abilene in the mornin'."

None of the customers who were in the saloon during the shooting had left. As the day wore on, the place filled up. A lot of the customers were happy for Susie now that she was the manager. A lot of hugs were exchanged. Whenever Susie spotted one of her regular customers, she went to them and informed them she was no longer one of the working girls. Most of them took it well as all of the girls were beautiful anyway, and they wouldn't mind visiting them.

There was one particular man who was not happy at all. His name was Alfred Walker. He was a short man, about thirty, and very thin. He owned a dress shop in town and his wife ran it for him. Once a month he paid Susie a visit. He was always trying to give her new dresses and other presents. He had convinced himself that one day he would leave his wife and run off with Susie. When Susie told him she was out of the business, he almost cried. He left the saloon and stood outside for a full hour. Then he went back inside. He found Susie and went to her. She was talking with two other men, but Alfred grabbed her by the arm and took her over to a corner. "I'm leaving my wife," he began. "We can go off together and start a new life."

"Just what are you talking about Alfred," said Susie. "Go on back home. Go home to your wife. I never wanted to be with you other than as a customer. Now go on home." Alfred grabbed Susie by the arms now and started shaking her. "I love you," he said. "We were meant to be together."

"Stop it Alfred. Stop it right now," said Susie. "Now let go of me and I mean right now." Alfred let go of her and stepped back.

When he did, Susie gave him a very hard slap. Dan was a few tables away and heard the slap. He came over to see what was happening. He saw Susie in the corner and Alfred standing in front of her. Alfred reached into a pocket on his jacket and pulled out a derringer.

"You're just a stupid whore," Alfred said. "And to think I was ready to leave my wife for you. Well you won't be anybody's whore anymore."

Dan saw the derringer but before he could get out his Colt, the derringer fired. Susie was struck and fell to the floor. Dan looked at Alfred, "drop that right now." Alfred didn't say a word. He turned to face Dan with the derringer pointed at Dan. As soon as Dan saw the derringer pointed at him, he fired. Alfred was struck in the chest and was dead before he hit the floor. Dan ran over to Susie. There was blood all over her right side. She looked up at Dan. "I don't think it's bad," she said. "It doesn't feel bad anyway. I think went in one side and out the other."

"You stay still," said Dan. "Someone go get Doc Barnes." Dan grabbed a clean towel from behind the bar and held it over Susie's wound. "Now let's stand you up and get you to the office. You let me know if we're hurting you."

They made it to the office with no trouble. Dan cleared off the desk, got some blankets and a pillow, and put them on the desk. Then he picked up Susie and laid her on the desk. "Now you lay still," said Dan. "Doc Barnes'll be here shortly. I think you're right. It doesn't look bad at all."

Sean, Michael, and Jon had been at a table at the other end of the saloon. They had no idea anything was happening till they heard the first shot. They headed toward the shooting but before they got there, Dan had killed Alfred. Sean and the boys made everyone clear a path so Dan could get Susie to the office. They followed them into the office. "How you doin' Susie?" asked Sean. "From what I can see, it don't look bad at all."

"It doesn't even hurt right now," said Susie. "Dan got there before Alfred could shoot me again."

"Dan's had some day today," said Sean. "Two men shot in one day. Maybe it'll be quiet for a while now."

"I hope so," said Dan. "I don't fancy bein' a gunman."

"You're not a gunman," said Sean. "You're just a man defendin' himself. There's a big difference."

Doc Barnes arrived and went to Susie. "Well let's see what we have here," said Doc. "We need to get you out of this dress and your under things. I suggest we cut them. That'll cause you less pain."

"Go ahead and cut Doc," said Susie. "They're ruined anyway and I'm not shy."

Doc cut off her dress and slip and such and covered her breasts with a piece of one her slips. "You are very lucky," said Doc. "That bullet went through and missed your ribs and other important things. It's a good thing it was a small bullet. A .44 would have probably got your last rib. I'll clean you up and you'll be just fine." Doc cleaned her up and then gave her some instructions. "Now you take it easy for a few days," said Doc. "Don't lift anything for two weeks. Keep it clean. If it looks strange or anything while it's healing, come see me. Our only worry is infection. Now's who's payin'?"

"How much is it Doc?" asked Dan.

"$3.00," said Doc. Dan reached into his pocket paid Doc. Doc nodded his head and left.

"That man don't beat around the bush when it comes time for his fee does he?" said Sean.

"He's always been that way," said Susie. "Even when he first came to town. I don't know if anyone has ever not paid him when he asked."

"Well he's in the big city," said Sean. "If he was out in the middle of nowhere, he'd be takin' meals and such for his fees. A lot of people out there don't have any money at all. Now I think we should get Susie wrapped up with something and get her to a bed. Then some of us better get back out on the floor."

There was a room in the back that Sam had used from time to time. It had a nice bed in it and all the necessaries. Dan wrapped Susie up and carried her to the room and put her in bed. "You know I can walk don't you Dan?" said Susie.

"I know you can," said Dan. "But I didn't mind carryin' you. No I didn't mind at all." Susie pulled Dan to her and gave him a kiss on the cheek.

"Now you get back to work now," said Susie. "I'll be fine."

Dan nodded his head yes and went back to work. Marshal Turner was there and wanted to talk with Dan. "I talked with Sean and his men. They tell me they really didn't see what happened," said Mark. "So what happened?"

"Alfred shot Susie so I shot Alfred," said Dan. "I reckon he was upset because Susie told him she was no longer one of the working girls. Susie'll be all right. The bullet from his derringer went clear through her right side and missed any vitals."

"I thought you were s'posed to check your weapons when you come in now," said Mark. Sean had come over and was behind Mark and heard the conversation.

"That's right," said Sean. "Be we don't frisk everyone that comes in. We rely on their honesty. This happened in Abilene too after we started havin'em check their weapons. Someone can slip in a small pistol or knife anytime if they want. It'd be a lot a trouble to frisk every fella that came through the door."

"Well now I gotta go tell that man's wife he got himself shot in a saloon over a working girl," said Mark. "I reckon everyone in town but her knew that he was comin' here at times. I hope you'll be goin' back home soon," Mark said to Sean. "You Federal boys cause too much work. I'll send over the undertaker for the body." Mark then nodded his head and left.

Sean then turned to Dan. "Are you gonna be all right?" asked Sean. "You've had a lot goin' on the last couple days. Some folks need some time after a killin'."

"I'll be fine," said Dan. "I didn't think I would be, but I am. Work'll be good for me. In fact I know you'll want to look at the books before you leave. We can do that right now if you want."

"No, I'll take a look in the mornin'," said Sean. "Train leaves at ten. That'll give me plenty a time for a good breakfast and time for the books."

~~~~

The rest of the day was uneventful. Sean and the men stayed till closing time and then went to their hotel rooms. They all got up at daylight and had a good breakfast. Sean then went to the telegraph office and sent the following.

Maggie O'Rourke
Abilene Kansas

Train leaves St. Louis this morning<<stop>>be home soon<<stop>>all is well here

Love and miss you
Sean

When Sean got to the saloon the first thing he did was go see Susie. She was sitting up in bed and having some coffee. "How are you doin' darlin'?" Sean asked her. "Did you sleep all right?"

"I did," she answered. "I haven't slept that good for a long time. Dan brought me in some coffee, and we'll be having some breakfast. Would you care to join us?"

"Thanks for the offer but I've already had mine," said Sean. "I'll be lookin' at the books, and then our train leaves at ten. I'll get Dan after you two have had your breakfast. I believe I'll go back up front and give the place a good look over. I'll tell'em to go ahead and clean up that mirror too. I'll stop in before I leave." Sean nodded his head and left. He passed Dan with a tray of food on the way up front. "Come get me after you eat," said Sean. "We'll get them books looked at."

When Dan was finished eating he found Sean, and they went to the office. "Well here's what I've got for you," said Dan. "I've got everything sorted out. This book has all the employees and their wages. This book lists our beer and liquor inventory and the dollar amounts. This book has all other expenses such as furniture, food, lights and such. This book will show what we took in each day. At the end of each week, I'll figure expenses and income and all profits will go to the bank and that amount will show on deposit slips from the bank. I believe that's everything. As I said before, we'll keep $3000 in the safe here for any unforeseen expenses and the rest will go to the bank. We can stay in touch however you want."

"Everything sounds good to me," said Sean. "When I get back, I'm sure Maggie will tell me how she wants to handle things. Now you take care of Susie for me and make sure this place stays the best place in town as it always has been."

Dan extended his hand to Sean and they shook. "We'll do you a good job," said Dan. "I'll make sure Susie heals good and doesn't get to doin' things too soon. Now you do me a favor."

"Sure Dan, what is it?" asked Sean.

"Don't go gettin' yourself shot," said Dan. "There's a lotta bad men out there."

"I'll do my best," said Sean. "Now I'm gonna go tell Susie good bye."

Sean went to the back room. Susie was sitting on the side of bed and it looked like she was thinking about getting dressed. "You get yourself back in bed young lady," said Sean. "If you don't, I'll have Dan hide all your clothes."

"I was just sitting here thinking," said Susie. "I'll be hiring a new girl to take my place. I'm gonna try and see if I can get me a red head. And I hope she's Irish too."

"Sounds good to me," said Sean. "I have this thing for red heads myself. Now I'll be leavin'. If you need anything, I mean anything at all, get ahold of me." The Sean bent down and kissed her on the cheek. Susie gave him a hug and then a kiss on the cheek.

"I feel foolish about getting shot," said Susie. "I had a derringer in my pocket, and I didn't think to pull it."

"If that fella had his gun on you already, he would have shot you before you got yours out," said Sean. "You just never had a

gun pulled on you before, and you probably had a hard time be-
lieving it."

"That's true. That was a first for me. I hope it never happens
again. If I even think someone might do that, I think I'll be better
prepared. Now tell Maggie to come see us soon," said Susie. "You
keep yourself safe too."

"I will," said Sean. He tipped his hat to her and then left.

The men and Dog were waiting on Sean. They checked out of
their hotel and went to the train station. The train left on time.

Sean and the men spent a night in Kansas City and then took
the stage to Abilene the next day. The stage ride to Abilene was
uneventful. Maggie, Betty, and Martha were there waiting when
the stage pulled in. All three couples hugged and kissed for a good
while and then went their separate ways. They did not see each
other until the next morning. Maggie didn't ask Sean one question
about St. Louis until breakfast the next morning. As they were
eating, she asked Sean to tell him about everything that happened.

"Well darlin', we talked to the local law when we first got
there to find out if they were tied up with the saloon or not," Sean
began. "It seemed that they weren't. Then we visited Susie. She
showed us her bruises and such from where they had beaten her.
Then we went over to the saloon and she pointed out the ones
who did it. I broke my finger bones when I had a fight with some
fella they called Mountain, and he was a mountain. After I got
him knocked out, we told the other ones they was gonna get a
beatin'. They tried ta shoot it out and they're dead. There was one
of'em missin' at the time. After I went into the office and convinced Owens he should sell to me, that fella that was missin'
shot'm right after he signed the deed over. That fella shot a deputy and the deputy killed'm."

"So how did you convince Owens to sell to you?" asked Maggie.

"Just used my regular charm," said Sean. "Not really. I convinced him that he didn't want ta die and that he could have all the money that was in the office safe. I didn't know it at the time, but there was over $38,000 in that safe."

"So how do you think Susie'll do?" asked Maggie.

"She'll do fine," answered Sean. "I didn't want to tell you in a telegram because you might get upset, but Susie got herself shot. It's not bad at all. Just got her right side, but not bones or vitals hit."

"Who in the hell shot Susie and why?" asked Maggie.

"It was some customer of hers," said Sean. "She told all her regular customers that she would no longer be one of the working girls. One of'em got upset and pulled a derringer on her. Dan killed that fella."

"Well who's Dan?" asked Maggie.

"Dan was workin' at the saloon. He was probly the only honest man there," said Sean. "I found out that he had his own place in New York before the war and was on his way to California to be a partner with his uncle in a gambling house and saloon. I asked him to help Susie learn the ropes while his wife got better. She took sick and they were waiting on her to get better before they went on to California. Well his wife died. She got somethin' called cancer. Dan's gonna stay on now. Dan shot another man there too."

"And what was that about?" asked Maggie.

"Well I decided we would have a weapons policy like we got here," said Sean. "This one fella wouldn't give up his gun and tried to shoot Dan. Dan killed'm."

"Sounds like Dan might be a good man to have around," said Maggie. "So I hope you saw to it that all the employees are receiving a good wage."

"Yes I did," said Sean. "Susie rounded up all the former employees that were there before Sam was killed. I gave'em all another $20 a month on top a what they were gettin'. I told Susie we'd give her $350 a month as manager and Dan $300 a month as assistant manager. Did I do good darlin'?"

"Yes you did," said Maggie. "We'll check on things from time to time. If it goes well, maybe we can pay them more or give them a bonus from time to time."

"Besides that money in the office safe, I found out that we do business at the Bank of St. Louis," said Sean. "Just take a guess. How much money do you think would be in our account at that bank?"

"I have no idea," answered Maggie. "Maybe $50-60,000?"

"Darlin', we have $155,000 in that account," said Sean.

"Damn, that's a fair amount," said Maggie. "Do you suppose that was in there when Sam was still alive or do you figure Owens put it there?"

"I got no idea," said Sean. "That Owens was a weasel. I kinda figure Sam had that money in there and Owens didn't wanna take it out yet and arouse any suspicion about anything. It's hard ta say. I reckon it's ours now. Got any big plans?"

"No I don't," said Maggie. "We had more money than we would ever spend in several lifetimes before we got that money. Let's just enjoy the thought that we would never have to work again ever in our lives if we didn't want to. Besides, you're a lawman. You'll be a lawman for a while. You're good at it. It's what you do. So did the Judge have anything new for you to get into?"

"No, it's been quiet for a while," said Sean. "I guess we can sit back and wait for the cattle drives to get here next spring."

"Well I doubt if it'll be quiet around here for that long of a time," said Maggie. "But we can hope for that."

CHAPTER FIVE

It did stay quiet in Abilene for the rest of the summer and the fall, but it was not quiet in western Kansas and the Nebraska Territory. The Cheyenne and other tribes were constantly raiding. The army had no luck trying to catch them. They could not get them to stand for a pitched battle. It was always hit and run. Then hit and run someplace else. Custer was not having his usual Custer's Luck.

~~~~

The Bozeman Trail was established in 1863. It went from the gold fields of Montana and what is now Wyoming to the Oregon Trail. The trail was basically animal trails that the game and buffalo had used for years made wider to accommodate wagons. This seemed like a good trail at the time, but the local Indians had used this trail for years to hunt their game, and they were not happy about the white men being there and interfering. There were several fights during the years of the trail's use. In 1863, the Bear River Massacre occurred. Some volunteer cavalry units slaughtered a lot of Shoshone. Women and children were killed too. Some witnesses said that the soldiers took women and children and smashed their heads against rocks. That was after the women were raped first. In 1865 at the Battle of the Tongue River, a large group of Arapaho were defeated.

The largest group of Indians in the area were the Sioux. Their Chief was a man named Red Cloud and he led his men in several attacks on people and soldiers on the trail. This became known as the "Red Cloud War." He was relentless and never let up. The army built three forts to protect the trail. They were constantly being harassed. Usually, the Sioux did not attack the forts. They attacked when small parties came out to gather wood and cut hay. A lot of soldiers were lost.

There was a young warrior with Red Cloud who was starting to make a name for himself. His name was Crazy Horse. He had been in several fights with the soldiers and was getting a good reputation for being very brave. Some thought that bullets couldn't harm him. On Dec. 21, 1866, a party was sent out from Fort Phil Kearny to gather wood. A party of forty to sixty Sioux warriors attacked the party hoping to draw out more soldiers from the fort. This attack took place in full view of the fort. The ruse worked and soldiers were sent out to help the attacked party. The relief party consisted of 27 cavalrymen, 2 scouts, and 51 infantryman. They were commanded by a man named Captain Fetterman. The cavalrymen were armed with 7 shot Spencer carbines. The two scouts had Henry rifles, and the infantry was armed with muzzle loaders. The officers were armed with their revolvers.

When the relief force went out, the Sioux quit the attack on the wood cutting party and fled, but six warriors stayed behind and were used as a decoy for the relief force. They taunted the soldiers and finally the soldiers followed them looking for glory. The soldiers figured the only Sioux out there was the small force that had attacked the wood cutting party. When the soldiers reached the ambush spot, they were set upon by over a thousand warriors. The fight was over in less than thirty minutes. The Sioux had very few firearms at this time, and it was discovered later that only six of the soldiers died from bullet wounds. The rest were killed by arrows, lances, and war clubs. All of the bodies were mutilated but one. The body of a nineteen year old bugler was found covered by a buffalo robe. His bugle was all bent up and bloodied where it looked like he had used it for a weapon. It was believed that the Sioux honored his bravery by not mutilating him. Most of the tribes were strong believers in courage and bravery. It is strongly believed that Crazy Horse made the plans for this massacre. There were now repeating rifles in the Sioux's possession, 27 Spencers and 2 Henry's. They also got the revolvers and muzzle loaders that were carried by the infantry.

Fort Phil Kearny expected to be wiped out any time, but the Sioux did not attack the fort. Instead they went to their winter camps. Everyone was looking for someone to blame. Naturally they put the blame on the fort Commandant, but he swore that he told Captain Fetterman that he was not to go past a certain point, and he had witnesses to that effect. He had watched Captain Fetterman from the fort and had seen him go farther than he was instructed, but he made no effort to get him to return. Some believed him about telling Captain Fetterman not to go past a certain point, but if this was true, why didn't he make an effort to get Fetterman to return? This became known as "The Fetterman Massacre." This was the Army's worst defeat by the plains tribes at that time.

Attacks continued all along the Bozeman Trail the next spring but the Indians lost more and more warriors because the army had rearmed the soldiers with new breech loading rifles. Whenever the Indians would attack, they usually waited till the soldiers fired a volley and then when they were reloading their muzzle loaders, they would attack. These new breech loaders were a big surprise to the Indians and it cost them dearly. At the Fetterman fight, less than twenty Sioux were killed. In the fights after that, hundreds lost their lives. They still did not give up or stop the attacks. They wanted the white men off their land.

~~~~

At Fort Leavonworth, the 10th Cavalry was having a hard time. Most of the officers didn't want to be there, and the army was having a hard time getting recruits. They wanted coloreds who could read and write, or had some type of skill, but they had to give up on that.

When Sam Carver got there, they made him a Sergeant and gave him eighty men to look after. Some of the men were veterans of the war, but most of them were former slaves and had never been on a horse and never fired a gun of any kind. Sam did his best but progress was slow. After the Fetterman fight, the Army considered sending the 10th to that area, but finally decided that they were not anywhere near being a fighting force and did not send them.

Sgt. Carver was out drilling some of his men one day when he heard a familiar voice from behind. "Put someone else in charge of that detail Sgt. and come over here and talk to me," the man said. Sgt. Carver turned around saw Captain Pierce standing there. He immediately came to attention and saluted. Captain Pierce returned the salute. "At ease Sgt.," the Captain said.

"Johnson, take charge while I talk to the Captain. Now pardon me Captain, but weren't you s'posed to be goin' to Fort Riley with the 7th?" asked Sgt. Carver.

"I did go to Ft. Riley Sgt.," said Captain Pierce. "When I told Mister Custer things he didn't want to hear, he suggested that I get the hell out of his Regiment. I did what he said and here I am."

"Are you sure you wanna be here sir?" asked Sam. "We got a long way ta go before we're ready for anything. Most a these white officers don't wanna be here. Most a these recruits don't know spit. I got a few veterans but none of'em was cavalry. I know we got a Commandin' Officer, but I heard another staff officer was s'posed to come here and turned it down and retired. We don't see too many officers anyhow."

"Well you're going to see me Sgt.," said Captain Pierce. "I'm your troop Commander. Now get your men formed up and I'll introduce myself."

"Yes sir," said Sam. Johnson had been drilling the men for a few minutes while Sam talked to the Captain. They had turned into an unorganized mob in those few minutes. "Johnson, you are relieved. You men fall into formation and I mean now and do it smart. Dress it up." In a few minutes, the Sgt. came to attention and saluted Captain Pierce again. "The troop is formed Captain," he said. The Captain returned his salute.

"At ease men," Captain Pierce started. "My name is Captain Ben Pierce. I am your troop Commander. Sgt. Carver is now your 1st Sgt. Together, he and I will turn you men into a fighting machine that will be second to none. It will take time, but it will be done. I have high standards, so you will have high standards. I know most of you believe that most white folks, including army officers, believe that you are totally worthless and are good for nothing except maybe digging latrines. We will prove them wrong. I will not tolerate insubordination of any kind. If you ever have a problem with anyone, including other white officers, you come to 1ˢᵗ Sgt. Carver and he'll come to me. I will take care of it. No one but me is going to give my men a hard time. Anyone shirking their duty will be disciplined. Anyone who deserts and gets caught will be shot. We are at war men. We are at war with the Indians of the plains and sooner or later we will be out there fighting. Do not worry whether you will be a coward under fire or not. Anyone who has ever been under fire has been afraid. You must learn to control your fear. We will go places where there are white folks we are supposed to be helping and these folks will treat you badly. You must learn to not be bothered by this. We will gain everyone's respect by being the best damn troop in the Army. Now I hope you men understand what I want. 1ˢᵗ Sgt. Carver, call the troop to attention."

"Yes sir. Troop atten-hut," said Sam. "The troop is at attention sir." Sam saluted the Captain. Captain Pierce returned the salute.

"Pick out your best man and tell him he's acting Corporal and to continue drilling," said the Captain. "Tell him if he does a good job, he'll be a real Corporal shortly. After you get that done, come to my office." The Captain then left.

"Yes sir," said Sam. "Johnson, you're acting Corporal now. Continue the drill. When I get back, I better not see a mob like I did a little while ago. You'll be shovelin' shit for a month if I do."

"Yes 1ˢᵗ Sgt.," said Johnson. 1ˢᵗ Sgt. Carver then headed to Captain Pierce's office.

Sam reported to the Captain's office as ordered. "Sir, Sgt. Carver reporting to the Captian as ordered," Sam said.

"I told the troop that you were now their 1st Sgt.," said the Captain. "Here are your new stripes. Get them sewed on as soon as you leave this office. Now you are here because I know you were not in the cavalry, but you know horses. I have these books and they are all about cavalry formations and such. You must learn everything in these books so between you and me, we can teach the men. They must understand that care of our horses is very important. Any man not taking proper care of his mount will be disciplined. It might be some time before the unit is up to strength, and we have all of our equipment and mounts, but we will do the best we can with what we have. I am counting on you 1st Sgt. I know you will not let me or the unit down."

"No sir Captain, I will not let you or the unit down," responded Sam. "All of the troop will learn everything in these books one way or the other. Will there be anything else sir?"

"No 1st Sgt., you are dismissed," said the Captain. Sam gave the Captain a salute and after the Captain returned his salute, he did an about face and left the office. He went straight to his quarters and sewed on his new stripes.

A few minutes after Sam left Captain Pierce's office, another officer made his way into Captain Pierce's office. He was a young Lieutenant just out of West Point and this was his first assignment. "Is there something I can do for you Lieutenant?" asked the Captain.

"No Ben, I just stopped in to jaw a little," said the Lieutenant. "So I hear you made that nigger a 1st Sgt."

"First off Lieutenant, I never gave you permission to call me by my first name," said Ben. "You will address me as Captain

Pierce. Secondly, you will not use that word in my presence. I'm sure you know what word I'm talking about. That 1st Sgt. Is a very good man. He's been in more combat then you'll probably ever see in your lifetime. If I ever even hear about you slandering me or my men, I will take you out and beat you till you can't stand. Do you understand me Lieutenant?"

"I understand that threatening another officer is against regulations and I can report you and have you brought up on charges," said the Lieutenant.

"That's true Lieutenant," replied Ben. "But If I hear that you have done that, I will come after you and when I get done with you, your momma won't be able to recognize you. Now do we understand each other Lieutenant?"

"Yes sir, I believe we do," said the Lieutenant. "I'll be leaving now."

"Lieutenant, don't forget to salute me," said Ben. "Regulations you know." The young Lieutenant came to attention and saluted. After Ben returned his salute, he did an about face and left.

The young Lieutenant must have put out the word that Captain Pierce didn't like the word nigger because Ben never heard that word one time in his presence during the next couple of months. Everything was going well. More recruits were coming and the men were learning well. Then the unthinkable happened. There was a cholera epidemic in western Kansas. Several of the men died. There were several deaths in most of the units on the frontier. It would take some time for the unit to recover from this disaster.

CHAPTER SIX

Everything was quiet in Abilene. Susie and Dan had been keeping in touch with Maggie and Sean. Cookie and Barbara had been on their belated honeymoon for three weeks now, and Betty was doing the cooking. Michael helped a lot in the kitchen but every once in a while he grumbled about not being able to play the piano. Betty's food wasn't as fancy as Cookie's and Barbara's, but there were no complaints from anyone. Cookie and Barbara would be back any day now. Sean could tell that Michael would be relieved.

It was the first week of November now. There was a chill in the air but the weather had been pleasant most of the time. It was Saturday morning and Maggie and Sean were at their table getting ready for breakfast when the postal clerk came in with a letter for Sean and Maggie. "It's from Susie," said Maggie. "I'll open it and read it to you." The letter went as follows:

October 23

Dear Maggie and Sean,

Things are going very well here. There has been no trouble of any kind since my accident. I have a new girl hired.

Her name is Kathleen Jameson. She is a beautiful red-head and the men love her. I thought the other girls would be jealous of her but they all have become great friends. She had been a school teacher in Philadelphia. Her husband was killed during the last days of the war, and she decided to go to California. She had been working her way west from town to town making just enough money in one town to move on to the next. She decided this was taking way too long and that she needed a way to make money quicker. While in Cincinnati, she decided to try the oldest profession. She met a few girls, and they introduced her to their Madam. Things went well for her there and when she had enough money to move on, she did. I was close to the train station one day when I noticed her getting off a train. I saw that she was alone, so I went over and introduced myself. I took her to "The Palace" and showed her around. She's been with us for a month now. I think she'll stay a while.

There's one more thing I should tell you. Dan and I are getting sweet on each other. He's a very good man. He tells me he has deep feelings for me, but he feels guilty because his wife hasn't been gone that long. I have deep feelings for him too. We'll see what happens.

Well back to business. Business is very good, and the books are in good order. We look forward to your visit in the near future.

Much love,

Susie

"Sounds like everything is well in St. Louis," said Maggie. "When do you think we should pay them a visit?"

"We could probably go as soon as Cookie and Barbara get back," answered Sean. "Michael and Jon can take care of everything while we're gone. Should we take Jeb with us?"

"I think we can leave Jeb here," said Maggie. "I think we can take care of ourselves since we'll be together most of the time."

"You know that dog will miss you, don't you?" said Sean. "That dog loves you."

"Jeb loves you too," said Maggie. "I see that look in his eyes when you take off for parts unknown and he can't go."

"Well he can miss us both again," said Sean. "He did good when we went on our honeymoon. I think Michael likes havin' him around."

That evening, the saloon filled up as usual. Every table was taken, and the bar was full. It was around nine o'clock now, and Betty and Michael had just closed the kitchen. Michael came out and played the piano while Maggie sang. There was a huge applause as usual when she was finished. Maggie was making her way over to Sean's table when two rough looking men came in. They stopped and read the sign and walked over to the bar and turned in their gunbelts. As they stood at the bar waiting for the drinks they had ordered, Jeb walked over beside them and began a low growl. One of the two men was a head taller than the other one. The shorter man heard the low growl and turned around and saw Jeb with his teeth showing. "Whoever owns this mongrel dog best git him away before I kill'em," he said. Sean had been watching and made his way to the bar.

"That's my dog," said Sean. "You musta done somethin' he didn't like, or he wouldn't be a growlin' at ya."

"I never done nothin'," the man said. "Now call'm off before I kill'em."

"Now just how are you goin' ta kill my dog?" asked Sean. "You just turned in yer gunbelt, and you was s'posed ta turn in all weapons. That includes knives too. You gonna kill my dog with yer bare hands? Lemme tell you somethin' mister. Ole Jeb here can rip out your throat before you can reach fer any weapon you got hid somewhere. Now if I was you, I'd move real slow like and drop any weapon you got hid on the floor. Do it now mister or I'll turn Jeb loose on ya."

Very slowly, the man reached inside his jacket and pulled out a small .32 revolver and dropped it on the floor. Michael had been watching and had worked his way around and was behind the bar now. When the man dropped his .32 on the floor, the other man made a quick reach for something that seemed to be tucked in his pants. Michael pulled his pistol and cracked the man over the head. He fell to the floor. Sean reached down and pulled a small pistol from his pants. He got right in the other man's face. "Just why didn't you check these pistols like the sign said?" said Sean. "Was you figurin' on shootin' someone in here tonight?" The man didn't answer. Sean pulled a pistol and cracked him over the head. He fell to the floor unconscious. Maggie came over to Sean.

"Why do you think Jeb was after them two?" Maggie asked. "You don't suppose he knew that they still had some guns on them do you?"

"I don't know but wouldn't that be somethin' if he did," said Sean. "Mebbe he could smell them pistols."

"Well when them fellas was here tryin' ta kill Robert, Jeb didn't go after them," said Michael.

"I think that when that happened, Jeb was with Maggie and not close to Robert or them fellas," said Sean. "I got me an idea. Tomorrow we'll get someone to come in and not turn in all their weapons. It might hafta be someone Jeb don't know. We'll try it with people Jeb knows. Then I'll get some strangers off the street. I'll tell'em what we're doin' and give'em some free drinks. For right now, let's get these two down to the jail. We'll run'em outta town tomorrow."

~~~~

The first person that Sean got to help out the next day was Jason. Jason came into the saloon wearing a jacket and had a gunbelt strapped on. He went straight to the bar and turned in the gunbelt. Inside his jacket was a shoulder holster with a .44 in it. Jeb was there at the bar and didn't pay Jason any mind. Then Sean got the blacksmith to do it. The results were the same. Jeb paid no attention to the blacksmith. Then Sean went out into the street and grabbed a total stranger. He explained what he was doing and promised the man several free drinks. The man agreed. He already had on a gunbelt so Sean gave him the shoulder holster with the .44 and a jacket to cover it up. The man walked into the saloon and stopped and acted like he was reading the sign. Then he proceeded to the bar and turned in his gunbelt. Jeb was there. As soon as he turned and started walking from the bar to a table, Jeb was on him and growling. Sean came over and called Jeb off. "Thanks a lot mister," said Sean. "Take off that shoulder holster and Tom there at the bar will give you a bottle of whatever you like. If you need anything after that, we'll git it for you." The man got a bottle of rye and took a table in a corner and started enjoying himself.

"So let's try it again," said Sean. This time Sean got a derringer for a different stranger instead of a bigger pistol. The results were the same. After the stranger turned in his gunbelt and walked away from the bar, Jeb was on him. Sean got the derringer back and got the stranger a bottle.

"So what do you think a that?" said Sean. "Ole Jeb here can smell them guns. Let's try it with a knife and see how he does." Instead of getting another stranger, Sean used one of the men he had used earlier. This time, he had the man put a big pocket knife in a pocket and tuck a big hunting knife in the back of his belt. The man turned in the gunbelt and walked away from the bar. Jeb was on him. Sean called him off and had the man give him the hunting knife. Then he had the man move again. As soon as he moved, Jeb was on him again. Sean got the pocket knife and thanked the man again. "You can have more free drinks tomorrow," Sean told the man.

"Well Maggie, what do ya think a that?" exclaimed Sean. "We got us some dog here."

"Yes we do," said Maggie. "I never would have believed it if I hadn't seen it. Maybe Dog can smell guns and knives too. Where's Jon anyway?"

"He's probably with Martha," said Michael. "Them two should just get married."

"Maybe they will one day," said Maggie.

"Well we'll see how it goes tonight," said Sean. "It's Sunday and we won't be full like we are on Saturday but we should have a good crowd.

They did have a good crowd. Jon and Dog were there. Jon wasn't surprised when Sean told him about Jeb. "These'r some good dogs we got," said Jon. "I don't think anything they do would surprise me." That evening, Jeb went everywhere that Maggie did. Whenever a new customer came in, Maggie always made her way over to them so Jeb could check them out. There were no incidents that evening.

~~~~

The next morning Sean went to the jail and let out the two men. He handed them their weapons and then gave them some instructions. "All right you two, this is how it's gonna be," Sean began. "Here's yer guns but they're not loaded. I'll give you one hour to get a meal, and then you're leavin' town. Someone'll be watchin' you. If you try ta load them guns before you git outta town, I'll be after you and I'll send you ta hell. Now git movin'. If I ever see you back in town, I'll send you ta hell."

"You got a name mister?" the taller one asked Sean.

"O'Rourke, Federal Marshal Sean O'Rourke," answered Sean.

"We won't ferget you," the tall one said. "No, we won't ferget you."

"That's good," said Sean. "I wouldn't be able ta sleep at night if you was ta forget my name. Time's a wastin'. Better git movin'." The two men strapped on their gunbelts and then went over to a café and had some breakfast. Then they got their horses from the livery and headed south out of town. Sean went to the saloon and had some breakfast.

"I see you got them fellas out of town," said Michael. "Did you find out who they were?"

"No, I didn't bother to ask their names," said Sean. "I probly should've. They didn't seem too smart. I don't think I'll get any trouble from them."

After the two men were out of town about a mile, they stopped and loaded their pistols. "Billy, why do you s'pose O'Rourke didn't ask us our names?" the tall one asked the other one.

"I reckon he didn't think we was worth knowin' Bob," the other one answered. "We'd a had ta give fake names ifn' he'd asked us. If he knew we was kin to the Hawks, he'd a probly killed us."

"Yer probly right Bob," said Billy. "I hear he's the best there is with a pistol and a long gun."

"Well let's git back over ta Missouri and let everyone know O'Rourke's still in Abilene," said Bob.

When Sean had finished breakfast and was having some more coffee with Maggie, the postal clerk showed up with another letter. "We must be popular," Sean said to Maggie. "Two letters in three days. That's gotta be some kinda record."

"Well who's it from?" asked Maggie.

"It's from Jug and Lolita," answered Sean. "It's postmarked Ft. Worth."

"Well read it," said Maggie. "I hope things are well with them." The letter went as follows:

Nov. 1

Maggie and Sean,

Things are well here. We got us a good herd. Josh and Wayne are good cowmen. The rest of the boys are good too. I got two Mexicans and two colored boys working here too. Everyone gets along fine. Haven't had any trouble from the Comanches. Most of the trouble with them is farther west. We still get along good with the

Kiowa. I let them have a beef or two when they need it. Flying Eagle died a while back. Bear Claw is the new Chief. We get along fine. There's been some rustling going on down here but I haven't had no trouble. The spread next to mine was having some, and they finally caught one of them. They hung him. Before they hung him, they found out his name was Hawk. I thought you'd like to know that.

Lolita sends her love and we'll be seeing you come late spring or early summer.

Jug

"Damn," said Sean as he finished the letter. "I was hoping we'd never hear the name Hawk again."

"Well look at it this way darlin'," said Maggie. "Since they hung one down there, that's one less that could be out there causing us trouble."

"That's true but when the Hawk women and kids went back to Missouri , they had to be goin' back to kin," said Sean. "Could be another passle of'em. Maybe their name's not Hawk. Maybe Grammaw Hawk had brothers and sisters back in Missouri that are just as mean or meaner than she was. There's a lotta trouble over in Missouri right now, and it's not just them fellas that's robbin' them banks. We need ta find out what Grammaw's maiden name was or if she had sisters or brothers."

"I don't know how we'd ever find that out," said Maggie. "Maybe your new boss could get a hold of some officials in Missouri. Maybe somebody might know something."

"I'll send'm a telegram and see what he can find out," said Sean. "I'll go do that now." Sean went to the telegraph office and sent the following:

Federal Judge Robert Sharpton
Federal Court House
St. Louis

Judge<<stop>>rustler in Texas named Hawk<<stop>> Grammaw Hawk from Missouri<<stop>>can we find out her maiden name and if she had sisters and brothers<<stop>>Hawk women went back to Missouri after shootouts<<stop>>must have kin somewhere

O'Rourke

It wasn't an hour later when Sean got a response. It went as follows:

Federal Marshal O'Rourke
Abilene Kansas

O'Rourke<<stop>>will see what I can find<<stop>>may take some time

Judge Sharpton

That night after the saloon closed, Sean and Maggie decided to soak in the tub for a while. They had made love and were now holding each other. "I think tomorrow I'll go around and ask everybody in this town if they're originally from Missouri," said Sean. "Maybe sooner or later, I might run into someone who might know something. There's a lot of new people in town we don't know and more are coming all the time. You can ask the customers here. The men just love to talk with you. Maybe you'll find one that knows somethin' and he'll spill everything he knows."

"Maybe so," said Maggie. "Now let's quit worrying about the Hawks. I want you again right now."

~~~~

The next morning after breakfast, Sean went all over town trying to find anyone who was from Missouri or knew anything at all about the Hawks or their kin. He had some pleasant conversation, but no one knew much or anything about the Hawks except what they knew about what had happened around Abilene. Sean had Jon asking around town, but he wasn't having any luck either. A full two weeks went by, and there was nothing from Judge Sharpton. They had not found out anything in Abilene. It was Saturday night and the saloon was full again. About nine o'clock a group of four men came in. They really looked tired and beat up. Maggie went over to talk with them. "You boys look worn out to me," said Maggie. "Just what have you been doing to get this tired?"

"We been laying track all day," one of them said. "I'm Jim and that's Tom, Sam, and Fred. You gotta be Maggie and I bet that's your picture on the wall."

"Yes, that's me," said Maggie. "Any of you boys carrying any weapons?"

"We don't even own any guns or knives and if we did we'd be too tired ta carry'em around," said Tom.

"Well you boys follow me and I'll show you to a table," said Maggie. "Any a you boys from Missouri?"

"I am," answered Jim. "And I'd follow you anywhere."

"Well that's good to know," said Maggie. "Now what'll you have? Take a seat and I'll get it for you."

"Bring us a couple bottles a rye and four glasses," said Sam. Maggie went to get their drinks. Sean had seen her with the four boys and went over and asked her about them.

"I got one from Missouri," said Maggie. "I'll let him drink a little and then sit down with them and see what I can get out of him." Maggie took the bottles and glasses over to their table. Jim paid her. "You boys get started," said Maggie. "I'll be back in a short while and see how you're doing." All four of them thanked Maggie and told her not to forget to come back. "I won't forget boys," said Maggie. "I always mingle with my customers. Now excuse me. Enjoy your drinks." Maggie did some mingling and when the four men had finished one of the bottles of rye, she went back to their table. Jim grabbed a chair from another table for Maggie and she sat with them.

"So you boys have been laying track," Maggie began. "Sounds like hard work to me. Why did you come all the way from Missouri to lay track here? Isn't there any railroad work in Missouri?"

"There's more work over this way," said Jim. "Back in Missouri things are pretty slow . Out west is where the railroads need to build. We could 've went to work on that transcontinental railroad for the Union Pacific or whoever it is, but I heard they're using a lot a Chinamen and not payin'em spit. I won't work for an outfit like that. Any man breaks his back workin' for the railroad should get paid proper. Don't matter where he's from or what he is."

"So where are you from in Missouri?" Maggie asked Jim.

"Some little bitty place that really don't have a name," said Jim. "Everybody kinda lives back in the hills and minds their own business. There's a general store and a saloon and that's about it. The county seat is bout twenty miles away. There's a County Sheriff, but he don't do nothin' or at least he hasn't done nothin' since that shoot out with Red Hawk."

"So you know the Hawks," said Maggie.

"Hell yes, I know the Hawks," said Jim. "I know the Slaughters too. They was a bad element in our county."

"Mind if I ask you about the Hawks and the Slaughters?" asked Maggie.

"No pretty lady, you can ask me anything," said Jim.

"So Jim, what do you know about the Hawks and the Slaughters?" asked Maggie.

"Well three of the Slaughters married three of the Hawks," Jim began. "There was a lot more of'em on each side, but everybody in the county thought it was somethin' cause three from each famly married three from the other. There was Pearl, Buck, and Bud on the Slaughter side. Then there was Red, Ruby, and Goldie on the Hawk side. Pearl married Red. Buck married Ruby, and Bud married Goldie."

"So why were they the bad element in the county?" asked Maggie.

"Well the Slaughters were whiskey makers and the Hawks were all horse and cattle thieves," answered Jim.

"So did they ever have trouble with that Sheriff?" asked Maggie.

"No, they kept him paid off," said Jim.

"Well you said something about a shootout and the Sheriff," said Maggie.

"Well that really wasn't the Sheriff's fault," said Jim. "Ole Red had shot and killed a feller in the next county while he was stealin' the man's horses. The Sheriff went out to talk to him and was tellin' him he better lay low for a spell. Well Red was drunk and didn't wanna listen to the Sheriff. He grabbed a pistol and started shootin' at the Sheriff. The Sheriff had to shoot back to keep from gettin' kilt. Red got kilt. After that, Pearl and all her kids, and she had a bunch too, moved to Kansas. Pearl was the Grammaw Hawk that got kilt out here a while back."

"So what are the other Hawks in Missouri up to these days?" asked Maggie.

"Well later on, some of the Hawks came to Kansas to be with Pearl, and the rest of'em stayed in Missouri makin' whiskey with the Slaughters," said Jim. "They started passin' laws about taxin' whiskey and such. The law started givin'em a hard time so a bunch of'em moved down to Arkansas. I heard they was in the Ozarks somewhere. I know some of their kin stayed in Missouri but I don't know who or how many or what they're doin'."

"So Jim, how is it you know so much about the Hawks and the Slaughters?" asked Maggie.

"Well lovely lady, in that county, almost everone is related," answered Jim. "I'm some kinda distant cousin to the Hawks. Why did you wanna know all this?"

"Well Jim, there was a rustler that got hung a short while back in Texas and his name was Hawk," said Maggie. "My husband is a Federal Marshal. He's had to kill several of the Hawks. We're hoping there's not more Hawks out there causing trouble."

"So that famous lawman is your husband," said Jim. "Everbody's heard a him. Well you can tell him everthing I told you. I don't know no more'n that. One thing I do know though. Everbody on both sides a the family was fruitful and multiplied. Buck and Ruby had a huge passle a kids and so did Bud and Goldie. I don't figure any of'em is doin' any kind a honest work for a livin' seein' as how they was raised."

"So what did your family do back in Missouri do for a living?" asked Maggie.

"They was farmers," answered Jim. "I tried it but it weren't for me. I left home and got a job on the railroad on a bridge gang. When the war started, I joined the Union and was with a road crew. We went all over fixin' bridges and track where the Rebs had blowed it up and such. Made a lot a folks back home ticked off when I joined the Union. I said hell with'em. I never had no slaves, and I weren't gonna fight so some rich plantation owner could keep his."

"I'm glad you feel that way," said Maggie. "I'm sorry you other boys have been left out of the conversation."

"We don't mind at all ma'am," Sam said. "It's pure pleasure just sittin' near you."

"Well thank you Sam," said Maggie. "Now please call me Maggie. How about I get you boys another bottle on the house?"

"Sounds good ta us," said Tom. "But can we get it a little later. I'd like to pay a visit to one of your girls. If I drink too much now, I'll probly pass out and not be able to do what a man should."

"I understand," said Maggie. "I'll get you a bottle later but for now, I'll bring over a couple of the girls." Maggie was back in a few minutes with the girls. The girls sat with them for a few minutes and then Jim and Tom went with them upstairs. About a half hour later, Tom and Jim came downstairs and Fred and Sam went upstairs. When Fred and Sam came downstairs, Maggie went to their table and asked if they wanted another bottle yet.

"I think we'll finish this bottle here and then head out," said Jim. "We got a busy day tomorrow. We don't get Sundys off."

"Well the next time you come in the first bottle is on the house," said Maggie. "I sincerely hope you boys have enjoyed our establishment."

"I can assure you that we have," said Jim. "I'm sure we'll be back as soon as we can."

"I look forward to seeing you boys," said Maggie. "Now I must attend to my other customers. It's been a pleasure." Maggie nodded her head and left to mingle with other customers.

"I'll be dreamin' bout her tonight," said Sam. "I never seen a woman that's as good lookin' as her. Damn, I just been with a woman. I'm ready ta go again."

"Control yerself," said Jim. "We'll be back before ya know it. Now let's get this bottle finished and head back." The boys finished up and headed out. They all waved to Maggie as they went out the door.

When the last customer was out the door at closing time, Maggie and Sean sat down at their table and had a drink. "You was with them boys a good while darlin'," said Sean. "You musta found out somethin'."

"I found out a lot of stuff," said Maggie. "I'm not sure it'll be helpful but let me sit here a minute and I'll tell you all that boy told me. My feet are tired."

"Well put your feet up here on my lap and I'll give'em a rub for you," said Sean.

"That sounds inviting," said Maggie. She slipped off her shoes and placed her feet on Sean's lap. He began working on them. He could tell that she liked what he was doing. "Keep rubbing while I talk," said Maggie. "Now here's what I was told. Grammaw Hawk's maiden name was Slaughter and her first name was Pearl. She married a man named Red Hawk. Two of her brothers, Buck and Bud, married two Hawk sisters. Buck married Ruby and Bud married Goldie. There was probably more brothers and sisters but these three Slaughters married those three Hawks. The Slaughter side of the family was whiskey makers and the Hawk side was horse and cattle thieves."

"Sounds like a good clan," said Sean.

"Jim said they were all fruitful and multiplied a lot," said Maggie. "Pearl's husband Red got killed by the Sheriff but it wasn't really on purpose."

"And just why was that?" asked Sean.

"Well the Sheriff was being paid off by the Hawks and the Slaughters," Maggie began. "Red killed a man in another county when he was stealing the man's horses. The Sheriff went out to his place to tell him to lay low for a while. Red was drunk and started shooting at the Sheriff. The Sheriff had to shoot him to keep from getting killed. After that, Pearl and all her kids moved to Kansas. Jim said she had a bunch of them too. Later on, more of the Hawks came out to Kansas. The Slaughters and what was left of the Hawks stayed in Missouri making whiskey until they started passing some laws about taxing whiskey, and the law started giving them trouble. A bunch of them moved down to Arkansas and are in the Ozarks somewhere. Jim said a few of them stayed in Missouri, but he doesn't know where they are or what they're doing."

"Well I would bet that whatever they're doin' isn't honest work," said Sean. "So how did that Jim fella know all this?"

"He's from the same county as them," said Maggie. "He said he was some kind of distant cousin."

"Well now we know the name Slaughter and that there's more Hawks out there," said Sean. "So how's your feet now?"

"My feet are good," said Maggie. "The rest of me needs looked after now. Let's go."

CHAPTER SEVEN

The next morning, Sean had Michael and Jon join him and Maggie for breakfast. Sean had been wondering about the four men who said they were working for the railroad. He was especially concerned about the one who said he knew about the Hawks and Slaughters and was a distant cousin to the Hawks. After they had eaten and were sipping coffee, Sean spoke. "Boys, I'm curious about them four boys," said Sean. "That Jim fella said a lotta stuff about the Hawks and the Slaughters."

"Just who'r the Slaughters?" asked Michael.

"According to that Jim fella, Grammaw Hawk's maiden name was Slaughter," answered Maggie. He said there was a whole bunch of the Slaughters and Hawks. Jim said he was a distant cousin to the Hawks."

"Did he say where they were now?" asked Jon.

"He said a bunch of them came out to Kansas to be with Grammaw," said Maggie. "But there's still a bunch of them in Missouri and Arkansas. Jim said the Slaughters were whiskey makers and the Hawks were cow and horse thieves."

"So what are you intendin' to do young Sean?" asked Michael.

"I think I'll ride out to where the rail spur is bein' built and check up on them boys," said Sean. "Maybe they was givin' Maggie a line a crap or maybe they do work for the railroad. At least I'll find out if they do work for the railroad."

"When will you be going?" asked Maggie.

"I'm gonna get my gear ready soon as I finish my coffee," said Sean.

"Do you want us to go with you?" asked Jon.

"No, I'll go by myself," answered Sean. "It's not far out there. I should be able to get out there and get back before supper."

"Do you want Dog to go with you?" asked Jon.

"No, keep him here," said Sean. "Maybe you can see if he can smell guns and knives like Jeb does."

Sean finished his coffee and rounded up his gear. He took his Winchester, Sharps, and the two pistols he always wore. He made sure he had plenty of ammunition and that his spyglass was in his saddle bags. Maggie made sure he had some food. She loaded him up some biscuits and some jerky and made sure he had plenty of water. He gave Maggie a long hard kiss and was on his way.

The spur was less than a half day's ride so Sean took his time and kept alert. There were very few trees and brush and the land was mostly open plain with a few rolling hills. Sean stayed off the skyline as best he could. After about three hours, he heard the railroad workers well before he saw them. The sound of them driving in the spikes could be heard a good ways off. As he got closer he could hear the foreman yelling obscenities at his crew. As Sean got closer, the foreman saw him before his crew did. He stood there quiet for a minute and watched Sean ride in. When the foreman quit yelling, his crew stopped for a minute to see why he was quiet. Then they saw Sean. Sean rode up to the foreman.

Before Sean could speak, the foreman noticed that his crew wasn't working and he started with the obscenities again and told them to get back to work. Then he looked up at Sean.

"What can I do for you Marshal?" asked the foreman.

"Nothing, I just rode out here to see how far along you are," said Sean. "Looks like you'll be in Abilene before too long." Sean was looking at the crew. Jim was there with the other three boys who had been to the saloon. Jim looked at Sean and waved to him.

"How's that good lookin' wife a yers?" yelled Jim. "We sure did enjoy yer place. Hope ta be there again soon."

"Get back ta work," yelled the foreman. "You won't be a goin' nowhere if ya don't get no work done."

"Looks like you got a good crew," said Sean. "You sure you need ta yell at'em that much?"

"I think they like it," said the foreman. "Anyway, we're movin' right along."

"Well I'll be goin' now," said Sean. "Maybe I'll see you in town soon."

~~~~

Sean rode for about an hour then stopped by a small tree and had some jerky and biscuits. He let his horse graze a little while he was eating. When he was done eating, he got his spyglass and looked all around. After a thorough look all around, he was on his way. He had been riding for another half hour when he got a feeling that he was being watched. He stopped his horse and looked around. He reached forward with his right hand and petted his horse on the neck. As he was petting his horse, a bullet slammed into the right side of the horse's neck just missing his hand. A split second later he heard the shot. Sean let himself slide off the rear of the horse as it reared up and started falling to the left. He dropped to the ground and crawled behind the horse. The horse kicked its' legs a few times and then died. Before Sean could look to see where the shot had come from, two more bullets slammed into the dead horse. Sean took off his hat and keeping as low as possible, he took a quick look around the horses rump. He spotted their smoke. It was coming from a small rise about three hundred yards away. As soon as he pulled his head back behind the horse, two more bullets slammed into the dead horse. The sharps was under the horse's body but Sean was able to pull it from it's scabbard. As he reached up and tried to get his spyglass from the saddlebag, two more bullets slammed into the horse. Sean was able to get the spyglass without being hit. The sun was at Sean's back so he could use the spyglass without it giving off a glare. He slipped it up beside the saddle bags and keeping his head as low as possible, he took a look. He spotted the two shooters laying in the high grass on the top of the rise. Two more bullets slammed into Sean's dead horse. Sean ducked back down for a second then looked through the spyglass again. He thought he saw some movement to the right of the shooters. He waited a few minutes then took another look. There was another man about fifty yards to the right of the shooters. It looked like he was holding their horses. He was pacing around a little. Sean thought he looked he looked like he was getting impatient and wondering why they hadn't killed him yet. Sean ignored the two shooters and kept watching the man holding the horses. Sean took the Sharps and held the barrel against the end of the horse's rump but the muzzle did not stick out for the shooters to see. The man with the horses must have noticed that he was getting careless because he moved back behind the rise. Sean decided that he would go ahead and take a shot towards the man and the horses. Maybe it would spook the horses and they would run off. Two more bullets slammed into the dead horse. Sean picked a spot that he thought would be close to the man and the horses and fired. As soon as he fired, he reloaded. The shot worked. The three horses got spooked and came running Sean's way and the holder was running behind them. Sean took aim and dropped him. He reloaded and took aim on the closest horse. He fired and the horse reared up and fell over dead. He reloaded again and took aim on another horse. The shot rang out and the horse let out a scream and fell to the ground kicking. The third horse was still running toward Sean. Sean could hear one of the shooters calling the horse at the top of his lungs. "Get back here Billy. C'mon boy. Damn you Billy. Get back here," he kept yelling. When the horse got close to Sean, it stopped and reared up. Then it walked right over to Sean.

"Good boy Billy," Sean said to the horse. "Don't know why you stopped here but I'm glad you did." Sean dropped the Sharps and pulled his Winchester from its' scabbard. Billy was close enough for Sean to get his reins. Sean didn't think the shooters would take a shot now. Billy was the only horse around that wasn't dead so Sean figured the shooters would concentrate on him and not the horse. Sean grabbed the reins then pulled Billy so he was between Sean and the shooters. Keeping his Winchester in his right hand, he got up quickly and put his left foot into the stirrup and held the reins with his left hand. He grabbed the saddle horn with his left hand and told Billy to make tracks. Billy took off running. Sean was hanging on the left side of Billy Indian style so Billy's body was between him and the shooters. A couple of shots rang out but Billy kept running. Sean rode that way for a few hundred yards then stopped Billy behind another small rise. He got off of Billy and gave him a once over to make sure he hadn't been hit. Sean was impressed when he looked at Billy. Billy was black with a white blaze and four white socks. He was about fifteen and a half hands. Sean looked at his teeth and figured he was only four years old. "Damn boy, you're a fine lookin' animal," said Sean. "How'd ya end up with that shooter. If you live through this, I'm keepin' you." Sean let Billy have a short rest. Then he mounted. "All right Billy, we're gonna do more a the same," said Sean. "Let's hope they're shootin' at me and not you." Sean gave Billy a kick in the slats. Then they headed right toward to shooters. When they got to within two hundred yards, Sean got back down on Billy's left side and rode parallel to the shooters. The shooters were totally surprised and were standing taking shots at Sean. Sean slipped the Winchester over the saddle and brought Billy to within a hundred yards of the shooters. He took aim as best he could and fired. One of the shooters was struck in the chest and thrown to the ground. The other shooter was so surprised that his partner had been hit that he took off running for the closet cover he could find. Sean slipped up and into the saddle and headed right for the shooter. The shooter saw that he wasn't going to get to any cover and he turned to take a shot at Sean. As soon as he shouldered his rifle, Sean fired his Winchester and the shooter was thrown backwards to the ground. Sean stopped Billy right next to the shooter and dismounted. The shooter wasn't dead yet. He was bleeding from his mouth. He tried to point his rifle at Sean. Sean just kicked the rifle away and stared down at the man. "Just who in the hell'r you and why you tryin' ta kill me?" asked Sean.

"Go ta hell you sombitch," said the man. "You mighta got us, but you can't get us all. We'll git your ass yet."

"So you gotta be a Hawk or a Slaughter," said Sean. "Which is it?"

"Name's Jeremiah Slaughter and I'll tell you right now. There's a bunch a us and we won't quit till yer ass is dead," said the dying man. "We'll git yer damn deputies and their women too. We got special plans fer you and that red-headed bitch a yers. We're gonna skin you and her and hang yer hides on our barn doors."

"Looks ta me that you'll be dead shortly so I'll help you out," said Sean. "Wouldn't want you ta suffer." Sean pulled a pistol and put a bullet into Jeremiah's forehead. Then he sat down and let his thoughts overtake him. "So this shit is startin' all over again," Sean said to himself. "I reckon I'll hafta kill'em all before it's over with." Sean sat there for another half hour or so and then got back on Billy. He rode over to his dead horse, pulled off his saddle, and put it on Billy. "I wish I could bury you boy but I got no shovel," said Sean. "Sorry." Sean got all of his gear and headed back to the railroad spur. He went straight to the foreman. "I need ta borrow Jim there for a spell," said Sean. "He'll need a horse too."

"Who's gonna do his work while he's with you?" asked the foreman. Sean reached into a pocket and pulled out a twenty dollar gold piece and threw it to the foreman. "Just git him a horse and keep your mouth shut," said Sean. "I don't need no guff right now." The foreman could see that Sean was dead serious, and he did as he instructed. As Sean and Jim were leaving the spur, Jim spoke.

"So what is it Marshal? What do ya need?" asked Jim.

"Three fellas tried ta bushwack me after I left here," said Sean. Óne of'em told me his name was Jeremiah Slaughter before he died. There's two more of'em. I want you ta look at'em and see if you recognize them."

"I know Jeremiah," said Jim. "I met him once back in Missouri. I'll be able ta tell you if it's him or not."

When they got to Jeremiah's body, Jim spoke right up. "That's him. That's Jeremiah," said Jim. Then Sean took him to the other bodies. "That one is Jeremiah's brother Gabby," said Jim. "His real name was Gabriel but they called him Gabby cause he never shut up. I don't know that other fella. Could be somethin' in his pockets or gear that might help out." They went through the man's pockets. They found a tin type. It was Ethan Hawk with a teenage boy beside him. It wasn't very clear but it could have been the dead man.

"So that son of a bitch could be a Hawk," said Sean. "Damn!"

"Marshal, I can be a big help if ya want," said Jim. "I could kinda be a deputy for you. I could kinda hang around and let you know if I see any Hawks or Slaughters I know."

"What makes you think I can trust you?" asked Sean. "You said you was a distant cousin to the Hawks."

"I done told Maggie that I was with the Union durin' the war," said Jim. "Them sons a bitches hate me fer that. They just as soon kill me as look at me. Take me on and I'll prove it to ya."

"Well let's get back to the spur," said Sean. "We'll spend the night there and get to town in the mornin'." They went back to the spur and spent the night there. They had a meal there and Jim informed the foreman that he no longer worked there. The next morning Sean and Jim headed back to

Abilene. Sean gave the foreman another ten dollars for the horse Jim was riding.

When they got close to where the dead bodies were, Jim asked Sean if they were going to stop and bury them. "I saw a coyote on my way over here," said Sean. "He looked a little skinny. Probly could use a good meal. Maybe his family could too. We'll get their guns and any valuables they might have on'em. I'll come back out any bury my horse and get them saddles and such if they're still here."

"So you say you'll come back out and bury your horse but you won't bury them men," said Jim. "Why would you bury your horse and not the men."

"Red was a good horse," said Sean. "He got killed cause I got a little careless. I shoulda known someone was out there. I had a feelin'. I said I wouldn't bury them men but there's an undertaker in Abilene now. I tell him they're out here and if he wants ta bury'em, I'll pay'm for it outta the buryin' fund."

"So what's the buryin' fund?" asked Jim.

"It's somethin' I started a while back," started Sean. "Whenever me or my deputies kill someone, we take their guns, horses, and such and sell'em. We use the money to get'em buried. Whatever is left goes to the buryin' fund. If the next fella that gits killed don't have no money, we use the fund to get'm buried."

"Most other folks'd keep that money," said Jim. "Why don't you?"

"I don't need it," answered Sean. "I'm a part owner in the saloon plus I have my lawman's pay and any reward money I claim. I own a fancy saloon in St. Louis now too."

"So why are you a lawman?" asked Jim. "It's a dangerous job."

"Someone's gotta do it," replied Sean. "There just too many bad people out there. Besides, I'm good at it."

"So will you take me on as a deputy?" asked Jim.

"I'll use you for a bit and see how you work out," said Sean. "Are you any good with a gun?"

"When I was with the railroad during the war, we was always gettin' ambushed by rebs," said Jim. "I had me a Sharps carbine for a while. Later on I got me a Spencer. I know how ta use'em. I had a LeMat revolver for a while. It got took. I think some officer stole it. Never did find out."

"Where'd you get the LeMat?" asked Sean.

"I got it off a reb officer I killed one day around Nashville," said Jim. "He was trying to stick me with his saber. I was outta ammo for my Sharps. He came right at me on his big red horse, and I clubbed him knockin'm off his horse. I clubbed him some more. Got his horse too but they made me give it to some officer. I heard stories about you after the war. They said you was one a them sharpshooters that was shootin' the Corporals and Sergeants. Was that true?"

"I was one of'em," said Sean. "We had a whole unit doin' it. Let's get movin'. Maggie's gonna be plenty worried bout me." Jim didn't say another word and they moved out.

When they got into town they rode straight to the saloon. Maggie was standing just inside the door and looking out when she spotted them. She ran outside and jumped up grabbing Sean. She jumped so hard that Sean was knocked out of the saddle and they fell to the ground holding each other. They laid there in the street and kissed for a good while. "Damn, I guess you missed me," said Sean as they got back to their feet.

"We've all been worried to death about you," said Maggie. "What happened and where's your horse and why is Jim with you?"

"Well darlin', the shit is startin' all over again," started Sean. "After I left the railroad spur where Jim was workin' yesterday, I got bushwacked. There was three of'em. Ole Red got killed but I got them killed. I found out that two of'em were Slaughters. Not sure about the other one. This horse belonged to one of'em. His name is Billy. I'm keepin'm. I got Jim here to see if he could identify them three. I'll be tryin' him out as a deputy for a while." Michael and Jon came out from the saloon now.

"So young Sean, did I hear you say that the shit is startin' again?" asked Michael.

"Yes you did," answered Sean. "And they say they're gonna get all of us and our women too."

"I guess we'll just hafta be ready for'em at all times," said Jon. "Well it's been a little quiet around here for a short while anyway."

"Jim can have the back room while he's here," said Sean. "So Jim, just what is your last name anyway?"

"It's Stewart," answered Jim. "My Pa's name was Stewart and my Ma was a Nolan. I don't know how we got to be related to the Hawks."

"Well I wanna give these horses a rest, get somethin' ta eat, and then head back out there to bury Red, and get the rest of them fellas gear," said Sean. "Michael, go over to the undertakers and tell'm I got three customers for'em if he'll go get'em. Jon, I'd appreciate it if you went back out with me and bring Dog along."

"I'll be ready when you are," said Jon.

Michael went to the undertaker who said that he would not turn down any business. He told Michael that he would have a wagon ready whenever Sean was ready to go. Maggie showed Jim his room and then they all sat down for a meal. As soon as they were finished, Sean, Jon, Jim, Dog and the undertaker headed out. As they got closer they could see the buzzards circling. They saw Red first. A couple of buzzards were sitting on him but they hadn't got started picking at him yet. One of the other dead horses had been chewed on a bit. From the tracks it looked like it had been a coyote. The three dead bodies had not been molested yet. They threw them on the undertaker's wagon along with the dead men's saddles and remaining gear. Sean and Jim started digging a hole for Red while Jon and Dog kept watch. The ground was hard so they couldn't go very deep. They used their horses and ropes and dragged Red into the hole. After the hole was covered with the dirt, they placed as many big rocks on the grave as they could. With two other dead horses there on top of the ground, Sean figured that the coyotes wouldn't take the time to dig up Red. If they did, they'd have to work some. Sean stood there by the grave for a minute and told Red what a good horse he had been. Then they headed back to town.

"As soon as we git back to town, round up all their gear and see if the general store'll buy it," Sean said to Jon. "Jim, you can do whatever you want. I'll be with Maggie for a good while. You probly won't see me till tomorrow."

When they got to town, Sean went ahead and paid the undertaker. Jon rounded up the dead men's gear and took it to the general store. Michael took the horses to the livery for them. Jim went to his new room and fell asleep on the bed. Sean and Maggie went to the bath house. They spent a few hours in the tub and then went to their room. They were not seen again till the next morning.

Michael and Betty and Jon and Martha were already at the regular table when Maggie and Sean came downstairs. "Cookie just started some fresh coffee," said Michael. "Should be done shortly." Jim came walking into the saloon now.

"Come on over here and join us," said Sean. "You've not been formerly introduced. Everbody, this is Jim Stewart. Jim, that big Irishman there is Michael O'Connor and that's his wife Betty. This other fella is Jon O'Brien and this fine lady is Martha. Jim here is gonna be a deputy for a while. Jim, consider yourself sworn in."

"Pleased ta meet you all," said Jim. "I hope I can be of some help when the time comes."

"Well let's have some coffee and breakfast," said Sean. "Then I'll take Jim over to Walter's and get him some decent weaponry. We coulda kept some a them guns from those three dead men but the guns looked liked them three didn't take good care of'em. I want my boys to have good weapons." As they were eating breakfast, Sean reminded everyone that every caution was to be taken. Sean could see that Jim was amazed at Jeb and Dog. "Them are two a the best dogs anywhere," said Sean. "If we don't like someone, they don't like'em. If they don't like'em, they're in bad trouble. These two can rip out a man's throat before that man can pull a gun or knife. Jeb here bit a man's hand clean off."

"I reckon I'll stay on their good side," said Jim.

After breakfast, Sean took Jim over to the Gunsmith. "Walter, this here is Jim Stewart," said Sean. "Just took him on as deputy. Jim, this is Walter Black." They shook hands.

"He'll be needin' some good weaponry," said Walter. "I don't have any Winchesters right now but I got a Henry that I just traded for. It's in real good shape. I fired it yesterday." He handed the Henry to Jim. Jim shouldered it and worked the action.

"Nice," said Jim. "I had me a Spencer once but I never shot a Henry before. This thing holds a whole lotta bullets."

"Yes it does," said Sean. "When you're a lawman, you need ta make sure you're not outgunned. Now have you got a good pistol Walter?"

"I got a Remington that I just got done convertin'," said Walter. "We can go out and try it out if you want. We'll take the Henry too."

"Yep, let's go try'em out," said Sean. "I gotta see if Jim here can hit what he shoots at."

Walter got a buckboard and they headed out of town. They found a likely spot and Walter set up some targets for Jim. He put up some boards about a hundred yards out for the Henry and some boards about thirty yards out for the pistol. Jim fired the Henry first. There were two targets and Jim fired five shots at each one. All ten shots hit the targets. Each group was around eight inches. "Not bad," said Sean. "If that had been a man, you'd a hit'm. Now give that pistol a try." Jim fired the pistol. He didn't shoot from a draw. He just pulled the pistol and took careful aim and fired. Every shot hit the target. "That's good," said Sean. "Now when we have some time, I'll teach you how to draw and shoot. Remember now, them targets aren't shootin' back at you."

"I been shot at lots a times," said Jim. "I'll be all right."

"When you got shot at durin' the war it was different," said Sean. "Them were soldiers tryin' ta kill you because it was their duty. Some a these fellas we'll be up against aren't like soldiers. They kill and hurt folks cause they like it and they think they can get away with it. They're just some mean sons a bitches. Well that's enough lecturin'. Let's get on back. We'll take the guns but we don't need any ammunition. Still got plenty."

When they got back to Walter's shop, Walter gave the weapons a quick cleaning and got some cleaning equipment for Jim. Sean paid Walter and he and Jim left. "We'll take that Henry back to your room and then I'll take you around town and introduce you to folks," said Sean.

"I'll pay you for these guns," said Jim. "I got a little on me and you can take the rest outta my pay. How much is my pay anyway?"

"Forty dollars a month," answered Sean. "And we can claim any rewards that are posted on any outlaws we get. Don't worry bout payin' for them guns. I always get good guns for my men." Jim took the Henry back to his room. Then Sean took him around town and introduced him to everyone. Jim was amazed that everyone seemed so nice. After they had visited most of the businesses and people, they headed back to the saloon. They sat down at the regular table, and Sean got them some coffee. "Now Jim, what you're gonna do here is mainly keep your eyes open and let me know if you recognize anyone who could be a Hawk or a Slaughter or may be their friends," said Sean. "Durin' the day you'll spend most a your time out wanderin' the streets. When it gets dark, you'll spend most a your time in the saloons. There's a few other saloons in town now. You can have a beer once in a while but if I catch you drunk, I'll hurt you a bit and then fire you. Do you understand?"

"I won't let you down Sean," said Jim.

"Now if you do see someone you recognize, come and get me," said Sean. "Try not to let them recognize you if you can. Here's a badge for you. Make sure you wear it where it can be seen. Now get out there and keep your eyes open." Jim gave a nod and headed out into the street. Michael came over to the table.

"So how's our new friend?" asked Michael.

"Well he can shoot when he's got time to aim proper," said Sean. "He'll be all right after I work with him some. Let's hope he don't get recognized and get himself killed. Think I better send the Judge a telegram and tell'm what's goin' on now. I'll have Maggie write a letter to Susie and Dan and tell'em we won't be visitin' for a while. I think Maggie was lookin' forward to goin' to St. Louis again. I reckon we'll go when we can. Thanksgiving's not too far off. Hope we don't have trouble then."

"We'll be all right Sean darlin'," said Michael. "We took care of this kind of trouble before. We'll do it again."

"Keep that good attitude," said Sean. "Now I'm goin' to the telegraph office." Sean sent the following telegram.

Federal Judge Sharpton
Federal Court House
St. Louis

Judge<<stop>>have found out about Hawks and Slaughters<<stop>>bushwacked by two Slaughters and another man<<stop>>I killed them<<stop>>before dying one Slaughter said they would kill me and my men and our women<<stop>>we are ready for them<<stop>>Jim Stewart is new deputy

O'Rourke

Sean told the telegraph operator to find him if there was any reply. Sean went back to the saloon. An hour later, a telegram arrived for Sean. It went as follows.

Federal Marshal O'Rourke
Abilene Kansas

Be careful<<stop>>you are needed

Judge Sharpton

Sean went back to the saloon. Michael was practicing his piano. Maggie and some of the girls were at a table drinking coffee. Sean went to the regular table, and Maggie came over and joined him. "You look worried darlin'," said Maggie. "Is something going on now?"

"No everything's all right," said Sean. "I just sent a telegram to the Judge and told him what was goin' on. I want you to write a letter to Susie and tell her we won't be there for a while."

"I can do that," said Maggie. "Is there anything else on your mind?"

"I was just thinking about Thanksgiving," said Sean. "I was hoping to get through it without any trouble."

"We'll handle whatever comes," said Maggie. "In the meantime, I'll tell Cookie that he can plan on putting together a good feast again. We'll have a good time."

~~~~

The time leading up to Thanksgiving was uneventful. Sean still made sure everyone was always vigilant. Cookie kept a shotgun and a pistol in the kitchen. Tom wore a pistol on his hip in full view. Betty and Martha had pistols on them. Maggie had two pistols on her and Jeb never left her side. Michael had on one pistol belt and another pistol was tucked in his belt. A shotgun was beside the piano. Jon carried two pistols and Dog was always close by. There were the two shotguns at each end of the bar. Sean wore his two pistols and he had his ten gauge strapped under his regular table. Everything seemed quiet.

Thanksgiving day came and they all had a great time. Barbara's and Cookie's feast was spectacular. After the meal, Michael played the piano and they all danced. There were very few customers in the place. The few that were there that day left as soon as the meal was over. One of Maggie's girls Sally, had taken a liking to Jim and they seemed to be having a good time. They danced a little after the meal and then were not seen the rest of the evening. Finally around 2am, they all decided they had enough and went their separate ways. Cookie and Barbara had left about an hour before this. Michael and Betty were still there talking to Maggie and Sean when Jon and Martha left with Dog. Jon and Martha had only been gone for a few minutes when they heard the shots. There was at least six shots. "Those are shotguns," said Sean. "You women stay here and take cover. Shoot anyone who comes in the door if it's not me or Michael." Sean grabbed the ten gauge from under the table and Michael got the shotgun from beside the piano. They ran out the door staying low expecting to be shot at. No shots were fired at them. They waited a little and then worked their way to where the shots had come from. Jon and Martha were dead in the street. They had taken shotgun blasts in the back. Where was Dog? About fifty yards from the bodies, they found Dog. He had taken a shotgun blast but he still had ahold of one of the shooter's throats. The shooter's hands were still clutching a shotgun. Sean had a hard time holding the tears back. "Sons a bitches," yelled Sean. "These sons a bitches don't know a damn thing bout death. I'm gonna teach'em." Jim had heard the shooting and got up to see what was happening. When he came into the back door of the saloon, Betty fired a shot at him but missed.

"Hold up, hold up," said Jim. "It's me Jim. What's happening?"

"We don't know Jim," said Maggie. "Me and Sean and Michael and Betty were in here when the shots were fired. Sean and Michael went out to see what's going on. If you go out there, you better let them know who you are or you might get accidentally shot. It's pretty dark." Jim went outside and kept himself low. In the distance he could see two men standing in the street. Jim yelled to them.

"It's me Jim. Is that you over there Sean?" Jim said.

"Yes it's me and Michael," said Sean. "Come on over. Looks like the shooters are gone." Jim walked over to Sean. He looked at the man that Dog had killed.

"I seen this man before," said Jim. "Can't remember his name but I seen him with Jeremiah sometime back."

"It's hard to tell but it looks like there was four of'em. There's only three now." said Sean. "That's Martha's place over there." Sean went over and looked behind Martha's place. "They had their horses back here. One of'em is still here." said Sean. "I should be able to track'em at daylight." Sean went back over to the bodies. "Martha had taken two blasts. Jon took two and then one of'em got close and shot'm again after he was down. His jacket is all burned. Yep, I'm gonna teach these sons a bitches about death.

Let's get Jon and Martha over to the undertaker. Jim, you bury Dog in the morning."

"What about this other fella?" asked Jim.

"Don't worry about him." said Sean. "I'll take care a him." They got the bodies to the undertaker and then went back to the saloon. Maggie and Betty were anxiously awaiting the news. "They killed Jon and Martha," said Sean. "They killed Dog too but he got one of'em first." Maggie and Betty broke into a good cry.

"Why would anyone shoot Martha," cried Maggie. "She's never hurt anyone."

"She was Jon's woman," said Sean. "I'll be trackin'em at daylight. There's three of'em. I'll be takin' Michael with me. Jim, you'll be stayin' here since you might recognize some of'em if they would double back on us. If you're not sure about someone, don't hesitate. Disarm'em and tie'em up and put'em in the jail. If they don't wanna be disarmed, you shoot'em. You hear me? You shoot'em. Don't waste time talkin'. Shoot'em."

"I'll take care a things," said Jim. "You just be careful out there."

Sean and Michael had everything ready and they headed out at daylight. They took two extra horses with them. Sean took the dead outlaw from the street and threw him up on one of the horses. "What are you gonna do with him?" asked Michael.

"You'll see," said Sean. "You'll see." When they were a few miles out of town, they came to a small grove of trees. Sean dismounted and checked out the trees. "That one in the middle'll do," said Sean. Sean got a rope and threw it over a big limb. Then he made a noose and placed it around the dead man's neck. He tied off the rope at the tree's trunk. Then he moved the horse and dead man was hanged."

"The man's already dead," said Michael. "What good did that do?"

"I'm not done yet," said Sean. He reached into his saddle bags and pulled out a piece of white canvas and pinned it to the front of the dead man. On it was some writing. It said the following in big letters. "I am scum. I am a backshooting son of a bitch. My momma should have killed me at birth."

"Damn Sean, that's a mouthful," said Michael. "So do you think this helps anything?"

"It makes me feel better," said Sean. "I'm hopin' that some a his kin find'm here. Maybe they'll get so mad they won't think straight."

"So are you thinking straight?" Michael asked.

"I am," said Sean. "I am. Now let's get moving. If they stopped ta eat or rest their horses we'll be on'em before too long."

"Maybe they want us to catch up," said Michael. "Maybe they'll have an ambush set up for us."

"That's always a chance ya take when you're trackin' someone," said Sean. "Let's keep movin'." After another hour the trail split. They had been heading south but now one horse went east and the other two went west. "I'd say they're tryin' ta double back on us," said Sean. "They'll head north after a bit. We need to try and cut them off. We'll head back toward town and try to get them before they get to town. We'll ride hard and when we get close to town we'll split up. I'll go after the two and you go after the other one. "They took off riding hard. After a hard ride they split up. "Now find yourself a good spot and wait for'm," said Sean as they split up. "Don't worry about shootin' the wrong person. There was only three sets a fresh tracks out there," said Sean. "Whoever you see will be one of Jon's killers."

When Michael got close to town, he took a position on a small knoll that had some brush near the top. He tied his horse where it couldn't be seen from the south. He took his Winchester and waited. Sean found himself a good position too and waited. He had some brush for cover and his Sharps and Winchester with him. He kept a good watch with his spyglass. After about a half hour, he saw some movement in the distance. There were two riders coming. They were around eight hundred yards away now. In another two hundred yards they would be in the middle of a perfect killing zone. It was totally flat with absolutely no brush or trees of any kind. Sean waited until they were right where he wanted them to be. He took aim with the Sharps. The Sharps barked but before the bullet had reached its' mark, Sean had re-loaded and was taking aim again. The first bullet found its' mark. One of the horses reared up and fell over dead. The second bullet struck the other horse. It reared up and fell dead too. Both riders fell to the ground. It took them a few seconds to get their wits back. When they did, they got down beside their dead horses and tried to pull their rifles from their scabbards. Sean didn't want to kill them just yet so he took careful aim at one of them. The man's legs were sticking out where Sean could clearly see them. Sean fired. A second later he heard the man scream in pain. The bullet struck him on the backside of his left knee. The bullet went through and tore off the man's kneecap. The man was six hun-dred yards away but as loud as he was screaming, it sounded like he was right beside Sean. The other man had retrieved his rifle and began firing shots in Sean's general direction. Sean could tell that he was using a Spencer. The man fired seven shots then after a short time, he fired seven more. Sean was way out of range for the Spencer. Sean decided he would play with the man for a while.

Every once in a while, Sean would take a shot that was very close to the man but not hitting him. The man was starting to get very rattled now. After a few shots, he stood up and began yelling towards Sean. "Come out here and fight me face to face you sombitch," he kept yelling. "Come on out you gutless sombitch." Sean laughed to himself and then took careful aim. The Sharps roared again. The bullet struck the receiver of the Spencer, and the rifle was torn from the man's hands. The man stood there and began a streak of cuss words that Sean hadn't heard since he had been in the Army. Sean got Billy and slowly rode toward the two men. When he was about a hundred yards from the two men, the one who had been cussing pulled a pistol and began firing at Sean. He fired six times and started trying to reload. Sean kicked Billy into a gallop and they headed right at the man. He rode right up on the man and had Billy ram him with his chest. The man went down hard. His pistol went flying. He got back up in a few seconds and starting cussing Sean again. Sean walked over to him, pulled a pistol and cracked him over the head. He hit the ground unconscious. Sean looked over at the other man. He was still screaming some and was bleeding badly. Sean took a piece of rope and tied it around the man's leg as a tourniquet. "Gotta get that bleedin' stopped," said Sean. "I want you alive when I hang you." The man never said a word. He had on a gunbelt but the holster was empty. It must have gone flying when Sean shot his horse. It wasn't anywhere close that Sean could see. After the bleeding was stopped, Sean tied the man's hands behind his back. He tied the other man's hand too.

Michael had not seen any riders when he heard the shooting in the distance. He could tell by the sound that it was Sean's Sharps. He figured if he heard the shooting, the other rider had heard it too. He watched and waited for another hour and then rode to where the shots had come from. He found Sean and the two men with no problem. He could see a lot of blood near the man who had been shot in the knee. "So what do you need me to do now Sean?" asked Michael.

"I want you to stay here with these two," said Sean. "That other one has gotten past us. I'd say he's in town somewhere. I'll go take care a him, and I'll send a buckboard out for these two. If that other fella comes to and starts giving you hell, knock'm out again."

"Are we gonna hang'em?" asked Michael.

"Yes we are," answered Sean. "They committed murder and murder is a hangin' offense."

Michael never said another word. Sean mounted up and headed for town.

~~~~

Jim was on the sidewalk in front of the saloon when he saw a man come into town riding hard. The man went straight to the livery. Young Billy was there. The man said a few words to Billy and then handed him the reins to his horse. Jim couldn't make out his face yet. The man went into one of the other saloons in town. Jim went to the livery and looked at the man's horse. There was a sawed off double barreled shotgun in a scabbard. Jim pulled it from the scabbard and checked it out. He could tell that it had been fired not long ago. Both barrels were dirty from shots that had been fired. Jim went over to the saloon and peered in a window. The man was at the bar with a shot of whiskey in front of him. Jim could see the man's reflection in the mirror. The man was Chance Slaughter. Jim knew him from back in Missouri. Jim pulled his pistol and let it hang down to his right side as he entered the saloon. He knew that Chance could see his reflection in the mirror too. Chance's right hand slipped down to his pistol. "Chance Slaughter," yelled Jim. "I'm Deputy Jim Stewart. Grab that pistol by the butt with your left hand and drop it on the floor. Do it now." Jim raised his pistol now.

"I know you," said Chance. "You're that blue belly son of a bitch from back home. We been lookin' fer you."

"You don't gotta look no farther," said Jim. "Now do like I say or I'll shoot you dead."

"You blue belly's were always a bunch a cowards," said Chance as he started turning around. He started turning to his left, and was drawing his pistol as he turned. Jim did not see him drawing at first. Chance's pistol had just cleared the holster. He was bringing it up to fire when Jim fired. The bullet caught Chance in the chest. He hit the floor dead. Jim cocked the hammer on his pistol again and walked over to the body. Then he turned and faced everyone in the saloon. "Any a you friends a his?" Jim shouted. "If you are, you best get your ass outta town now or pull your pistols and go to work." No one said a word. After a period of silence the bartender spoke.

"I never seen that fella before," he said. "What did he do?"

"Him and three others murdered a deputy and his woman last night," said Jim.

"I heard the shootin', but I didn't go out to see what it was about," said the bartender. "Well you got one a the sombitches. Won't hafta worry about hangin' him now."

Sean had just gotten to the edge of town when he heard the shot. He dropped off his horse at the livery and went looking for where the shot had come from. "That shot came from that saloon over there," said Billy. "Some man came in on this horse here. Your deputy came in and saw the shotgun on the man's saddle and went over to the saloon. Not long after that, I heard the shot."

"Thanks Billy," said Sean. "You stay inside for a while in case there's more shootin'." Sean went into the saloon. Jim was at the bar beside the dead man on the floor. Jim's pistol was still in his hand. Sean walked over to him.

"This here is Chance Slaughter," said Jim. "He wouldn't give up his gun. He tried to draw on me and I killed him."

"Good work Jim," said Sean. "We got the other two just outside a town. I'll go tell Maggie we're all right. Then I'll get a buckboard and go get Michael and them other two. You go tell the undertaker we got him some more business. Get that man's body outta here and get his valuables and guns and such before the undertaker gets him. We'll sell'em later." Jim did as instructed and Sean went to the saloon to let Maggie know all was well.

Sean told Maggie all that had happened. He could tell that she was relieved but still extremely upset. "You're going to hang those two aren't you?" she asked.

"Yes I am. I'm gonna do it out by the trail so if any more of'em come along, they'll see what happens to their kin," said Sean. Maggie nodded her approval. Sean left to get the buckboard and some rope. He instructed Jim to stay in town and keep his eyes open. There could still be more of them. Sean got the buckboard and ropes and headed out of town. It wasn't long before he got to Michael. Both men were unconscious.

"That one fella came to and started cussin' me bad so I cracked him again," said Michael. "I think that other fella passed out from lack of blood."

"Well Jim got the other one for us in town," said Sean. "The fella forced a shootout and Jim killed'm. Jim said his name was Chance Slaughter. Well let's throw them two up on the buckboard and go find a good tree. Throw their saddles and such up there too. We want the tree close to the trail so if any more of'em come to town, they'll see what happens to their kin around here."

"We could go over where you hung that other fella," said Michael.

"We could but I want a different trail covered," said Sean. "I'd say word'll get out pretty quick anyway." They headed east of town. Sean figured that any Slaughters or Hawks would come from that direction. They found some nice trees a few miles out. Sean stopped the buckboard right underneath one of them. He threw two ropes over a good limb and made some nooses. Then he tied off the ropes at the trunk of the tree. He took his canteen and threw some water on the faces of the two men. The one who had been shot in the knee didn't come to. He was dead. The other man woke up and started cussing again. Sean stood him up in the buckboard and put a noose around his neck. Then he stood up the dead man and put a noose around his neck. "You got anything to say before I send you ta hell where you belong?" asked Sean. "Oh by the way, my deputy killed Chance in town a little while ago."

"The boys'll have fun when they skin that red-haired bitch a yours," the man said. "I'll see you in hell."

"I already been," said Sean as he swatted the horses and the buckboard was pulled out from under the two men. It took a good while for the man to strangle to death. When he was done kicking, they headed back to town.

When Sean finally got back to the saloon, Maggie was upstairs crying in their room. Sean took ahold of her and together they had a good cry. After a good while Sean asked Maggie if there was anything special she wanted for the funeral. "I just think we should have it as soon as possible," said Maggie. We don't want to have a viewing. Their bodies were pretty torn up."

"I'll go talk to the undertaker right now," said Sean. "I'll tell him we want it before noon tomorrow." Sean went straight to the undertaker. "We want to have the funerals for Martha and Jon before noon tomorrow," said Sean. "There won't be any viewing."

"I don't know if I can do that Marshal," the undertaker said. "There's these other fellas you brought me already."

"To hell with them fellas," said Sean. "You'll have the funerals before noon tomorrow or you can forget about me gettin' you any more business ever again. Coyotes gotta eat too. Now if you gotta pay someone a little extra ta get the graves dug and such, don't worry bout the cost. Just get it done."

"All right Marshal, it'll be done," said the undertaker.

~~~~

Over half the town showed up for the funeral. There was no Minister so Maggie and Sean said some words about Martha and Jon. There was another smaller grave right beside Jon's grave. Jim had not buried Dog earlier as Sean had told him. He thought it would be nice if Dog was buried next to Jon. No one objected.

CHAPTER EIGHT

Everyone stayed vigilant. Everyone who had anything to do with the saloon was armed. All of the girls had pistols on them. After two days, Sean decided he would ride out to where he had hanged the men. He took Jim with him and left Michael at the saloon. Jeb was with Maggie as always. They rode to where Sean had hanged the first man. The rope had been cut, and the body was missing. The rope was still hanging from the tree and had a note tied to it. Sean took a good look at the surrounding area and then took the note from the rope. "Yer a ded man marshle" it said.

"Well some a the sons a bitches'r close," said Sean. "Let's go see if they cut down them other fellas too." They rode over to where Sean had hanged the other two men. The ropes had been cut, and the bodies were gone. There was some wagon tracks leading to the west. "Let's get back to town and get supplied. "I'll be trackin' this wagon."

"Them tracks look ta be a day old'r so," said Jim.

"I know they are," said Sean. "But maybe they won't think I'll be out here after'em. Maybe they think I'm gonna stay holed up in town."

"Maybe they did this to draw you out from town so they could ambush you or get Michael or Maggie while you're gone," said Jim.

"Listen, anybody can kill anybody anytime," started Sean. "All they gotta do is be willin'. They killed Jon and Martha when we was all in town. Nobody can protect themselves every minute of every day. All a killer's gotta do is watch and wait for that one minute when you're not ready for'm. Now let's get to town and get supplied."

When they got back to town the first thing Sean did was go to Maggie and tell her what he was doing. "Darlin', I'll be gone for who knows how long," started Sean. "Them bodies I hung got cut down. I'll be following some wagon tracks. They headed west. Don't make sense ta me. Them Dog Soldiers could be raidin' over that way. You and Michael keep yourself safe while Me and Jim'r gone. Keep Jeb with you at all times. Anybody you don't know gives you a hard time or looks suspicious, let Jeb have'em."

"You be careful out there darlin'," said Maggie. "If there's as many Slaughters as there was Hawks, you'll have your hands full."

"I'll be fine darlin'," said Sean. "I got careless a while back and got ole Red killed. That will not happen again. Them Slaughters'r gonna think the wrath a the Lord is comin' down on'em. They started this and I'm gonna finish it." Sean gave Maggie a hug and a kiss and got his gear ready. They had a pack horse with plenty of food, water, and ammunition. Sean wore two pistols as always and had his Winchester and Sharps in scabbards on his saddle. The ten gauge was on the pack horse. Jim had his Henry and two pistols. They told everyone goodbye and headed out.

They had followed the wagon tracks about an hour when Sean saw that the wagon was joined by two horses. After another hour, two more sets of tracks joined the wagon. "Well there's five or six of'em," said Sean. "I'd say they're expectin' me to track'em. You keep your eyes peeled. Some of'em'll probably split off to one side or maybe both sides . Hard to tell when they'll do that. It's hasn't been cold lately. I'd think they'd be buryin' them bodies before too long. They should be gettin' ripe."

About dark, they found some fresh graves and where the wagon and other men had spent the night. "We'll spend the night right here," said Sean. "No fire. We'll probably take'em tomorrow."

"Just how'r we gonna do that?" asked Jim. "There's only two a us and five or six of them."

"You just do what I tell you and when I tell you and everything'll be all right," said Sean. "Now I don't think we'll have any trouble but we'll take turns standin' watch anyway. I'll go first. I'll wake you when I get tired." Sean stood watch for over four hours. He spent most of the time trying to guess what these Slaughters were up to. He fell asleep easily when Jim took over, but he woke about every hour and looked around. At daylight they had a cold breakfast and headed out.

They had traveled about two hours when Sean stopped. "You see what I see," Sean said to Jim.

"I don't know what you're seein'," said Jim. "I see them wagon tracks and them other horse tracks. What else is there ta see?"

"They're hard ta see on this hard ground so I'll show you," said Sean. He dismounted and walked over to a spot just off the trail they were following. He pointed to a spot on the ground. "These'r unshod pony tracks," said Sean as he pointed them out to Jim. "They're maybe two days old."

"What'r they doin' this far east?" asked Jim. "I thought they was farther to the west. What tribe you reckon it is?"

"Probly Cheyenne," said Sean. "Probly came over east lookin' ta steal some horses or kill some buffalo hunters before they got over west to the herds."

"So what're we gonna do now," asked Jim. "We shouldn't be out here traypsin' around with them Injuns around."

"The Cheyenne'r my friends," said Sean. "We won't have no trouble from them."

"And why is that?" asked Jim.

"I lived with the Cheyenne after my folks was killed by white outlaws," said Sean. "I'll tell you all about it another time." They rode for another hour before they came to where the trail split. The wagon had gone straight ahead. Two horses went to the left. Sean dismounted and studied the tracks. These two horses with the wagon are tied behind it and there's no riders. The tracks are lighter. The two horses that went to the left are carrying two riders. The tracks are deeper."

"How in the hell do you know that?" asked Jim. "I can't see no difference in them tracks."

"Take my word for it Jim," said Sean. "One a these days I'll show you how ta track. Now should we follow the wagon or the horses that split off?"

"I'd say them fellas want us ta follow the wagon," said Jim. "They could be set up and waiting for us somewhere."

"That's what I'd say too," said Sean. "I figure they're maybe only an hour ahead of us now. With all this open ground they'll be lookin' for a nice rise ta shoot from. The wagon'll stay on low ground. We'll follow the wagon till we find a likely spot that they might try to bushwack us."

The ground was endlessly flat. Finally they could see a big rise to the left. It was maybe a half mile ahead. "The shooters'll be on that rise. The wagon'll stop down below and wait," said Sean. "We'll swing way around to the left and come up on'em. They might not be as dumb as I think they are and have a man watchin' their back. We'll see. Let's move."

They swung way out to the left till they were just to the other side of the rise. Then they moved slowly toward the rise. The sun was at their back. They took advantage of what little cover there was. They were around a thousand yards from the rise now. Sean got out his spyglass. The two horses were hobbled about fifty yards from the top of the rise. Three men were laying near the top of the rise with their rifles ready. The fourth man was covering the trail they had used to get there. Not one of them was looking Sean's way. "That's a lotta open ground," said Jim. "How'r we gonna do this?"

"It'll be dark in a few hours," said Sean. "We'll wait till dark and then slip up on'em if they stay put."

"Won't they think somethin's up and move if we don't show up over there before too long?" asked Jim.

"They might," answered Sean. "We'll sit tight and see what they do." After a couple of hours Sean took another look through the spyglass. It looked like a couple of them were arguing. Sean figured it was about why he hadn't showed up when they thought he should. They argued some more but they stayed put. Right before dark, Sean saw them eating some biscuits and jerky. When it got dark, three of them bedded down while one man stood watch.

"We'll wait about an hour and then slip up on'em," said Sean. "We'll ride a few hundred yards and then go in on foot."

"Well I never slipped up on anyone in my whole life," said Jim. "I'm bout as noisy as an ox in a china closet."

"You'll be fine," said Sean. "You worry too much. Just watch me and do what I do. I'd like to take at least one of'em alive if we can. Two'r three would be even better. Might get one of'em ta talk. Don't take no chances though. I don't wanna be buryin' you."

"I don't want you buryin' me either," said Jim. They rode the few hundred yards closer and dismounted.

"Just drop the reins," said Sean. "Billy and this pack horse won't wander far with them reins down. That horse a yours'll probly stand too. Now I'll take the one standin' guard first. Then you unhobble their horses and move'em down the rise some. Don't let'em make no noise. I'll take out the other three."

"Are you sure?" asked Jim. "I can get one of'em for you."

"I'll be all right," said Sean as he moved out to get the guard. It wasn't quite pitch dark. Sean slipped up on the guard and knocked him out with a pistol butt. He tied him and gagged him in case he might come to before Sean got the other three. Jim unhobbled the two horses and was moving them. One of them let out a little whinny. One of the men woke up and sat up to see what was going on. Just as he sat up, Sean cracked his head with a pistol butt. When he cracked the man's head, another one of them woke up and reached for a rifle that was beside him. Sean was able to crack the man's skull before he got the rifle around to fire. While he was hitting the third man, the fourth man woke up and had his rifle ready to fire. A shot rang out. The man was pushed backed down. Jim had seen what was happening and pulled a pistol and killed the man. "You get these other two tied up and I'm gettin' a horse and goin' down to the wagon," said Sean. Sean found a bridle and put it on one of the horses and jumped up on it bareback. He took off down the rise toward the wagon. As he got closer, he heard a voice. "Buster, is that you?" Sean heard that a couple of times and then shots were being fired at him. He hunkered down low on the horse and rode straight at the man. The man fired several shots and missed. When Sean was around ten yards from the man, the horse was struck by a bullet. Sean knew the horse was hit and jumped off to the horse's left and rolled. The man stood there in disbelief. The horse slammed into him as it was falling. Sean got up as quickly as he could and looked around. No one else was there. The horse was on top of the man. His chest was crushed. He was gasping for air and blood was coming out of his mouth. "Are you a Slaughter?" Sean asked the man. The man just looked at him and smiled. "You're gonna die mister," said Sean. "Can't do nothin' for you. Won't hurt nothin' for you to talk now." The man smiled at Sean again. It looked like he was trying to say something but he died before he could get it out.

Sean walked back up the rise to where Jim and the other men were. "Let's tie them up tight and get some sleep," said Sean. "I'm tired." They went down to the wagon tied the men to the wagon and then rounded up the horses. We won't gag them fellas tonight," said Sean. "One of'em'll surely be awake and yell and wake us up if some Cheyenne slip up on us."

"I heard Injuns don't like ta fight at night," said Jim.

"They don't," said Sean. "But if they catch someone asleep they can kill'em without too much fightin'. We'll be all right. Get some sleep." Jim shook his head a little and then spread out his bedroll. Sean was asleep before Jim even laid down. Jim got back up and threw a blanket over each of the three men.

The next morning, Sean was up at daylight and had a fire going. "We'll have us a hot breakfast this mornin'," said Sean. "I missed my coffee yesterday."

"Should we be havin' a fire when we're not sure where them Injuns are?" asked Jim.

"I told you them Cheyenne were my friends," said Sean.

"Well what if them aren't Cheyenne?" What if they're Comanche or Kiowa?" asked Jim.

"Well I'm friends with the Kiowa too," said Sean. "Now if them'r Comanche and they find us, they'll be wantin' our scalps. I still say they're Cheyenne." The coffee was done. Sean poured himself and Jim a cup. "You get some bacon fryin' Jim," said Sean. "We'll have some bacon and biscuits for breakfast. You do that while I talk with these fellas. Jim did as instructed.

"Any a you boys feel like talkin' ta me this mornin'?" asked Sean. One of them replied.

"You go ta hell O'Rourke," he said.

"Which one a you boys is Buster?" asked Sean. "That other fella that was at the wagon was asking for Buster when I rode down on'm." No one said a word. "Well boys, it's clear ta me that you came here ta kill me," said Sean. "There won't be no lawyers or juries out here. I'm gonna kill you. I got plenty a rope too, but I had an idea come to me durin' the night. You boys wanna know what it is?" No one said a word. "Well boys, this fire here is gonna attract them Cheyenne out here," said Sean. "If you wasn't so stupid you woulda seen their tracks and got the hell outta here. Them Cheyenne'r my friends. I'm gonna give you to them as a gift. I'll tell them you was at Sand Creek. They'll kill you slow."

"You wouldn't do that to no white man," said one of them.

"You boys'r just scum. You're not even people," said Sean. "Do you even know why you're supposed ta kill me and my men?" No one spoke. Sean stood up and looked to the west. He could see some riders way in the distance. "That'll be them Cheyenne," said Sean.

"So if we talk you won't give us ta them Cheyenne?" asked one of them.

"That's right boys," said Sean.

"Well I'm Buster. Buck is my Pa," Buster began. "Buck and Bud was Grammaw Hawk's brothers. We was sposed ta kill you and your men and women if we could. If we didn't get it done, come spring when the cattle drives are coming to Abilene, a bunch of'em was gonna rustle a herd and come into town as plain old cowboys. They'd fit right in. Then they could could kill you easy."

"Where are they now?" asked Sean.

"We got some all over. We even got some in Abilene. Your woman might be dead now if they got a chance at her," said Buster. "Others are holed up in "The Nations." My Pa and Bud's in Arkansas."

"So you'd go out and kill folks just cause your Pa told you to?" asked Sean.

"Didn't you used to do what your Pa said?" asked Buster.

"My Pa never told me ta kill anyone that didn't need killin'," said Sean. "Them Hawks were thieves and murderers. They broke the law and paid for it."

"I reckon we don't see eye ta eye," said Buster.

"You other boys got anything ta say?" Sean asked. Nothing was said. The Cheyenne were getting closer now. Sean walked out to greet them. In perfect Cheyenne, Sean spoke. "Come in friends and I will share some food with you. I am "Shooter". I am "The one who kills with the long gun and the big pistol." Blue Swan was my mother-in-law and Black Wolf was my bother-in-law." There were six of the Dog Soldiers. The one who appeared to be the leader spoke.

"I know of you," he said. "Many stories were told about you. I am White Horse. Why are you here, and why do you have those men tied to the wagon?"

"Let's have some coffee and some food and I will tell you," said Sean. Jim was in disbelief. He had never been close to an Indian in his whole life. Now there were these Cheyenne Dog Soldiers right there and having a meal with them. They wore paint and smelled like buffalo grease.

The Dog Soldiers liked the coffee and enjoyed the biscuits and bacon. Then they got down to business. "I'm giving you these men as a gift," said Sean. "They were at Sand Creek and killed many women and children. You may have their horses and guns too."

Jim didn't know what Sean had said to the Dog Soldiers but he could see the looks on their faces change toward the end of the conversation. The Dog Soldiers got up and rounded up the horses and weapons. Then they untied the men from the wagon and stood them up. They had them line up and put a noose around their neck that would get tighter if they struggled. They were tied one behind the other. The leader nodded his head at Sean and they left. The three men had to keep up or strangle. Buster was yelling at Sean as they left. "O'Rourke, you're a son of a bitch," Buster kept yelling. "You said you wouldn't give us to them Cheyenne if we talked."

"I lied," yelled Sean as they left.

"What do you reckon them Dog Soldiers'll do to them men?" asked Jim.

"Don't you be worryin' about it," said Sean. "I was gonna hang'em anyway."

"How many more more of'em you think'll be tryin' ta kill us?" asked Jim?"

"No way a knowin'," said Sean. "You said there was a buncha them Hawks and Slaughters. We had ta kill a buncha them Hawks. Seemed like every time we killed one, two of'em took his place. Now we need to be gettin' back ta town. Buster said there was some of'em in Abilene."

"We gonna bury them fellas?" asked Jim.

"Ta hell with them fellas," said Sean. "Get your gear packed and let's get movin'."

Maggie knew that Sean could take care of himself but she still worried. There were more new faces showing up in town all the time. It was getting harder to judge people. A new boarding house had opened up and a lot of new people were staying there. There was a young couple staying there who looked and acted like newlyweds. They called themselves Clara and Darrel Stockton. They had arrived the day that Sean and Jim had left. They were waiting on a partner to arrive. They were going to open up another general store. They took some of their meals at "Maggie's Place." Darrel would have a beer once in a while but never any whiskey. Clara never drank at all. Their first day in town they went around and introduced themselves to everyone. The townspeople thought they were nice and that it would be nice to have more than one general store. The third morning in town, Clara and Darrel were up early and appeared to be going to a café for some breakfast. It was a little cool outside and Clara had a shawl over her shoulders. Darrel had on a jacket. Michael and Betty had gotten up and were walking to the saloon. The couples approached each other in the street. They stopped and greeted each other. They were about ten feet apart . Michael had tipped his hat to Clara. Before he had his hand back down, Clara had pulled her shawl off of her shoulders. She was holding a sawed off double barreled shotgun. Betty saw the shotgun and reached into her purse and pulled out her .32. Darrel was reaching into his jacket for something too. Michael pulled his pistol and fired before Darrel had his pistol out of his jacket. Darrel hit the ground dead. Clara had the hammers on the shotgun cocked now and was almost ready to fire. Betty fired her .32 first. The bullet struck the shotgun and when it did, Clara pulled a trigger and the shotgun fired. Before Clara could raise the barrel of the shotgun to fire again, Betty put a bullet in her forehead. Michael was on the ground. The blast from the shotgun had caught him just below his left knee. He was bleeding terribly. Betty screamed for help. Doc Rawlins had been up early and was getting ready to go on a call when he heard the shots and then the screaming. He ran straight to Michael. He reached into his bag and pulled out some straps and put a tourniquet around Michael's leg. "I need some help here," Doc yelled. "We gotta get him to the office quick." Several men were there and carried Michael to Doc's office.

Maggie was coming down the stairs in the saloon and started running for the street when she heard the first shot. Jeb came with her. She had a pistol in her right hand. By the time she got to the street, the shooting was over. Michael was being carried to the Doc's office. The young couple was dead in the street. A crowd was gathering around the dead couple. After a few minutes the crowd disbursed but there were still two men looking down at the dead bodies. Maggie stood on the sidewalk in front of the saloon. The two men who had been looking at the bodies turned and stared at Maggie. Then they started walking toward her. At first Maggie didn't think that they were armed but they started reaching into their jackets. Maggie didn't hesitate. She raised the pistol and fired. Jeb had seen the men coming toward them. He took off toward them before Maggie had fired. Maggie shot one of them and he hit the ground dead. Jeb got the other man by the throat. He got out one scream before he died. Maggie walked over to the dead men and looked them over. She had never seen them before. She had met the young couple and wasn't suspicious about them. She went to the Doc's office.

Betty was crying uncontrollably. Michael was on an examination table trying to tell Betty that everything would be all right. Doc Rawlins had cut away Michael's pants and removed his boots. He was silent for a moment. Then he spoke. "I've got to take the leg below the knee," he said. "There just too much damage. I can't save it. If I don't operate soon infection will set in, and then we could lose him."

"Go ahead Doc and git it done," said Michael. "Don't worry Betty darlin'. I'll get me one a them wooden legs and we'll be dancin' in no time."

"I've got chloroform," said Doc. "Now my wife will assist me. I want you two to leave now. We'll see you when it's done." Betty and Maggie gave Michael a hug and left. Doc got his wife and got to work.

Maggie and Betty started back to the saloon. Sean and Jim arrived in town before they got to the saloon. As they rode in they saw the dead bodies laying in the street. Maggie and Betty saw

.

Sean and Jim and waited on the sidewalk in front of the saloon. Sean and Jim dismounted and went to the girl and young man first. "I know these two," said Jim. "That's Sara and Tobey Slaughter. They're Bud and Goldie's grandkids." Then they walked over to the two dead men. "I'm not sure about these two," said Jim. "I know I seen'em before back in Missouri, but I can't be sure who they are." They walked over to Maggie and Betty.

Maggie ran to Sean and began crying as she wrapped her arms around him. "What the hell went on here?" asked Sean. "Where's Michael?" Betty was crying now.

"Let's go in and get off the street," said Maggie. Betty looked like she was about ready to faint so Jim helped her off the street. They all sat at the regular table. Maggie began telling Sean what had happened. "That young couple came into town the day that you and Jim left," Maggie began. "They were staying at the new boarding house. They called themselves Clara and Darrel Stockton. They told everyone they had a partner coming, and they were going to open another general store in town. They seemed like a newlywed couple and were so nice. They went around and introduced themselves to everyone. This morning they tried to kill Betty and Michael. Michael and Betty killed them but Michael took a shotgun blast in his left leg below the knee. He's at the Doc's now. Doc couldn't save his leg.."

Sean held his tears back. Anger was building in him. "Well what went on with them two men?"

"When I heard the shooting, I went outside with a pistol in my hand," started Maggie. "Some men were carrying Michael to the Doc's office. I saw the young couple dead in the street with a crowd around them. The crowd disbursed but those two men stayed a while and kept looking at the dead bodies. Then they started staring at me. They started toward me and were reaching for something in their jackets. I didn't hesitate. I shot one and Jeb got the other."

"Well Jim said that girl and guy was Sara and Tobey Slaughter," said Sean. "They're Bud and Goldie's grandkids. Jim's seen them other two back in Missouri, but he's not sure who they are. Jim, you go back out there and go through all of'ems pockets and such. Bring all the guns and everything here." When Jim went out to the street, Sean went over to the bar and got a bottle and some glasses for everyone. "I figure we could all use a drink," said Sean. Sean filled the glasses. Betty was shaking but she managed to take a sip. Jim came back into the saloon.

"Them two men each had a pistol in a shoulder holster and a knife on their belts," said Jim. "They had $40 between'em. There was nothin' on'em that would say who they are. That girl had this here little purse. There's a derringer in it but nothin' else. The guy had a pistol on'm and $50 and nothin' else."

"Thanks Jim," said Sean. "Now tell the undertaker he can have'em. Then come on back and have a drink."

No one said anything for a while then Sean spoke. "Doc knows what he's doin'," said Sean. "He probably done hundreds of amputations durin' the war. Michael's in good hands. We'll get'm healed up good cause we got us some killin' to do. If there's any of'em left when we get done, they'll be wantin' to go back to wherever their ancestors come from. Them sons a bitches thought Sherman was the Devil himself. Well they haven't seen nothin' yet." They stayed at the table and sipped their whiskey, but no one spoke for over an hour. Tom came over and asked if anyone wanted to eat. Everyone said they would wait till they heard about Michael.

An hour later, Doc Rawlins' wife came into the saloon and announced that Michael had come through the surgery all right and was sleeping. Everyone could come and see him if they wanted, but he would not wake up for several hours. They all went to see Michael. Doc was there cleaning up his instruments and everything. "He'll sleep for a good while," said Doc. "One of you can sit with him if you'd like. I'd say he won't wake up for six or more hours. All we have to worry about now is infection. I'll do my damndest to make sure that don't happen."

"Thanks Doc," said Sean. "I think me and Maggie and Jim'll go get somethin' to eat now. I spect Betty'll want to sit with Michael for a while."

"I'll sit with him for a while and then I'll come over and eat," said Betty. "I'll go back over later so I can be there when he wakes up." Betty stayed and the rest of them went back to the saloon.

Not one word was spoken while they ate their meal. Then Maggie spoke. "How are we going to get all of them Sean?" asked Maggie. "There might be more of them than there were Hawks, and we don't know who they are."

"Well there's five less of'em," started Sean. "Nine less countin' these here in town."

"Did you hang any of the one's you tracked?" asked Maggie.

"Not this time," answered Sean. "Jim here killed one and a horse killed another one. Them other three won't be killin' no one ever."

"Well what did you do with them?" asked Maggie.

"I give'em to some Cheyenne Dog Soldiers as a gift," answered Sean. "I told'em that them three was at Sand Creek and killed women and children."

"You're right. They won't kill anyone ever again. I hope they die slow," said Maggie. "So how did a horse kill that other one?"

"I was riding straight at'm and gettin' close," said Sean. "He was shootin' at me and missin'. When I was close, he hit the horse. I slid off the horse and the horse slammed into him when it fell. It crushed his chest."

"Well did you get any information out of any of them?" asked Maggie.

"I found out that one of'em was named Buster and his Pa was Buck," started Sean. "They was supposed to kill all of us. He said there was more of'em in town. He also said that if they didn't get us killed that come spring, a bunch of'em would rustle a herd and come into town like plain old cowboys. They'd fit right in and be able to kill us easy. He said Buck and Bud'r in Arkansas. There's more of'em holed up somewhere in "The Nations.""

Betty came back to the saloon and tried to eat but she couldn't get any food down. She was too upset. "I'll just have some coffee now and go back over and sit with Michael," she said. "I know he doesn't know I'm there, but I feel I need to be there."

"We'll keep alert in case there might be more of'em in town," said Sean. "If Michael would happen to wake up soon, tell'm he's in our thoughts." Betty finished her coffee and headed back to the Doc's office. "I'm goin' over and talk to Jason," said Sean when Betty was out the door. "I want him to help us keep an eye out. He can maybe watch the Doc's office. Might be that someone might wanna go there and finish the job. Then me and Jim'r gonna go around this whole damn town and find out about every damn person in it. Make sure everyone here is armed."

Jim stayed with Maggie while Sean went to talk with Jason. Jason was in the back room straightening up. "Jason, I could use another set of eyes," started Sean when Jason came out of the back room.

"I'll do whatever I can to help out," said Jason. "I didn't see the shootings, but I know about Michael. I met that young couple too. Nobody would suspect them of anything."

"I'd like you to keep an eye on Doc's office," said Sean. "I don't want anyone goin' in there and finishin' the job. If you see anyone goin' there that you don't know or aren't sure of, you put a gun on'em and hold'em for me. Anybody don't cooperate, you kill'em. Don't hesitate. Watch your back too and don't let nobody get behind you."

"This ten gauge'll demand some respect," said Jason as he reached behind a counter and pulled out the shotgun.

"Thanks Jason. Now me and Jim'r goin' all over this town and find out everything we can about everybody in this town," said Sean.

"There's a lotta new faces in town," said Jason. "You take care now." Sean went back to the saloon and got Jim.

There were two other saloons in town now, and Sean decided they would go there first. The first one they went into had about twenty customers. Four of them were standing at the bar. The others were scattered out at different table. Sean walked up to the bar while Jim stayed just inside the door. "What brings you in here Marshal?" the bartender asked.

"I came in here to see if there were any Slaughters or maybe some Hawks in here," said Sean.

"I don't know but a few a these people's names," said the bartender. "The ones I know aren't Slaughters or Hawks."

Sean turned his back to bar and looked out over the saloon. "Any a you in here a Slaughter or a Hawk?" asked Sean. "I don't 'spect you'd tell me if you were." Nobody said a word. Sean went to each man in the place and asked him his name and if he was any kin to the Slaughters or Hawks or if they knew anything about them. Jim kept a close watch. After Sean had questioned everyone he had a few words for them. "The Slaughters and the Hawks are scum," he began. "They're thieves, murderers, liars, and cowards. If I find out that any of you have lied to me, I will hunt you down and kill you. Won't be no judges or lawyers or trials or nothin'. I will kill you. Thank you for your time."

It was the same at the next saloon. No one knew anything or said anything. Sean and Jim then went to every business in town. He went to the newspaper office first. Sean figured that maybe a newspaper man was always curious about people and might have noticed something.

The newspaper had grown some since it first started. The owner had hired another man who could run the press. No one there knew anything. Sean and Jim headed to the livery. It was still the only livery in town and if anyone wanted horse care, that's where they had to go.

~~~~

Jason was out in front of his store sweeping off the sidewalk when he saw two men walking in the street he didn't recognize. They were walking in the direction of Doc's office. Jason had the ten gauge just inside the door of his store. He opened the door of the store and stepped inside. He grabbed the shotgun and made sure it was loaded. He also had some more shells in his pockets. His son Greg was inside. "Son, I don't know for sure but there could be some trouble," said Jason. "You stay inside and keep low." Jason watched the two men. They both had on pistol belts.

They went right to Doc's office. As soon as one of them put their hand on the door knob, Jason walked out into the street with the ten gauge pointed at them. "State your business at the Doc's," said Jason. The two men froze for a moment and then turned to face Jason.

"Whoa Mister. No need ta be pointin' that scattergun at us," one of them said. "We're just goin' in there and check on an old friend." Jason cocked the hammers on the ten gauge.

"You're a liar Mister," said Jason. "Now real easy like you drop them gunbelts."

"You got no call ta be callin' me no liar," said the man. "I don't take kindly ta be called a liar." Greg had not done what Jason had told him. He knew that his father kept a Spencer rifle in the back room. Greg knew where it was and how to use it. When he saw his father cock the hammers on the shotgun, he went for the Spencer. It was already loaded. When he got back up front another man had appeared. He had slipped behind Jason without Jason seeing him.

"Get them gunbelts dropped or I'll shoot you where you stand," said Jason.

"I don't think you'll be shootin' anyone," came a voice from behind Jason. The two men by Doc's office were laughing now. The man behind Jason had a pistol out but it was down to his side and not pointed at Jason.

"You can drop that scattergun if you want," said the man who had spoken from across the steet. "You're most likely gonna die if ya don't."

"Don't do it Pa," yelled Greg from inside the store. "I got this one on your back covered."

"Sounds like you're just a kid in there," said the one behind Jason. "You don't have the stomach to shoot nobody." Then he started raising his pistol. Before he had it up to fire, the Spencer barked and the man was knocked to the ground. As soon as the Spencer fired, the two men in front of Doc's went for their pistols. One barrel of the ten gauge went off and then the other one. The two men were thrown backwards. One of them was right in front of Doc's door and when the blast knocked him backwards, he went through the door. Doc was in the back with Michael and Betty and came running to the front.

"Just what in the hell is going on out here?" yelled Doc. "Who the hell are these two?" Jason reloaded the shotgun and walked across the street.

"I reckon they was figurin' on finishin' off Michael," said Jason. "There's another one out here in the street." Doc looked at the two who had taken the shotgun blasts. They were dead. Then he went to the one in the street.

"This one's not dead yet but he will be soon most likely," said Doc. "Let's at least get him off the street."

As soon as Sean and Jim heard the shots, they went running. When they got there, Doc was with the one who was not dead yet. "What happened here?" Sean asked.

Jason went over to Sean. "Them two by the Doc's office said they were there to visit an old friend," said Jason. "I knew what they was up to and told them to drop their gunbelts. I got careless and another one got behind me. Greg shot him and I shot them two. This one in the street's not dead yet." Sean looked down at the man.

"That's one a Bud's boys," said Jim. "Don't recognize them other two. His name's Buford."

"He's gonna die isn't he?" Sean asked Doc.

"I'm pretty sure he is," said Doc. "That bullet went pretty close to his heart. Can we get him off the street?"

"We can get him off the street but I don't want him in the same place where Michael is," said Sean. They picked up the wounded man and took him to the sidewalk just down from Doc's office. "I'm gonna ask him some questions now," said Sean. "I doubt he'll talk but I'm askin' anyway." Sean knelt down beside the man. "Well Buford, you been shot ta hell," said Sean. "Got anything to say before you go?"

"I'll see you in hell O'Rourke," said Buford. "There's more of us. It may take a while but we're gonna kill you dead. You'll get careless one a these days and we'll blast you ta pieces. Your momma won't recognize you."

"Can't you come up with somethin' better'n that ta say?" said Sean. "I heard shit like this before."

"I hope they make you watch while they skin that red-headed bitch a yers," said Buford.

"Well Buford, it appears to me that you're suffering," said Sean. "If your horse was sufferin' I'd put it outta his misery. Reckon I can do that for you." Sean pulled a pistol and put a bullet through Buford's head. Not one person acted surprised about this. After a moment, Doc Rawlins spoke.

"Was that necessary?" he asked Sean.

"No it wasn't but I feel better now," said Sean.

"You're gonna end up being just like the men you been killing," said Doc.

"No Doc, I'll never be nothin' like them," said Sean. "Men like them like killin' and hurtin' folks. If some old man tells'em ta go kill someone, they do it. They don't question it or nothin'. They're stupid, mean, and nasty and they do it. I kill ta keep me and my people alive."

"You know they don't see things the way you do," said Doc. "They couldn't care less about O'Rourke's law."

"Well Doc, right now it's O'Rourke's law or no law at all," said Sean.

Jason and Greg went back to the store. Once inside the door, Jason spoke. "I'm glad you didn't do what I said son," said Jason. "You saved my life and probably Michael and Betty's. How are you feeling now?"

"I didn't want to shoot that man Pa," said Greg. "But he would have killed you. I had no choice. I feel bad Pa. I hope I never have to do something like this again."

"I hope so too," said Jason. "Let's go tell your Ma what happened. I don't want her getting anything second hand."

~~~~

Jim got the undertaker and the bodies were removed. Maggie and Sean went into the Doc's to check on Betty. She was sitting beside Michael's bed with her pistol in her hand. "There's three more of'em we won't hafta worry about," said Sean. "I'd say things'll quiet down for a while. Seven a them been killed today. If there's more of'em in town, they'll probly lay low or get outta town for a while. That undertaker's gonna be a rich man if this keeps up."

"Let's talk about something else," said Maggie. "So Doc, how long should Michael stay here?"

"I want him here two more days at least," said Doc. "I'll be needin' to change them bandages regularly and make sure there's no infection. Now when you do take him home, I'll have to see him every day. Bandages will still need changed until we see some good healing started. I'll have something for the pain if Michael wants it. Knowing Michael, he probably rather have some bourbon. We'll see how it goes. Now if you'll excuse me, I have a baby to deliver just outside of town. If anything happens or doesn't seem right, my wife can help. She's actually a good nurse."

"I'm going to stay here with Michael," said Betty. "Could you bring me over something to eat later on?"

"We sure will," said Maggie. "We'll see you again in a few hours."

"Michael's liable ta be sick when he wakes up," said Sean. "I seen men be sick after they wake up after they used that chloroform stuff on'em. Don't be scared Betty. I think it's a normal thing." Betty nodded her head and Maggie and Sean left.

"I think we should have Michael and Betty come to the saloon and stay while Michael heals," said Maggie as they walked back to the saloon. "I think if we're all together we can keep a better eye on ourselves."

"I think so too," said Sean. "I don't know what Betty will say about that but I can just hear Michael. "Nobody, and I mean nobody is gonna run us out of our house" is what he'll probly say. Anyway, Jim's been spendin' a lot of time with Sally now so the back room should be available." Maggie got quiet. She looked like she was in deep thought. "What is it darlin'?" asked Sean. "You got a very strange look on your face."

"I was just thinking," said Maggie. "What kind of man would send his grandkids out to kill someone? I don't understand. What's wrong with those people? Don't they care about human life at all? I just don't understand. How can there be people like that?"

"Them people don't think like we do. Remember Mose Crandall." started Sean. "If they think they been wronged, it don't matter how many of'em it takes to right that wrong. I killed Grammaw Hawk. In Buck and Bud's eyes I wronged 'em. It's gotta be made right. It don't matter that Grammaw Hawk led a pack a murderers and thieves. She was their sister."

"So we need to get Buck and Bud," said Maggie.

"That'd be a good start," said Sean. "They're probly givin' the orders. But maybe another one of'em would step up and take over if we did kill Buck and Bud."

"So do we have to kill all of them?" asked Maggie.

"I don't know," said Sean. "We just gotta keep this up till they get tired of it and quit. We killed a lot a them Hawks. We thought they finally quit but I'd say they didn't. That rustler that Jug said they hung down in Texas was named Hawk."

"Well maybe they'll just rustle cows down there and leave us alone," said Maggie.

"Rustled cows'r gonna end up comin' here sooner later come spring," said Sean. "Buster said there was some of'em in "The Nations" and if he didn't get us killed, they were gonna rustle a herd and drive'em here and come in as ordinary cowboys. They'd fit right in and be able ta kill us easy. I wish I knew what Jesse was up to. He went down there with Dawn to visit her folks some time back. Maybe he's heard somethin'."

"I'd say that if Jesse heard or knew anything, wherever he was, he'd get ahold of you," said Maggie.

"You're right," said Sean. "Jesse's a good man."

CHAPTER NINE

When Jesse and Dawn went to visit her folks, they really didn't have an idea what they wanted to do. What started out as a short visit got longer and longer. They decided to stay. Jesse built them a cabin and they set up housekeeping. They had a nice garden and Jesse did a lot of smithing. They liked it there. No one gave them a hard time about anything. The Osage didn't care that Jesse was a colored man and Dawn was Osage.

Thanksgiving had come and gone and Christmas wasn't far away. Jesse was at the Indian Agent's place one day seeing if he could get horseshoe nails and other supplies. While he was there, he saw a newspaper on the counter. "Mind if I take a look at this paper?" Jesse asked the Agent.

"No, help yourself," the Agent said. "I never knew your kind could read."

"What do you mean my kind?" asked Jesse.

"I never meant no offense," said the Agent. "I just never met any colored folks who could read. I guess I know more white folks who can't read cause I know more white folks." Jesse didn't say anything else. He just unfolded the paper and read. The paper was from Abilene. There was a huge headline on the front page. "Deputy Federal Marshal Gunned Down In The Street" it said. Then the story went on about some woman who was killed too and that one of the killers was killed by a dog. The deputy was Jon O'Brien but the woman's name wasn't given. Jesse finished the story and then handed the paper back to the Agent.

"Where's the nearest telegraph?" asked Jesse.

"The onliest one I know that's close is just north of the boundary of the Cherokee land," said the Agent. "There's a little town there and they have a telegraph. Probly two days hard ride from here."

"Thank you kindly," said Jesse. "Don't forget about my supplies. I gotta be goin' now." Jesse went home to tell Dawn about what he had read in the paper.

"What are you intending to do?" asked Dawn.

"I'm goin' to a telegraph and see if Sean needs me," said Jesse. "There's s'posed ta be a telegraph in some little town just north a Cherokee land. The Agent said it was a hard two days ride."

"I'll get you some food packed and fill you some canteens," said Dawn. "You get up there soon as you can and get back to me. I'll be wanting to know what you're going to do."

"If Sean needs me, I'll be goin'," said Jesse. "Now I'll go tell your folks what I'm doin' and ask them to look out for you while I'm gone." Jesse talked to Dawn's folks and then got his horse ready. "I'll ride hard and be back as soon as I can," said Jesse. He gave Dawn a kiss and a hug and then was on his way.

~~~~

It was a hard two days ride but Jesse found the town and telegraph with no problems. He sent the following telegram.

Federal Marshal O'Rourke
Abilene Kansas

Do you need my help<<stop>>will do whatever is
needed<<stop>>will wait for reply

Jesse

Now you make sure you mark that urgent. I'll be in town
waitin' for a reply. Jesse still had the badge that Sean had given
him when he was in Abilene. He pulled it out of a pocket and put
it on. The telegrapher looked at him in amazement. "You one a
O'Rourke's deputies?" he asked Jesse.

"Yes I am," answered Jesse. "Now you make sure I get that
reply real quick like when it comes in."

"I sure will deputy," said the telegrapher. "I just never seen
me no colored lawman before."

"Well don't your worry about what color I am," said Jesse.
"You just worry bout this here badge. Now I'll be goin' over to that
saloon or whatever that is over there." Jesse went to the saloon.
There were two men standing at the bar when he went in. They
had glasses of whiskey in front of them. They gave Jesse a good
stare when he walked in. Jesse went over to a table and sat down.
The two men at the bar turned around and kept staring at Jesse.
Then one of them spoke.

"Looks like that nigger thinks he's gonna drink in here Orry,"
he said.

"That nigger's wearin' a star there Nate," said Orry. "Best
leave'm alone. He might be one a them O'Rourke men. I hear
they're all damn good with their fists and their guns."

"I never seen me no nigger I couldn't take in a gunfight," said Nate. "Them monkey's are lucky they can even get their guns loaded."

Jesse had heard enough. He stood up and got right in front of Nate. "Go ahead and try and pull that pistol white trash," said Jesse. Nate pulled back his jacket exposing a tied down Colt on his right side. Orry was on Nate's left and moved over out of the way. Nate went for the Colt. Jesse didn't go for his pistol. He reached out and grabbed Nate's right arm before his hand got to the pistol. He took Nate's arm with both of his hands and slammed it down on the edge of the bar. Jesse could hear both of the bones snap. Jesse grabbed Nate's pistol and stuck it in his belt. Then Jesse turned toward Orry.

"You'll have no trouble from me deputy," said Orry. "If you remember I told'em it'd be best if he left you alone. I don't wear no pistol either. I got a Sharp's carbine out on my horse I use for critters and such."

Nate was screaming in pain and cursing at the top of his lungs. Jesse got tired of the cursing and cracked Nate over the head with his own pistol. He fell to the floor in a heap. "You got any short boards around here?" Jesse asked the bartender.

"I can probly find some," said the bartender. "What do ya need boards for?"

"I'm gonna set this fool's arm," said Jesse. "It's a good thing he's out. It'll hurt some." The bartender was gone for a minute and returned with some boards. "I'll need somethin' to tie these on with," said Jesse.

"I got a apron you can tear up and use," said the bartender. "I'll need two bits for it." Jesse reached into Nate's pocket and found some change. He gave it to the bartender. Jesse gave the man's arm a yank. He was satisfied that the bones were set properly and placed the boards and strapped them to the arm.

"I never seen nothin' like this before," said Orry. "A man breaks a man's arm and that man wants ta kill that man. Then that man sets his broke bones. Who da thunk it?"

"Can I get you somethin' to drink?" the bartender asked Jesse.

"Have you got anything ta eat here?" asked Jesse.

"I got some bacon and beans," said the bartender. "I can heat'em back up."

"Go ahead and heat'em up and I'll have a whiskey while I'm waitin'," said Jesse. The bartender put the food on the stove and got Jesse's drink. Jesse sat back down at the table. Orry walked over to the table.

"Mind if I join you deputy?" asked Orry.

"I don't mind," said Jesse. "You sure you wanna set down with a colored man. You know if you get too close it might rub off on you."

"What might rub off?" asked Orry.

"My skin color. What'd you think I was talkin' bout?" said Jesse.

"I never did think anything like that," said Orry. "I never been round too many colored folks. I'm from Maine. Don't remember how I got here."

"Why you call colored folks niggers?" asked Jesse.

"I reckon I was raised that way," answered Orry. "Guess I don't know no better. So are you really one a them O'Rourke deputies?"

"Yes I am, or I was over in Abilene for a while," answered Jesse. "What's your last name Orry?"

"It's Carpenter," answered Orry.

"Well Orry Carpenter, you seem like a nice fella," said Jesse. "How'd you end up with this fool and what's his name?"

"I needed some work and he hired me ta help him move some cows," said Orry. "I was gonna have a drink and move on. We got them cows moved the other day. This fella's name is Slaughter, Nate Slaughter. I never knowed he was like this or I wouldn't a hired on with'm." The bartender brought Jesse's food to him. Jesse didn't talk while he ate.

Sean and Maggie were at their table when the telegraph operator came with the telegram for Sean. "It's from Jesse," said Sean. "He found out about Jon and Martha. He says he'll do whatever he can to help out. He's waitin' for a reply." The operator was still there because he figured there would be a response. Sean sent the following.

Jesse Strong

Slaughters   kin   to   Hawks   trying   to   kill us<<stop>>Michael wounded lost left leg<<stop>>many Slaughters killed<<stop>>more holed up somewhere in Nations<<stop>>heads of clan Buck and Bud in Arkansas<<stop>>need your help<<stop>>you are still sworn in

O'Rourke

Jesse was waiting at the saloon when the operator brought him the telegram from Sean.

"You got some paper and somethin' ta write with?" Jesse asked the operator. "I gotta reply ta this." The operator pulled out a pencil and some paper. Jesse sent the following to Sean.

Marshal O'Rourke

Abilene Kansas

Will see what I can find in Nations<<stop>>will stay in touch

Jesse

"Now you get that sent and mark it urgent," said Jesse. "Won't be no reply this time." The operator left and sent the telegram. "Well Orry, do you reckon you can show me where you and Nate took them cows?" asked Jesse.

"I can do that," said Orry. "Is them cows rustled?"

"I don't know but I bet they are," said Jesse. "Ole Nate's kin got a feud goin' with my boss over in Abilene. Some Slaughters killed a Federal Deputy and his woman and shot another one and he lost a leg. Need ta find out if Nate here is with them other Slaughters. I guess a bunch a them Slaughters been killed too."

"What'r you gonna do bout Nate while I show you where them cows are?" asked Orry.

"Don't know yet," said Jesse. "I'll wake him up in a bit and ask him a few questions. Maybe he don't know nothin' bout this feud."

Nate wasn't awake an hour later so Jesse threw some water in his face. Nate woke up and started swearing. "What the hell did you do ta me nigger?" yelled Nate. "What the hell's this shit on my arm? Did you break my arm you sombitch?"

"Watch your mouth boy or I'll break the other one," said Jesse. "Now you settle down and answer some questions."

"The hell I will," said Nate. "Just who the hell do you think you are anyway?"

"Name's Jesse Strong, Deputy Federal Marshal Jesse Strong," answered Jesse. "Now you're gonna answer some questions or I'll haul your ass up ta Abilene and let a friend a mine hang you. I'm sure you heard a Federal Marshal O'Rourke."

"Yeh I heard a him," answered Nate. "Everbody knows a that bastard. He'll be dead afore too long."

"And why's that?" asked Jesse.

"You'll not get another word outta me," answered Nate.

"Well Nate, there's already been a bunch a your kin killed tryin' ta kill O'Rourke," said Jesse. "He knows there's a bunch a you down here in 'The Nations' and that Buck and Bud's in Arkansas. He'll find you and kill you. How many more a you gotta die before you quit? Do you know what my boss does for a livin'? He kills men. That's what he does. He's very good at it. He can shoot your eyes out at five hundred yards with his Sharps, and he can kill you at a thousand. Nobody better than him with a pistol either. If you blink you miss his draw. He can put three holes in your chest, and it'll sound like only one shot got fired. He can sneak up on a Cheyenne Dog Soldier too. How many men you killed? Probly none a facin' you. Trash like you can only shoot men in the back or helpless folks who can't fight back."

"Yer a talkity nigger," said Nate. "Why don't you shut up fer a spell and give my ears a rest."

"I'll quit talkin' for a while but I'll give you somethin' ta think about while your ears are restin'," said Jesse. "If I find out that them cows'r rustled, I'm gonna hang you."

"Yer a lawman not no hangman," said Nate. "You can't be hangin' no one."

"Rustlin's a hangin' offense," said Jesse. "We got no judges and juries out here boy. You're gonna get hung." Nate never said another word. He just turned pale and started shaking. "Orry, you get all our horses ready," said Jesse. "Nate here'll be goin' with us." Orry did as instructed. Jesse put Nate up on his horse. "You behave now or I'll tie you to that horse and you won't like how I do it."

Orry told Jesse that the cows were only a half day's ride away so it wasn't long when they had them in sight. "There's a stream over there and plenty a grass," said Orry. "Them cows wouldn't wander far even if nobody was a watchin'em." Jesse gave everything a good look. There was a stream over there and there was a small grove of trees beside it. Smoke could be seen coming from a campfire in the grove. There must have been four to five hundred cows. They were spread out between the stream and where Jesse was. There was another grove of trees to their left. It was around five hundred yards from the stream.

"We'll swing way out to the left and come into that grove to our left," said Jesse. "There's some cows close to that grove. I should be able to see their brands." They swung out and came into the grove and dismounted. They tied the horses and Jesse put a gag in Nate's mouth and tied him to a tree. "You stay back here and I'll go take a look at them cows," said Jesse. Jesse didn't need to leave the grove. He could see the brands on the cattle as plain as day. He went back to Orry. "Them cows is rustled," Jesse said. "I know them brands. I got me an idea."

"Is your idea gonna get me shot?" asked Orry. "I came out here to show you where them cows were, not ta get shot."

"You'll be back with the horses," said Jesse. "Now take off your jacket and hat. You'll be changin' with ole Nate here." Orry muttered something to himself and took off his jacket and hat. Jesse untied Nate from the tree and took off his hat and jacket. Then he put Orry's jacket and hat on Nate. Then he picked up Nate and put him on Orry's horse.

"Why you puttin' him on my horse?" asked Orry. "That's my horse and I like'm. You're gonna get Nate and my horse shot aren't you?"

"We'll see," said Jesse. "Now you'll get Nate's horse. It's a better horse than yours, probly stolen too. "Jesse then tied Nate's left hand to the saddle horn and tied his right arm to his body so he couldn't untie his left hand with his fingers. "You stay with the horses," said Jesse as he led the horse back to the other side of the grove.

Orry wanted to see what Jesse was up to. He made sure the horses were tied good, grabbed his carbine, and followed Jesse. At the other side, Jesse had the horse pointed right at the campfire in the grove of trees. He took the gag from Nate's mouth and then removed the horse's bridle. He gave the horse a slap on the rump and then took the pistol he had taken from Nate and fired it into the air until it was empty. Then Jesse let out some rebel yells. The horse took off at a dead run toward the campfire. The cows also got spooked and were starting to stampede. If Nate was yelling anything, it couldn't be heard over the noise of the stampeding cattle. When the horse was maybe a hundred yards from the campfire, some shots were fired. Jesse counted six shots before the shooting stopped.

"What kinda man are you?" said Orry. "You sent him down there knowin' them down there would shoot at anyone ridin' down on'em like that."

"You forget purty quick," said Jesse. "Ole Nate tried ta kill me when we first met."

"Well yer still a cold man," said Orry. "A cold man."

"Well this cold man's alive," said Jesse. "Now we'll just sit tight and see what them fellas over there do. They might come over here lookin' for whoever done the shootin' after they find out they killed their own man or they may high tail it or they may try ta round them cows back up. If you're gonna leave you best git goin'."

"I better stick with you," said Orry. "I'm likely ta git myself kilt if I'm out there by myself."

"That's good thinkin'," said Jesse. "Get us some jerky outta my saddle bags. We can eat a bit while we're waitin' ta see what them fellas might do." Orry got the jerky. They sat down and ate and watched. It wasn't a half hour later when two riders came out of the grove by the stream. They rode on line but were about fifty yards apart. They were headed right for the grove where Jesse and Orry were hiding. When they got closer, Jesse could tell that they had Winchester rifles across their saddles. "Are you any good with that carbine?" Jesse asked Orry.

"I can drop a deer at a hundred and fifty yards," said Orry.

"Well deer don't shoot back," said Jesse. "Keep low behind that tree and brush as best you can. Keep your sights on the one on the left. I'll take the one on the right. Do what I tell ya and when I tell ya." The two riders were now within a hundred yards of the grove. They looked and looked but couldn't see Jesse and Orry. They moved toward the grove very slowly now. When they were fifty yards away Jesse yelled, "you boys drop them guns right now or we'll kill you." The two riders hesitated for a moment and then charged right toward the grove. "Shoot, shoot now," yelled Jesse. Orry fired the carbine and the rider was thrown backwards out of the saddle. Jesse fired his Spencer and the other rider was thrown from his saddle. "Stay put over there," Jesse yelled to Orry. "We'll wait a bit before we see if they're dead or not." Jesse knew for sure that the one he had shot was dead but he saw the other one move a little. Jesse went over to him with his Spencer ready. The man was on his back looking up at Jesse. He had been hit in the chest. He should have been dead but wasn't yet. His pistol must have fallen out of it's holster because it was empty. His Winchester was laying about ten feet from him. He looked up at Jesse.

"Who in the hell'r you?" he asked. "Was some a them cows yours?"

"No boy. I'm Deputy Federal Marshal Jesse Strong," said Jesse.

"You one a O'Rourke's deputies?" asked the dying man.

"Yes I am," answered Jesse.

"That was our brother you tied up and sent down there," said the man. "That was a rotten thing ta do."

"So all a you'r Slaughters?" asked Jesse.

"I guess it won't hurt ta tell now," the man said. "I'm shot ta hell and dyin'. Us three'r brothers. I'm Jethro and that's Mathew over there. You must already know Nate. We—, we—, we was gonna —." Jethro gasped one last time and died. Orry finally got up and came over to Jesse.

"We gonna bury them fellas?" asked Orry.

"I reckon we will," said Jesse. "Maybe them boys had a shovel over at their camp. Be a lot easier than scrapin' out a hole with a pan or a stick. Git their horses and we'll take'em over there by the stream where they had their camp. Orry got the horses and they threw the bodies across them. Then they got their horses and went over to the stream. Nate's body was close to where they had their fire. He had been shot through the head and heart. Jethro and Mathew had taken him off the horse and laid him down. There was a lot of supplies at the campsite. It looked liked the boys were intending to be there for a while. Jesse found a shovel. The ground was soft by the stream so the graves were dug in no time. Jesse said a few words over the graves. There was a wagon there too. Jesse took some boards from the wagon and made markers for the graves. He put the names on the markers.

"Why'd you put them names on there?" asked Orry.

"I want their kin to know these boys is dead," said Jesse. "Chances are they was buildin' up a herd and more of'em would be showin' up sooner 'r later. We best high tail it before some of'em do show up."

"I'm keepin' this Winchester," said Orry. "Mathew won't need it now."

"No I don't reckon he will," said Jesse. "Best check it and make sure he don't have it marked some way. You wouldn't want ta get shot cause some a his kin saw you with his rifle. Go ahead and take his pistol too. I'll be takin' these other guns and sellin'em. I bet they got more ammunition on that wagon too." Orry checked the rifle and the pistol and there were no markings that he could see. There was more ammunition on the wagon. There was also some food supplies. "I gotta be gettin' back ta my wife," said Jesse. "She'll be gettin' worried bout me."

"Where's your wife?" asked Orry.

"She's in Osage land," said Jesse. "She's Osage. Her folks is lookin' after her while I'm gone. What'r you gonna do?"

"I'm ridin' with you if you don't care," said Orry. "I still don't wanna get caught out here alone with all that's been goin' on."

"Well if you're goin' with me, get all them horses rounded up," said Jesse. "We'll pack up all this stuff and take it and the horses with us. Wouldn't want anything ta go ta waste."

~~~~

It took two and a half days for Jesse to get home. Dawn was outside doing some chores when she saw Jesse in the distance. She ran all the way to him. Jesse got down off his horse and picked her up and spun her around and kissed her. "I missed you woman," said Jesse.

"I missed you too Jesse," said Dawn. "Who's your new friend and what's with all these horses and such?"

"This fella here is Orry Carpenter," started Jesse. "He helped me some. These horses and all them supplies belonged to some cattle rustlers. They won't need'em now."

"So you're sayin' them rustlers is dead?" asked Dawn.

"It was their idea, not mine," answered Jesse.

"Who were they?" asked Dawn. "Did they have anything to do with what's goin' on in Abilene?"

"I don't know if they're in on it or not but they know about it," responded Jesse. "Their names is Slaughter and the Slaughters been the ones tryin' ta kill Sean and his men."

"So what are you going to do to help Sean?" asked Dawn.

"There's s'posed ta be more a them Slaughters somewhere in "The Nations," said Jesse. "I'm gonna see if your Pa or Uncle John will ride with me through some a the other tribes land and see if we can find'em."

"Well Pa's been poorly lately," said Dawn. "I'm sure Uncle John will ride with you. He and Sean are good friends. They're always talkin' about how Sean and them run out them outlaws."

"Well how bout you fetch Uncle John or one of the elders and they can take these supplies and give'em to any folks that might need'em," said Jesse. "Me'n Orry'll take care a these horses."

Dawn was gone for a few minutes and returned with her Uncle John. There was another young woman with her. Before anyone else could speak, Dawn took the young woman over to Orry and introduced her. "Orry Carpenter, this is my cousin Laura Brownshirt," said Dawn. "I thought you might like to meet her. Pretty, isn't she." Orry was kind of embarrassed. He could see that Laura was too. When he quit blushing he spoke.

"I'm proud ta make your acquaintance ma'am," said Orry. "And Dawn is sure right. You are very pretty."

"You're embarrassing me Orry," said Laura.

"I didn't mean to Miss Laura," said Orry. "I thought Dawn already done that." Everybody let out a laugh.

"Woman, we got important business ta take care of, and you're match makin'," said Jesse. "Laura looks like she don't need no help attractin' men. Orry, you can go talk ta that sweet young thing while me'n John talk if ya want."

"I'll talk with her after I hear what you two got ta say," said Orry. "No offense Miss Laura."

"None taken," said Laura. Dawn and Laura went to the cabin while the men talked.

"So what's going on?" asked John. "Where'd these horses and supplies come from?"

"Got'em from some cattle rustlers," answered Jesse. "Their names was Slaughter. The Slaughters been trying ta kill Sean and his men. They killed Jon O'Brien and wounded Michael. Michael lost his left leg."

"So I take it them rustlers is no longer with us?" asked John.

"That's right," said Jesse. "There's s'posed ta be more a them Slaughters somewhere down here in "The Nations." I told Sean I'd look around and see what I could find out. I would like it if you would ride with me. I could use your help on some of the other tribe's land."

"Of course I'll ride with you," said John. "Sean is my friend. We'll take Charlie Redhorse with us too. He's our best tracker, and his eyesight is really good. He sees things long before anyone else does. When will we leave?"

"I figure we'll leave at daylight," said Jesse. "Is that all right with you?"

"We'll be ready," said John. "Now what are you going to do with these horses and supplies?"

"I brought them here for the elders to pass out to whoever needed them," said Jesse. "Tell whoever takes them horses that they was probly stolen. I wouldn't take'em off Osage land till I checked for brands or changed'em. You can pass out them guns too."

"I thought you was gonna sell them guns," said Orry.

"I was but I don't need the money," said Jesse. "Was you fig-urin' on gettin' a cut on the money from them guns?"

"I guess I was but it don't matter," said Orry. "The folks here probly need these guns more'n I need any money. Besides, if I had any money, I'd just spend it anyway."

"So Orry, what'r you gonna do now?" asked Jesse.

"I'll just stick with you," said Orry. "Been interesting so far."

"It might get real interestin' before we're through," said Jesse. "If we run into some a them Slaughters they might wanna kill us."

"So nothin'll be any different than it has been so far," said Orry.

"I reckon not," said Jesse. "Just might be more of'em this time. Well John, I'm gonna go spend some time with my woman. Orry, I'll send that sweet young thing out for you to be with." Jesse went to the cabin and sent Laura outside. He stood in the doorway for a moment. "Don't nobody bother us for a few hours unless we're bein' attacked 'r somethin'."

"You can stay at my cabin tonight," John said to Orry. "Jesse and Dawn need ta be alone for a while. "I'm sure Laura'll make sure you get fed today." Laura went over to Orry and took his hand.

"You're a might forward aren't you Miss Laura?" said Orry.

"You like me. I know you do," said Laura. "At least you like the way I look."

"I do like the way you look but I don't know you," said Orry.

"Well that's what we're doing," said Laura. "We're getting acquainted. Now let's take a long walk and talk."

"With your looks you should have all the young men after you," said Orry.

"I am what white folks call a breed," said Laura. "My father was half negro and half Osage and my mother was half Osage and half white. I'm not quite sure what that makes me. Some of the young men don't want me because of this. Some older men want me but I do not want them. I don't want a man who is twenty years older than me. So how old are you Orry Carpenter?"

"I just turned eighteen not long ago," answered Orry. "How old are you Miss Laura?"

"I am seventeen and will be eighteen in a month," said Laura. "And please quit calling me Miss Laura. Laura will be just fine."

"All right M--, I mean Laura," said Orry. "I don't understand all this breedin' stuff. People is people. Some'r a different color. Why should that bother anybody?"

"Did you fight in the war for the blue?" asked Laura.

"I was too young," answered Orry. "My folks wouldn't sign for me ta join. I thought bout runnin' off one time and joinin' up but one day I seen this train come into town. It was full a wounded soldiers. I never seen so many men missin' arms and legs and such. I never thought bout signin' up after that."

"Where are you from Orry?" asked Laura.

"I'm from Maine. That's way up to the northeast," said Orry. "It can get mighty cold up there sometime. I don't miss that a bit."

"When did you leave there and what have you been doing?" asked Laura.

"I left up there soon as the war was over," said Orry. "I s'pose like a lotta fools I wanted to go west. This is a far as I got. I been driftin' around doin' whatever I could to make a dollar. My folks'r still up there. I write'em ever so often."

"It's good that you stay in touch with your parents," said Laura. "So why are you with Jesse now?"

"I hired out ta help some fella move some cows," started Orry. "We got the cows moved but I found out later that them cows was rustled. I was with the fella that hired me at some saloon when Jesse showed up. That fella picked a fight with Jesse, and Jesse broke his right arm. I seen that Jesse was a deputy right off. Anyway, I went with Jesse to show him where we took them cows, and that's where we found out they was rustled. There was some shootin', and them rustlers is dead. I stayed with Jesse cause I didn't wanna be out there by myself with all that went on. I'll be goin' out with Jesse and John tomorrow too."

"Why are you going with them tomorrow?" asked Laura. "You're not a lawman."

"No I'm no lawman but I like Jesse," said Orry. "He's a good man."

"He is a good man," said Laura. "Dawn got herself a good man when she got him. Now let's go to my place. You can meet my folks."

"Isn't it a might early for me ta be meetin' your folks?" asked Orry. "I only met you a short while ago."

"You don't meet many nice girls do you Orry?" asked Laura. "It's only proper for a young man to meet a girl's parents when they first see each other."

"Well I been with some girls before but usually their folks was runnin' me off," said Orry. "That one time a girl named Jenny and me was in a hay loft. Her Pa caught us. I thought he was gonna kill me with a pitch fork. I never understood that. It was her idea to go up there, not mine. Never seen Jenny after that. Then old man Bowden saw me kissin' his daughter, and he took after me with a shotgun. It's a good thing he only had bird shot in that thing. I got a few pieces in my back side."

"Well my father won't shoot you or take after you with a pitch fork," said Laura. "My mother and him are good people. You be nice to me, and they'll be nice to you. Now let's go. You'll be having dinner with us."

Laura's parents were sitting out in front of their cabin when Lonnie and Orry arrived. "Momma, Poppa, this young man is

Orry Carpenter," said Laura. "He came in with Jesse today. He helped him with some rustlers." Laura's father stood up and shook Orry's hand.

"Pleased ta meet ya young man. I'm MIke" said her father. "How'd Laura latch on ta you?"

"Poppa, don't be that way," said Laura. "Dawn introduced us."

Orry took off his hat and gave Mrs. Brownshirt a nod. "You are a very beautiful woman Mrs. Brownshirt," said Orry. "I can see where Laura gets her looks."

"I like this young man," said Laura's mother. "You'll be staying for dinner, and I won't take no for an answer. You may call me Kathy."

"I'd be pleased to dine with you and your family Kathy," said Orry.

"Don't be overdoin' the manners boy," said Mike.

"I didn't mean to sound that way," said Orry. "My folks taught me to be respectful when I meet new people."

"You got some good folks," said Kathy. Now you and Mike can talk while Laura and me get dinner ready." The women went inside and the men stayed outside and talked.

"So where you from Orry?" asked Mike.

"I'm from Maine. It way up to the northeast if you didn't know," said Orry.

"I heard of Maine but I wasn't sure where it was," said Mike. "I did know it was up north somewhere cause I heard about some a them Maine boys durin' the war. Heard bout this Officer named Chamberlain. They say he was a real fighter. They say his Maine boys helped hold the line at Gettysburg. Don't really know where Gettysburg is. Somewhere in Pennsylvania they say. You fight in the war?"

"No sir, I was too young," said Orry. "My folks wouldn't sign for me. I just turned eighteen not long ago. I thought about runnin' off and joinin' up one time but one day I saw a train load of wounded men and that changed my mind."

"There weren't a lotta fightin' around here durin' the war," said Mike. "There was some over in Cherokee land. Some a them were for the north and some were for the south. Still a lotta bad feelin's over there in a lotta places. I couldn't a cared less about it. Didn't bother me all them white folks killin' each other. Still don't understand why some poor dirt farmer'd go out and fight so some rich plantation bastard could keep his slaves. Nope, don't understand it."

"They probly thought they had to go along with their state," said Orry. "Some folks think the Federal Government should have no say in what a state does."

"I kinda know about that stuff," started Mike. "Back in the old days we had a lotta clans in our tribe. Each clan didn't always wanna do what the big chief in the big clan wanted. If a big chief is gonna jump off a cliff and says I gotta follow'm, I'm not a gonna. Ifn' he wants ta kill hisself that's his business. He can go on and I won't git in his way. Enough a that. How'd you help Jesse?"

"Some fella hired me ta help move some cows," started Orry. "Found out later that them cows was rustled and the fella that hired me was named Slaughter. Them Slaughters got a feud goin' with Marshal O'Rourke. That fella tried ta shoot Jesse but Jesse broke his arm. Then I took Jesse to where them cows was. There was a shoot out and them rustlers is dead. There was three of'em. They was all Slaughters."

"Never heard a no Slaughters," said Mike. "Wonder who they are."

"I caught a glimpse of a telegram Jesse got from Marshal O'Rourke," said Orry. "They're kin to the Hawks."

"Oh, I know bout them Hawks, bad bunch," said Mike. "I heard a bunch of'em got killed a while back." Laura came to the doorway and told the men to come into dinner. Orry pulled out Laura's chair and then Kathy's."

"Don't be over doin' them manners," said Mike. "Told ya that once already."

"Just bein' polite. Looks like a nice spread Kathy," said Orry. "I haven't had a good home cooked meal for a long time."

"Well I hope you enjoy it," said Kathy. "Laura did most of the work." The food was passed and everyone dug in.

"This is very good Laura," said Orry. "It appears that you're a good cook."

"Thank you," said Laura. "Now what did you and Poppa talk about?"

"We was talkin' bout them rustlers and a little bout the war," said Orry.

"So Poppa didn't get started talking about the old days and how they were so much better than how things are now," said Laura.

"The old days were a lot better," said Mike. "We weren't on no reservation then. We went where we wanted and did what we wanted. No white folks told us what to do."

"Well back in the old days there was a lot of scrapes with the Pawnee and Comanche," said Laura. "Somebody was always raiding somebody. Somebody was always getting killed."

"That's enough," said Kathy. "I don't much care for having to stay on this reservation but that's the way things are for now. Some day it'll be different. Now let's enjoy our meal and try to be pleasant. So Orry, did you go to school up in Maine."

"Yes I did Kathy," said Orry. "I made it all the way to the sixth grade. I know my sums and I can read real good. My writin's a little sloppy but most folks can read it. I even read some Shakespeare stuff. Never understood it, but I read it. He sure talks funny."

"Who the heck is Shakespeare?" asked Mike.

"He's some famous writer Poppa," said Laura. "He wrote a lot of famous plays and such. I heard a this one called "Romeo and Juliet." These two young people fall in love but her parents hate his parents. They end up killing themselves in the end."

"Seems ta me if they was so much in love they coulda run off together instead of killin' themselves," said Mike.

"That's true Poppa but Shakespeare wanted it to be tragedy, not a story with a happy ending," said Laura.

"Remind me not ta read any a Shakespeare's stuff," said Mike.

"All right Poppa, next time I see you with a Shakespeare book in your hand I'll remind you not to read it," said Laura. "Momma, Orry and I are going outside and take a short walk before it gets dark. I'll clean up after I get back."

"You go on now," said Kathy. "I'll take care of things. Go talk to your young man." Orry excused himself and he and Laura went outside and started walking.

"You got nice folks," said Orry. "You mother is a good woman. I can tell. Your father sounds a little rough but I bet underneath he's a good gentle man."

"Yes, he is," said Laura. "Are your folks like that?"

"Pretty much I'd say," said Orry. "My Pa likes ta think he's always in charge but he knows he won't do nothin' unless my Ma says it's all right. My Pa wears the pants in the family but only cause Ma says so."

"So tomorrow you're going out with Jesse and John," said Laura. "Will you come back this way when you're done?"

"I will," said Jesse. "And when I do I'll come a courtin'. Now come over here ta me and and put your arms around my neck. Looks ta me like you're wantin' kissed so I best oblige you." Laura and Orry wrapped themselves together and kissed. It was a very long kiss. "I think we better do that again just ta make sure we're doin' it right," said Jesse.

"Oh we're doing it right," said Laura. "It feels so right that you better take me home before we go too far."

"One more kiss and I'll take you right to your door," said Orry. The kiss lasted a very long time, but they unwrapped themselves and Orry walked Laura home. "We'll be leavin' at daylight," said Orry. "I'll be back this way soon as I can. I'll miss you."

"I'll miss you too Orry," said Laura. "Keep yourself safe out there and get back soon as you can. I'll be waiting for you." Orry nodded his head and left for John's cabin. Laura went inside with a smile on her face.

"Why you smilin' girl?" asked her father.

"Because Poppa, Orry is a very good kisser," answered Laura.

"So is that boy gonna hafta marry you to protect your honor?" asked Mike.

"No Poppa, we just kissed," said Laura. "Orry was a perfect gentleman. He says next time he comes, he'll come courting."

"In the old days he'd hafta give me ten horses for you," said Mike.

"Gee Poppa, it's good to know that you think I'm worth at least ten horses," said Laura.

"You're worth a lot more than ten horses girl," said Mike. "You need ta know somethin' about your young man and keep it in your mind."

"What's that Poppa?" asked Laura.

"He's ridin' with Jesse," said Mike. "Jesse's a lawman. Lawmen don't usually live too long around here. If he's with Jesse, they'll take him for a lawman too even if he's not wearin' a badge."

"I know that Poppa," said Laura. "I'll be worrying about that some."

"Well he seems like a real nice boy," said Mike. "Let's hope he don't get careless out there."

"Thanks Poppa, it's nice of you to say that," said Laura. "Now I'll be going to bed. Goodnight Momma. Goodnight Poppa."

"Goodnight girl," said Mike.

CHAPTER TEN

The next morning, Jesse, Orry, John, and Charlie Redhorse left at daylight. They were heading south when they left. John thought it would be a good idea to head south and then turn east. They would ride to the border of Cherokee land and then head north to the border of Osage land and then head west. Then they would head south again and go into Creek land.

It took a week to go through all of the Osage land. They kept spread out but they didn't find any sign of any white men or herds of cattle. It was the same on Creek land. When they went into Chickasaw land they did find some white men but they were traders who were trying to sell the Chickasaw some old cap and ball rifles. They said they hadn't seen any cattle herds anywhere they had been. In Choctaw land they came across a whiskey trader. Jesse busted up all of his whiskey barrels and told him if he saw him on Indian land again he'd shoot him. The trader left cursing. In Cherokee land Jesse had to beat some brave senseless. The brave didn't think much of Jesse being a lawman, and he called Jesse one too many names. It was almost Christmas now and it was snowing some. They were at the northern border of

Cherokee land. Jesse decided to go to the small town that had the telegraph.

"John, you and Redhorse can head on back if you want," said Jesse. "I'll be goin' to the telegraph office and tellin' Sean what we been doin'. I'll be goin' home soon as I get that done."

"We will stay with you Jesse," said John. "The telegraph is not far but you could still run into some trouble."

"All right, let's get that done and then git home before too much a this snow falls," said Jesse.

~~~~

When they got to the small town, Jesse sent the following telegram to Sean.

Federal Marshal O'Rourke
Abilene Kansas

Three Slaughters killed same day I sent last telegram<<stop>>Jethro Mathew Nate<<stop>>had stolen cows<<stop>>was in Kansas just outside Cherokee land<<stop>>went all through Osage Creek Choctaw Chickasaw Cherokee land<<stop>>no Slaughters or cows<<stop>>snowing now<<stop>>will wait for reply then head home

Jesse

"Now you mark that urgent and I'll be over at that saloon waitin' for a reply," said Jesse. Jesse and all of them went over to the saloon. "Let's go in and see if he's got anything ta eat," said Jesse.

"Redhorse and I will stay outside and wait," said John. "The owner might not want us inside."

"It's gettin' cold out here," said Jesse. "You're comin' inside. If the owner has any objections, he'll hafta take'em up with me." John shook his head but he and Redhorse followed Jesse and Orry inside. The place was empty. They bartender was leaning against the bar. "You got anything ta eat today?" asked Jesse.

"I got some son of a gun stew on the stove," said the bartender. "You don't 'spect me ta feed them Injuns do ya?"

"Them Injuns is my deputies," said Jesse. "And I'd take it real bad if you was to refuse to give my men somethin' ta eat. I'd take it so bad that this place might just git torn apart and who knows. It might just catch on fire."

"Well all right but don't be tellin' no one that I give food to your Injun deputies," said the bartender. "Somebody would burn my place down then."

"Well if that happened, you could get a hold a me and I could arrest'em," said Jesse. The bartender muttered something to himself and then brought all of them a plate of stew. "This isn't bad," said Jesse after he took a bite. "If someone did burn your place down, you could probly get a job at some café somewhere."

"Already done that," said the bartender. "Wanted my own place. Tired a workin' for other folks. Thought this little town might grow some but don't look like it's gonna. Maybe someday."

Just as the men finished their meal the telegram from Sean arrived for Jesse. It went as follows.

Jesse Strong

Snowing here too<<stop>>seems quiet here now
<<stop>>maybe will be quiet till spring<<stop>>
telegraph me in one month<<stop>>go home<<stop>>
thanks and Merry Christmas

Sean

"Well boys, Sean says it's quiet up there now," said Jesse. "Let's saddle up and head home. I wanna go past where we buried them rustlers. Might be some sign. What'r you gonna do Orry?"

"I'd like to go with you Jesse If it's all right," said Orry. "I got a little money and I can pay for my keep some."

"You wanna see that sweet young girl again," said John. "Don't worry. You can stay at my cabin. You'll earn your keep though."

They were about an hour away from where they had buried the three men when Redhorse spotted some fresh tracks. He stopped and dismounted and looked at the tracks carefully. "There's six of them," said Redhorse. "Three of the horses are un-shod. Tracks are less than an hour old."

"They look to be headed the same way as us," said Jesse. "Let's just move on easy like. Maybe they'll break off before we git where we're goin'. Anyway, let's keep our eyes peeled."

The tracks didn't break away. They were leading right to where the three men were buried. When Jesse knew for sure where they were going, he had everyone swing out to the left. They would come in on the backside of the grove they had used earlier. When they got to the grove, everyone stayed back while Redhorse worked his way to the other side. He came back in a short while. "I can't see much from here," said Redhorse. "It's too far. They started a campfire. I'll slip over to the stream to their left and get as close as I can."

"Don't get yourself caught," said Jesse.

"I won't get caught," said Redhorse. "Whoever that is over there is not worried too much about getting themselves spotted. If they was, they wouldn't have made a fire. They must be meetin' somebody." Charlie took his time and made his way to the stream. He was around four hundred yards from the six men. There was some brush and a few trees along the bank so he had no trouble slipping up on them. He got within fifty yards of them and decided that was close enough. There were six men. Three of them appeared to be Pawnee. "Just what would them Pawnee be doing with these white men?" Redhorse thought to himself. One of the white men was standing and looking at the graves.

"We was s'posed ta meet some Slaughters here," said the man. "But them names on them markers aren't the names a the ones we was s'posed ta meet. We was s'posed ta meet Chester and Butch. I reckon we'll stay here a few days and wait and see if they show up."

"They damn well better show up Brownie," said one of the other white men. "They wanna hire us for a killin' they better show up or they'll be the ones gettin' kilt."

"They'll be here sooner or later Bobby," said Brownie. "They done give us a down payment. They'll come."

"How much will each of us get when it's done?" asked one of the Pawnee in perfect English.

"When O'Rourke and his woman is dead we'll get $500 a piece," said Brownie.

"I will enjoy skinning O'Rourke and his woman," said the Pawnee. "It's been a long time to wait. I have a special knife that I keep razor sharp just for him. He killed two of my brothers many years ago. He was with the Cheyenne then."

"That's why you're here Bighorse," said Brownie. "We heard you was good with that knife." The other white man had made some coffee and it was ready now. The other men set around and drank coffee but didn't talk while the other man got some food ready. Redhorse studied each man carefully. The three white men all had two pistols and a knife on them. All three of them had Winchester rifles on their saddles. The three Pawnee each had rifles and knives on them. One of them had a Henry and the other two had Spencers. They had McClellan saddles on their horses and each one had a bow and a quiver full of arrows tied to it. "They stole them saddles from the cavalry," Redhorse said to himself. "I'd rather go bareback than sit on them things." After Redhorse thought he had seen and heard enough he worked his way back to the others.

"What did you find out?" asked Jesse when Redhorse returned.

"Let me catch my breath for a minute," said Redhorse. In a few minutes he spoke. "There's six of'em like we figured," said Redhorse. "Three white men and three Pawnee. One white man is called Brownie and another is called Bobby. I never heard a name for the other white man. One of the Pawnee is called Bighorse."

"So did you find out what they're doin'?" asked Jesse.

"They're hired killers," answered Redhorse. "They are supposed to meet Chester and Butch Slaughter. They hired them six ta kill O'Rourke and his woman. Them six already been given a down payment. That Pawnee was sayin' that O'Rourke killed his two brothers many years ago. He's intending to skin O'Rourke and his woman."

"Well boys, what do you think we should do bout them fellas over there?" asked Jesse.

"Why you askin' us?" asked Orry. "You already got it in your mind to go over there and kill them fellas. Don't matter that there's six a them and only four a us."

"You got a better idea?" asked Jesse. "Them fellas been hired ta kill my friend and I'm not gonna let that happen. Now any a you got a good idea on how ta do it?"

"I'll slip back over there a little before dark and see if they're keepin' anyone on watch," said Redhorse. "They seemed confident to me. I bet they won't have a man on watch. If they don't, I'll steal their horses tonight and we'll take'em at daylight."

"What if they have a man on watch?" asked Orry.

"I'll take him," said Redhorse. "An Osage could always slip up on a Pawnee or a white man."

"Well let's get ourselves fed and get some rest. No fire a course," said Jesse. "We'll take turns standin' watch at dark." The men had some jerky and biscuits for their meal. Right before dark, Redhorse slipped away. "I reckon if we hear some shootin', things didn't work out," said Jesse as Redhorse left.

Jesse took the first watch and it wasn't long when Redhorse returned. "They don't have a man on watch," said Redhorse. "I'll sleep for a few hours and then get their horses."

"You sure you can get all six a them horses?" asked Jesse. "I'm not worried bout them white men but them Pawnee might be more alert."

"Them Pawnee been hangin' round white folks too long," said Redhorse. "They won't be no problem."

Jesse stood watch for about three hours and then woke up Orry. "Don't be firin' no guns unless you hafta," said Jesse. "Anything happens, wake me up. Wake up Redhorse in an hour if he's not up yet. He'll be goin' after them horses then. Don't be shootin' him by accident when he starts comin' back with them horses."

"I'll be fine Jesse," said Orry. "Git yerself ta sleep. I'll wake ya if anything happens." Jesse drifted off to sleep and an hour later Redhorse was on his way to steal the horses. It wasn't two hours later when Redhorse had made it back with all six horses. "How in the hell did you do that?" asked Orry. "You went over there and stole six horses and got outta there without gettin' yerself shot. How'd you do that. Them horses shoulda made some noise."

"Horses like me," said Redhorse. "That's why I always been such a good horse thief. Now help me hobble these horses so I can get back to sleep." Orry and Redhorse took care of the horses and Redhorse went to his bedroll. An hour later, Orry woke up John for his watch.

"Anything goin' on?" John asked Orry.

"No, just Redhorse gittin'all them horses," said Orry.

"I knew he would," said John. "Horses like him. Now get some rest. Could be awful busy come daylight."

Orry was asleep in no time. Two hours before daylight John woke everybody up. "Everybody make sure they're loaded up and got plenty of ammunition," said Jesse. "Take a knife if you got one." Everyone checked their weapons and ammunition. "Me and Redhorse'll slip up on'em on foot," said Jesse. "We'll be goin't the way Redhorse went when he slipped up on'em. John, you and

Orry'll be comin' across the open field and be bringin' our horses. You'll be walkin'em. We'll leave them other six here. There's almost no moon so if they did hear you, they won't see you till you're right up on'em. Try ta keep them horses quiet. Go nice and easy like. Don't take off till me and Redhorse been gone for maybe fifteen minutes."

Orry and John did as instructed and were moving fifteen minutes after Jesse and Redhorse left. They moved slow. Orry was wondering if John could see any better than he could because he thought maybe Indians could see better in the dark. It was slow going but they made it to the campsite without being detected. Jesse and Redhorse were already there.

It was not quite daylight yet. Jesse and the men could see bedrolls around the still smoking fire but it was too dark to see the men in the bedrolls. Jesse felt uneasy. He had Orry and John tie the horses. Then they lined up about ten feet apart with their weapons ready and waited for the daylight. When it was just barely light enough to see, they could tell that the six men were not in their bedrolls. "Get down now," Jesse yelled when he knew the men were not in the bedrolls. Just as he yelled, He heard the twang of some bowstrings. An arrow flew past him just missing him as he hit the ground. Orry was not so lucky. An arrow caught him in his left shoulder. He was going forward to get down and when he hit the ground, the arrow shaft broke off. He wanted to scream in pain but he held it back. He still had ahold of his Winchester. As he looked up to see what was happening, one of the Pawnee was charging him. The Pawnee had a hatchet in his right hand and was yelling some kind of war cry. Orry took quick aim and fired. The bullet struck the Pawnee in the chest and threw him backwards but he didn't go down. He charged Orry again. Orry chambered another round and fired. This time the Pawnee was struck in the forehead and the back of his head was ripped off. He fell dead a few feet from Orry.

The other Pawnee who had shot an arrow at Jesse had switched to a repeating rifle. He had backed off some and was sniping at Jesse and the men. No one had been hit. He would fire a few rounds rapidly then quit for a moment and then fire some more. He wasn't worried about running out of ammunition. "He's trying to keep us pinned down," said Jesse. "The rest of them have skedaddled. I bet they figured out where their horses are. Redhorse, get on your horse and see if they're over there where we left them horses. We'll keep this one over here covered while you get mounted. Redhorse gave Jesse a nod and headed to his horse. Jesse and John laid down some fire on the lone shooter. Redhorse mounted his horse and took off without being hit.

There was no more firing coming from the lone shooter. Jesse made some moves to try and draw fire but no shots were fired. "He's either been hit or he's skedaddled too," said Jesse. "I'll work my way toward him. John, you and Orry try and keep me covered. Jesse moved toward the lone shooter's position slowly using what cover he could find. When he reached the spot where the shooter had been, he saw a Henry rifle there on the ground. The lever was down and looked bent. There was also a bow laying there. The bowstring had been cut. Jesse stood there and looked around carefully. He scanned the whole area around him as best he could. He turned back toward John and Orry. His Spencer was cradled in his left arm and he motioned to John and Orry with his right arm letting them know that the shooter was gone. Just as he lowered his right arm, he heard someone running up on him from behind. When he turned, the Pawnee was just about to strike him with a big hunting knife. The knife was in his right hand and the Pawnee had just made a leap for Jesse. He was so close Jesse couldn't turn his rifle to fire. Jesse dropped his Spencer and grabbed the Pawnee's right arm with his left arm. With his right hand, Jesse grabbed the Pawnee by the front of his pants. With Jesse's strength and the momentum of the charging Pawnee, Jesse lifted the Pawnee up over his head. As hard as he could he threw the Pawnee to the ground. This probably would have killed or knocked unconscious most men but the Pawnee got back up and came at Jesse with the knife again. Jesse quickly pulled his pistol and put a bullet in the Pawnee's chest. The Pawnee was thrown backwards to the ground but got back up and charged Jesse again. This time Jesse put a bullet in his forehead. He didn't get back up.

Redhorse was on his way back now. Jesse was with Orry now, seeing what could be done for him. "That arrow's gotta come out," said Jesse. "I'll give it a yank. We can hope that the head don't come off. If it does, I'll hafta dig it out."

"Git it done," said Orry. "If I get ta yellin' too much just punch me out."

"All right boy, here goes," said Jesse as he gave the arrow a yank. Orry let out a loud scream as Jesse yanked out the arrow. The head stayed on the shaft when it was pulled out. "That's a metal arrowhead," said Jesse. "That Pawnee made it outta some cook pot or somethin'. Good thing for you boy. Metal head less likely ta break inside you. Now I'm gonna heat up my knife and slap it to your wound. It'll stop the bleedin'. Redhorse had dismounted now and went to Jesse.

"The three white men and the Pawnee called Bighorse took off on them horses," said Redhorse. "They headed west. I watched them till they were outta sight. How's the boy doin'?"

"I got the arrow out. I'm gettin' ready to slap some heat on it," said Jesse. "He'll be all right in a month'r so." John got a fire going and Jesse's knife was ready in no time. Orry let out another yell when the hot knife was on him.

"I need to get back to that telegraph and let Sean know what went on down here," said Jesse. "Redhorse, I want you to go with me. John, you take Orry back with you."

"Are we gonna bury them fellas?" asked Orry.

"Not this time," said Jesse. "We'll round up their weapons and such and move out."

"Shouldn't we stick together," asked Orry. "Them other four might come after us. They was s'posed ta meet them two Slaughters too. What if they meet up with them. They'll be six of'em. I can ride and shoot."

"You need ta get to a bed and rest up and heal," said Jesse. "You go ridin' all over the place you'll get a fever and die on us. No boy, you're goin' back. You go easy John. If Orry gets ta where he can't sit a horse, make him a travois. Me'n Redhorse'll see you in a two'r three days. Let my woman know what I'm doin'.'" Jesse and Redhorse took off for the telegraph office and Orry and John headed back to "The Nations."

Jesse and Redhorse made it to the telegraph office without incident. Jesse sent the following telegram.

Federal Marshal O'Rourke
Abilene Kansas

Ran into six killers hired by Slaughters on way back from telegraph<<stop>>three white men and three Pawnee <<stop>>killed two Pawnee<<stop>>four got away headed west<<stop>>were to meet Chester and Butch

Slaughter<<stop>>Slaughters never showed<<stop>>one white man called Brownie and one called Bobby <<stop>>no name for other one<<stop>>Pawnee that got away called Bighorse said you killed two brothers years ago<<stop>>heading back to Nations<<stop>>will stay in touch

Jesse

John and Orry made it back home with no trouble. They moved nice and easy and Orry was able to sit his horse the whole time. When they got back to the village, the news traveled fast that Orry had been wounded. Laura was all over her parents insisting that Orry stay with them so she could care for him. Her father grumbled a good bit but he gave in. "I warned you that somethin' like this could happen," said Mike. "He can work off his room and board when he heals up some."

"I got an extra bed at my place that I can bring over for you," said John Littletree. "If you need more blankets and such, I have them too."

"We got blankets and such but we could use that bed," said Laura. "We'll put it close to the fire so Orry can be nice and warm. Orry, you come on in and sit down while we get your bed set up." Laura and Orry walked into the cabin. Laura snuck a kiss when she thought no one was watching. It wasn't long and Orry was sound asleep on the bed.

The next day Jesse and Redhorse made it back. Dawn ran to him and grabbed him like she always did. She grabbed his arm and led him to their cabin. "Let me take care a my horse and I'll be right with you," said Jesse.

"I'll take care of your horse," said Redhorse. "Your woman wants you right now."

CHAPTER ELEVEN

When Michael finally woke up at the Doc's office, he looked at Betty and smiled. Then he leaned over the side of the bed and threw up. Betty had placed a bucket beside the bed on Michael's right but Michael spewed to his left. Doc's wife came running when she heard Michael vomiting. "That happens sometimes when they use that chloroform," she said. "He'll be all right. I'll get it cleaned up." Michael finished his business and then looked at Betty and smiled.

"I guess I lived through the surgery," said Michael. "I must still be a tough old bird. I heard that a lotta boys died from shock durin' the war when they had arms'r legs cut off." Betty took a towel and wiped off his mouth.

"Of course you lived you big Irishman," said Betty. "You can't be leavin' till I say it's time and it won't be time for a long time to come. Now are you in pain? Doc's got some stuff if you need it."

"It's probably that laudanum stuff," said Michael. "I hear it tastes just awful. I'd rather have some bourbon."

"You can't have any whiskey till Joseph says so," said Doc's wife. "He'll be back shortly and he'll be changing your bandages.

You may ask him then about the whiskey. I can get you the laudanum now if you want."

"I'll wait a bit," said Michael. "It does hurt but not too bad right now. I do feel like I have a fever."

"That's normal after a surgery," said the Doc's wife. "A fever is a sign that your body is fighting off bad things. Of course a high fever for too long can be bad." She put her hand on Michael's forehead. "Your fever is not high," she said.

"What's your name anyway?" asked Michael. "You and doc been in town all this time and I don't know what your first name is."

"It's Cora," she answered. "I was named after my grandmother."

"Well Cora, thanks for taking care of Michael," said Betty. "When can he have something to eat?"

"I would say probably not till tomorrow," answered Cora. "He'd probably just throw it back up. We'll ask Joseph when he gets back. You can have more visitors now if you feel up to it. I know Maggie and Sean will want to see you. I can go tell them Michael is awake if you'd like, or if you'd rather I was here, I'll sit with Michael while you go Betty."

"I'll go tell them and come right back," said Betty. It wasn't but a few minutes and Maggie and Sean were there. Maggie hugged Michael as best she could. Sean just looked at his friend and smilled.

"Don't you all fret any," said Michael. "I'll be up and dancin' in no time. I'll get someone to make me a wooden leg and I'll get Jason to make somethin' so I can fasten it to my knee. This won't affect my piano playin' one bit either."

They had been talking for a while when Doc Rawlins got back. "I hate to break up the party, but I think it's best that you all step out for a spell," said Doc. "I need to change his bandages now. You won't want to watch. You can come back when I'm done." Everyone stepped out. Doc and Cora got busy changing Michael's bandages.

"So Doc, Cora here says I can't have any whiskey till you say so," said Michael.

"That's right," said Doc. "That's what I told her. Are you in much pain now?"

"It hurts some but not a whole lot," said Michael. Doc put his hand on Michael's forehead.

"Your fever is slight which is good," said Doc. "Did you throw up yet?"

"I did right after I woke up," said Michael.

"Well if you don't throw up any more and the pain isn't bad enough that you need laudanum, you can have a little whiskey in a couple of hours," said Doc. "And I mean just a little. No more than a couple of drinks."

"I'll be a good patient Doc," said Michael. Doc and Cora finished with the bandages and all of them came back in to see Michael. "Doc says I can have a little whiskey in a couple of hours," said Michael. "I think I'd like some good bourbon Sean darlin'."

"Good bourbon it'll be," said Sean. "I'll get a bottle of that new stuff we got from that drummer a while back. I had some a that at Sally's last time we were in Kansas City. It's the best bourbon I ever had." They talked and talked and soon two hours was up. Sean had gone to the saloon and returned with a bottle and glasses for everyone. Sean filled the glasses.

"I think we should have our toast young Sean," said Michael. "It seems like it's been a long time since we had our toast. Now seems like a good time."

"I agree," said Sean. "Raise your glasses." Sean was about to start when Doc walked back in. "We're having a toast Doc," said Sean. "Would you like to join us?"

"What are we toasting or who are we toasting to?" asked Doc.

"Join us and you'll see," said Sean. Doc nodded his head yes, and Sean filled another glass. "Now here we go Doc," said Sean. "Here's to not getting killed." Everyone repeated the toast.

"That is a good toast Sean," said Doc. "You wouldn't be offended if I used it sometime would you?"

"No, go right ahead anytime Doc," said Sean. "Michael and me would be honored."

"I will then," said Doc. "Now would you mind stepping outside for a few minutes Sean? I need to talk to you." Sean nodded and he and Doc went outside.

"What is it Doc? What do you need?" asked Sean.

"Sean, I've never had a patient like Michael before," started Doc. "I've done hundreds and hundreds of amputations and almost every patient says they'd rather be dead than be one legged or one armed. That is, the patients who could talk. A lot of them mope around for years after the surgery. Michael is taking this so well. He must really be a remarkable man."

"He is Doc," said Sean. "He knows he's got a lot to live for. He enjoys life and he likes people. He'll do well. We might hafta slow down on his deputy duties or maybe give them up altogether. Anyway, he's got a good woman in Betty and plenty of good friends and he'll do fine."

"I'll do some research and send some telegrams," said Doc. "They've been coming out with all kinds of new things since the war did so much damage to people. They got artificial limbs and things now. I don't know how good they are, but they might be worth a try."

"Well Michael figured he could get someone to make him a wooden leg and then get Jason to make something so he could strap it to his knee," said Sean. "Michael's figurin' on dancin' before too long."

"It's good that he has that attitude," said Doc. "Now let's get back inside. Don't want anyone thinking we were talking about something bad."

When they went back inside, Maggie spoke first. "What were you two talking about?" asked Maggie.

"Maggie darlin', Doc and I were discussing what a good patient Michael has been, and that's the gospel truth," said Sean.

"That must be true," said Michael. "Cause I never have heard you use the word gospel in all the time that I've known you."

They all talked a little while longer. Michael had his second drink of whiskey and was asleep shortly after his glass was empty. "If you'd like to spend the night here Betty, I can bring in a cot for you," said Doc.

"I'd like that if it wouldn't be too much trouble," said Betty. "I want to be with him." Doc brought in the cot and some blankets. Maggie and Sean went back to the saloon.

On the way back to the saloon, Sean pulled Maggie to him and hugged her hard. "I love you darlin'," said Sean. "I just wanted to say that."

"I know you love me darlin' and I love you too," said Maggie. "Let's make sure everything is all right at the saloon and then go soak in our tub."

"Sounds wonderful," said Sean. "Let's hope nothin's goin' on." All was quiet at the saloon so Sean went to the bath house and got a fire going and started heating the water. They were all over each other for the first hour in the tub. Sean heated up some more water and they held each other and soaked. "You know darlin', Christmas is close and I haven't done any shopping at all," said Sean.

"I don't need or want anything for Christmas," said Maggie. "I already have the best man any woman could hope for, and we have the best friends. What more is there?" Talk like that got Sean heated up again. A good while later they were soaking again. "Let's find us a tree and put it up soon," said Maggie. "We really enjoyed our tree last year."

"We'll have one tomorrow," said Sean. "Jim can stay in town while I go get us a tree."

The next morning Sean let everyone know what he was doing, and then he took off for the tree. He found a nice spruce tree at the same place where they got the tree last year. He got back to town without any trouble. Sean made a stand for the tree and they put it the same place as last Christmas. They decorated it the same way as last year. Whenever anyone had something for the tree, they just put it on.

~~~~

After two days at the Doc's place, Michael was allowed to leave. Maggie and Sean tried to get Michael to stay in the back room at the saloon but Michael would have no part of it. Doc came over twice a day to change bandages until it wasn't necessary any more. Maggie and Sean were visiting Michael when a telegram arrived. "It's from Jesse," said Sean. "He found out about Jon and Martha and wants to help out. I'll tell'em what's goin' on and ask him to see what he can find out in "The Nations." The operator was still there so Sean wrote the telegram and had it sent. "I was hopin' ta hear from Jesse," said Sean. "He's a good man." It wasn't long and the operator returned with another telegram for Sean. "Well Jesse's gonna see what he can find out down in "The Nations" and he'll stay in touch with us," said Sean. "Maybe he'll get John Littletree or someone to help him out."

~~~~

Michael was healing very well. It was only a week till Christmas when another telegram arrived from Jesse. It told about killing the three Slaughters and finding nothing in "The Nations." Sean replied and told Jesse to go on home and wished him a Merry Christmas. It was only two days later that another telegram arrived. This one told about the six hired killers and that four of them got away heading west. Three of them were white men and three were Pawnee. The two killed were Pawnee. The Pawnee that got away was called Bighorse and he said Sean killed two of his brothers years ago. One white man was called Brownie and another one Bobby.

~~~~

After Sean read the last telegram he went to the jail to look at wanted posters. Maybe there would be someone by those names who was wanted. There was nobody on any of the posters who went by Brownie or Bobby. Sean decided to go to the telegraph office and see if the Judge had ever heard or seen these names on a wanted poster. Sean sent the following telegram.

Federal Judge Sharpton
Rederal Court House
St. Louis

On going feud with Slaughters<<stop>>one deputy killed another wounded badly<<stop>>many Slaughters killed<<stop>>do you know of hired killers calling themselves Brownie or Bobby<<stop>>quiet here now<<stop>>Merry Christmas

O'Rourke

"You get that sent and if a reply comes, you get it to me quick," Sean said to the operator. "I'll be at the saloon or visiting Michael at his place."

"Sure thing Marshal," said the operator. Sean left for the saloon. He got a surprise when he went inside. Michael was sitting at his piano playing and singing.

"What do ya think Sean darlin'?" said Michael. "I haven't lost my touch have I?"

"No Michael you haven't," said Sean. "Maybe you're even better than you were."

"I'm gettin' better with these crutches too," said Michael. "When my stump gets tougher I'll get someone to make me that wooden leg. It'll have a foot on it too and it'll be hinged so it can bend like your ankle does. Maybe I'll be able to wear a boot over it.

I reckon the hardest part'll be learnin' to keep my balance so I won't need the crutches. I'll get me a fine looking cane so I can look sophisticated."

"Who you reckon can carve out a leg like that?" asked Sean.

"I don't know but I'll find somebody," answered Michael. "There's some carpenters in town now and some of them do some fancy carvin' for furniture and such. I'm sure one of 'em'll see if they can get it done. I'll probly hafta get on my horse from the right side now when I want to ride or maybe I'll get me and Betty a fancy carriage."

"Sounds like you got it all figured out," said Sean.

"So what's goin' on with them Slaughters now?" asked Michael.

"Well Jesse got three more of 'em killed down close to "The Nations" and went all over down there, but didn't find any more of 'em or any more rustled cows," said Sean. "On his way back home he come across six hired killers who were s'posed ta meet some more a the Slaughters. Three of 'em was white men and three of 'em were Pawnee. Two of the Pawnee got killed. Supposedly I killed two brothers of the other Pawnee some years back. I sent a telegram to the Judge hopin' he might know somethin' about two of them white men. One calls himself Brownie and the other calls himself Bobbie. Hopefully he'll get back to me soon."

"Let's get sometin' ta eat now," said Michael. "Seems I got my appetite back and then some."

"It could be because it takes a lot of strength to move around with them crutches," said Sean. "You're a big man Michael. Takes a lot of strength to move you around."

"Well I'll be movin' over to that table and havin' a meal now," said Michael.

"Get yourself seated and I'll go tell Cookie and Barbara we need some plates," said Sean. Maggie and Betty were over at the bar, and they came over to join them.

"Get two more plates," said Maggie. "We'll be joining you."

"I'll get us a pot of coffee too if that's all right with everyone," said Sean.

"Coffee's good for now," said Michael. "I might have a drink after I eat."

"Coffee's good for me," said Maggie.

"I'll have some coffee too," said Betty. "Then I'll join this big Irishman for a drink after we eat."

Everyone was just about done with their meal when the telegraph operator arrived. "It's from the Judge," said the operator. "I'll hang around for a bit to see if you need to send a reply." The telegram went as follows.

O'Rourke

Have heard of man called Bobby Lee Jackson and another called George Washington Brown<<stop>>calls himself Brownie or GW<<stop>>one rode with Bedford Forrest<<stop>>both wanted in Missouri for multiple murders<<stop>>keep alert<<stop>>no descriptions<<stop>>Merry Christmas

Judge Sharpton

"Well what did the Judge have to say?" asked Maggie.

"He's heard of them two fellas Jesse told us about," said Sean. "One's called Bobby Lee Jackson and the other one is George

Washington Brown. Calls himself Brownie or GW. He didn't have any descriptions. One of'em rode with Bedford Forrest. Both of'em are now wanted for multiple murders in Missouri."

"Well we took care of hired men before," said Michael. "We'll take care of'em this time too." Jim came into the saloon now and joined them at the table.

"Nothin't goin' on in town now that I can see," said Jim. "Maybe it'll stay that way all winter."

"We hope so too," said Sean. "Say Jim, you're from Missouri. You ever heard of a fella calls himself Brownie or GW. His full name is George Washington Brown."

"I heard a him," said Jim. "He rode with Bedford Forrest durin' the war. I heard he killed a lot a prisoners and he loved to shoot colored folks. I heard he was at Fort Pillow when they killed all them colored soldiers. They say he's a crazy sombitch."

"Do you know what he looks like?" asked Sean.

"I never seen'm," said Jim. "But they say he's a short skinny man. Got long blonde hair and a white eye. They say he packs three pistols and a Henry rifle. They say he wears a cavalry saber that got broke in half and he's got it sharpened up."

"How'd you know all that?" asked Sean.

"Hey where I come from in Missouri everybody is related or knows everybody else's business," said Jim.

"Well have you ever heard of a fella calls himself Bobby Lee Jackson?" asked Sean.

"I heard a him too," answered Jim. "Calls himself Bobby Lee after Robert E. Lee and Jackson after Stonewall Jackson. Fancies himself a great General. He rode with JEB Stuart."

"What's he look like?" asked Sean.

"They say he's a real tall man and has black hair," said Jim. "He wears a full beard, but they say there's one way for sure that you'd know him if you seen him close up. He has a double barreled shotgun that's cut off so short that he wears it like a pistol on his right hip. They say he's quick with it too. Last I heard a him he was s'posed ta be down in Arkansas."

"Well Buck and Bud were s'posed ta be in Arkansas," said Sean. "Probly them that hired those two boys. Well now we got some idea what them two might look like. Hope they stay holed up till spring."

~~~~

Christmas came and they had good a celebration at the saloon. Barbara and Cookie made a great feast. Maggie did some singing, and Michael played his piano. The blacksmith was there too and played his fiddle. There was drinking and dancing well into the night. It was after 2am when the celebration finally died down.

It snowed hard that night. When Maggie and Sean woke up shortly after daylight it was still snowing hard. "We may as well stay in bed and snuggle," said Maggie. "There won't be much going on today. There must be a foot or more of snow out there already."

"Sounds good to me," said Sean. "Can't think of anyone I'd rather be snowed in with. Let's get to that snugglin'."

Around 11am they decided they were hungry and got up and got dressed. When they went downstairs, Betty, Michael, and Jim were at their table drinking coffee. Barbara and Cookie were in the kitchen. "Damn, I didn't expect to see anyone down here this morning," said Sean. "How much snow we got out there anyway?"

"Over a foot," said Michael. "You can measure the wet mark on my crutches if you want."

"You're doing good if you can get around in this stuff Michael," said Sean. "It's hard enough with two good legs." Maggie had let Jeb out the back door to do his necessaries and came to the table.

"I know it's late but I think I'll have some ham and eggs," said Maggie. "Anybody else want anything?"

"We already had some breakfast," said Betty.

"I'll have some ham and eggs too," said Sean. "But I want some taters too if they have any."

"I'll tell Barbara and Cookie," said Maggie. Maggie went back to the kitchen to tell them what they wanted but she didn't see Barbara or Cookie. "They were in here just a minute ago," Maggie said to herself. "Wonder where they are now." Maggie looked all around but couldn't find them. Then she looked out back. There were tracks leading to the ice house. She pulled up her dress and went to the door of the ice house. She opened the door and stuck her head inside. She could hear some heavy breathing and some clothes rustling. She backed out and went back inside and went to the table.

"You got a strange look on your face Maggie," said Sean. "Is somethin' wrong?"

"No, nothing's wrong," said Maggie. "Just Barbara and Cookie are in the ice house seeing if they can melt some ice."

"I guess we'll get some breakfast when they get done," said Sean. "Or we can go fix it ourselves."

"That sounds like fun," said Maggie. "I haven't cooked at all for ages and you've only cooked over a campfire when you're out on the trail. Let's go." Maggie and Sean went to the kitchen.

"They got the stove hot," said Sean. "You get some eggs, and I'll cut us some ham. I'll cut up some taters for you too." Sean got some grease and started frying the taters. When he thought they were done enough, he put the ham in with them. Maggie took another skillet and started cooking some eggs. Sean was getting excited as he watched Maggie. He got behind her and put his hands on her breasts.

"We'll have to cook more often if you're going to be like this," said Maggie. She pulled up her dress and dropped her undergarments. It was short and intense but they were able to get done without burning the food. Maggie had just put her dress back down when Barbara and Cookie came back inside.

"Did you melt any ice?" Sean asked them. Both of them turned beet red.

"We tried," answered Cookie. Barbara and Maggie started laughing.

"Well we tried out your kitchen while you were gone," said Maggie. "Everything seems to be in working order, and I mean everything." They all laughed. Maggie and Sean carried their food out to their table.

"Looks like you two can still cook a little," said Betty.

"Not much to ham, eggs, and taters," said Sean. "We had us a little dessert in there too."

"Nothing wrong with that," said Betty. "Me and Michael been having a lot of dessert lately too."

"You people need ta quit talking like this," said Jim. "I'll be needin' to go see Sally again."

"Go on and see her," said Sean. "I'm sure she won't mind. Jim didn't need any coaxing. He left very quickly.

~~~~

It didn't snow anymore. In a couple of days it warmed up and all the snow melted. It was a muddy mess outside. The next week it got very cold and all the mud froze. With all of the ruts and wagon tracks on the road it was very hard to walk. It stayed frozen for a couple of weeks. Michael made it the whole time without falling once.

Michael found a carpenter who was willing to make his wooden leg. He told Michael that he would have one made in around a month. He warned Michael that this would be just a start. It could take a while longer to get it sized right and make sure the hinge would work. And then they would get with Jason and figure out how to make it so it would strap to his knee and such and not be too uncomfortable to his stump. Michael waited patiently.

The rest of January was cold but there wasn't much snow. There was some snow in early February, but it didn't stay long. In the middle of the month, the carpenter was working on getting Michael's leg sized. It took another week but he got it as good as he thought he could. "It may look too short but you'll have to have a lot of padding between the wood and your leg and it will take a while for your leg to build up calluses on your stump," said the carpenter. "Take your time and don't rush things. I'd say you'll be dancin' in no time. It'll fit right in your boot if you do wear your boots. I did some good work if I say so myself."

"You have my deepest thanks," said Michael. "I'll get over to Jason's and see what he can come up with." Michael paid the carpenter and left with his new leg.

Jason was waiting on a customer when Michael arrived. Michael took a seat on a wooden box and waited. When the customer left, Jason went over to Michael. "I see you have your new leg," said Jason. "Looks like that fella did a nice job. Let's take a look at your leg and take some measurements."

Jason took a tape measure and measured around Michael's leg above the knee and the distance from there to where the top of the wooden leg would be. "All right Michael, here's what I'll try," said Jason. "On the top of the wood I'll fasten some leather. It'll be a foot above your knee for starters. Your leg will fit into it kind of like a sock. There will be a lot of padding in it so your stump doesn't rub against wood. There will be straps around it above and below the knee to hold it in place. They will be adjustable. They need to be tight to hold it on but not too tight so it's uncomfortable. We might have to figure out something to keep it from turning if it does turn and not stay lined up. If something doesn't work, we'll try something else. Does all this sound all right with you?"

"Sounds good Jason," said Michael. "Just get ahold of me when you're ready to give it a try."

"I'll have it ready within a week," said Jason.

"I'll see you then," said Michael as he left.

~~~~

A week later Michael was at Jason's store trying out his new leg. The first time he tried walking he fell. "Take your time Michael," said Jason. "It will tke a long time to get used to it. Now go nice and easy. Remember, that's not your real leg down there. It won't act like your real leg did." Michael got himself back up and tried again. He did a lot better this time.

"Jason, I'll wear it from time to time and longer each time so I can get used to it," said Michael. "I'm sure it will take a good while till we get it as good as we can. Now I'll be off and many thanks to you." Michael made it all the way back to the saloon without incident. He went inside and sat at their table.

"You're looking good Michael," said Sean. "How does it feel?"

"It'll take a lot of getting used to," said Michael. "It'll be awhile before I can switch over to a cane but I'll be there before you know it. I'll sit here a bit and then go for another walk."

Michael worked very hard for the next few weeks. He got discouraged a few times but he kept at it. By the second week of March, he could get around with the cane. He moved slowly but he was confident. It would still be awhile before he was dancing.

~~~~

While Michael was in Abilene healing and learning to walk with his new leg, Orry Carpenter was in Osage land healing from his shoulder wound. He had healed well during the first month. He was strong now and could do just about everything. He decided that it wasn't proper for him to be in the same house as Laura and not be married, so he moved into John Littletree's house. He helped John with whatever was needed, and he also helped out at Laura's house. He had stayed with them for a month and felt obligated to pay them back. In his spare time he courted Laura. They would be married in the spring. Several people got together and helped build them a small cabin.

Dawn and Jesse had been busy themselves. Dawn was fairly certain that she was with child. She had missed her last two times and she was having some morning sickness. Both of them were excited about their new edition. Jesse had been staying in touch with Sean at least once a month by telegram. Orry had gone with him every trip to the telegraph office. They hadn't had any trouble. Sean informed them that all was quiet in Abilene, but Sean asked Jesse if he would come to Abilene in the late spring so he would be there when the cattle drives started arriving. Jesse replied that he would be there by the end of April.

CHAPTER TWELVE

The rest of the winter was mild. Michael was doing very well and could move around without much trouble. There had not been even one fist fight in "Maggie's Place" the whole winter. There had been one small altercation in one of the other saloons, but it was just an argument over who would buy the next round. A couple of punches were thrown, but the men throwing the punches were so drunk that they missed their mark.

It was early spring now. The railroad spur and the cattle pens were done. Everyone in town anxiously awaited the cattle herds that would soon be arriving. Down in Texas, Jug Carter was just about ready to start the drive. He had three thousand head of cattle on his ranch and intended to start the drive with two thousand. As soon as the branding was done in another week, they would move out. Josh and Wayne were very good cow hands and were also good judges of men. Jug had himself a good crew. Besides himself, Josh, and Wayne, there would be twelve other men and a wrangler on the drive. Lolita would be doing the cooking. Jug also had another six good men who would take care of the ranch in their absence.

Finally the branding was done, and they were ready to start the drive. Jug had a talk with everyone the evening before they left. He wanted to make sure the men knew what they were getting into. "Men, I know you are all good cow men or you wouldn't be here," Jug Started. "This drive'll take two months'r more. You'll be in your saddles from daylight till dark. Then you'll be takin' turns on nighthawk. You go ta sleep on nighthawk and get somebody hurt'r killed, you'll have me to answer to. They'll be no fightin' amongst ourselves. Any man pulls a gun on someone and he's fired. If someone shoots another man, I'll hang'em on the spot. Now we'll be fightin' mother nature, border gangs, and mebbe some Injuns. I don't 'spect any a you men ta be heroes. Any time you see somethin' or think you see somethin' that could be trouble, you get to me. Don't be firin' your guns lessen I tell ya. We don't need no stampedes. Lolita'll be doin' the cookin' so you'll be well fed. Now there won't be no other women out there. Most likely we won't see no more women till the drive's done. You men've been good around my wife, and I'm sure you will be out on the trail, but if one a you gets outta line out there, I'll hurt you bad. And I mean bad. I expect every man that starts this drive to be there when we finish. Nobody gets any pay till the drives done. Any man who quits is on his own. You'll get no supplies from me. Any man who steals from me'll meet his maker when I catch up to him. Anybody got any questions?" No one said a word. "Well boys, get as much sleep as you can tonight and be ready to move at daylight," said Jug. "Have yourself a dream about that bonus money I'll be givin' you if we get a good price in Abilene."

Jug and Lolita didn't sleep well that night. Jug kept tossing and turning and this kept Lolita awake. After about an hour of this, Lolita rolled Jug onto his back and sat on top of him. "What is it darlin'?" asked Lolita. "A big man like you shouldn't be worried about this drive. That's what you're thinking about, isn't it?"

"Yep it is," said Jug. "I know I got good boys and such and been on plenty a drives, but this'll be one long drive. Plenty a bad things could happen out there."

"Bad things can happen anywhere," said Lolita. "We could have had trouble with rustlers and Comanche down here but we didn't. You're a good man Jug, and you have a good crew. We'll probably have some kind of trouble out there, but we'll handle it. We always do. Now, since we're both awake we may as well make the most of it." Jug didn't neet any coaxing.

They moved out at dayhlight. It wasn't long and the herd was stretched out and moving at a nice pace. The weather was perfect for the first week. It rained during the second week but it didn't storm. It rained several hours during the day but not during the night. None of the streams that they had crossed had been swollen, and no cows were lost during the crossings. Near the end of the third week, the man riding drag thought he had seen some Indians following the herd so he eased his way toward the middle of the herd where he knew Jug would be. Jug saw him coming and waited for him to catch up. He was a young colored man, and he seemed to be shook up. His name was Billy Blackburn. He rode up to Jug. "We got some Injuns follerin' us," said Billy. "They know I seen'em but they're stayin' back. Maybe they're hopin' some cows'll stray off and they can get'em."

"Well you ease on back to the drag. I'll get Pedro and see if maybe we can talk with'em," said Jug.

"Why would you need Pedro?" asked Billy.

"Well Billy, some a these Indians out here speak Spanish," said Jug. "Probly more of'em know Spanish than they do

American. Let's hope they're Kiowa. I'm in good standin' with them. I'd say they was Kiowa. If they was Comanche, you wouldn't be here talkin' to me. Now ease on back and keep your eyes peeled." Pedro Martinez was at the middle of the herd. He could speak perfect English.

"We're gonna go see what them Indians want," said Jug. "Billy says some been follerin' us for a spell. "Yer not afraid a Indians are you Pedro?"

"I'm not afraid of them," said Pedro. "But you won't see me setting down to dinner with any Comanches."

"Well I'm hopin' these is Kiowa," said Jug. "I know one a their Chiefs." Jug and Pedro eased their way to the back of the herd. They could see four Indians a few hundred yards back. Jug could see that they weren't wearing any paint. He and Pedro rode up to them. The Indians stopped and waited on them.

"Any a you speak American?" asked Jug. The four Indians all looked at each other. Then Jug had Pedro speak.

"Habla Espanol?" said Pedro. One of the Indians spoke right up.

"Ask him what tribe they are," said Jug. "If they say they're Kiowa, ask'em if they know Bear Claw." The Indians were Kiowa, and Bear Claw was their chief. They said that Bear Claw wanted to have council with them. "You go tell Wayne and Josh that I'll be gone for a spell while I meet with Bear Claw and ta keep the herd movin'," said Jug to Pedro. "Tell Lolita too. She knows Bear Claw and won't be worried. Then get back here. You'll be translatin' for me." Pedro did as instructed and came back to Jug. They followed the four Kiowa to their village. It was a two hour ride. Bear Claw was sitting in front of his lodge when they rode in. He recognized Jug right away. Jug went straight to him. "It's good to see you again my friend," said Jug. "I hope all is well with you and your people." Pedro translated.

"I can see that you are doing well," said Bear Claw. "All is not well with our people. There are just too many white people. The buffalo hunters are slaughtering our herds. I do not understand how a man can kill our buffalo and just take the hides and tongues and leave the meat to rot. They have no respect for what the great father has given us. If we kill the buffalo hunters, then the blue soldiers and the rangers hunt us. Sooner or later there will be a great war to drive the white men from our land. Many of us will die fighting, but we would rather die honorably than to starve to death. Now that the big war to the east is over, more and more blue soldiers come. The buffalo are usually here this time of year but they have not come. My people are hungry. We would like some of your cows. We just need enough to last us till we find the buffalo herds again. They must be farther to the west. Our band is small and we will not need many."

"You helped me when I needed it so I will be glad to help you out," said Jug. "Will fifty head be enough to get by?"

"That is very generous," said Bear Claw. "We will be able to dry plenty of meat for our journey."

"Tell you what else I'll do for you," said Jug. "If you run into any other white folks out here, they'll be convinced that you stole them cows. I'm gonna write you out a bill of sale."

"What is a bill of sale?" asked Bear Claw.

"Well white folks is big about seein' things in writin'," said Jug. "To some folks, the writin' means that somethin' really happened."

"So you mean that to some white men, a man's word is not good enough," said Bear Claw. "It must be written down for other white folks to see."

"Somethin' like that," said Jug.

"I will never understand white people," said Bear Claw. "A man's word has always been good enough for the Kiowa. If everything has to be written down, wouldn't that make you go crazy?"

"It can make you crazy if you let it," said Jug. "Anyway, I'm gonna write down on this piece of paper that I sold you those cows. It will say that for the price of fifty cows, you let me graze my cows on your land. My name will be on this piece of paper. If anyone questions you about those cows, you show them this piece of paper. Tell them I took a herd to Abilene if they want to see me."

"You are a good man Jug Carter," said Bear Claw. "I do not understand this writing, but you have our thanks. The children will not be hungry tonight. Are you still with that woman who was with you when you came to us before?"

"Yes I am," answered Jug. "She is with the herd. She's our cook too."

"She is a fine looking woman," said Bear Claw. "She will give you many handsome children."

"Yes she will," said Jug. "Now I better be gettin' back. We'll cut out them cows when we get back. I'll have a couple men drive'em back toward your village. Now these cows is Texas longhorns. They're wild and can be nasty sometimes. Tell your men to be careful."

"We have been stealing cows in Texas for many years," said Bear Claw. "There are so many of them on some of the ranches down there that the white men don't know for sure how many they have. My braves can handle the cows."

Jug and Pedro went back to the herd and the fifty head were cut out. Jug had Perdo and another man drive them back toward Bear Claw's village. They were less than half way to the village when several braves met them and took the cattle. Pedro and the other man got back to the herd right before dark. Not one man questioned why Jug gave fifty cows to the Kiowa. That night after the men were fed and Jug and Lolita were bedded down, Lolita asked Jug some questions about Bear Claw. "Did Bear Claw remember you from before?" asked Lolita.

"Yes he did darlin'," answered Jug. "And he remembered how good lookin' you are. He said you would give me many handsome children."

"Well maybe after this drive we can get started on that," said Lolita. "So how are things with Bear Claw's people?"

"They're probably like most of the tribes out here on the plains," said Jug. "There's too many white folks and more comin' all the time. They want all the land. Don't matter who was here first. The buffalo hunters are slaughtering the buffalo herds. Bear Claw's people are hungry because the buffalo herds that usually come over this way are probly farther west now. That's why I give'm them fifty cows."

"You know Jug, our ranch was probably Comanche or Kiowa land at one time," said Lolita. "Should we give it back?"

"That's a good point," said Jug. "I don't know where to draw the line. Do you tell all them white folks comin' west that they can't come out here? Your folks was Mexican. The Spanish came to Mexico a long time back and run off the local Indians. The ones they didn't run off they turned into slaves and such. And they forced their religion on'em. Then the Mexicans had a revolution and run off the Spanish. So now the Mexicans run off or fight with the local tribes. I guess the French went to Mexico a while back and tried to take over. There's still fightin' goin' on there now. I don't know the answer. I guess some folks always been tryin' to force their ways on other folks ever since people been around."

"Jug, maybe someday you should run for a public office," said Lolita. "Sounds to me like you really care about people."

"I do darlin'," said Jug. "Now let's quit talkin' and have our way with each other."

~~~~

The next day they moved out at daylight as always. Jug was at the point talking to the lead man. "I'm goin' up ahead aways and make sure that stream up ahead isn't up," said Jug. "I mighta rained upstream. Be back shortly." Jug was gone about a half hour when he came across fresh tracks from another herd of cattle. The tracks were at least two days old. The other herd had been moving just west of them and was a day ahead. "Well we won't be the first herd to Abilene," Jug said to himself. "I s'pose there could be more up ahead of us too." Jug moved on till he came to the stream. It was not high and the other herd had crossed easily. He went back to the herd and found Wayne. "We'll bed down this side of the stream and cross in the morning," said Jug. "That other herd is two days ahead of us."

"Do you reckon that'll hurt us price wise?" asked Wayne. "First herd'll probly get the best price."

"I reckon I don't think it'll make any difference since this shippin' by rail outta Abilene is just gettin' started," said Jug. "I'd say them slaughter houses and meat packers are beggin' fer beef. It'll be a long time till someone hollers that there's too many cows."

"Hope you're right Jug," said Wayne. "I'll let the boys know we're beddin' down this side of the stream. Maybe some a the boys'll take a bath. I know I'm gettin' a little ripe."

Several of the men did take a bath. Some of them even washed their clothes. That night after they were sure everyone was asleep but the nighthawk, Jug and Lolita slipped into the stream and took a bath. They almost got caught by the nighthawk but they were able to get close to the bank and hide behind some brush. "I feel like a school girl who's out skinny dipping and almost got caught by her father," whispered Lolita.

"Well it'll be a good while before that nighthawk comes back this way," said Jug. "Let's not waste any time." Jug laid out the blanket they had brought with them and they wrapped themselves together. They finished and got back to the wagon before the nighthawk was back again.

It took a while to cross the stream but it wasn't long before herd was stretched out and moving at a good pace. They had been moving for a few hours when the point man spotted something ahead. He made his way to Jug at the middle of the herd. "There's a bunch a buzzards circlin' up ahead," said the point man. "There's a whole bunch of 'em. Gotta be somethin' dead'r dyin' not far ahead." Josh was with Jug and Wayne was not far from them.

"You get back to the point and keep the herd movin'," said Jug. "Me'n Josh'll ride ahead and see what's up there." Jug and Josh took off at a gallop. As soon as they got to the head of the herd they saw the buzzards. They moved ahead for another half mile. Josh spotted something first.

"Looks like there's a dead horse up there," said Josh.

"I see it too," said Jug. "Let's go over there slow like. Have that pistol a yours ready just in case. No tellin' what's over there." Jug and Josh both had their pistols out and ready as they approached the dead horse. When they were maybe fifty yards from the horse, they could see a man's foot just behind the horse. They dismounted and approached the dead horse. The horse had been shot in the neck. There was a dead man on the other side of the horse. He had been shot in the back of the head. His boots were missing and it looked like someone had gone through his pockets. He wasn't wearing a pistol belt and if he had a hat, it was missing. The saddle and bridle had been taken off the horse. "Tie these horses," said Jug. "We'll look and see if there's any more dead men around." It wasn't long and Jug found another body. This one had been shot two times in the back. His boots were gone and he had no pistol belt. He also had no hat and someone had gone through his pockets. Jug was looking again when Josh let out a yell.

"Jesus Christ," yelled Josh. "What in the hell could do that to a man? He's just ripped all to pieces." Jug came over and looked down at the dead man.

"That was a shotgun," said Jug. "It had ta been sawed off really short. Look at them burns. Whoever shot'm was no more'n three feet from'm. That fella's one sick son of a bitch. We'll keep lookin'. There's bound ta be more of'em." Jug was right. They found six more bodies. "We'll get these fellas buried when the herd catches up to us," said Jug. "Looks ta me that some rustlers killed these men and took their herd. Josh, you head back and tell'em we'll be stoppin' long enough ta bury these boys." Josh had just started back when Jug thought he heard someone's voice. He kept his pistol in his hand and stood quietly. He heard the voice again. It was a very low whisper. Jug walked to where he heard the whisper. There was a man laying in the brush. There was blood all over his chest and blood coming from his mouth. Jug went to him and dragged his body over to a tree and put his back against the trunk so he could set up. The man tried to speak and finally got out a word.

"Rustlers," he gasped. "Killed us and took the herd."

"Easy now mister," said Jug. "I'll get you some water." Jug went to his horse and returned with a canteen and gave the man a drink.

"I'm Don Johanson," the man gasped. "That was my herd. We had twelve hundred head. They come on us when we just got done eatin' our supper. Don't know how many they was. I got hit early and crawled off. I know you can't help me mister, but would you get word to my wife. Send a telegram to Ft. Worth, and they'll get it to her. Her name is Sandy."

"I'll do better than that Don," said Jug. "Your herd's headin' ta Abilene just like my herd is. My good friend Federal Marshal O'Rourke lives in Abilene. When we get closer, I'll work my way around your herd and get myself into Abilene before they get there. My friend don't take kindly to murder and rustlin'." Jug could tell that Don didn't have much longer to live. He could barely set up without help.

"I heard one a them call someone Brownie, and I swear I saw a Pawnee brave with'em," said Don. "That might be of some help. My brand is a simple DJ." Don took a couple more hard gasps and then died. Josh was back with some of the men and some shovels.

"I see you found another one," said Josh.

"Yeh, he wasn't quite dead yet," said Jug. "Said his name was Don Johanson and they had twelve hundred head. Rustlers come at'em right after they ate supper. Killed'em and took the herd."

"We gonna do anything bout that?" asked Josh.

"Yes we are," said Jug. "When we git closer ta Abilene, I'm gonna git around that herd and git inta Abilene before they do. Sean'll be ready for'em."

"Reckon we can git any of'em hung?" asked Josh.

"We will if there's any of'em left alive when we get done with'em," said Jug. "Somehow I don't think they'll be any hangins. Men like that don't give up. Ya gotta kill'em outright. Now let's get these men buried and git movin'."

That night when they were bedded down, Lolita and Jug had a serious talk. "You're going to help Sean kill those rustlers aren't you?" Lolita asked Jug.

"Yes darlin' I am," said Jug. "Them rustlers killed ten men and took their herd. That coulda been us instead a them. Men like that gotta be stopped, or they'll do it again and again thinkin' they can get away with it. Don't you worry darlin'. I'll make sure it's them that get killed and not me."

"Quit trying to reassure me that everything will be all right and kiss me," said Lolita. Jug obliged her.

The next week on the trail was fairly quiet. It rained for a couple of days and there was even some lightning and thunder, but the herd behaved well. One of the days after it had rained, the point man spotted a lot of unshod pony tracks. He brought Jug up to the front of the herd to take a look at the tracks. Jug studied the tracks as best he could. "I'm no expert at this but I'd say there was maybe thirty of'em," said Jug. "Looks like they might be follerin' that herd ahead a us. I'd say they was Comanche or

Cheyenne. Just guessin' a course. I figure since we already seen some Kiowa, these tracks weren't made by no Kiowa. I'll be ridin' point now. You ease on around the herd and tell the boys ta have their guns ready. Tell Lolita ta keep that scattergun beside her on the wagon." The point man did as instructed and the herd moved on. After another four hours, Jug saw that the unshod pony tracks broke off from the cattle trail and headed northwest. "They been follerin' the cattle trail hopin' to hide their tracks," Jug said to himself. "Wonder what they're up to now. Probly figurin' on doin' some raidin' somewhere." That evening when they set up for the night Jug let everyone know that the pony tracks had gone off to the northwest. "I still want you boys ta keep alert tonight and tomorrow," said Jug. "They might just be circlin' back to hit us."

Nothing happened that night. They had been moving for about two hours the next day when the point man came riding back to the center of the herd looking for Jug. "Got a bunch a riders comin' our way from the west," he said. "Looks like mebbe a troop a cavalry."

"I guess I'll ride out and meet'em," said Jug. Jug rode out to meet the oncoming riders. It was a troop of cavalry. It was something Jug had never seen since the war. It was a troop of colored cavalry. A Captain was at the head of the column and his 1st Sergeant was with him. Jug waited for the Captain to stop the troop and then approached him. "Howdy Captain, can we help you with anything out here?" said Jug.

"I am Captain Pierce and this is 1st Sergeant Carver," said the Captain. "We are Troop C with the 10th Cavalry."

"Well Captain, I'm Jug Carter from Texas," said Jug. "Now can we help you with anything?"

"Some Comanche war parties have been raiding up this way," said the Captain. "But we haven't found any sign for a while."

"Well Captain, we come across some unshod pony tracks yesterday," said Jug. "They was follerin' the cattle trail and then broke off to the northwest. I'm guessin' there was mebbe thirty of'em. You foller the cattle trail south, you'll come across their tracks."

"My thanks to you Mr. Carter," said the Captain. "We'll be moving out now."

"Hey Captain, before you take off there's mebbe somethin' you should know," said Jug.

"And what would that be?" asked the Captain.

"That herd a cattle that's just ahead a us is a rustled herd," said Jug. "They killed all the men and rustled the herd. We found one a the men still alive and he told us what happened before he died."

"I wish I could help you Mr. Carter but that is a civil matter," said the Captain. "We have orders to pursue, kill, or capture the hostiles who have been raiding. I'm sure when you get to Abilene, Marshal O'Rourke will take care of the rustlers."

"So you know Sean O'Rourke?" asked Jug.

"Yes, I know him," said Captain Pierce. "He's a good man. 1st Sergeant Carver knows him too. It sounds like you know him too."

"I was a deputy of his for a while," said Jug. "He gave me a stake so I could go to Texas and start a ranch. You know Captain, we'll be settin' up camp for the night shorty. You and your men can set up with us for the night if you want. You can get a fresh start in the mornin'. Them horses a yers look like they could use a rest."

"You're right about the horses," said Captain Pierce. "We've been pushing hard."

"Well if them is Comanche you'll never get close to'em ifn' ya don't push hard," said Jug. "Them Comanche'r some tough sons a bitches. They'll ride a horse till it won't go no more and then make it go some more. After it dies, they'll eat it and then steal another one."

"Yes I've heard all kind of stories about Comanche," said Captain Pierce. "And I'm beginning to believe most of them."

"Well let's quit jawin', and you and your men come on over to our wagon," said Jug. "My wife'll be makin' some good eats for supper tonight. We butchered a steer the other day. Probly a long time since you and your men had any beef."

"Yes it has been a long time," said Captain Pierce. "We been eating hard tack and salt pork for a good while. Anything different'll be a good treat."

"Well get your horses taken care of, and we'll have us some coffee while we're waitin' on supper," said Jug. The soldiers got their horses taken care of and some sentries were posted. The coffee was ready, and they all sat around and relaxed. Jug introduced the Captain to Lolita. "Captain Pierce, this good lookin' woman is my wife Lolita," said Jug. "She's one hell of a cook too."

"I am pleased to meet you Mrs. Carter," said the Captain. "I hope the trail is not too hard on you."

"As long as Jug is with me everything seems easy," said Lolita. "So do you have a wife Captain?"

"No, I am a bachelor," answered the Captain. "I was engaged once but it never worked out. She decided she couldn't be a camp follower. I guess it was best to find that out before we got married instead of after. Her folks never liked me anyway."

"Some folks are like that," said Lolita. "No one is ever good enough for their daughter. Now please excuse me and I'll get back to work."

"So Captain, how do you like commandin' colored troops?" Jug asked the Captain.

"I'll tell you Mr. Carter," started Captain Pierce. "So far, these are the best troops I've ever commanded. They put any white troops I ever had to shame. Now we have not had an engagement with any of these Indians out here yet, but I'm sure they will do well. Some of my men fought in the war. 1st Sergeant Carver was with the 54th when they assaulted Fort Wagner."

"Was you in the war Captain?" asked Jug.

"Yes I was. I seen the elephant more times than I wish to remember," answered the Captain.

"Sean used to talk once in a while bout a colored deputy he had," said Jug. "I believe his name was Jim O'Rourke and he was in the 54th till he went into the cavalry. Sergeant, did you know Jim?"

"I surely did," answered 1st Sergeant Carver. "He was my Platoon Sergeant till he went to the cavalry. He was a good man. He was best friends with another Platoon Sergeant named Jesse Strong. Them two together was somethin' ta watch under fire. Never seen nobody like them. Their men woulda followed'em to hell. Sure wish I coulda seen Jim before he got killed. Mebbe I'll see Jesse some day. He was the strongest man I ever did see. I seen him pick up reb soldiers clear over his head and thrown them off the wall at Fort Wagner."

"Sounds like a good man to have on your side," said Jug. "So Captain, how'd you come ta know Sean?"

"I was in the 7th Cavalry," started Captain Pierce. "Custer had sent a telegram to O'Rourke and asked him to scout for the cavalry. O'Rourke told'm no so Custer sent me and another officer to Abilene to see if we could talk O'rourke into changing his mind. We got into a little scrape with him. Wasn't much of a scrape. That other officer and I got our asses kicked."

"So how did you end up with these colored troops?" asked Jug.

"Custer wasn't too happy about us not being able to convice O'Rourke that he should scout for us," said the Captian. "Custer didn't like it when other officers spoke their minds, which I did, and he told me to get myself out of his unit. I did and here I am."

"I never met Custer but I heard about him," said Jug. "They say he was a glory huntin' son of a bitch. They say he was the youngest General in the Union Army, and his men followed him anywhere he went."

"Yes, he was the youngest General," said Jug. "And yes, his men did follow him. He always led the charges. Most officers that did that got themselves killed. Somehow, he didn't. Custer's luck I reckon."

"Well these Indians out here aren't soldiers like the soldiers you know," said Jug. "They're fighters, but they're not gonna line up and let you shoot at'em. You'll find all that out. Custer will too. If he don't, his luck'll run out."

It wasn't long until food was ready. Captain Pierce and his men said that it was the best meal they'd had since they left home. The soldiers bedded down that night with their bellies full. They were up the next morning and on the move at daylight. "My men and I thank you for your gracious hospitality," said the Captain. "Good luck to you for the rest of your drive."

"You're most welcome," said Jug. "Now you be careful if you come upon them Comanche."

"We will," said the Captain. The troop mounted and took off.

It wasn't long and the herd was moving again. They would push a little harder today and maybe tomorrow. Jug wanted to stay no more that a day behind the rustled herd.

CHAPTER THIRTEEN

Buck and Bud Slaughter were holed up just outside of a small town in Arkansas just across the border from Missouri and not far from "The Nations." They had been there for a good while. The law in Missouri had been giving them a hard time because of their whiskey operation. The problem wasn't because they were making illegal whiskey. The problem was that the local law wanted a bigger cut of the operation. Some of the local lawmen in Missouri had mysteriously disappeared. They had no problems in Arkansas. Business was booming, and the clan did some rustling too. The local law had married into the Slaughter family. The local Sheriff was a young man. He married one of Buck's granddaughters. He had one deputy who also married one of Bud's granddaughters. There was no regular judge in the county. There was a Circuit Judge who came through every so often. The Judge liked his whiskey and he became good friends with the Slaughters.

When Pearl Hawk was killed in Kansas, Buck and Bud swore that they would have their vengeance. They bided their time and waited. Chester, Buck's oldest son, and Butch, Bud's oldest son, were convinced that their Pas were going to forget about what happened to all of their kin. They just couldn't believe that they didn't ride out to Kansas and kill everyone who had anything to do with their kin's death. They didn't know their Pas as well as they thought. The Slaughters don't forget anything and always deal out any punishment that they deam proper. They fully intended to kill O'Rourke, his deputies, and their women. It may take a while, but it would be done no matter the cost.

The next year, Bud's sons Jeremiah, Gabby, and a cousin of theirs were sent to Kansas to kill O'Rourke. When word got back that Jeremiah, Gabby, and their cousin was dead, Bud's oldest grandson Chance and three others were sent out. The four of them killed one of O'Rourke's deputies and his woman but they had gotten themselves killed.

Buck and Bud both knew that the cattle drives to Abilene would be starting soon so they sent three of Buck's sons, Nate, Jethro, and Mathew to Kansas and "The Nations" to gather a herd. They figured that it wouldn't be a problem for some plain looking cowboys to slip into Abilene and kill O'Rourke if other plans failed. In the meantime, they had Chester and Butch hire some reliable hired killers.

When Buck's son Buster found out that Chance and his troop had been killed and hung, he came up with a plan of his own. His plan failed. Buck never found out that Sean had given his son to Cheyenne Dog Soldiers.

Bud's grandkids, Sara and Tobey, were next to make a try. They got themselves killed but managed to badly wound one of O'Rourke's deputies. Two of their cousins were killed that day too. Bud's son Buford and two others were killed when they were sent to finish the job on the deputy.

When word got back that Nate, Jethro, and Mathew had been killed, Buck and Bud both went into a rage. Couldn't any of their offspring get the job done? They were raised better than that. It was winter now, but come next spring, Buck and Bud would go to Kansas and take care of O'Rourke and his bunch themselves. The only thing that would stop them was if the killers hired by Chester and Butch got it done before they got to them.

~~~~

It was a mild winter but there was an influenza epidemic. Several people in the county died. The two granddaughters who had married the local lawmen and their infant children died. Bud's wife Goldie died. Bud had gotten pneumonia. Several members of the clan had gotten sick but had recovered. Bud fought the pneumonia for almost a month before he died. Buck was determined to go to Kansas even if he had to go by himself. As winter wore on and on, Buck's hatred grew and grew.

In the early spring Buck sent Chester and Butch back to Kansas. They were to get back with the hired killers and rustle a herd. If the killers wanted more money, that wouldn't be a problem. They could keep all the money from the sale of the stolen cattle. That should make them rich men. They would still be expected to kill O'Rourke and his bunch. Buck would be waiting for them in Abilene. Chester and Butch took most of what was left of the male population over the age of sixteen with them when they left. There were eight of them all together. Once a herd was rustled, they would send a rider to Abilene with a letter for Buck telling him when to expect the herd in Abilene. They would leave the letter at the Post Office under the name of Jim Davis.

Buck kept one grandson with him. Buck didn't have the stamina to ride a horse for very long. He would be going to Kansas in a nice looking carriage. Buck figured an old man and his grandson in a carriage wouldn't arouse any suspicion. The day before he was to leave, one of his granddaughters, Alice, decided she was going with them. Ruby begged and pleaded with her but she made up her mind that she was going. "They done killed my brother Chance and my Pa," said Alice. "I know Sara got killed but someone's gotta make sure them sons a bitches get what's comin' to'em. I'm goin' and that's that." Alice's mother never said a word one way or the other. She had become very withdrawn since they found out that Jethro had been killed.

They packed plenty of food and water for the trip. They would take three horses on the trip. One would pull the carriage. One would be a pack horse, and Tommy would ride the other one. The horses would take turns pulling the carriage. They would take plenty of guns and ammunition. Buck wore one Colt on his right hip and had a smaller pistol in a shoulder holster. His grandson, Tommy, wore a tied down Colt. Tommy was only fifteen but he was pretty much full grown. He also had a Winchester rifle on the pack horse. Alice kept a .32 in her purse and had a derringer hidden somewhere in her under garments. They had two double barreled shotguns with them in the carriage. They were 12 gauges and one of them was sawed off. Everyone had extra shells on them and there was plenty more on the pack horse.

When they were ready to leave for Abilene, Ruby stood on the front porch of the house and spoke her mind. "You're intendin' ta git this whole famly kilt you old fool," Ruby began. "You and that stupid brother a yers bit off more'n you could chew when you got into it with that O'Rourke fella. That man's a killer. That's what he does. He's good at it. The onliest folks this clan ever kilt was folks that weren't lookin' fer it or got shot in the back. Pearl's dead. Gettin' your whole clan kilt won't bring her back. There, I spoke my piece. Now git the hell outta here and go git yerself kilt. Don't 'spect me ta be here if by some miracle you make it back."

"Woman if I see that big ass a yers again, I'll be kickin' it out the door a my house when I git back," yelled Buck. "Good bye God riddance you ole bitch." Ruby shook her head and went in the house. Buck said giddap and the carriage pulled away.

~~~~

Two days later, Ruby and the remaining members of the clan loaded up wagons and headed back to Missouri. They still had the old family homestead and that's where she was headed. She wouldn't have any trouble with the law. If she did get back in the whiskey business she would do her best to make sure the local law was satisfied.

~~~~

The trip to Abilene was uneventful. It had rained on them one day but had quit by night fall. When they got to Abilene, Buck put the carriage and the horses at the livery stable. He got them rooms at a boarding house and registered under the name Jim Davis. He told everyone he was traveling with his grandchildren and they would be meeting some relatives who were on one of the cattle herds coming up from Texas. He checked at the Post Office when they had arrived in Abilene but there was no letter yet. On his way back to the boarding house he saw Jim Stewart in the street. He saw that Jim was wearing a badge too. He was sure that Jim had seen him, but there was no reaction so Buck figured that Jim hadn't recognized him. When Buck got back to the boarding house he told Alice and Tommy about seeing Jim Stewart. "I just seen Jim Stewart out there on the street," said Buck. "He's a distant cousin to the Hawks from back in Missouri," said Buck. "It didn't look like he knew who I was. He was wearin' a damn badge too. That means he's one a O'Rourke's men. Sombitch wore blue durin' the war too. It'll be a pleasure killin' him too."

"You reckon he'd know who we are?" asked Alice.

"He might, but I doubt it," said Buck. "If he's seen you, it was a long time back. Mebbe when the war first started. You two growed up some since then. Yer looks have changed some too. Ifn' you run into'm on the street and he says anything to you or asks who you are, tell'm your name is Davis and you gotta git back to yer grandpa. Don't be havin' no long converstion with'm. Alice, yer a good lookin' girl. Young boys'll be wantin' ta flirt with ya. Flirt all ya want but don't be sayin' nothin' bout yerself'r yer family. Let them boys do the talkin'."

"I know how ta handle boys," said Alice. "Most of'em don't have sense enough ta pour piss outta a boot. I'll be all right."

"So what are we gonna do with ourselves while we're waitin' for the herd ta git here?" asked Tommy.

"We'll just be takin' it easy," said Buck. "This might be one a the few times in yer life that you don't got a bunch a chores ta be doin'. While we're waitin', we'll figure out who's who in this town. We need to know what O'Rourke looks like and who his men are. We need to know who their women are too. I hear that O'Rourke's woman is a beautiful redhead. She won't be hard ta spot. We know that one a O'Rourke's men got wounded too. Maybe we can spot him too. I'll do some askin' around and see what I can find out. Don't you two be gettin' nosey. I'll be doin' that."

~~~~

The next morning when they were eating breakfast at the board-ing house, Buck struck up a conversation with the woman who owned the place. "Pardon me ma'am, me and my grandkids are new in town," began Buck. "Is there any law in this town? I did see a young man wearin' a badge yesterday. Is he the law here?"

"He's just one of Sean O'Rourke's deputies," said the owner. "Sean's other deputy got his left leg shot off a while back."

"So is O'Rourke the law in town?" asked Buck.

"Sean O'Rourke is a Federal Marshal," said the owner. "We really don't have any local law here yet. Sean just happens to live here in Abilene. Him, his wife, and his deputy Michael are part-ners in that saloon just down the street aways. It's called "Maggie's Place." Michael is the one that got his leg shot off. Why'r you askin' me all these questions? You seem awful inter-ested in the law around here."

"I didn't mean to sound that way ma'am," said Buck. "It's just that we're meeting some relatives who are coming up from Texas with a herd. We heard it'll take a couple months'r more ta get here from Texas. Them cowboys'll be wantin' ta blow off some steam and could get a little rowdy. I'll be worryin' bout my grandkids if them boys git ta shootin' off their guns and such."

"I think a lotta folks in town'r worried bout that too," said the woman. "Some'r worried about the rowdiness but others are lookin' forward ta makin' some money off them boys. Them boys won't git too rowdy in "Maggie's Place." They make'em check their guns and knives or they don't git in. They don't put up with no fightin' either."

"That's good to know," said Buck. "Mebbe one a these days no one'll hafta carry a gun."

"I hope that too," said the woman. "Probly won't see that in our lifetime though."

"Well ma'am, thank you for the good breakfast," said Buck. "Me and the grandkids got a few things to do now. We'll see you at supper." They excused themselves and then went to Buck's room. "You two can walk around town today and see what you can see," said Buck. "Remember, don't be sayin' nothin' bout your family. I'm just gonna set on some sidewalk and read a newspaper if this town's got one. Then a little later I'll pay that saloon a visit. I'll leave my guns back at the room." Alice and Tommy took off and Buck went looking for a newspaper to read. He found the newspaper office. There was a stack of newspapers outside on the sidewalk and a can that had a note on it that said 5 cents. Buck put 5 cents in the can and went looking for a chair to sit on. He found a chair in front of the Leather Goods store. Jason was outside sweeping the sidewalk. "Pardon me sir, would you mind if I sit in that chair there and read my paper?" Buck asked.

"No sir, go right ahead," said Jason. "I'm Jason Hunter and this is my store. And you are?"

"I'm Jim Davis," said Buck as he extended his hand to Jason. They shook. "I'm here with my grandkids. We're meetin' some relatives who'r sposed ta be with one a them herds comin' up from Texas."

"Well the first herds should be showing up before too long," said Jason. "Towns been waiting a long time for this. That McCoy fella's gonna be a rich man soon."

"Who's McCoy?" asked Buck.

"He's the man that talked the railroad into coming to Abilene," said Jason. "Not sure what kind of deal he made with the railroad, but I'm guessing it'll make him a lot of money. It'll help them ranches down in Texas too. They can finally get their herds to the slaughter houses."

"You might make some money off the Texas boys too," said Buck. "That stuff you got in yer window looks like good stuff."

"Thank you," said Jason. "Me and my son made all that stuff. My boy's learning the trade real good. Well please excuse me, I have some chores inside to take care of. Nice meeting you."

"Nice meeting you too," said Buck. The paper was only six pages. Buck sat down and started reading. The whole front page was about Cheyenne and Sioux raiding parties to the west and how the army wasn't having any luck trying to subdue them. The rest of the paper was about the town and how it had grown in such a short time. There were a lot of advertisements on the last page. Buck decided it was time to visit "Maggie's Place." He walked in the front door and stopped and read the sign about turning in weapons. He looked all around and then went to the bar. Tom waited on him.

"Name's Tom. What'll you have?" said Tom. "Take a seat anywhere if you want, and I'll bring it to you."

"Thanks, name's Jim," said Buck. "I'll have a glass a rye. I'll just sit down at this table right behind me." Buck sat down and Tom brought him his drink. Buck paid him and Tom returned to the bar. Over to Buck's right was a big one legged man playing the piano. A woman was sitting beside him on the piano bench. "That's gotta be that deputy named Michael," Buck said to himself. Buck looked over to his left. Jim Stewart and a woman was sitting there with another man and a red headed woman. "That's gotta be O'Rourke and his woman," Buck muttered to himself. Then Buck noticed the painting of Maggie on the wall. "Jesus Christ," Buck said to himself. "Women didn't look like that when I was a young buck. Damn she's a looker." Tom could see that Buck couldn't take his eyes off the painting.

"That's Maggie," said Tom to Buck. "That painting don't do her justice either. That's her over at that table there. See for yourself." Buck didn't say a word. He just looked over at Maggie.

"I can't be lookin' at no woman that looks like that," said Buck. "Just even thinkin' bout a woman that looks like that'd kill me. I'm not ready ta die yet." Buck finished his drink and then had another one. He saw Jim looking at him a couple of times but he was still convinced that Jim didn't recognize him. He finished his drink and then left. Jim was watching him as he was leaving.

"That old timer sure looks familiar but I can't place'm," said Jim to Sean. "I know I've seen that face somewhere."

"It'll probly come to you," said Sean. "This town'll be overflowin' with people when the first herds get here shortly. Probly be several people show up that might look familiar. We got three saloons in town now. I bet we'll have more shortly. They'll be puttin' up tents and bringin' in more women. Them Texas boys'll have all kinds a choices on where to spend their money. I'm goin' outside and look around a bit. Maggie, I'll be back shortly. Jim, you go make some rounds of the town." Sean went outside and stood on the sidewalk in front of the saloon. He looked throught the window and could see Michael playing his piano. The he thought to himself. "If I was gonna shoot Michael I could shoot right through this window and shoot him in the back," Sean thought to himself. "In the dark, a shooter could do it without being seen. I'm movin' that piano." Sean went back inside and went straight to Michael. "We're movin' your piano," said Sean. "We're puttin' it back in the corner and we're gonna turn it so your back's not facin' the window."

"I guess that would be wise," said Michael. "All this time it's been settin' there like that, and we never thought about it."

"Well we're thinkin' bout it now," said Sean. "That things heavier'n hell. I'll get Tom and Cookie to help move it." Sean rounded up Tom and Cookie and they got the piano moved. They put it at an angle so Michael could still see what was going on in the saloon but the piano still gave him some cover if someone decided to take a shot at him. Sean went back outside and decided to walk around town a bit. Not many people were out. A young man was walking down the street. Sean stopped and watched him for a while. Sean had never seen him before but there were a lot of people in town now that Sean had never seen. This young man was wearing a tied down Colt. The young man knew that Sean was watching him. He walked right up to Sean.

"Is there something I can do for you Marshal?" Tommy asked Sean. "I seen you watchin' me."

"I watch everbody," said Sean. "Goes with the job. I see you got that Colt tied down. You're kinda young ta be a gunman."

"I'm fifteen," said Tommy. "How old you gotta be ta be a gunman?"

"I reckon there's no set age," said Sean. "Most men don't tie down their pistol unless they're expectin' ta be drawin' it quick like."

"Well rest easy Marshal," said Tommy. "I'm no gunman. I just tie my gun down cause I'm kinda skinny and I don't like ta feel it floppin' around on my leg. I reckon I don't really need ta wear this thing in town. I always wear it when I'm out workin' somewhere."

"So what's your name young fella?" asked Sean.

"Name's Tommy Davis," answered Tommy. "Came here with my Grandpa and my cousin Alice. We got some kin we haven't seen for a long time. They're s'posed ta be comin' here on one a them cattle drives."

"Well it won't be long and some a them herds'll be showin' up," said Sean. "Hope your kin's not a rowdy bunch. Some a them boys'll be wantin' ta blow off some steam after two'r more months on the trail."

"Well I haven't seen them since I was real little," said Tommy. "Don't know if they even drink'r not."

"Well hope you don't hafta wait too long on your kin," said Sean. "I gotta go talk to someone now. See you around." Tommy gave a nod and they went their separate ways. Sean went to Jason's store. Jason was inside straightening up."

"Mornin' Sean, what can I do for you today?" said Jason.

"Nothin' really," said Sean. "I just came over ta remind you that you're still the Justice of the Peace in town."

"I didn't forget Sean," said Jason. "Why'd you come over to remind me about that?"

"Well Jason, in the absence of any other local law in town, you're the local law," said Sean. "Them Texas boys'll be here shortly. I don't think you should do too much Justice of the Peacin' lessen it's absolutely necessary."

"That's what I was figurin' too," said Jason. "I figure it'll take a little while ta see what them boys'r gonna act like once they get ta town. I'm hopin' most of'em'll behave."

"I reckon we'll find out soon enough," said Sean. "Well I'm goin' back to the saloon now. See you later."

As Sean was walking back to the saloon, he passed an attractive young girl. He tipped his hat to her and went on. He had no idea that this young girl was Alice Slaughter. Alice had really been enjoying being in town. She had met several young men and was on her way to meet one now. She had met him earlier in the day when he was working at his father's store. He convinced her that they should meet later for a walk. His name was Frank Hogan and his father owned a new general store in town that had just opened. They met in front of the store and started their walk. They went all around town and then went out of town. They were about a half mile out of town Frank was conviced that it would be a good time to steal a kiss. They were walking and talking and he stopped and pulled her to him and kissed her. She didn't object so he kissed her again. This time the kiss was longer. She still had no objections. Frank felt very confident now. He kissed her again but his time he slipped his right hand down on her backside and put his left hand on her right breast. He thought he was doing good and then he felt something pushing against him down below. He pulled back and looked down. Alice was holding a derringer and had it right against his privates. "What in the hell is that?" yelled Frank.

"Just what do you think it is Franky boy," said Alice.

"But I thought ----. We were----. You been leadin' me on," yelled Frank.

"I let you kiss me Franky boy," said Alice. "That don't give you permission to put your hands all over me. When I want someone's hands all over me, I'll let'em know. Now git. I can walk myself back to town."

"I wouldn't walk you back ta town if you paid me you bitch," said Frank as he started back to town.

"Don't be name callin'," said Alice. "I'm pretty good with this thing." Frank never said another word. He took off running and probably ran the rest of the way to town. Alice put the derringer back into hiding and started back to town. When Frank got back to town, he spotted Sean on the sidewalk in front of the saloon.

"Marshal, Marshal. That crazy bitch pulled a gun on me," gasped Frank.

"Slow down and git your breath boy," said Sean. Frank took a few minutes and got his breath back.

"I took that bitch for a walk and she pulled a gun on me," said Frank.

"First off, I don't think you should be callin' her a bitch even though I have no idea who you're talkin' bout," said Frank. "And somehow I doubt that she pulled a gun on you for no reason. Now just who in the hell'r you talkin' bout?"

"It's that new good lookin' young girl that's been walkin' round town," started Frank. "Just got into town the other day. I met her at my Pa's store and later on we were havin' a walk."

"So all you did was go on a walk and she pulled a gun on you," said Sean. "That's hard to believe. C'mon, tell me what you done."

"Well I kissed her," said Frank.

"So you kissed her and she pulled a gun on you," said Sean. "Are you sure that's all you done?"

"Well my hands did move around some on her," said Frank.

"Sounds ta me like she didn't want your hands all over her," said Sean. "Lucky she didn't shoot you."

"She had that thing stuck right against my privates," said Frank.

"So it is a good thing for you she didn't shoot," said Sean. "Now look boy, you be nice to a girl and she'll be nice to you. Treat her like she don't wanna be treated and she'll sure as hell let you know. I'd say she sure as hell let you know she didn't want handled like that. Now git away boy and go do some growin' up." Frank mumbled something to himself and left. Maggie had seen Sean out talking to Frank and asked what it was all about when he went back into the saloon. "Oh, that boy put his hands on that new girl in town," said Sean. "He put'em where she didn't want'em and she stuck a gun in his privates."

"Good for her. He got what he deserved," said Maggie. "I think I've seen that new girl around town. She wasn't carrying a purse. She must have had her gun somewhere else."

"Well women got all sorts a places to hide things," said Sean. "Speakin' a which, how bout we go upstairs and check out some a your hidin' places." Maggie didn't say a word. She grabbed Sean by the arm and they went to their room. While they were busy in their room, a rider came into town and went to the Post Office. He left a letter for Jim Davis and then was on his way.

The next day Buck went to the Post Office and got the letter. Chester had let him know that they had rustled a herd and should be in Abilene in another week. There was one herd ahead of them. When they got to town they would get together and come up with their plan to kill O'Rourke and his bunch. Buck got with Alice and Tommy and gave them the news. "We got a week to kill before they git here," said Buck. "That's plenty a time to learn all we can bout the whole bunch of'em. I need you two ta be on your best behavior. Alice, I heard bout you and that boy. Don't be pullin' no guns on nobody. Just tell them boys if they're horny they can use their hands." Alice let out a laugh. "Boy, I know you talked to that Marshal," said Buck. "I reckon he seen that tied down Colt a yours. Don't be wearin' it anymore till I tell ya."

"I already told'm I probly wouldn't wear it anymore in town," said Tommy. "And when's everybody gonna quit callin' me boy?"

"When yer full growed," answered Buck.

CHAPTER FOURTEEN

Down in "The Nations," Laura and Orry had gotten married and were sort of on their honeymoon. No one saw them at all for the first week. On the second week they came out of their cabin briefly to take care of any necessaries and went right back inside. It was the same for the third week. It was getting to be the latter part of April, and Jesse would be going to Abilene to help out Sean. Orry got it in his head that he should go too. Of course Laura didn't want Orry to go. "We just got married, and you want to go traypsin' off with Jesse and probably play lawman," said Laura. "You just healed up from that arrow, and now you wanna go get bullet holes in yourself. I'm too young to be a widow."

"Look Laura, Jesse's my friend and he might need my help," said Orry. "If he went by himself and somethin' happened to'm, I couldn't live with myself. You got to understand."

"I understand but I don't like it," said Laura. "If you're dead set on goin' I expect you ta bring me back somethin' nice from that town. Don't matter what it is just so it's nice."

"I'll do that," said Orry. "I reckon we're leavin' in the mornin', so we best make the most of our time."

Jesse and Orry left the next morning right at daylight. They took plenty of food, water, arms, and ammunition. They took two extra horses with them. One of them was used as a pack horse. It took them a week to get to Abilene. The weather had been good and they didn't have any problems. Jesse hadn't said a lot to Orry about him coming along but when he did say something, he let him know that he should have stayed with his new wife. There was no arguing at all. Jesse just spoke his piece and that was it. It was morning when they got to Abilene. They went to the livery and got their horses taken care of. They left most of their gear there and told Billy they would be back after it. Both of them wore pistols and they took their rifles with them. Jesse had his Spencer and Orry had his Winchester. When they got to the saloon, Maggie and Sean, Michael and Betty, and Jim and Sally were at their regular table drinking coffee. Sean spotted Jesse first and went over to him and gave him a hug and a handshake. "It's good to see you my friend," said Sean. "I'm sure everybody here is glad to see you." Maggie got up and gave Jesse a kiss on the cheek. Betty did the same. Jesse went to Michael and shook his hand.

"It's good to see you again Michael," said Jesse. "Sorry bout your misfortune. I'll make'em pay. Now I want you all to meet Orry Carpenter. I met him sometime back. He's helped me out some." Orry went to everyone and shook their hand.

"Jesse, you don't know this fella here," said Sean as he pointed to Jim. "This is Jim Stewart. He's been a deputy for a while now. He's helped me out quite a bit." Jesse extended his hand and he and Jim shook. "Well you men take a seat and have some coffee," said Sean. "I'll get us some more. We'll get us some breakfast too." After they ate, the women left and the men stayed. Jesse started the conversation.

"So is anything goin' on right now that you know of?" asked Jesse.

"We're just waitin' for somethin' ta happen," said Sean. "We got descriptions of two of them hired killers, and they got that Pawnee with'em. We'll know'em when we see'em. Spottin' that Pawnee'll be easy if he's still with'em. Jim here is from Missouri, and he's a distant cousin to the Hawks. He knows what a lotta them Slaughters look like, and he hasn't seen any of'em in town since them last ones got killed. I figure when them cattle herds git here they'll show up. They could be with a rustled herd or just be workin' as cowboys with a herd. They could just slip inta town when all them cowboys'r here. There'll be so many people in town that it'll be hard to watch for anyone who's wantin' to do harm. From now on, I don't want any of you goin' anywhere by yourself. Michael, don't let Betty go anywhere by herself. Jim, you been hangin' round with Sally. Don't let her go round town alone. Anytime one a you men gotta do somethin', another man goes with you. Goes for me too. Now I guess all we can do is watch and wait. Jesse, you and Orry can have the back room. We'll git another cot in there so you don't hafta sleep in the same bed."

"Orry and me'll go back to the livery and git the rest of our gear," said Jesse. "Be back shortly." When they got back to their room, Sean had already put the extra cot in the room.

"You go ahead and take the bed," said Orry. "You're a big man. I don't think you'd fit on this cot anyway."

"We can trade off if you want," said Jesse.

"No that's allright," said Orry. "If I get in that big bed by myself I'll be thinkin' too much bout Laura and won't be able to sleep."

"Suit yourself," said Jesse. "If you change your mind, just lemme know."

~~~~

The next few days were uneventful. The men remained vigilant. By this time, Buck and the grandkids knew about everything there was to know about O'Rourke and his bunch. It was easy to get people to talk when nothing was suspected. The barber was very helpful. They knew where Michael and Betty lived and which room at the saloon was Maggie and Sean's room. They knew about the bath house out back. They found out where Jim and Sally stayed. They found out about Jesse Strong and this new man Orry. Everybody had heard of Jesse. He was the colored man who shoved a bowie knife into a man's skull and the blade stuck out below his chin. They knew that Jesse and Orry stayed in the back room of the saloon. All Buck needed was for the boys to get to town, and they could wipe out the O'Rourke bunch once and for all.

~~~~

Jug Carter's herd was still a day behind the rustled herd. He figured that when he was four days from Abilene he would ride ahead and let Sean know. He made up his mind that Lolita would go with him. The men could do their own cooking for a few days. They grumbled a bit, but then Pedro came forward and told them that he could cook and they wouldn't be disappointed. He would do all the cooking if he didn't have to nighthawk. Everyone was agreeable to this. Wayne and Josh would be in charge in Jug's absence. When the herd got to Abilene, they would set tight till they got word from Jug.

When the herd was four days from Abilene, Jug and Lolita left the herd. The distance that the cattle herd took to go four days could be made by a man on horseback in less than two. It could be done in one day if he rode hard and had another horse. Jug and Lolita took two extra horses with them. He wanted to make sure they got to Abilene well ahead of the rustled herd. They would ride at a good pace but not so hard that they would have to worry about losing a horse.

After they got around the rustled herd, they soon found out that there was another herd ahead of the rustled herd. They made it to Abilene in a little over a day and a half. They went straight to the livery and then to "Maggie's Place." Sean was just starting out the front door. He almost ran into Lolita. "Oh my gosh, you made it," said Sean as he picked up Lolita and hugged her. Maggie saw them and ran over. Sean put Lolita down and gave Jug a hug and a handshake. Maggie and Lolita hugged each other. Betty came over and hugged her too. "Where's Michael?" asked Jug. "Isn't he here today?" Jug and Lolita didn't know what had happened to Michael. Michael was sitting at their table and yelled over to Jug.

"I'm over here Jug," said Michael. "I just don't get around as well as I used to. It's good to see you my friend. Lolita is still as gorgeous as ever." Jug and Michael shook hands, and Lolita gave Michael a kiss on the cheek.

"Well we got some important stuff to talk about," said Jug. "We best get down to business. I almost forgot about Jon. Where's Jon?"

"I'll tell you all about Jon when all the boys'r here. I'll get'em rounded up and we'll get started," said Sean. Sean rounded up

Jesse and Orry and then got Jim. They went to the regular table, and Sean got all of them a drink.

"Jug you've not met these other fellas," said Sean. "This fella to my left is Jim Stewart. He's been a deputy for a while. This great big man is Jesse Stone. He was my deputy sometime back. This other fella is Orry Carpenter. He's helped out Jesse some." All of them shook hands. "Now what have you got for us Jug?" asked Sean.

"Well the first herd to Abilene will be here tomorrow," started Jug. "Then the next day another herd'll be here. That herd is rustled. We come upon a bunch a dead men on the trail. We found one that was still barely alive. His name was Don Johanson. It was his herd. He had twelve hundred head. The rustlers hit'em right after supper. Don was hit early and crawled off. The rest a his men got killed. There was ten of'em total. He said he heard one of'em call another one of'em Brownie. He also said he swore he saw a Pawnee brave with'em. He asked me to get word to his wife. I promised him that I would and that I would let you know what happened. He said his brand was a simple DJ. That was about all he said before he died. My herd is a day behind the rustled herd."

"That is good news for us Jug," said Sean. "That Brownie fella is a hired killer. The Slaughters hired him ta kill all of us."

"Who in the hell'r the Slaughters?" asked Jug.

"They're blood kin to the Hawks," answered Sean. "They been wantin' ta get us ever since I killed Grammaw Hawk. Her maiden name was Pearl Slaughter. She had two brothers, Buck and Bud and they got a passle a offspring. Some of'em been tryin' for us for a while. We killed several already. More keep comin'. That's what happened to Michael's leg. Bud's grandkids come ta town and acted like respectable people. Nobody woulda thought they would do anything bad. They tried to kill Michaal and Betty. Michael and Betty killed'em but Michael took a shotgun blast. Four of'em ambushed and killed Jon and Martha Thanksgiving night. We got'em killed."

"What kinda man sends his grandkids out to do a killin'," said Jug.

"I'd say we'll be findin' out shortly," said Sean. "Now Jug, you and Lolita can have your old room back. Maggie and the girls'll make sure it's ready for you. Damn, it's good to see you. It's good that all of you are here. It's gonna get ugly around here in the next few days. Let's have us a toast. Sean filled all the glasses again. "Here's to not getting killed," toasted Sean. Everyone repeated the words. "Jug, you and Lolita go get settled in," said Sean. "I want all of us to meet back here for supper. We'll talk about how we're gonna handle things."

Supper time rolled around and when they were finished with their meal, the women excused themselves and the men got down to business. Sean started talking first. "Well boys, that rustled herd'll be here day after tomorrow," Sean began. "That don't mean they don't have people in town already. We got names and descriptions for two a them hired killers. One of'em is called George Washington Brown. They call'm Brownie or GW. He's a short skinny guy with long blonde hair and a white eye. Wears three pistols and carrys a Henry. He also has a cavalry saber that's been broke off and sharpened. Booby Lee Jackson is a tall man with black hair and sports a full beard. He wears a sawed off shot-gun on his right hip like it was a pistol."

"I seen his work," said Jug. "One a them dead men we found on the trail got shot up by him. He was ripped ta pieces."

"That Pawnee that's with'em goes by the name a Bighorse," said Sean. "I reckon that don't matter. We see a Pawnee, we kill'm. Now we don't know how many of'em there are out with that herd plus they could have more in town. I was thinkin' that me and one other man could go out and do some scoutin'. Jim and the rest of you will stay in town. Jim might recognize some a the Slaughters if they show up." Just then, Buck came into the saloon and went up to the bar and ordred a drink. Jim watched him closely.

"I swear I seen that old man before," said Jim. "I still can't place'm."

"Well he's been tellin' folks his name is Jim Davis," said Sean. "He's in town with two a his grandkids. That grandson a his was sportin' a tied down Colt when I first seen'm but he hasn't worn it since. That granddaughter a his packs a gun too. Young Frank Hogan put his hands on her in the wrong place. She stuck a gun in his privates."

"Maybe we better watch that bunch a little closer," said Jim. "Remember that young couple that tried to kill Michael and Betty. Everbody thought they was a nice young couple, but they was really Slaughters. I seen them two new kids around town, but I can't say as I seen'em before. Could be they was real little when I seen'em. They look a might different now."

"Well we're do our scoutin' and be back well before dark," said Sean. "That is unless we mess up and get ourselves shot or some-thin'." Sean was setting at the table so he could look out over the saloon and keep an eye on everything. He saw a familiar face coming toward him. "Bill Thompson, figured you'd be here when the first herds showed up," said Sean. "Got plenty a money with you?" There's three herds close now." They shook hands.

"I got plenty of money but I'm not the only buyer in town," said Bill. "There two more that I know of. They're over at one a my hotels now. So it looks like the whole town is excited about this. I hope them boys don't get too rowdy. I seen your sign about weapons. I doubt them boys'll like that."

"Well there's other saloons in town," said Sean. "They can go there if they want. Now I got somethin' important to tell you Bll."

"Well what is it?" asked Bill.

"The first herd'll be here tomorrow," started Sean. "The second herd'll be here the next day. It's a rustled herd. Them fellas bringin' in that herd killed the whole crew and took the herd a ways back. I intend ta kill'em or see'em hang. If somethin' would happen to me, a fella named Don Johanson owned that herd. His brand was a simple DJ. We give our word that we would git word to his wife and we intend to send her the money for the herd. How bout you tell them other buyers about the stolen herd."

"I'll do that Sean," said Bill. "They might not care who they pay for the cows as long as they get cows. They might be more concerned bout the cows than they are the previous owner. If they get cows, they make money, and the railroad makes money. You understand what I'm saying don't you Sean?"

"I do," answered Sean. "You tell them other buyers if they buy one steer with a DJ brand on it, I'll throw'em in jail for buyin' stolen cattle. I might even accuse them of bein' involved in the rustlin' and murder of Johanson and his men. Them are hangin' offenses."

"I think they'll see things your way when I tell them what you said," said Bill. "I believe I'll go tell them right now. I'll be seeing you. Tell your beautiful wife I said hello."

"I will Bill and thanks," said Sean. "Now boys, Jug and me'll be goin' out in the morning. Orry, consider yourself sworn in. You boys remember what I said. Nobody does nothin' alone. Always be in pairs. Jim, you keep your eyes peeled and let the others know if you spot any Slaughters. Don't take after'em yourself. Now if them Texas boys find their way here, make sure they know what the sign says. If they don't like it, there's other saloons in town. Don't take no crap off any of'em. Try to be polite if you can. Don't talk'em ta death either. Crack their head if you hafta. If you do crack a head, remember them boys may have friends around. Don't let nobody pull a gun on you. If you even think one of'em might pull on you, stop'em as best you can. Ole Jeb'll be there too. He can smell a gun or a knife on someone. If someone checks his gun and Jeb gets ta growlin' at'm, that fella's still got a gun'r knife on'm. Jeb's quick too. He can get a man's throat before that man can get his pistol pulled. Michael'll be wearin' his pistol and have a shotgun by the piano. I'll make sure Tom wears his pistol. Cookie'll have a rifle and pistol in the kitchen with him. Maggie'll have her pistols on her. We always have the shotguns at each end of the bar. Betty always has her pistol with her. We got enough firepower to wipe out a whole regiment if we have to. Now anybody got anything they think needs said?" No one did. "Well git your rest tonight," said Sean. "See you all at daylight."

No one stayed up late or did any drinking that night. Michael quit playing his piano early, and he and Betty were home before dark. Business at the saloon was slow so they closed up at midnight. Jug and Lolita had gone to bed early. Maggie and Sean could hear Jug snoring as they passed their door. Sean had stayed up with Maggie even though Tom was there. He was feeling a little frisky when they got back to the room. "You should go to sleep darlin'," said Maggie. "You might be busy tomorrow."

"How could anyone go to sleep with you next to them?" said Sean. That was all the coaxing that Maggie needed. An hour later they were sound asleep. Sean woke up before daylight and got dressed. Maggie woke up and started to get dressed. "You go back to sleep darlin'," said Sean. "You'll be havin' a long day yourself."

"All right darlin', I'll go back to sleep," said Maggie. "Don't be getting yourself shot. See you when you get back. I love you."

"I love you too Maggie," said Sean. "I'll do my best to keep from gettin' shot." Sean gave her a kiss, grabbed his gear and went downstairs. Cookie had come in early so he could make the men a good breakfast before they left. "Didn't expect ta see you this early," said Sean. "I was all set ta make my own breakfast. Looks like Barbara is sleepin' in today."

"She woke up and I told her to go back to sleep," said Cookie. "She didn't argue."

"Well today's the day," said Sean. "The first herd's comin' in today. We'll get us an idea how them Texas boys'r gonna act. Now you make sure you have them weapons in the kitchen. Let's hope they never need used."

"I don't figure there'll be any trouble to speak of today," said Cookie. "With only one herd comin' in there won't be that many of them. Shouldn't be no more that twelve or so. Now when we start having several herds here at the same time, that's when we'll have trouble. Anyway, I'm not worried about them cowboys today or even tomorrow. I'm worried about the fellas that's trying to kill you and your men. Any man sends his grandkids to kill folks has gotta be nothing but pure evil."

"You're right about that Cookie," said Sean. Jug came downstairs now.

"Mornin', hope coffee's ready," said Jug. "I gotta have my coffee first thing in the mornin' ta get goin'."

"Cookie's gettin' everything fixed for us," said Sean. "You got all your gear?"

"I got my Spencer and pistol and plenty of ammunition," said Jug.

"I got a Sharps for you and plenty a shells for it," said Sean. "We'll take plenty a water and food with us just in case. I'll have my spyglass too. There's a lotta open country out there." The other men started showing up now. Jesse and Orry were first. Michael showed up with Betty and Jim. The coffee was ready now, and they all had a cup. Cookie served Sean and Jug breakfast first. Then he started cooking for the others. Sean and Jug finished eating and headed to the livery for their horses. Sean told the men to take care as he was leaving.

They had ridden for a couple of hours when they came upon the point rider of the cattle herd. The rider noticed the badges on Sean and Jug right away. He rode over to them. "What can I do for you Marshal?" asked the point rider.

"Where's your foreman?" asked Sean.

"He's should be about halfway back," said the point rider. "We got'em stretched out purty good. He won't be far from the wagon I'd say."

"Thanks fella," said Sean. "And if you didn't know it, you're bringin' in the first herd to Abilene."

"We thought we was," said the point man. "Mebbe I'll git me some bonus money." Sean and Jug rode back to the middle of the herd. They went to the wagon and asked where the foreman was."

"That's him on that big black, Marshal," said the cook. "Is there some trouble or somethin'?"

"I just need ta have some words with'm. That's all," said Sean. They rode over to the foreman. "Name's O'Rourke and this is my deputy Jug Carter," said Sean.

"I heard a both a you," said the foreman. "My name's Thompson, Ben Thompson. I'm the owner and foreman. Now what can I do for you?"

"Well first off, your herd'll be the first herd to Abilene," said Sean. "There's buyers there waitin' on you."

"That's good," said Thompson. "I got 2000 head. Will them pens hold all of'em? "They made'em big enough ta hold 3000 head," said Sean."

"That's good. It's been a long trail," said Thompson. "I might not set a horse fer a week after this. Now what is it I can help you with?"

"Have you had any trouble from rustlers on the trail?" asked Sean.

"We had some Injuns try ta steal a few head," said Thompson. "We cut out a few head for'em and they left us alone. We had some problems with the weather. Lost one man durin' a stampede. But no, no trouble from rustlers or any border gangs."

"Have you got good men that you really trust?" asked Sean.

"These boys been with me since I started my ranch," said Thompson. "We fought Comanches, Mexican bandits, and land grabbers down in Texas. I trust these boys with my life."

"It's good that you have a good crew," said Sean. "There's a herd behind you. Belonged to a fella named Johanson."

"I know Don," said Thompson. "What do you mean they belonged to him."

"Rustlers killed the whole crew and took the herd," said Sean. "They don't think anybody knows it. Jug here's got a herd behind the rustled herd. He came upon the dead men, and they found Johanson just barely alive. He told'em what happened before he died."

"Sons a bitches," yelled Thompson. "If you need help gettin' them rustlers, me and the boys'll be glad to help you Marshal."

"You go ahead and get your herd in," said Sean. "When you get your business taken care of, take your boys over to "Maggie's Place." I'm part owner in that saloon. You'll see a red headed beauty there. That's Maggie and she's my wife. Tell her I said that you and your men could have a drink on the house. There's somethin' your men should know though. We make everyone check their guns."

"I don't know if my boys'll cotton ta that," said Thompson. "Us Texas boys feel naked when we're not heeled."

"We got plenty a girls too," said Sean. "Best lookin' gals in town. Tell'em if they feel naked they should go see them girls. They won't need their pistols when they're with them girls."

"I'll tell'em Marshal," said Thompson. "Now don't go gettin' yerself killed. Maybe I'll see you in town. Adios." Sean and Jug waved goodbye and moved out. Sean and Jug worked their way to the end of the herd.

"After we get past the end a this herd, we'll ride on till we come upon that stolen herd," said Sean. "We gotta be careful and not get spotted. If they are a day behind this herd, we'll be able to get back to town before dark. We'll head out in the night and maybe we can bushwack'em as they wake up in the mornin'. Should be enough moon tonight to see all right."

"I wish we knew how many of'em was in town," said Jug.

"So do I," said Sean. It wasn't long until they spotted the rustled herd. They headed back to town and were not seen.

When they arrived back in town, the last of the first herd was being put in the pens. They had already started loading the rail cars. Sean and Jug took their horses to the livery, and then went to the saloon. He rounded up everyone and told them his plan. "Boys, we're goin' out tonight," started Sean. "We'll find their camp and have at'em at daylight. Me, Jug, Jesse, and Orry will be goin' out. Jim'll stay here cause he might recognize someone. They don't know that we know they rustled the herd. They shouldn't suspect anything. I'll find the nighthawk and take him out. The rest of'em should be at the campsite. There shouldn't be more than ten or twelve of'em. We are not gonna yell at'em and tell'em ta give up or anything like that. We're just gonna start shootin' and kill'em all before they get a chance ta kill us. Anybody don't have the stomach for that speak up now." No one said a word. "Well try ta get as much rest as you can. We'll be pullin' out at 2am."

~~~~

About two hours later, Ben Thompson and his whole crew showed up at "Maggie's Place." He walked up to the bar, took off his gunbelt and laid it on the bar. His men followed him and put their gunbelts on the bar. Sean saw him and went over to him. "I see you made it here," said Sean. "Tell your boys to have a seat. We'll bring'em whatever they want."

"I figured we'd come here first," said Ben. "This way the boys won't be liquored up and not wanna give up their guns."

"They'll be glad they came here," said Sean. Maggie's girls were already starting to mingle with the boys. Maggie herself brought over some bottles and glasses. Those young cowboys were speechless when they saw Maggie. Ben was too at first and then he spoke.

"You gotta be Maggie," said Ben. "Sean was right. You are sure beautiful. You gotta be the most beautiful woman I ever did see." Then Ben noticed the painting on the wall. He looked at it. Then he looked at Maggie. "If that's you on the wall it don't do you justice," said Ben.

"Maggie, this is Ben Thompson and his boys," said Sean. "Their first drink is on the house."

"I'm pleased to meet you," said Maggie. "I hope you and your men enjoy our establishment."

"I'm sure we will," said Ben. "Sean said you had the best lookin' gals in town and from what I can see, he's most likely right. How's the food in this place? I'm tired a bacon and beans."

"We have the best cooks in town," said Maggie. "I'm not sure what they're fixing this evening but if you try it and don't like it, we can fix you a steak or some ham."

"I'll have whatever they got," said Ben. "I can eat bout anything."

"Someone'll bring you a plate shortly," said Maggie. "Now I must mingle with my customers."

Cookie brought Ben a plate and some fresh baked bread. Ben wolfed it down in about two minutes and asked for some more. "I guess you liked the food," said Cookie.

"Best I can remember eatin' for a spell," said Ben. "Don't know what it is but it sure eats good."

"Glad you liked it," said Cookie. "I'll bring another plate right away and some more bread."

"That fella's a mighty good cook," Ben said to Sean. "I might steal him and take'em back ta Texas. My wife can cook. We been together for fifteen years, and as you can see, I haven't gained no weight."

"Cookie and his wife Barbara both cook for us," said Sean. "I bet they could write down some recipes that you could take back to your wife. Barbara's half Mexican, and she makes some really good stuff sometimes."

"My wife is strictly a meat and taters woman," said Ben. "I been a cow man for a while now. I plumb forgot what chicken tastes like."

"Well when you get back, sweet talk her some," said Sean. "Let her know you'd like somethin' different but be nice about it. Maybe she makes the same stuff over and over because she thinks that's what you want. If you eat it and don't say nothin', she'll think it's all right."

"That might work," said Ben. "I reckon I'll find out."

"So how long you stayin' in town?" asked Sean.

"I'll be here one more day then head back," said Ben. "I told my boys they could stay as long as they wanted. They'd still have a job if they got down there in a month. I figure the one's that stay'll run outta money in two, three days. I give'em a bonus too, but with all these saloons and stores, they'll get it spent. I seen a leather goods shop. I might stop there tomorrow. My old saddle is about wore out."

"The fella that runs that store is Jason Hunter," said Sean. "He's a good man. He'll treat you right and give you a fair price."

"I seen a gun shop in town too," said Ben. "Some a my boys been wantin' them new Winchesters."

"Well that's Walter Black and he'll probly have some," said Sean. "He does all my firearm work for me. I got my conversion pistols from him. I got my big Sharps and my other guns from him too."

"I might get me one a them new pistols," said Ben. "I reckon it's nice not havin' ta worry bout wet powder and caps."

"It sure is," said Sean. "When I pull a pistol, I need to know for sure that it's gonna fire when I squeeze that trigger."

Ben ate his second plate of food and then told Sean he was going to knock around town and see what he could see. "I thank you for your hospitality," said Ben. "I don't 'spect my boys'll be any trouble tonight. They seem ta be happy here. Remember what I said. If ya need any help with them rustlers, me and the boys'll be glad ta help."

"I'll keep that in mind," said Sean. "If I don't see you again tomorrow, you have a safe trip back home."

"I thank you," said Ben. "Adios amigo."

~~~~

Most of Ben's crew stayed at Maggie's Place till around midnight. About that time they decided they would try another place while they still had some money. They kissed all the girls goodbye, got their gunbelts, and were on their way. There weren't any other customers in the place when the cowboys left so Maggie decided to go ahead and close up. Sean had gone to bed earlier and was sound asleep when Maggie came to bed. He didn't wake when she climbed into bed.

Sean woke up around one thirty and got himself dressed. Maggie was still asleep but he gave her a kiss on the cheek anyway. Jeb was at the foot of the bed as ususal. "Jeb, you look after Maggie while I'm gone," said Sean. "Don't let nothin' happen to her." The boys were already downstairs waiting on Sean. "Well let's get our horses and git this done," said Sean. "Looks like we got plenty a moon so we'll be able ta see good. You all got plenty a ammunition, right?" Everybody nodded their heads yes.

The street was completely deserted as they headed to the livery. There were no lights showing in the other saloons in town. "Them Texas boys quit early tonight," said Sean. "Must be savin' some money for tomorrow." Everyone got saddled up. They were moving in no time. It was a good night for riding. The moon was almost full, and the sky was full of stars. After a couple of hours, they spotted the smoke from a dying campfire. It was a quarter of a mile from them. There were some trees and brush just ahead to their left. "We'll head to them trees and brush," said Sean. "You boys'll stay here while I go take care a the nighthawk." They made their way to the trees and brush. Sean went after the nighthawk. He rode Billy slowly and pulled his jacket collar up around his neck. He talked low and slowly like he was talking to the cows. He even sang a little. If the nighthawk spotted him first, he would probably think that it was someone who was coming out to replace him.

It took Sean a while but he finally spotted the nighthawk. He had gotten off his horse to relieve himself, and Sean spotted him when he mounted his horse. Sean rode toward him. "Yer a might early," said the nighthawk. "I still got a couple hours yet."

"Couldn't sleep," mumbled Sean as he rode up to him. As he got next to the nighthawk, he pulled a pistol and before the man could react, Sean cracked his skull. The man fell from his horse in a heap. Sean dismounted and took out a knife and cut the man's throat. He left the body there and let the horse wander. Sean mounted and slowly moved toward the camp. He counted ten bedrolls around the fire. He could plainly see the Pawnee brave because the side of his shaved head glowed in the moonlight. Sean could see the long blonde hair of the one called Brownie and the black full beard of Bobby Lee Jackson. There was a makeshift rope corral for the remuda. Sean cut the ropes and let the horses wander. Then he went back to the other men. "I got the nighthawk," said Sean. "I cut the ropes on the corral they made for the remuda. There's ten of'em around the fire. I seen that Pawnee and Brownie and Bobby Lee Jackson. It'll be light enough ta shoot good in a couple hours. We'll spread out about ten yards apart and move to about fifty yards from'em. We'll tie the horses in these trees. They won't have no cover but their saddles and that wagon. I'll get over to our right so if anyone gets behind that wagon I'll have a clear shot at'em. Now let's move and move quiet. When we get there, we won't have much cover either. If there's no brush or anything where you stop, lay as flat as you can. Don't shoot till you hear me cut loose with the Winchester." The men eased up on the camp and waited.

It had just gotten light enough to shoot good when the Pawnee got up and went to relieve himself. He walked about ten yards from his bedroll and did his business. He started looking around. Something wasn't right. Orry didn't know if the Pawnee had seen him or if he had seen that the horses were gone. Orry was about to fire when Sean's Winchester barked. The Pawnee was struck in the head and hit the ground dead. When the other men sat up in their bedrolls to see what was happening, Sean and all of them cut loose. Four of the rustlers were struck on the first volley. Somehow, some of the rustlers had managed to get their pistols and were returning fire. Sean was working the lever on his Winchester as fast as he could. He saw Brownie trying to get behind the wagon, and Sean put three slugs into him before he fell. Jug and the rest of them were firing as fast as they could too. Sean was about to fire on Bobby Lee when someone else's bullet struck Bobby Lee's forehead. Sean emptied his Winchester and pulled a pistol and was about to fire when he noticed that it was quiet. Jug and the others were reloading but there was no fire coming from the rustlers. Sean yelled for the others to cease fire. He waited a few moment for the gunsmoke to settle down and then walked slowly over to the camp. Every one of the ten rustlers had been hit multiple times. None of them were breathing. The shootout was over in less than two minutes. Sean and his men had not been wounded. "Jesus H. Christ," said Orry. "They're all shot ta hell. I never seen nothin' like this."

"Better them than us," said Jesse.

"What'r we gonna do with these bodies?" asked Jug.

"Let's throw some stuff off that wagon and then throw them on," said Sean. "We should be able to round up some horses to pull that wagon ta town. That undertaker'll shit hisself when he sees this." Sean rounded up some horses for the wagon, and the boys loaded the bodies. They went through their pockets as they were loading them. Brownie and Bobby Lee both had several hundred dollars on them. The Pawnee had $200 on him. There wasn't $50 between the rest of them. They rounded up all of the rustler's weapons too. "I'm gonna keep Bobby Lee's scattergun. Might come in handy sometime," said Sean. "When we get ta town, I'll see if Ben and his boys'll take this herd on inta town." It wasn't long and they were on their way back to town.

CHAPTER FIFTEEN

Sean didn't know it, but Chester Slaughter had slipped away form the herd sometime during the night and was in town. He found out from someone at one of the saloons that the old man who called himself Jim Davis was staying at the boarding house. Chester had found his room and was sound asleep in a chair beside Buck's bed. When they woke up, Buck had Chester stay in his room while he and the grandkids had their breakfast. Buck would get something for Chester to eat and bring it back to the room. Buck had his meal and then went to a café and got something for Chester. Alice and Tommy went back to their rooms. Chester ate his food like he hadn't eaten for a month. "Didn't they feed you out on the trail?" asked Buck.

"We had plenty, but bacon and beans get old if ya eat it all the time," said Chester. "Now have you got us a good plan Pa?"

"I do son," said Buck. "I know where every one a his bunch lives. There's more of'em than we thought but that won't be no problem. We'll get'em tonight one at a time. We'll git that one legged deputy and his woman first. We'll be cuttin'em. Don't want no guns used till we get O'Rourke and his woman. He'll be last. Him and his woman got this real big ugly dog. They say he likes ta rip out throats. They say he bit a man's hand clean off once too. That dog sleeps in their room. One a his deputies is the biggest darky I ever saw. Him and another deputy sleep in a back room of their saloon. Another a his deputies and his Mexican woman stay in a room upstairs in the saloon. He's a big man but we'll get'm. Maybe one a you might wanna have yer way with the Mex before we kill'r. Now do you remember Jim Stewart?"

"Yeh, I remember him Pa," answered Chester. "He fought with them blue bellys."

"Well he's here in town, and he's one a O'Rourke's deputies," said Buck. "He might recognize you if he sees you. He's been stayin' with some whore named Sally. I know where too."

"It's been a long time Pa," said Chester. "I bet he don't remember me."

"Well you be careful and if you see'm out there, try not ta let'm see you," sid Buck. "Pull your hat down and your collars up'r somethin'. Don't look'm in the eye. I been here all this time, and he don't know me or Tommy'r Alice."

"Alice, what the hell is Alice doin' here?" asked Chester.

"Couldn't be talked out of it," said Buck. "She said O'Rourke and them gotta git what's comin' to'em. They done killed her brother and Pa. Now you git yerself back out to your herd. Tell the others that when they bring the herd in today to just act like reglar ole cowboys. They best not do nothin' to attract attention to themselves. We'll all get together after the herd is sold and everything. I'll let all a ya know what ta do and when ta do it. Now go on now Chester. I'll see you back here later."

"All right Pa," said Chester. "See ya in a few hours." Chester had put his horse in the livery when he had come to town. There was no one there at that time of night, so he put his horse in an empty stall and gave it a little grain and some hay. He left a note on the stall door. It said the following. "Got in late. Leevin' in mornin'. Pay you then." Chester pulled the collar on his jacket up and pulled his hat down low on his forehead and started for the livery.

Jim was at the saloon standing by one of the front windows and looking out into the street. He had a cup of coffee in his hand. Michael was at his piano trying out a new tune he had written. Betty was behind the bar cleaning glasses, and Maggie was still upstairs. Cookie and Barbara were in the kitchen getting ready for the day. Tom would be there in a half hour or so. Jim was talking to Michael as he was looking out the window. Then Jim noticed Chester on the street. He didn't recognize him at first. He thought hard on who that man was and then it came to him. He was sure it was Chester Slaughter. Chester was past the saloon now and walking away. Jim never said a word. He put down his coffee cup and pulled his pistol. He went out onto the sidewalk in front of the saloon. Chester was about fifteen yards from him. "Chester Slaughter," yelled Jim. "I know it's you. Stop or I'll shoot you." Chester kept moving. "Last warning Chester," said Jim. Jim cocked the hammer on his pistol but had it down to his right side. Chester stopped now. He started turning to face Jim. He was drawing his pistol as he was turning. Jim fired as soon as he saw Chester bringing the pistol around to fire. Chester was struck in the chest and thrown backwards but he didn't go down. Before Jim could fire again, Chester fired. Jim was struck in the left shoulder and the force of the bullet almost turned him sideways. As he was being turned, he managed to cock his hammer and fire another round. Chester was struck in the forehead and thrown backwards to the ground. Then Jim fell to the ground.

Maggie and Jeb were just coming down the stairs when she heard the shooting start. She ran the rest of the way down the stairs and grabbed the double barreled shotgun that was at the end of the bar. She already had two pistols on her. Michael had picked up the shotgun that he always kept by the piano and stayed at his piano bench so he could use the piano for cover if necessary. He told Betty to stay low behind the bar. Maggie and Jeb went out onto the sidewalk. Maggie had the shotgun ready. Jim was laying on the sidewalk and bleeding from his left shoulder. Jim looked up at Maggie. "That's Chester Slaughter out in the street," said Jim. "I believe he's killed." Maggie yelled for Cookie and Betty to help her get Jim inside. They got Jim inside and then Tom showed up. Maggie sent Tom after the Doc. Maggie kept the shotgun in her hands. She and Jeb went out into the street to see if Chester Slaughter was dead. Several people were on the sidewalk now trying to see what had happened. Chester was dead. The first shot should have killed him outright but somehow it hadn't. The bullet to his forehead had torn off the back of his skull. It was a few feet from him in the street and was covered with blood and brains. Maggie thought she might throw up but she didn't. She went back to the saloon.

Buck and the grandkids had also come a running when the shooting had started. They were on the sidewalk when Maggie had first come out of the saloon. Alice and Tommy wanted to run over to Chester but Buck stopped them. "You can't go over there," Buck said to them. "If ya do they'll figure out who we are. Jim Stewart's not dead yet. He'll put two and two together."

"That's your oldest boy layin' there dead in the street Grandpa," screamed Tommy. "Don't you feel nothin' right now. Don't you got no feelins'?"

"I got feelins' boy," said Buck. "But us goin' over there and gettin' dead isn't gonna get O'Rourke and his bunch dead."

"Well I'm gonna git some of'em dead right now," screamed Tommy.

"Me too," said Alice. Both of them went to their rooms and were back in a few minutes. Tommy had his Colt on and tied down. Alice was carrying the sawed off shotgun. When they entered the street, the people on the sidewalk had already started to disburse. Alice carried the shotgun in her right hand and let it hang down so it was partially covered by her dress. When they came to Chester's body in the street, they paused for a moment and then moved on.

In the saloon, they had taken Jim to the regular table and Betty was cleaning his wound and trying to get the bleeding stopped while they waited for Doc. Michael was still at the piano. Maggie had gone for some clean linen for bandages. It was in the storage room behind the bar. She still had the shotgun. Jeb was with her. Cookie and Barbara were back in the kitchen.

Alice and Tommy entered the saloon. They looked straight ahead and there was no one there. They looked to the right and saw Michael partially hidden by the piano. Michael saw them when they first came in and had the shotgun right next to him on the bench. Before Michael could say anything, Tommy pulled his Colt and was firing at Michael. Michael got farther behind the piano. Alice cut loose with the shotgun with both barrels and wood splinters from the piano went flying everywhere. Maggie and Jeb came running back when the first shot was fired. Tommy was firng at the piano hoping bullets would go through and get Michael. Alice was fumbling with the shotgun trying to reload it. Tommy was empty now and was reloading. Maggie aimed the shotgun at Alice and fired. Michael had seen they both were re-loading and he grabbed his shotgun, moved from behind the pi-ano a little and took aim on Alice and fired. The blasts from Maggie's and Michael's shotgun struck Alice at the same time. As soon as they had fired, Jeb had Tommy by the throat. It was over quickly.

When the shooting had started, Buck gave in and grabbed the other shotgun and his two pistols. By the time he got to the sa-loon, the shooting had stopped. He came into the saloon with the shotgun ready. He saw his grandkids dead on the floor and with-out a tear or a flinch, he spotted Maggie and starting taking aim on her. Maggie had seen Buck but didn't have her shotgun up and ready to fire. Michael had seen him and was ready. He fired the other barrel and Buck was thrown backwards. Before he hit the floor, Jeb was on him. Buck was probably already dead but Jeb tore out his throat anyway. Maggie dropped her shotgun on the floor and started crying uncontrollably. Then Betty started crying. Jeb got close to Maggie. After a few minutes, she quit crying and started hugging Jeb. Jeb licked her on the cheek as she hugged him. Jeb had blood all over his mouth so now Maggie had blood all over her face.

Tom finally got back with Doc. "Just what in the hell went on in here?" screamed Tom as he saw the dead bloody bodies. "That's an old man and those other two'r just children." Then he saw the blood on Maggie's face. "Maggie, are you hit?" asked Tom.

"No, that's not my blood," said Maggie. "Jim over there is the only one that needs medical attention. It's too late for these oth-ers." Jim stood up and walked over to Buck's body. Then he thought for a moment.

"I'll bet you a hunnerd dollars that this here is Buck Slaughter," said Jim. "Chester was his oldest boy. I bet Chester came inta town ta see him and was goin' back ta that rustled herd. I really can't recognize them kids. I'd bet they're grandkids."

"Well if you'll sit down now I'll take a look at your shoulder," said Doc. "Yep, you're lucky. It went clean through. Someone did a good job cleaning you up too. Not much more I can do now except bandage you up and tell you to take it easy." Doc bandaged Jim up and made him a sling to wear. "I'll check on you in a couple of days and make sure there's no infection. Now has anyone got ahold of the undertaker yet?"

"We haven't yet," said Michael. "But if he was in town, he should know by all that shootin' that he'll have some more business." The undertaker walked into the saloon just as Michael had finished talking.

"Who's paying for all this?" the undertaker asked.

"They are," said Maggie. "That old man hired some men to kill us. He should have some money on him or somewhere." Maggie went through Buck's pockets. There was $2000 in big bills and a couple of hundred in small bills. Maggie handed the undertaker $100. "That's way more than enough to get them three in the ground," said Maggie. "Now would you please get these bodies out of here as soon as you can."

"Yes Maggie. My help will get them shortly," said the undertaker as he turned and went out the door.

~~~~

When Sean and the men got back into town, The undertaker's help was just starting to remove the bodies from the saloon. They rode their horses right up to the saloon but left room for the undertaker's men. They left the wagon in the street. "Tell your boss there's a bunch more dead bodies in that wagon," said Sean. "Now would someone please tell me what the hell went on here?" Maggie heard Sean outside and went to him. She hugged him and kissed him several times.

"Jim believes that the old man was Buck Slaughter and them two young ones were his grandkids," started Maggie. "Jim spotted Chester Slaughter in the street. They had a shootout. Chester's dead but Jim got hit in the shoulder. After that shootout, we took Jim inside and was waiting for Doc when them two young ones came in and started shooting. Me and Michael and Jeb killed them. So are you and the boys all right?"

"Yes we are darlin', answered Sean. "We killed eleven of'em out there. It was quick and none of us got hit." Jug walked into the saloon and looked around.

"Where's Lolita?" Jug asked.

"She must be up in her room," answered Maggie. "I haven't seen her yet today."

"That's where she most likely is," said Jug. "I told her that if she heard any shootin' she was ta stay in her room, lock the door, and have a pistol ready. I'll go check on her." Jug eased upstairs and knocked on the door. "It's me darlin'. I'm back and in one piece," said Jug. The door slowly opened and Lolita was standing there with a pistol held low in her right hand. She dropped the pistol and went to Jug and hugged and kissed him till she was out of breath.

"I missed you Jug," said Lolita. "I prayed to the Saints that you would come back to me in the same condition that you left."

"I missed you too woman," said Jug. The he picked her up and carried her to their bed.

~~~~

When all of the bodies were removed from the saloon and the wagon load of bodies was gone, several of them got together and cleaned up the place as best they could. When they were finished, they all sat down for a drink. Jug and Lolita had finished and were downstairs now. Sally had heard that Jim had been shot and was there making over him. "What would you all like?" asked Sean. "Will it be Irish Whiskey or bourbon or both?"

"Let's start with the Irish and finish with the bourbon," said Michael.

"Sounds good to me," said Sean. "I'll round up some bottles and glasses for everyone." Sean was bringing glasses to the table when Ben Thmpson came into the saloon. "Come on over and join us," said Sean. "I need ta talk to you anyway. Don't worry bout that pistol. I know you're not gonna shoot anyone." Ben went to the table and had a seat.

"I heard a rumor that you got them rustlers kilt," said Ben.

"Yep, we did," said Sean. "That brings us to you. That Johanson herd is still out there. How bout you and yer boys bringin' it in. I figure it'd be the right thing ta do. Hell I'll pay you and your boys for your time. I got some money off them killers. When the herd gets sold, we'll get that money to Johanson's wife and tell'r what happened to Don and that we made things right."

"Sounds all right ta me," said Ben. "I'll have a drink with you and then see if any a my boys is sober enough ta get that herd in here." Sean made sure everyone's glass was filled.

"Here's to not getting killed," toasted Sean. "Everyone repeated the words and took a drink."

"Just what was that stuff I just drunk?" asked Ben.

"That was Irish Whiskey," answered Michael. "Smooth, isn't it."

"It surely is," said Ben. "A fella could drink too mucha that stuff if he wasn't careful. Well thanks for the drink. I'll go round up my boys." Ben gave a nod and left. No one said a word for a good while. Maybe five minutes later Maggie spoke.

"I hope all this killing is over for a while," said Maggie.

"I hope so too," said Sean. "Jim, I know you're a wounded man but I need you to get over to the undertakers and see if you can identify any of them other bodies before they get put under."

"I'll go over there after we have our drinks," said Jim. "Sally can help hold me up."

"I'm not goin' anywhere near no dead bodies," said Sally. "You're strong enough ta git over there by yourself."

"Just kiddin' Sally," said Jim. "I can move around all right."

"Well Jim, the first thing you're gonna do after you get healed up is go over to Missouri and Arkansas and find out who's left in that clan," said Sean. "We haven't heard a peep outta Bud Slaughter. He could be around here yet."

"You know you could get me killed if you send me over there," said Jim.

"Well we been tryin' ta git you killed out here and it hasn't worked yet," said Sean. Everyone let out a good laugh.

"All right boss, I'll go," said Jim. "I'll git on over to the undertakers right now before I git ta drinkin' too much." Jim had another drink and then went to the undertakers. All of the dead bodies were laid out behind the parlor. Jim knew he had seen several of these men back in Missouri but he wasn't sure of their names. He was sure that Butch Slaughter was one of the dead men. He went back to Sean and gave him the news. Butch

Slaughter is one a those dead men over there," said Jim. "He was Bud's oldest son."

"Well that's one less of'em ta worry bout," said Sean.

"I seen several a them others but I don't know their names," said Jim. "They gotta be kin to them Slaughters." Just as he finished talking, the woman who owned the boarding house came into the saloon and went straight to Sean.

"Marshal, that old man and those two youngsters were staying in my place," said the woman. "Their things are still in their rooms. What should I do with it?"

"Go ahead and take it out of the rooms and put in your lobby," said Sean. "One of us will be over and take it off your hands shortly."

"Thank you Marshal," said the woman. "It just gives me chills thinking about those three. They were so nice. Who would have thought that they would try to kill anyone. I thought that about that other young couple too. How am I going to know who I can trust to be a good and honest boarder?"

"Just always hope for the best," said Sean. The woman shrugged her shoulders and left.

~~~~

With all of them there at the table it didn't take long to finish the bottle of Irish Whiskey. They started on the bourbon. After a couple of shots of bourbon, Sean decided he would go over to the boarding house and get the belongings of Buck and the two young people. Jesse went with him. There were four small valises in the lobby. A Winchester was on the floor beside the valises. Sean and Jesse took them back to the saloon. They laid them on the table and started going through them. The one that belonged to Alice had some clothes and a .32 pistol in it. There was ammunition for it and some ammunition for another weapon that was not in the valise. Tommy's valise had another set of clothes and ammunition for his Colt and the Winchester. Buck's valise had a set of clothes and plenty of shotgun shells. There was also ammunition for his pistols. Folded neatly and laying at the bottom of the valise were two letters. One was from Bud Slaughter and addressed to Butch Slaughter. The other one was not really a letter but kind of a "Last Will and Testament" of Buck Slaughter. Sean read the one from Bud first. It went as follows.

Butch,

Now that yer Ma is ded and I will be very soon from this coffin sikness, you are the hed of the famly now. I spect you ta do yer duty and git O'Rourke and his bunch kilt. You always been a good son and I always been proud a you. I'll see you on the streets a glory.

Yer lovin Pa Bud

"Well it looks like Bud's no longer with us," said Sean. "Wonder why Buck had this letter and it never got to Butch."

"Only Buck knows that and he's dead," said Jesse. "Read that other thing." Sean unfolded it and started reading. It went as follows.

Last words of Buck Slaughter

Famly, if any a you are reding this it is cause I am ded. Since I am ded, O'Rourke better be ded to. If he is not, I wil come back from the grave and haunt al a you til you are ded. When I left Arkansaw Ruby sed she wuldn't be ther when or if I got bak. She most likely went bak to the homested in Missouri and took the rest a the clan with her. I loved that woman fer a lotta yeres but she culd be a mene bitch at times. Mebbe I'll see O'Rourke in hell.

Buck Slaughter

"Maybe you will Buck Slaughter," Sean said to himself. "Maybe you will."

Here ends The Sean O'Rourke Series, Book 4, *O'Rourke's Law or no Law at All*. Continue reading for a preview of The Sean O'Rourke Series, Book 5, *Quiet Times?*

The Sean O'Rourke Series
Book 5

Quiet Times?

by

Michael E. Cook

CHAPTER ONE

After Sean read the letters that Buck had in his valise, he asked everyone to come back to the table and join him. He filled everyone's glass again and told them to take a sip. Then he spoke. "I found two letters in Buck Slaughter's valise," Sean began. "One was from Bud and was addressed to Butch, and the other one was kind of like a "Last Will" and such from Buck. The one from Bud said that Butch would be the head of the family cause Goldie was dead and he was dying of the coughin' sickness. I reckon he meant pneumonia. Bud said that he was always proud of Butch and he expected him to get us killed. I have no idea why Buck had this letter and it didn't get to Butch."

"Well what did Buck have to say?" asked Maggie.

"He just said that if anyone was readin' this it's because he's dead and I better be. If I'm not dead, he's gonna come back and haunt all of'em till they're dead," Sean said. "Then he said that Ruby probly took the rest a the clan back to the old homestead in Missouri."

"Well maybe this'll be the end of it," said Michael. "Was there anything else?"

"Ole Buck said that maybe he'd see me in hell," said Sean.

"Well maybe we're all going after what we've had to do," said Maggie. "I do recall something about "Thou Shall Not Kill." We've been doing a good bit of that lately."

"I been tellin' some a the ones we killed that I'm sendin'em ta hell, but I don't really believe in hell," said Sean. "I seen too much ta make me believe that there's somethin' that could be worse than what happened in the country the last several years." No one spoke for a few minutes. The undertaker came into the saloon and made his way to Sean's table.

"Excuse me Marshal," started the undertaker. "I discovered this on the body of that young girl when I was getting her ready." The undertaker handed Sean a derringer. "It was in her under-garments. I thought you might want it. I have no use for it."

"Thanks for bringin' it to me," said Sean. "Sorry to give you so much business all at once but it couldn't be helped."

"A man in my profession must take business when he can," said the undertaker. "Maybe one of these days you'll have all this outlawry under control and I'll be forced into waiting on folks to die of natural causes. Now good day to you all."

"You know Sean darlin', I think that man really likes his work," said Michael.

"Well if he doesn't, he sure came to the wrong place to set up shop," said Sean. "Let's have another drink. I feel like drinkin' today."

"We'll stay right here with you," said Michael.

"I'll have another one with you and then I'm goin' back out to the herd," said Jug. "Lolita, you can stay in town while I'm gone if you want. Ben and his boys'll bring in that other herd yet today and ours'll be in tomorrow. You can spend another night on that nice soft bed."

"I'd rather spend the night with my husband," said Lolita.

"Well Sean, looks like me'n Lolita'll be leavin' shortly and be back tomorrow," said Jug.

"You got a good woman there Jug," said Sean. "We'll see you again tomorrow." Lolita and Jug finished their drinks, then rounded up their gear and headed back to the herd. The rest of them stayed at the table and drank some more. After another hour, Jim decided it was time to see Sally. No one at the table talked much. They all finished their drinks and Sean went to the bar for another bottle. He came back to the table and filled everyone's glasses. He looked at Orry and spoke. "How bout you tellin' all a us bout yourself," said Sean. "Jesse told us you helped him some and you sure as hell helped us some here. We wanna know all about you. Start from the beginnin'."

"Well I was born up in Maine," started Orry. "It can get mighty cold up there sometimes. Made it through the grades all right. I just turned 18 not long ago. I thought about joinin' up durin' the war but my folks wouldn't sign for me. One day this train come inta town and it was full a wounded soldiers. I never seen so many men without arms and legs. After that I give up all thoughts a runnin' away and joinin' up. When the war ended I decided I was gonna go west. I didn't have much money. I kinda worked my way as I went. This is all the farther I got. I met Jesse at the little town just north a Cherokee land. I was in this saloon havin' a drink when he come in. I was with this fella named Nate Slaughter. He hired me ta help move some cows. I never knowed them cows was rustled. Anyway, Nate picked a fight with Jesse and Jesse broke his arm. I never seen nothin' like it. Nate went for his Colt. Instead a drawing his pistol, Jesse grabbed Nate's arm and broke it. Then he set it for'm. Would you a done that? If a fella wanted to kill me, I surely doubt I'd set his broken arm for'm. Anyway, I showed Jesse where them cows was. There was a fight. Nate and two others got kilt. They was all Slaughters."

"So that was maybe the first time you was ever in a gunfight," said Sean.

"Yes it was," said Orry. "I never shot nothin' 'cept deer and other critters. Jesse told me that them deer don't shoot back. I stayed with Jesse when he went down to "The Nations" cause I didn't think I'd live too long if I was out there by myself. Jesse's wife introduced me to this good lookin' young girl. She was Dawn's cousin. She's my wife now."

"That was mighty quick," said Michael. "Must a been one a them love at first sight things."

"It wasn't that quick," said Orry. "When Jesse went out with John Littletree, Charlie Redhorse and I went with'em. We went all over the different tribe's land lookin' fer rustled cows and such. We didn't find nothin'. After Jesse sent ya that telegram, we was headed back when we come across them six killers. We had a scrape and I took an arrow in my left shoulder. Jesse got it out. We killed two a them Pawnee and them others high tailed it. We got down ta Jesse's place and I stayed at Laura's place for bout a month healin' up. Then I stayed with John Littletree. Me'n Laura got married bout three weeks before we come up here ta help out."

"You best git down there to your new wife," said Sean. "I don't reckon she liked it when you left."

"She didn't like it, but I told her Jesse was my friend and I needed to help my friend," said Orry.

"Well you sure as hell helped Jesse and us," said Sean. "Now you're our friend too. That wife a yours got herself a good man. What do you think Jesse?"

"He's got a ways ta go but he's gettin' there," said Jesse. "If he sticks around with the likes a us, we'll get all the rough edges off'm."

"So Jesse, when you figure on headin' back?" asked Sean.

"How bout I stick around till a few more herds come in?" asked Jesse. "Not all them Texas boys'r gonna behave as well as Ben Thompson's crew."

"One thing I do know," said Sean. "They'll behave in our place or they won't be in it."

~~~~

Ben Thompson and his crew brought in the Johanson herd that day. A telegram was sent to Don Johanson's wife telling her what had happened to her husband and that she would receive a bank draft for the herd. Ben and his men spent the night in town. All of them headed back to Texas the next morning. Later that morning, Jug brought his herd into town. He got a good price and gave his men a good bonus. He also informed them that if they wanted to remain part of his crew, they would behave themselves in town.

The first thing Jug did after he got paid for the herd was to go to Sean. He wanted to pay back Sean for the money he had given him to help start the ranch. Sean flat out refused to take the money. "Jug, I don't mean to insult you but I won't take your money," said Sean. "Things have changed some since you were here last. I got more money than I could spend in several lifetimes. I don't remember if I told you or not, but me and Maggie own "The Palace" in St. Louis now. Sam Draper had a lotta money in the bank when we took over. Sometime when we're settin' around havin' a drink, I'll tell you all bout gettin' that place."

"You know I'm gonna feel awful guilty about that money," said Jug. "It don't set right with me."

"Well Jug, take that money and git some more land and cows," said Sean. "Maybe you'll have the biggest and best ranch in Texas one day."

"I'd still feel guilty," said Sean.

"Well I'll tell you what Jug Carter," said Sean. "Whenever I'm havin' trouble with some bad outlaws or somethin' like that, you can come and give me a hand. You can consider that as payment."

"I'd do that anyway," said Jug. "You're my friend and friends always help friends."

"You're a good man Jug. I'm still not takin' the money," said Sean. "Now why don't you take that woman a yours and you two enjoy the hospitality of our tub. I'm sure she'd want to scrape off some trail dust. We can all have dinner together later."

"I believe we will," said Jug. "We'll see you later for dinner."

~~~~

After going to the bath house to clean up, about half of Jug's crew went to Maggie's Place and the others went to other saloons. The boys who came to "Maggie's Place" grumbled a little about checking their guns but they had themselves a very good time. Some of the boys were downstairs drinking with some of the girls and the others were upstairs with some of the girls.

Sean and Jug and the rest of Sean's men and their women were at their regular table having dinner, when one of Jug's men stumbled into the saloon and fell to the floor just as he cleared the door. He was beaten up and bloody. Jug saw him and ran over to him. Tom was behind the bar and brought over some water and a towel. Jug noticed that the man's holster was empty. Jug sat beside him on the floor and lifted up his head. He gave him a drink of water and wetted down his face. "What happened boy?" said Jug. "Who done this?"

"Crooked card game," said the man. "I spotted'em cheatin' and called'em on it. Before I could do anything, two big fellas was whoopin' the tar outta me. Don't member how I got back here."

"Would you know them two fellas if you seen'm again?" asked Jug.

"Yes I would," said the man. "A woman was in on it too. She was behind me and lettin' them others know what kinda hand I had."

"Well boy, as soon as you can stand, me and some a the boys'll go over there and put a hurt on them fellas," said Jug.

"You know them card sharps'll be expectin' some cowboys ta go back there and do somethin'," said Sean. "They'll be waitin' for ya. I'll tag along ta make sure there's no gunplay. I want you and your boys ta leave their guns here."

"We won't need no guns fer what we're gonna do ta them fellas," said Jug.

"I'll go along too," said Jesse. Jug, the beaten man, and five of Jug's men headed to the other saloon. Sean and Jesse both had on their pistol belts. When they got to the saloon, Sean asked Jug and his boys to wait outside for a minute while him and Jesse went in first and had a word with the people inside. Jug agreed. Sean and Jesse went just inside the door and stood. The place got very quiet. Finally the bartender spoke.

"What'r you doin' here Marshal?" asked the bartender. "You're not local law. There's nothin' goin' on in here that's any a yer business."

"Git that scattergun you got back there and hand it to me. Then keep your hands up on the bar where I can see'm and I mean right now," said Sean. The bartender did as instructed. "Now ever one a you that's carryin' a gun is gonna drop it on the floor now and kick it over ta me." There were twelve men in the place and not one man did as Sean instructed. "I can kill six a you before any a you can git clear a your holster," said Sean. "I got another pistol too. Jesse here's mighty good with his pistol too. Now I'm gonna count ta five. If I don't see no guns on the floor before then, I'm gonna start shootin'. Most a you know me and you know what I can and will do. Sean started the count. Before he got to four the guns were on the floor and being kicked over to Sean. "Jesse, you take these guns and set'em just outside the door. These gentlemen, and I use that term lightly, can get them back when Jug and his boys'r done." Jesse got all of the guns outside and came back inside. "All right Jug, bring in that man a yers that took the whoopin' in here," said Sean. Jug came inside with the beaten man. The man could barely stand. "All right now boy, which a these fellas'r the card cheats?" asked Sean. The young man pointed them out.

"That woman with the blonde hair over at the bar is the one who was in on it," said the man. "Ever one a these fellas in here needs their asses whipped. Not one of'em lifted a finger ta help me while them two was workin' me over."

"All right young man, I want you to go back outside while we sort things out," said Sean. "Tell them other boys ta come on in." The man left and the others came inside.

Sean walked over to one of the card cheats. "You know mister, it's been my experience that card cheats always have a hide out gun," said Sean. "Hand it over."

"I already gave up my gun," said the cheat. Sean pulled a pistol and stuck it on the man's forehead. He waited a moment, then cocked the hammer. The cheat reached into his pants and pulled out a derringer. Sean took it. "Now the knife," said Sean. "You boys carry knives too." The cheat pulled back his jacket sleeve exposing a long dagger. Sean took it from him. Sean moved over to the other card cheat. He didn't have to say a word. The cheat pulled a derringer out of his right boot and a razor from his pants pocket.

"You know boys, I don't think you can be trusted," said Sean. "You two git your clothes off. I wanna see you two in your drawers pretty damn quick or I'll give that boy you whooped this pistol and let him shoot holes in ya." The two stripped as instructed. "All right Jug, they're all yours," said Sean.

As soon as the words were out of Sean's mouth, Jug and his men were tearing into the card cheats. Jug had gotten in one good punch on each of the cheats and then he started on other men in the saloon.

"So you just sat on yer ass and let them cheats beat the hell outta my boy," said Jug. "Well mister, you got a whoopin' comin' too. Jug tore into whoever was in front of him at the time. One time a couple of men grabbed Jug's arms while another one hit on him but Jug got loose and took the two men and cracked their heads together. The two men went down and didn't move. Jug and his men were outnumbered two to one but it didn't matter. Jug and his boys made sure all of them took a beating. The woman who was with the card cheats tried to run out a back door but Sean caught her and held her with her arm behind her back.

"I'm not into abusin' women," said Sean. "But if you don't stand still, I'll break that pretty little arm a yours right off." The woman didn't struggle anymore.

Jesse was enjoying watching the fight. It was almost over now. Josh and Wayne were holding up one of the cheats against the bar and taking turns hitting him in the gut. The bartender had stayed out of the fight but Jesse saw him duck down behind the bar and come out with a small club. He was about to strike Josh when Jesse spotted him and fired a shot into the ceiling. All of the fighting stopped and everyone looked around to see what the shooting was about. Jesse spoke. "That bartender got himself a club and was gonna brain that boy over there," said Jesse.

Jug ran over to the bar, jumped over it and tore into the bartender. Sean let him beat on him for a while and then went over to the bar. Jug and the bartender were on the floor and Jug was on top of the bartender beating on him. "Ya think maybe he's had enough?" Sean asked Jug.

Jug quit hitting on the bartender. "I reckon so," said Jug. "I'm gettin' tired anyway. C'mon boys. Let's let these fellas lay here and bleed for a spell." Jug and his boys left and headed over to "Maggie's Place." The cowboy who was beaten found his pistol among the ones that Jesse had set outside and put it back in his holster. Sean and Jesse waited a few minutes before they headed to the door. Sean still had ahold of the woman. The bartender pulled himself up behind the bar.

"That damn rancher's gonna pay fer these damages," yelled the bartender. "He's gonna pay I tell ya."

"Bill Thompson is a good friend a mine you piece a shit," said Sean. "He won't like it that you let cheatin' go on in his place. He won't like it that you let them cheats beat on that boy and didn't do nothin' ta stop it. He's in this town ta make money and he knows them cowboys won't go to a place where they'll get cheated. I'd say you'll be lookin' fer another job after I tell'em what really went on here. And I'll tell ya somethin' else mister. If you even look cross eyed at me on the street I'll blow your damn head off." Then Sean looked around at the other men in the saloon. A few of them were still unconscious but some of them were starting to get up now. "Any a you others got anything you want ta say ta me?" said Sean.

"This was none a yer business Marshal," one of the men yelled. "You had no call ta interfere."

"I didn't interefere," said Sean. "I just made sure it was a fair fight and nobody got shot. Now choke it down mister. You just got yer ass kicked and you deserved it. Git over it." Sean went out the door and started to "Maggie's Place." "Just what am I gonna do with you darlin'?" said Sean to the woman. "If you was a man I'd beat you till you couldn't stand. I know. I'll take you to Maggie and see what she says I should do."

"Please Marshal, turn me loose," said the woman. "I was just tryin' ta make some money. I never knew they'd beat on that boy like that."

"Sure, and I'm the Prince a Wales too," said Sean. "Now you walk along nice and behave and I'll let go a your arm. You take off runnin', I'll tell them cowboys know where ya went and let them have at ya." The woman nodded her head yes that she would behave and Sean let go of her arm. Jesse was several feet ahead of Sean. They had walked a little and Sean noticed that the woman was easing back. Sean stopped and turned to face her. "You're gonna run on me aren't you?" Sean said to the woman. As Sean was looking at the woman, he heard someone running on the sidewalk. He looked back to see. It was the bartender. He was running toward Sean. He had a double barreled shotgun in his hands. Sean pulled a pistol but the woman was right in the way so he couldn't fire. He grabbed the woman to push her out of the way. As he was pushing her, the bartender stopped running and fired the shotgun. Most of the buckshot hit the woman in the back but a couple of pieces hit Sean in his right thigh. The woman was knocked to the ground but Sean was still standing. Before the bartender could get the hammer cocked on the other barrel, Sean put a bullet in his chest. He hit the ground dead. Sean looked down at the woman. She wasn't dead yet but probably would be shortly. Jesse ran to get the Doc.

It didn't take long to get the Doc but by the time he arrived the woman was dead. Several people had gathered in the street to see what had happened. One of them was Bill Thompson. "What the hell is goin' on Sean?" asked Bill. "How come you killed my bartender?"

"Bill, soon as the Doc gits this buckshot outta my leg, I'll tell ya all about it," said Sean. "C'mon over to our place in a bit and you'll git the truth. I doubt you'll hear the truth if you go over ta your saloon. Them fellas over there are none too happy right now."

Maggie and everyone was in the street now checking on Sean. "Let's get you over to Doc's now and get that buckshot out of your leg," said Maggie. "Then you can tell us all about it." The under-taker heard the shooting too and came out to find that he had two more customers. He never said a word. He just walked back to his parlor and in a few minutes the dead bodies were removed from the street. He knew he would get paid.

~~~~

Doc had some whiskey so he let Sean have some good swallows before he probed for the buckshot. "Smells like you already had some whiskey," said Doc. "You probably won't feel a thing." Then Doc began.

"You're wrong Doc," said Sean. "I feel it plenty. Hurry up if you can. Gimme back that bottle." Doc let Sean have the bottle while he continued his work. It wasn't long till he was done.

"You'll be good as new in no time," said Doc. "Just keep them holes clean and you'll be fine. Neither one a them pieces hit bone."

"I thank you Doc," said Sean. "I'll do my best ta keep from bein' a customer in the future."

"As long as you're wearin' that badge, I'll probably see you on a regular basis," said Doc.

"I'm leavin' now," said Sean. "Talkin' ta you can be upsettin'."

~~~~

All of them went back to Maggie's Place and sat down at their table. "Jug told us all about the fight and such," said Maggie. "Now you can tell us about that woman and the bartender."

"Let's have some drinks and wait a bit," said Sean. "Bill Thompson'll be here shortly and he'll wanna know everything. If we wait on him, I won't hafta tell it twice."

"All right, I'll get us some more drinks," said Maggie. Maggie went to the bar and got everything. Lolita got some water and towels and then she and Maggie went around and cleaned the blood off of Jug and his men. "I sincerely hope the other fellas look worse," Maggie said to Josh.

"They do," said Wayne. "We made sure a that." Bill Thompson came into the saloon now and went to Sean's table.

"All right Marshal, tell me what happened," said Bill. "Every man I talked to at my place had a different story."

"Pull up a chair Bill," said Sean. Bill got a chair and sat down. "One a Jug's men got in a card game at your place," said Sean. "He found out it was crooked and a woman was in on it too. When he called'em on it, them two card cheats beat the hell out of'em. He was so beat up he barely got back here ta tell us. I had Jug and his boys leave their guns here and we went over there. I made everyone in there give up their gun. Then I let Jug and his boys have at'em. Jug and his boys was outnumbered two to one."

"So why in the hell did they beat up everybody and not just the card cheats?" asked Bill.

"I'll tell ya why mister," yelled Jug. "Cause them idiots sat around and done nothin' while them two worked over my boy. They deserved an ass whoopin' and they got it."

"So what happened with the woman and the bartender?" asked Bill.

"When the fight was over that bartender started yellin' at me and sayin' that the rancher was gonna pay for the damages," Sean began. "I told'm that he was a piece a shit and that he'd most likely be lookin' for a job after you found out that he was lettin' cheatin' go on in your place. And he also never done nothin' ta stop them cheats from beatin' up Jug's boy. I was takin' that woman who was workin' with the cheats over ta Maggie ta see what she thought I should do with her. That's when that bartender came runnin' at me with that shotgun. The woman was in the way and got shot. I killed the son of a bitch. Is that good enough for ya?"

"Well it looks like I need to get myself another bartender and some furniture," said Bill. "I'll do my best to make sure he's honest. Jug, I'm sorry this happened. You and your boys can have a drink on the house before you go if you'd like."

"Thanks Bill. I hope you do get yourself some good help," said Jug. "It was good luck this time. Sean was here ta make sure there was no gunplay and I was here with my crew. Any other Texas crew woulda rounded up all their boys and guns and the undertaker would be makin' some money."

"I'd say you were right," said Bill. "When things really get going around here, we'll definitely need to have some local law."

"Well for now we should enjoy the quiet times," said Sean.

"I guess we could call them quiet times," said Maggie. "There was only one beating and one fight today. I guess you could call it one fight even though there were eighteen or so men in it and only two people got shot and killed."

"Don't forget we had one more shot and wounded," said Sean.

Books By Michael E. Cook

The Sean O'Rourke Series

Book 1: A Killer For The Common Good

Book 2: A Killer For The Common Good—LAWMAN

Book 3: O'Rourke's Revenge

Book 4: O'Rourke's Law or No Law at All

Coming soon

Book 5: Quiet Times?

Available in paperback and eBook formats
at Internet retailers everywhere.

ABOUT THE AUTHOR

The Sean O'Rourke Series continues with Book 4 as Michael E. Cook takes us up to the summer of 1867. Michael hopes to keep your attention with plenty of fast action. The cattle drives have begun and some outside of the law try to take advantage of other's hard work. Michael will show you how our hero deals with those who would kill for the joy of killing and a dollar. As more and more settlers encroach upon land that belongs to the Plains tribes, Michael keeps you informed on actions taken by the tribes and some of the responses by the U.S. Army. Our young hero will stay a friend to the Cheyenne through the continuing series. Michael demonstrates to you how our hero's undying love for his family and friends and country will slowly but surely make the west a safer place to live.

Contact the author at: cookorourkeseries@gmail.com

www.ingramcontent.com/pod-product-compliance
Lightning Source LLC
Chambersburg PA
CBHW021943170626
46808CB00001B/10